MIKHAIL OSORGIN

The Riven Heart of Moscow

THE RIVEN HEART OF MOSCOW

(SIVTSEV VRAZHEK)

by Mikhail Osorgin

First published in Russian as *Сивцев Вражек* in 1928

Translated from the Russian by Svetlana Payne
Proofreading by Richard Coombes

Translation © Svetlana Payne, 2023
Introduction and comments © Svetlana Payne, 2023

Cover design by Ekaterina Milyukova/Olga Uvarova
The map of Moscow by Fred Boyle

Illustration on page 4 © 2023, Max Mendor

© 2023, Glagoslav Publications

www.glagoslav.com

ISBN: 978-1-80484-054-2
ISBN: 978-1-80484-055-9

First published in English by Glagoslav Publications in August 2023

A catalogue record for this book is available from the British Library.

MIKHAIL OSORGIN

The Riven Heart of Moscow

TRANSLATED FROM THE RUSSIAN BY SVETLANA PAYNE

GLAGOSLAV PUBLICATIONS

MIKHAIL OSORGIN
(1878 – 1942)

CONTENTS

ACKNOWLEDGEMENTS

(OR WITHOUT WHOM THIS BOOK
WOULD NEVER HAVE SEEN THE LIGHT OF DAY)

For many years I'd been hoping that, one day, there would arrive a time in my life when my age-old dream of translating *Sivtsev Vrazhek* into English, the availability of some spare hours in a day, and the requisite energy levels would all come together. Ironically, just such a context was provided by what otherwise would have been pure ill luck – the experience of lockdown. Working on my translation and dreaming about finally making this book available to the English-speaking world was what kept me sane in the days, months and years of COVID-induced isolation.

Hurdles to social life notwithstanding, there have been people whose help, support and belief in me and the project proved absolutely indispensable. I would now love to thank each and every one of them personally.

None of this would have happened without Daria Dubovitskaya. The fact that her day job is in development economics does not stop her from being a polymath. She is an amazing linguist and editor, a person with a magic touch when it comes to the music of words, an eagle eye when it comes to glitches and sloppiness, and a passion for literature in general and Osorgin in particular. I owe her an endless debt of gratitude.

Jim Handley was a treasure trove of 'speaks' and 'argots' – he is the one behind the most successful equivalents for the colourful expressions used by peasants and soldiers in the book. A novice in the world of Russia as it was in the early 20th century, his enthusiasm for the book and keen interest in the period provided a much-needed boost.

Chris Holifield and her team of editors from the Writers Service were incredibly thorough in their work on the text. Equally important to me was the fact that they became thrilled with the book and its fate, so much so that one of them even called the book 'a lost masterpiece'.

Judith Murray, my agent, contributed valuable notes on my translation and shared my passion for imagining prominent English actors playing various characters in the book. Her favourite candidate was Mark Strong as Protasov. The game, however, had been invented by my daughter whose personal favourite was Timothy Spall as Zavalishin.

Olga Makarova, lifelong enthusiastic promoter of Russian language and culture, a trusted teacher and a professional editor, proved to be a real colleague and friend.

Bella Kogan became a veritable well of ideas and contacts, always on the ball, always there to help.

I would like to thank Caroline Beddington – for a life-long interest in and support to my creative endeavours.

I was lucky to lure to my project two outstanding artists: Ekaterina Miliykova and Olga Uvarova. Ekaterina, daughter of a student of the famous Alexander Deineka, a graduate of the Stroganov University of Arts and Industry, an artist, designer, ceramicist and creator of batiks, an author of paintings sold to numerous private collectors all over the world and appearing in numerous exhibitions, only recently moved to the UK from Germany.

Her colleague Olga, a professional painter and a member of the Russian Association of Artists, worked for numerous publishing houses as an illustrator, on TV, and in the theatre as a costume designer. She now lives in Germany. The book cover they jointly created is the very essence of the book presented in paint.

10

Osorgin's photo on the back cover is reproduced by kind permission of Professor Oleg Lasunsky, the person almost single-handedly responsible for restoring Osorgin's name from oblivion in the late 1980s. A keen Osorgin enthusiast, he wrote numerous books and articles on him, and even corresponded with Osorgin's widow, who lived long enough to see her husband's name and legacy restored. Tatiana Bakunina (Osorgina) died in 1995. She was a direct descendent of the theorist and revolutionary Mikhail Bakunin, and inspiration for the character of Tanyusha in the book. Osorgin's photo came into Professor Lasunsky's possession as a result of that correspondence.

The amazing map of Moscow as it was at the time of the story was created by Fred Boyle – a young illustrator and designer from Windsor.

And finally, my husband, Ian Payne – an inspirer in despair and a purveyor of dreams, a wiper of tears and a cracker of jokes, the first listener to my ideas, the first reader of my texts, my strength, and confidence and love.

Svetlana Payne

DOLGORUKO

MALAYA BRONNAYA ST.

BOLSHAYA BRONNAYA ST.

TVERKOY BLVD.

SPIRIDONOVKA ST.

LEONTIEVSKY

MALAYA NIKITSKAYA ST.

BOLSHAYA NIKITSKAYA ST.

P O V A R S K A Y A

NIKITSKY BLVD.

DOGS' COURT

VOZDV

ALEX' DR II M'RY SCH

ALEXA GA

A R B A T S T.

PRECHISTENSKY

SYVTSEV VRAZHEK

STATE MUSEUM OF ART

ARBAT

CATHE- DRAL OF CHRIS

BLVD

D O R O G O M I L O V S K A Y A   S T.

PRECH STENKA

OSTOZHENK

KHAMOVNIKI DISTRICT

MIKHAIL OSORGIN, A WITNESS OF HISTORY

Truism or not, but time does fly. Before anyone has had the time to draw breath, the centenary of the Russian revolution of 1917 has been and gone, and yet, to this day, much remains to be discussed, analysed and agreed upon. The renewed interest in the literary works of Boris Pasternak, Mikhail Bulgakov et al. is part of this process, and the much-anticipated English translation of Alexander Solzhenitsyn's *The Red Wheel* has been hailed by many, and these are only a few examples. Recently, there has been an avalanche of new non-fiction publications on the subject: *Lenin on the Train* by Catherine Merridale; *October* by China Miéville; *Historically Inevitable: Turning Points in the Russian Revolution*, edited by Tony Brenton and many, many others. All these are worthy and noble attempts to unravel the complicated knot of events, ambitions, intrigue and geopolitics. Yet, for some bizarre reason, the name of a person whose insights were just as profound and prophetic – that of Mikhail Osorgin – remains firmly and unjustly forgotten.

It is, of course, logical to ask why this book might be of interest to anybody who is not Russian or a historian; why this obscure Russian writer who died a long time ago (in 1942) is worthy of anyone's time and money. Yet global events over this last year prove, once again, that he who does not learn from history is doomed to relive it in perpetuity.

The most newsworthy and horrifying event of 2022 was the unprovoked incursion of the Russian war machine into the independent state of Ukraine, marking the start of a hideous war. Numerous analytical errors and the myopia of Russian intelligence agencies aside, it had been widely believed that the war would be triumphantly finished within the space of three days; that the grateful Ukrainians would flock into their central city squares and welcome the invader with flowers. As dictates the age-old Slavic tradition, they should have welcomed their 'dear guests' with an offer of bread and salt, all artfully arranged on hand-embroidered towels. It is obvious now that those deluded agencies should have known better than believing their own PR about the military potential and morale of what was once referred to as the 'second most powerful army in the world'.

All these misguided calculations, by now, are history – to be researched, learnt from and used as a basis for future PhDs. To me, the really soul-destroying question now is this: how could a nation that had produced Pushkin and Tchaikovsky, Tolstoy and Dostoyevsky, Pavlov and Pavlova, Tsiolkovsky and Korolyov, Vavilov and Bulgakov, Solzhenitsyn and Shostakovich; the nation that had played a key role in the fight to crush the spine of the Nazi dragon and had pioneered space exploration; the nation that stunned the world with the beauty of its ballet and the courage of its own reinvention in the nineties – how could the same nation have become the perpetrator responsible for the immense suffering of women, the elderly and children, a wrecker of post-Second World War agreements and borders, a rapist, a pillager and the object of almost universal derision?

One cannot overestimate the courage and selflessness of those few people within Russia who are coming out into the streets to protest against the war, those who voluntarily submit themselves to Russian kangaroo courts and then do all they can to make their experiences known – even if it is too late, even if they had been perfectly placid over the war in Georgia and the annexation of Crimea. Now they are facing prison sentences but, of course, they are really risking something worse than that – sacrificing the safety, wellbeing, employability and even the very existence of their families, all this because of trying to remind the powers-that-be of the basic laws governing international co-existence in the 21st century.

Yet the overwhelming majority of protests and posts on Russian social media, as well as the coverage emanating from the front, steer way clear of addressing this fundamental question: what on earth is Russia doing in Ukraine (official propaganda notwithstanding)? Who really needs this war, and why? Instead, there are complaints of the paucity of ammunitions, rancid food rations and the inadequacies of their commanding officers. To paraphrase: complaints about the lack of comfort associated with committing murders and being slaughtered in return.

I have spent my life trying to share Russian culture with the English-speaking world. I have translated innumerable lectures, study tours, seminars – along with quite a few books of fiction and poetry. And now I find myself lost for words when trying to answer a very rational question: what good was all this cultural heritage if the nation that has produced it either commits or condones mass murder, rape and marauding?

And this is where the book I am offering to your attention, potentially, holds some answers.

Mikhail Osorgin was born in 1878, making him a mere eight years younger than Lenin and, effectively, a person of the same generation. When the First World War came to the Russian Empire, Osorgin was 35. By that time, he had experimented with various revolutionary movements and had even been arrested for his tangential interest in the ideas of Socialist Revolutionaries (the party of agrarian socialists and proponents of a democratic republic). Still, even this level of interest proved to be a bad move in the times of absolute monarchy in Russia, especially since the party itself was openly advocating terror as a viable tool for putting its agenda across. Still, social democrats had attracted a sizeable following that consisted, mostly, of people who were young, intellectually astute and eager to bring about change. The fallout did not take long: Osorgin received a prison sentence.

On the very eve of the First World War, due to a logistical blunder during transfer, he miraculously escaped the penitentiary and fled to Italy where, in exile, he finally started writing in earnest. After the breakout of hostilities, he returned to Russia illegally and tried to enlist as a volunteer, but his criminal record got in the way and he was turned down. He stayed on, writing articles in support of the democratic (if weak) February government, and was eventually hand-picked by Lenin to join the passengers of the infamous 1922 'Philosophers' Steamer' that carried the most prominent figures of the Russian intellectual elite into enforced emigration. The names of those on board that ship included the authors of what were destined to become classic works of philosophy, economics, theology and literature. Nonetheless, the times were still relatively 'vegetarian' (to quote Akhmatova), so instead of gunning the lot down, the newly-installed Bolshevik government simply expelled them to Danzig (today's Gdansk). A particularly charming house-keeping detail was that the passengers had been allowed only a couple of days for putting their affairs and baggage in order but received no means for further travel. The new Soviet power was nothing if not thrifty. After some time, Osorgin ended up in Paris, which is where his recent experiences crystallised into the sublime prose of *Sivtsev Vrazhek*, published in 1928. My translation of this is *The Riven Heart of Moscow* and this is why.

The original title (granted, a mouthful for a non-Russian speaker) is simply the name of a tiny crooked lane in the heart of Moscow, set back in a maze of similar lanes which form the ancient district of the Arbat, located within a stone's throw of the Kremlin and everywhere else that is of historic significance in the Russian capital. The name can be traced back to medieval Russian, and means a 'little ravine' ('vrazhek'), along which the long-since-disappeared river 'Sivka' ('grey') had once flowed. Osorgin used the name as a symbol of everything quintessentially and traditionally Russian – as it had been defined before the Revolution of 1917 – thus making the residents of this quiet street a perfect showcase for the impact produced by the tempestuous events of the early 20th century. Yet the title also suggests the idea of being 'split' or 'divided', bringing forth the subconscious notion of 'a chasm caused by something grey or murky'.

When the upward-projected and deceptively stable world, as it existed in the Russian Empire prior to 1914, started sinking, gradually but inevitably, into the quagmire of the First World War, the fallout from all those events proved to be something beyond a humanitarian catastrophe. Apart from killing millions of people and devastating the country, the war, as it affected the Russian Empire, set in motion mechanisms that later altered the course of global history. The events in Russia had forged a paradigm whereby the rights of an individual and other common-held assumptions about society were subjected to a radical revision. Humanism and altruism were disdainfully branded 'servants of the bourgeoisie'. Having proclaimed normal human ties not only obsolete but downright ludicrous and hostile to the Bolshevik doctrine, the new regime paved the way for crass, mercenary, mercantile, avaricious and self-serving ideologies that started mushrooming later in the 20th century. This gruesome legacy, to a large extent, informs the processes and trends observed in modern Russia.

It is true that the use of terror as a political tool was not invented by the Bolsheviks – it was as effectively used during the French Revolution of 1789. However, Russian tsars had also dabbled with it. Ivan the Terrible (who ruled from 1533 to 1584) had invented the institute of political police and used terror to eliminate his political opponents. Peter the Great (who ruled from 1682 to 1725) was supremely indifferent to the lives of the serfs whose bones became the foundation for one of his most famous projects – the city of Sant Petersburg. Nicholas the First (who ruled from 1825 to 1855) ruthlessly crushed the mutiny initiated by his fellow aristocrats who had tried to pioneer the evolution of absolute monarchy into a constitutional one. The famous Decembrist Uprising of 1825 was suppressed in a manner that, at the time, was considered to be extremely bloodthirsty.

Yet the Bolsheviks went further than most. They unleashed an all-embracing and methodical elimination of their own nation, a full-scale war waged not just against the political opposition, but against all and sundry. However, all this came later and is painstakingly reflected in the book. Still, the narrative opens with peaceful scenes describing the affluent period in Russia at the beginning of the 20th century.

The Russian Empire, as it approached the outbreak of the First World War, had every reason to be hopeful: by 1913 industrial performance was spectacular, grain imports were constantly on the rise, and the Russian currency (the gold *chervonets* – a nickname for ten rouble coins) was welcome all over the world. The foundations of the largely agricultural empire appeared solid and indestructible – where its God-fearing and tsar-worshipping peasantry, farmers and the countryside in general were seen as a collective keeper of traditional values, a guarantor of stability throughout society.

Yet at the same time there was another equally important development: the emergence and confident growth of the middle and professional classes – scientists, artists, industrialists. Many of them had been the product of a boost in access to education, be it Western or home-based, a phenomenon spawned by the abolition of serfdom in 1861 and the associated liberal reforms of the last quarter of the 19th century. Suddenly, the vital but traditionally put-upon classes (provincial clergy, teachers, doctors) could send their children to university, some even to Europe. Those newly-educated professionals, on returning home, felt they had a debt of duty to their native land. As a result, various liberal movements were founded, the most noteworthy being various campaigns for teaching literacy and finding urban employment for the rural poor. They embraced all things noble: education, duty, a high sense of societal integration, a debt of sharing with those less fortunate than themselves. The term 'intelligentsia' (allegedly coined by Chekhov) described just those people.

Was it any wonder, really, that they were the first to be swept away – in the beginning, by the First World War, then by the revolution of 1917 and the Red Terror that followed immediately afterwards? A process later termed 'negative selection' was set in motion then, and continues to this day. The brightest, the boldest, the most socially-aware, selfless and compassionate, have, through decades, either died at the fronts, or rotted in jail during the endless periods of mass terror, or been rooted out of their posts and kicked out of their professions, or booted into exile, or been allowed to leave the country under their own steam but ended up muzzled and demoralized.

If for decades a flower patch of human society is treated not with a growth-enhancing mixture of encouragement, civil liberties and personal security, but instead is perpetually scorched with a concoction of harsh chemicals such as fear, intimidation and the curtailment of any private initiative – personal or commercial, how can anyone wonder that the resulting crop is a profusion of thistles? Roses are beautiful, but when it comes to a struggle for survival, they are no competition for hardy weeds.

The book in your hands is among the very first testimonials of this exact process whereby the cream of the nation was all but eliminated and uniformity of thought started being rammed down everyone's throat. The same process validated systematic violence as an acceptable (and often preferred) tool of social engineering.

There are so many other brilliant things about this book, too. For example, its environmental message was way ahead of its time. Animals had featured in Russian literature before, but mostly for the purpose of characterising people. Osorgin goes further: nearly a hundred years prior to today's environmental wars he is full of sympathy for mice, birds, horses and even ants, as if crying out from the pages of his book: humans, stop and think what your poorly-thought-through actions are doing to the world around us.

The book is remarkable in many other ways – even its structure is incredibly innovative. The text reads almost as a film script where the camerawork zooms in and out of the infinitesimal to reach the cosmic.

How is it possible that a book of such literary brilliance, human perception, technical excellence and political prescience has not been better known up till now? I am certainly hoping to address this glaring injustice.

Svetlana Payne
January 2023

PART ONE

THE ORNITHOLOGIST

In the infinity of the universe, in the solar system, on planet Earth, in the country of Russia, in its capital city, Moscow, in the corner house in Sivtsev Vrazhek Lane, in the armchair in his study, sat a professor of ornithology, Ivan Alexandrovich. The light of his lamp, funnelled by the lampshade, shone onto his book, barely touching the corner of the inkwell, a calendar, and a ream of paper; and the professor was absorbed only in the part of the page showing, in living colour, the head of a cuckoo.

What the professor was ruminating about wasn't anything scholarly but something quite down to earth, specifically, how many more years he had left to live. These thoughts transported him deep into the forest, where the cuckoo called, and where the number of its calls foretold the number of years still ahead. Such was the popular belief, and it was no more far-fetched than any other prophecy. A cuckoo could be mistaken, but so could the doctors. And there wasn't a doctor alive who could predict if a person would fall under a tram.

The broad-faced, grey-bearded professor, as Russian as it was possible to be, did not want to die, but he had no fear of death either, since, in his youth and in his advanced age alike, he had been a man of substance and integrity. He had a name in scientific circles, but his love for his field was of a particular kind. His field was full of beauty: the colouring of the plumage, the singing, the nature around the birds, the birth of spring and the leave-taking of summer. His science was poetic. Each little bird that he knew and loved, he loved thanks to his in-depth knowledge. So, the professor had no intention of dying; he wanted to live, and live, and live. Still, how many years of life was it that the carefree bachelor bird was promising him?

The cuckoo called three times. The professor smiled, for he was not superstitious and was accustomed to his cuckoo clock. He shut the book, having marked the page with a scrap of paper. He gave a yawn – a good sign, since in his later years he had been suffering from insomnia. He raised himself, kneading his lower back with his fingers, gave another yawn, and, having put out the lamp, retreated to his bedroom.

An hour later, when the house was immersed in complete silence and the cuckoo had called four times, a mouse crept from under the bookcase and sat there, listening intently. All seemed to be in order; everything was asleep; there were no cat's eyes in view. The mouse twitched his tail, flared his nostrils, and set off. His route took him through the professor's bedroom. This one was a short sortie, only good for a few crumbs. A longer path would take him into the kitchen, but it was fraught with danger – that was where the cat lived. It would be better to venture through an alternative opening, behind the chest in the hallway. There was another hole in the floor there.

The mouse could only make out the nearest patch of floor and the contours of objects further away – just enough to get one's bearings. If only he had the eyesight of a cat! Having reached the door, the mouse squeezed his plump body underneath and used the tip of his tail to make sure that he had cleared the doorstep. Another stop and a frisson of anxiety. The ornithologist slept like the old man that he was, restless. He kept mumbling in his sleep, 'What? Why? Oh, but it doesn't matter!' At length, his breath became peaceful and he fell soundly asleep.

The professor had given his life to science. He could recognise any bird from afar, by a single tiny feather, its outline, its soft warbling; but could he place people as easily? He had become enamoured of his beloved's chirping song, and then their young chicks had hatched, all three of them. They had become fully fledged, grown up and flown away. Here and now, on the other side of the wall, lived his granddaughter, a young girl with no parents.

The old lady was still alive, the erstwhile chirper who had shared all forty years with the learned bird-lover. If only all his ornithological choices had been as impeccable. Still, life had been full of all sorts of things, especially in their youth… The old man stirred again in his sleep, and the tiny bundle of grey fur scuttled under the door into the adjacent bedroom.

It was stuffy there, pillows heaped high on the enormous bed, and the edge of the eiderdown had slid down. On the bed slept a tiny, silver-haired old lady. The professor's wife was curled up like a child, a glass of water on the bedside table, pills and some sweets in a paper cone. The armchair nearby was comfy, broken in. The room smelled of lavender and the past. There was nothing to fear here, so the tiny mouse crossed the rug unhurriedly, came to a halt, hunkered down and stopped to think. It was peaceful there like nowhere else, and like no other place; this one felt safe. The old lady breathed almost inaudibly, and her dreams were ordinary and down to earth. She slept with her lips pressed together tightly, her teeth resting in a glass of water.

The next room en route, by contrast, was one to dart across without stopping, as quickly as possible. The room was formidable, reverberant and deserted. Bedrooms, normally, smelled of comforting things, of the sweet everyday, but a reception room with giant windows and distant silhouettes was menacing. Something glistened in the mouse's line of vision and he sprang backwards, the nostrils and whiskers on his delicate muzzle all astir. Phew! Not so horrible after all; just the grand piano's glass footrests, that was all. But dear me! In this enormous world everything was menacing for a grey mouse, tiny and vulnerable! The mouse skirted warily round the huge grand piano, a thing capable of a deafening din with all its strings. The grand piano was the master of the house.

The professor played sometimes. 'Would you like me to imitate a nightingale? It goes like this: first, "whir", and "whi-i-r", and then lower, frog-like, "fr-r-r", and then the warble, and suddenly, a crescendo – no, it's impossible to demonstrate!' His wife, the old lady, Aglaya Dmitriyevna, played very well indeed, but was very difficult to prevail upon. 'No, my hands are too old, they are no longer nimble.' Tanyusha, the granddaughter, was a budding performer; now, she was the one who had the energy, and love of music, and the ability. Tanyusha was a student at the conservatoire. She performed at small concerts without trepidation. Still, the grand piano only really came to life when Tanyusha's professor, Eduard Lvovich, dropped by of an evening. That was the real thing, and it happened nearly every Sunday. On such evenings, the mice stayed up well into the small hours and aborted their nocturnal reconnaissance missions.

Eduard Lvovich was advanced in years, homely, a lack-lustre conversationalist but an amazing pianist. A composer, too. He took his tea with sweet biscuits that he loved. He had never in his life tasted vodka. Definitely a peculiar character.

Meanwhile the mouse was making his way back from the dining room. He happened on some crumbs: quite a pile, actually. He was on the point of venturing into the hallway when something suddenly crashed there, and the noise made him flee. He made a thorough scan of the dining room. It was time to retrace his steps, through the reception room, then the bedrooms, towards the bookcase, into the tiny crack in the floor, homewards. It was getting light. Darkness was scary but the light was scarier still. It was all scary, all the time.

The minute, grey bundle of eternal fear rushed through the rooms of the professor's flat and no one noticed a thing. No one knew that a whole family of mice was busy helping the worms eat away the wooden gussets of the floor and the sturdy, but not indestructible, walls. The Earth is cooling off, the mountains are being worn down, the rivers are getting shallow and sluggish; all things are seeking a point of balance, the energy of the universe is draining away – but not completely, not at all. The tiny mouse's tail lingered momentarily in view, and then disappeared.

The cuckoo called six times. The professor's bed squeaked. The sun brushed the edge of the curtain.

Along with the sunlight, a tiny swallow landed on the window, having just arrived from Central Africa.

A REMARKABLE DAY

The morning was born, a peach-faced morning in a white chemise, its milky-white wings flapping against the window panes. Just then the latch clanked and the window flew open. Suddenly face to face with the morning, Tanyusha squinted and felt the gentle waft, the cool of the day rippling down her nightdress. On tiptoes, she skipped back to her bed, to luxuriate a trifle longer, happy that the morning was full of the promise of a good day.

Early in the morning and by a window open wide – what could a sixteen-year-old girl reflect upon? Firstly, that today was a good day, and secondly, that it was Sunday. Instead of moving on to her next thought, she smiled for no particular reason. Then she ran down a mental list of things to do: telephone Lenochka and tell her she simply must come over in the evening. The lie-in was a treat, but just as appealing was the prospect of sluicing herself down with cold water. Then, having enjoyed her morning fill of coffee, the next task was to sort out the sheet music. That odd but loveable man, Eduard Lvovich, was going to play that night.

She wasn't the bird-loving professor's granddaughter for nothing; she had spotted the arrival of the swallows straight away. *I must be sure to tell Grandpa.* Only the previous day they had not been there, so today was surely the first day of real spring. The chiming of the bells, long and sonorous, the noise of the street below, now wide awake, and then the 'ch-r-r' of the swallows. Such a long life lies ahead of her! She ran her delicate fingers, the nails cut short – a musician! – along the newly rounded incline of her shoulder exposed by the sliding strap of the nightdress. Then abruptly, feet down onto the bedside rug, she ran up to the mirror, to have a close look at her own face. 'Nonsense, I am not so plain after all!'

By the time a girl turns sixteen she can trust her own eyes; Tanyusha made a brief pouting grimace but, for the time being, the mirror told her nothing about the mystery of a denuded shoulder. A minute later – and all was cold while the mirror reflected, for no one's benefit, or only for the passing swallow's – a hand raising the jug and water streaming down her body. Then a fluffy towel did its work, efficient and thorough. Here we go. Tanyusha was ready.

A photograph on the wall showed some people seated on a sofa and listening to music.

Once a loose button had been sown on, it had gone eight. It was Tanyusha's privilege to wake up her grandpa. She knocked on the door.

'Grandpa, do get up! The day's so lovely and there's some good news; the swallows have arrived!'

'Good morning, Tanyusha, I'll be right along!'

'Did you sleep well?'

'I did indeed, and you?'

'I did too. Oh Grandpa, what a day! I will get them to serve you some coffee.'

That day many houses in Moscow had their windows flung wide open, and out peeped many faces, some young, some old, some bleary, some fresh, squinting and listening to the bells. The old window putty, hardened, with balls of cotton stuck all over it, was crumbling; little glasses of acid were being removed[1] and emptied while the window sills were

....

[1]   It was placed there to absorb moisture. Before double glazing came along, houses used to use a so-called 'winter pane', inserted into the window for the cold months. The cotton balls were used to pack the cracks against drafts.

MIKHAIL OSORGIN

swept clean, and the fragments of debris tumbled down onto the streets. The sun, the air and the chime of the bells swirled into the upper-floor windows in dense eddies and dispersed on contact with the walls, the furnace and the furniture. The hearts of the religious folk were full of the joys of Easter, while the hearts of the non-devout sort were brimming with unadorned, visceral delight.

In the courtyard someone beat a rug; in the kitchen the cook filled a box with soil and planted some sprouting onions. At the corner of Malaya Bronnaya Street, a student bought some pickled apples on his way to Girshi,[2] loose pages of the Roman Civil Code pressed tightly under his elbow. Under the stone bridge, a boy, the tip of his tongue flitting around the corners of his open mouth, was busy casting a thread tied around a safety pin and hoping that something big would bite, his legs muddy up to the knees.

A tram clanged vehemently – but to no avail – as a constable of the city police, wearing white cotton gloves, tried to establish law and order in the face of the manoeuvres of two horse-drawn carriages and a drayman's cart.

That day, a student of the seminary who had been contemplating suicide for half of the previous year decided to put it off for a while longer; at the same time a lady doctor, unmarried and plain, blushing, invested in an inexpensive hat, the first one that she came across, but having done so, still went out wearing the old one, since she had learned the rigours of self-denial back in the days of her youth.[3] The

....

[2] A students' quarter in pre-revolutionary Moscow.

[3] Judging by the character's age, her formative years must have fallen in the 70s and 80s of the 19th century, hence there is a high probability of her being influenced by the Narodniks (The Narodniks were a politically conscious movement of the Russian intelligentsia in the 1860s and 1870s, some of whom became involved in revolutionary agitation against tsarism. Their ideology, known as *narodnichestvo* –

Reaumur[4] thermometer was optimistically speculating on a rise. All in all, it was a remarkable day.

....

acting on behalf of the people, the *narod* in Russia – was a form of agrarian socialism and subscribed to the code of a simple and virtuous life serving the people).

[4]   The Réaumur scale, also known as the 'octogesimal division', is a temperature scale for which the freezing and boiling points of water are defined as 0 and 80 degrees respectively. The scale is named after René Antoine Ferchault de Réaumur, who first proposed a similar scale in 1730. It was used widely in Europe, particularly in France, Germany and Russia.

GRAVEYARDS

And yet some windows never get opened; some windows are behind bars, like the ones in prison. Streaming in through the perennially dusty panes, the dull light falls on filing cabinets and shelves stuffed full with documents.

In Paris, Berlin and London, the cities where spring had come earlier, it sheepishly bypassed the old edifices and cast no rays into the windows of the diplomatic archives. Gentlemen of great intellect and learning, linguists and polymaths who knew how to think in codes, stood guard over those graveyards of paper densely covered with all sorts of writings, of technical drawings and negatives.

The sun believed that it was in charge of life on the Earth. It imagined the entirety of human existence as nothing more than the embodiment of the energy of its rays. It populated the polar north with the most advanced specimens of the organic world but, when the time was right, it created a horrendous catastrophe that destroyed all things living, did away with the culture of the poles and made the culture of the equator evolve to a most perfect level. It was contemptuous of the attempts made by the terrestrial organisms to adjust, of their struggle for survival; it made a negligible impact as far as the improvement of species and their welfare were concerned. Whether a polyp or a human being, all its efforts were futile without the sun, since its doings represented nothing more than the embodiment of the rays. Intellect, knowledge, experience, faith, just like the physical body, nutrition and death, amounted to nothing more spectacular than the transformation of solar energy.

Yet Man, puny and prone to frequent head colds, shrouded in swathes of fabric held together with miniscule buttons, had mounted a system of defence against the sun. He had erected walls and allowed only the requisite trickles of light inside; he had channelled those trickles to run along wires into sealed bulbs, and then decided to manage his life in his own way. He was dipping his quill in ink, writing, whispering and issuing orders.

The reams of paper covered with scribblings set in motion events leading to unimaginable sacrifice. The wires transmitted truths and falsehoods and stoked them, fomenting and nurturing facts, motives, reasons and pretexts. The human brain was fighting the sun and striving to subordinate living things to its lifeless, nefarious will. Man was eager to enclose a patch of land with fences, a city with ramparts, a state with boundaries, a race with skin colour, a nationality with traditions, history with the modern age, daily life with politics. The crafty and inquisitive brain had been building a pyramid of bodies, dead and alive, climbing along its slopes to the very peak and then collapsing and falling, bringing the pyramid down with it.

The sun was mocking him and he was mocking the sun. For all that, the last laugh was invariably on Man. The sun beamed down its energy, born of electromagnetic whirlwinds, with a force inconceivable to the human brain. The battering ram of solar rays struck the Earth, and everything that Man believed to be a fruit of his intellect perished as a result, while only what had been created by the sun was destined to survive.

A tight-lipped civil servant, buttoned up and self-contained, had converted, word by word, the coded letter and translated it into brisk and precise German prose. The emissary read it, smirked and gave his approval, since the letter had been complimentary about him. The emissary thought that he was privy to everything known to the upper echelons of Berlin, yet what he knew was merely a significant part of the whole. The upper echelons of Berlin were aware of everything, apart from what was known to a scrawny Serbian student. The student himself knew very little, practically nothing. He had been poisoned with a driblet of nationalistic venom, and was honourable, hot-blooded, sincere and prone to hysteria. He mastered the art of shooting by practicing on targets fixed to the wall of his chicken coop. The speckled hens and their shrill-voiced sultan could have paid a dear price for all this, but they had been in luck – all his bullets missed the mark. Once the little Serb refined his skills as a marksman, he decided to become a national hero. Such a plan could only ever work if he assassinated a national enemy, as no alternative methods of becoming a hero had ever been invented; and since quite a few Serbian boys had learnt how to shoot at a target affixed to the chicken-house wall, at least one of them was destined to try his chances on a different target – the Archduke's chest.

This might never have happened; but then something else would have happened instead. Whatever was to come, those in the archive rooms behind their dusty windows had an answer ready for all eventualities. The sun was making history; Man was merely providing his commentary, but believed himself to be the history-maker. That was why he encircled himself with walls and kept his windows shut, even in spring. He believed that the graveyard of documents and secrets, procured through friendships and espionage, was the signal station of the world and the pulse of the nation. They were numerous, those graveyards; and countries, rulers and nations were proud of them.

And although, in the flight of centuries and the whirling of nebulae, the aggregated power of those graveyards was no more significant than whether or not Lenochka would come along that evening to Sivtsev Vrazhek to listen to the music, in the lives of both Lenochka and the professor's household, just like in the lives of all those who ploughed the land, wrote books and composed music, tended the crops and loved their neighbour, who had lived before and would live in future, the role of those graveyards of paper was huge and decisive.

So just as the sixteen-year-old girl flung open her window and spotted the first swallow, the sparks from radio stations flew across the ether, crafty thoughts wormed their way into the brain of a diplomat, a hen on its roost tilted its head and, by chance, avoided the student's bullet, and a newspaperman's quill inflated the bubble of nationalistic hubris.

A horse planted its hooves in the moist and fertile soil, as it pulled forward the plough. The buds on the young birch tree swelled, the grass was green. Yet the farmer pushing the plough did not know that he would collapse onto the green meadow, next to the maimed birch tree, spread-eagled and stunned by a piece of cooled-down and reheated metal. No one could possibly know this. It was not important. And it passed without trace.

In paper graveyards, burial crosses disappear behind statistics. Once a number is rounded off, units vanish, surplus to requirements. He who had been ploughing his field had never existed, nor had the birch tree, nor the shell that cut it down. What had once been alive disappeared in the process of rounding off the numbers.

COSMOS

In the evening, the windows of the little house in Sivtsev Vrazhek were all aglow and radiating welcome.

Approaching the porch, Eduard Lvovich tilted his head upwards and, as numerous times before, paused to gaze at the red curtains in the living room. He felt a surge of something good and warm washing over him. His musical fingers, stiff from the cold seeping through the pockets of his unseasonably light coat, registered the influx of blood and all of a sudden started to tingle with new dexterity. He was running late, so when he finally did arrive, everyone had already assembled in the guest room, about to have tea.

Aglaya Dmitriyevna sat by the samovar, glasses and all, a large antique brooch prominently worn; the old professor was engaged in a heated debate with a young friend of his, the physicist Poplavsky, also a professor. Tanyusha and Lenochka were listening in. Lenochka's eyes were huge and round, set in a similarly round face that was now flushed. When listening, Lenochka looked amazed; when she was amazed her eyebrows would slide upwards and the button of her mouth burst open. As for Tanyusha, she knew how to listen while concentrating on the person speaking, how to contemplate him and his interlocutor, herself, Lenochka's endearing wonderment, and think about how much one ought to and would like to know. There were some other guests too: a deferential and disagreeably clever student called Ehrberg, along with Uncle Boris, the eldest son of the ornithologist and his wife – both the student and Uncle Boris totally unremarkable.

Eduard Lvovich let himself in, rubbing his hands. His usual place, to the left of Aglaya Dmitriyevna, had been kept vacant for him. On the whole, everything was as it should be, as it had evolved over the two or three years of their acquaintance.

Tea was being served, whilst the physicist Poplavsky and the old professor were still deep in discussion of the recent experiments by Michelson and Morley, involving the phase shift of light waves. The ornithologist was apprehensive: what if physics was powerless? 'Your luminiferous aether is suspicious! Too much has to be adapted and adjusted. You physicists are in a deadlock.' Poplavsky did not discount the existence of a deadlock but, honestly, did it really shake the foundations of science, and if so, how? One should simply wait and see.

After tea, everyone moved to the living room. The professor, Uncle Boris and Tanyusha snuggled up on the enormous sofa. Aglaya Dmitriyevna kept her place by the standing lamp, her knitting at the ready. An enraptured Lenochka perched herself on a chair. Poplavsky stayed in the darkest corner. Uncle Boris's wife lurked somewhere, too, imperceptible.

Eduard Lvovich performed somewhere every day, but what he loved best of all were the evenings spent here, on a Sunday, in the old ornithologist's household. Yet he was nervous. Eduard Lvovich was not old but seemed ancient: bald, with lank dishevelled tufts sticking out on the crown of his head, as well as on his temples. He had a lazy eye. Eduard Lvovich had stooping shoulders; he was embarrassed at his own homeliness and kept rubbing his hands.

He promptly installed himself by the grand piano but sprang right back up, then fussed over the revolving stool, making sure it was at the right distance from the keyboard. He struck a chord, hovered over the keys and got flustered all over again, scrutinising the lid on the grand piano and peeping underneath. Tanyusha was worried too now, and rushed forward to offer assistance. It transpired that the edge of the rug had got trapped under the piano leg. Uncle Boris's help was enlisted, and the stray piece of rug was manoeuvred out. Another chord; yes, that was better.

Eduard Lvovich had a stutter, so many of his consonants came out muffled and laboured. He said, 'I would like to p-play... That is, if you are interested... But I can d-do something else...'

Tanyusha was the first to grasp the real meaning of it all. 'Are you going to play your own piece, Eduard Lvovich, the one you mentioned last time? Is it ready?'

'Is it ready? I truly don't know... I n-nearly know... it is s-sort of an improvisation... My name for it is ... we could s-say it is "Cosmos".'

The physicist called back: 'Cosmos? That is... interesting! If anything could ever... completely... then it should be music...'

Lenochka sat there, amazement personified, and Eduard Lvovich asked, embarrassed, 'D-dare I suggest, could we make the room darker?...'

Tanyusha turned the lamps off, leaving only one to illuminate the old lady's handiwork.

And Eduard Lvovich started playing.

Lenochka's astonished gaze followed the composer's fingers, fluttering over the keys in semi-darkness, and his head, now tossed back, now cast forward. She was hearing sounds; those that were separate and those that merged, and thought that this wasn't anything like a tune, a dance, or an overture to an opera. She was also thinking that Eduard Lvovich was referred to as a genius, and that his left eye was wandering, and also that here she, Lenochka, was, listening to a man of genius playing the piano. She felt incapable of gathering her thoughts together into a coherent whole, and so her eyebrows kept rising in marvelled confusion.

Uncle Boris was glum. He was an engineer but nonetheless a failure. His wife was plain and looked prematurely old.

His knowledge was patchy in many areas, music being one of them. Beethoven, Grieg – he had heard of them, was aware of the names, but how did you tell them apart? *Scriabin means dissonance. Why is the piece that Eduard Lvovich is playing called 'The Cosmos'? The cosmos is something astronomical...* It would be nice if anything that exceeded Uncle Boris's level of comprehension turned out to be mere whimsical thinking or plain nonsense. If only it could always be so, Uncle Boris would have grown in his own eyes and proved to be a man of substance. Then again... *who says steam boilers are inferior to music? What do the lot of them understand about steam boilers?* Still, Uncle Boris was miserably aware that music was indeed superior to steam boilers and that this fact alone somehow belittled him, Uncle Boris, and rendered him wretched and uninteresting.

The old ornithologist sat, semi-recumbent, eyes closed. The sounds hovered above him, as if brushing him with their wings and soaring upwards. Now they whooshed in, in a tumultuous cluster, all croaking and clamour; now they chimed from afar, melodious and heart-rending. None of this was taking place on earth but somewhere nearby, no higher than the clouds or a flight of larks on the wing. *The cosmos as depicted by Eduard Lvovich is not frightening! It isn't even all that complicated or exotic, either – simply a portrayal of a Russian landscape. But how good it feels to be content in one's old age, and sit here, on this sofa, by one's sweet granddaughter, having access to something sublime that people call art. I am a professor, I am famous, I am old; I don't want to die but of course I can die, peacefully, like someone who has lived and accomplished a lot, like someone sure of himself and on his way out. The sounds are like flowers, the music like a verdant meadow: woodland, waterfalls. Eduard Lvovich, he is quaint but he is a master, someone who senses things accessible to others through science, thought and old age.*

In the boundless universe, among the nebulae, whirls and suns, fluttered a cooling planet that was Aglaya Dmitriyevna's

38

lamp. The old lady was listening and knitting, not dropping a stitch. What she heard pleased her and she was thinking, *There is little water left in the samovar and the embers are still hot. But the maid is sure to take care of it. Eduard Lvovich is a brilliant musician and a splendid teacher. Tanyusha is sixteen, let her get properly educated. Still, she will marry one day and this will take precedence over everything else. Music will help things along. Let her complete her historical studies, too, there is time. Tanyusha is an orphan, but a lucky one, one who has grandparents, alive and comfortably well-off. All this is very well but isn't he getting on a bit, music and all?* Aglaya Dmitriyevna stole a glance above her glasses and nearly lost a stitch.

Professor Poplavsky, nestled in his comfy chair in the darkest corner of the room, was thinking his private thoughts. *The universe is enormous; but to grasp the meaning of it we must imagine an atom. And the atom is not the limit. Eduard Lvovich is striving to comprehend the sum of things through music and its seven basic tones, but scientific knowledge can never be replaced with an intuitive insight. With seven spectral colours, we open up new vistas, and here we are, able to weigh, on a precise scale, the burning mass of a distant star, identify the complex composition of a celestial body, establish its age. But perhaps music, in its own way, opens our eyes to the ultimate truth as it follows the same route towards discovery and culminates in the same illusion of the universe. An astronomer studies a galaxy. Which one? For it no longer exists in the same shape! What we see through a telescope is the past of the stars, planets, nebulae. The sun was like this... well, eight minutes ago, a star was like that perhaps a thousand years ago, yet another star – ten or a hundred millennia past. A sublime illusion! Still, he, Eduard Lvovich, he does play beautifully. The greatness of music lies in the fact that it needs no words or figures to bring the message home; neither does it translate into any imperfect language. It is quite possible that no cosmos lurks behind those sounds; but try and render it in a language of words or numbers and you would end up with... well, Euclidean geometry.*

TANYUSHA

Tanyusha was perched on the sofa, her legs tucked under and her head pressed against Grandpa's shoulder.

To start with, she was mesmerised by the sound, then swept away by the novel harmonies. A miniscule, incandescent speck, she whirled hectically in the airless space, surrounded by eternal questions without answers, the questions posed by the stars, the planets and the nebulae; by the mundane that had progressed to the universal, by the universal that had regressed to the trifles of the everyday.

She didn't try to make out a cosmos in the music; she simply welcomed it into her soul and then, once in its orbit, made her home there. The unconscious flow of her thoughts subsumed everything else: her slender physical frame, the suffocating warmth of her grandpa's shoulder, the dimmed lights of the reception room and the hesitance of the sounds.

She filled the reception room with images and sat still, observing their emergence underneath the ceiling, their circular chain dance around the lamp, the disarray of their random encounters and the measured progression that followed. She was afloat, carried along by the sounds, beyond the constraints of the walls. She kept her mouth open so that the sound of her breathing would not interfere with the sounds. She willingly absorbed the new bales of unprocessed thought into the store of her intellect: the supply of new raw materials that would be processed not now but later, when the new morning had restored her equanimity. She had no fear; she was aware it would be difficult, but felt elated and earnest.

The Cosmos? That was not something Tanyusha had ever contemplated; the cosmos was all totality and completeness while she was on the threshold of her life, hardly out of the chaos of her childhood. She had barely started accumulating granules of genuine knowledge. She still lingered in the world of questions, primary perceptions; sublime, fragmentary and contradictory. She craved axiomatic clarity, and, rejecting theories, felt indignant about ambiguous solutions, dismissed the need for faith. She intuited that all of this was important, even the tickling hair in her grandpa's beard, but she had been so time-constrained, had so many things to do that she settled on a mental leap from the trifles (something to consider later) to a gigantic generalisation; from a rumpled fold of the tablecloth to things fascinating but terrifying, like, 'What's the point of life?' And then, especially, 'How should she live it?' It had occurred to her once, already, that the purpose of life was in the act of living, yet she was painfully unsure whether her conclusion had been correct. What if she had sinned against a higher purpose? Insulted the superior destination of being?

Once, in a conversation with her grandpa, Poplavsky had noted that three points in a single line of vision might not configure a straight line, that it was all relative. She did not quite grasp it but nonetheless felt agitated: what was she supposed to do, then, with what she had considered resolved, with what had been guiding her conclusions? How was it conceivable that her learned grandpa could dismiss it all with a smirk? Did he really have some bigger, sacred knowledge? As Poplavsky expounded on his peculiar points, his eyes took on a wistful expression. Grandpa, on the other hand, who should and did know better, was tranquil and in good humour.

'Don't you even mention such horrors in front of Tanyusha! She'll never be able to sleep now!'

True enough, that evening Tanyusha lay awake in her bed for quite some time, although what she thought about was not the points made but rather how on earth she was supposed to carry on if there was nothing, nothing at all that was completely and truly certain. That was when she intuitively guessed that there existed people who simply accepted the given and went on to build their happiness on that basis, whereas there were also those who had no foundations to build their happiness on, since the ground beneath their feet was forever aquiver with ever-changing questions. Her grandpa belonged to the former type, but then again, perhaps those who had such certainty were privy to something else, something superior to all questions, something unwavering? Yet this inquisitive mind of hers placed her firmly with the latter group.

Thus, her musical ear keenly attuned, she cherished the smithereens of sounds and merged them into a whole, splashed across the five threads of the stave. And so, all the while, Tanyusha sat there, listening to this strikingly unconventional but powerful improvisation by her teacher and pondering, simultaneously, matters private, trivial, pedestrian and mundane; but also profound, even if as yet unresolvable for the feeble muscles of her consciousness. Her own Cosmos was still in the process of creation.

Eduard Lvovich was approaching the final chords, his finale sounding almost like a melody. His journey, everything he had been searching for and making explicit, culminated with those few naïve sounds. Could it really be that it all was so clear to him? He finished playing but everyone stayed silent. He raised himself, rubbed his hands together, and cast a guilty glance towards the lamp. Aglaya Dmitriyevna, offering her approval, sent him a look over the rim of her spectacles. 'I wouldn't know where to start, it's ever so good. I quite lost myself in the music.'

It came out artless and to the point. The others were struggling to contribute but found there was nothing else to add. And so Tanyusha woke from her reverie and gave a sigh.

LASIUS FLAVUS

At the crack of a luminous dawn, the angel of life was sowing seeds in the damp black soil. The soil was ripe for sowing.

The sun was coming out, and the seeds, aquiver with anticipation, were gradually enveloped by the warm steam; they were swelling, bursting and thrusting out succulent white sprouts, atop the tiny threads of their roots.

The roots were reaching downwards, prospecting for some nutritious moisture and holding onto the rich particles of soil; the shoots were straining with all their might to straighten themselves, unfold miniscule green leaves and spread them towards the sun.

Then, after sunset, who should appear in the same field but the angel of death, carrying a basket overflowing with weeds. The angel would spread the seeds of discord and wickedness among the new green seedlings. By the morning, these green impostors would also be caressed by the dispassionate sun, while Man felt jubilant as he observed the lushness of his planted fields.

That year, He who does not exist but is Glorious and Almighty predicted victory to the angel of death. And so, when the spikes of the young grass started pushing forth their new ears, a certain ant, *Lasius flavus*, hastily clambered up a blade. He was not a hunter whose responsibility was to chase greenflies in the grass. The anthill at the edge of the forest held superb stocks of aphids and was well provided with their sweet nutritious sap. Nevertheless, the scouts had warned that trouble was brewing in the neighbourhood;

the ants' republic was facing the threat of invasion from the predatory tribes of *Formica fusca*, who had already crossed the construction site for the new railroad embankment and were mustering their forces by the turn-off in the field. It was not the impending war that frightened them but the danger of slavery. To make matters worse, all this was taking place at the very time when the tiny winged females had already returned from their first outing, having shed their wings, and were ready to lay eggs, and raise new generations of workers.

The first battle flared up in the heat of July. Jaws of steel clamped around the enemy's fragile tentacles and legs and hacked them off with a strenuous exertion of muscles. Masses of bodies clustered together and the stronger adversaries snapped the waists of the weaker.

The sandy path upon which the hostile armies engaged was now strewn with stumps of legs, splinters of jaws, trembling pellets of convulsing flesh. And all the while the murderous robbers shuttled back and forth along the roundabout pathways, dragging with them the captured pupae to ensure the future supply of slaves. Should some ravenous warrior sneak into the enemy's livestock pen and greedily suck a well-fed, thoroughbred aphid dry, in an instant he would find himself writhing on the ground, locked in deadly combat with the shepherd defending the property of his tribe.

The battle raged until the crack of dawn. The ant colony had already been surrounded by the ever-increasing armies of the pale-yellow enemy; but what happened next could never have been forecast by the best of the strategists among the ants.

The earth trembled, the booming shadows moved in closer, and all of a sudden, the anthill was wiped from the face of the earth by a powerful blow that had struck as if from nowhere. Chaos suddenly overtook the field as the enemies, still engaged in their unfinished conflict, were squashed by some invisible and inexplicable jolt.

The grass nearby faded, trampled underfoot; grains of sand were embedded into the bodies of the ants and suddenly there was not a trace of the well-organised armed forces. A fatal and irrepressible scourge of extermination passed by in the spheres unfathomable to even the sharpest of the intellects among the ants, maybe in some alien dimension – like some precipitous thunderstorm or global catastrophe.

It was not only the armies of the ants that had been eradicated. The planted fields perished too, stamped barren by soldiers' boots; and the young clumps of heather, trampled over and drooping, along with the millions of creatures alive and readying themselves to live – larvae, pupae, beetles, grass lice, field birds' nests, freshly unfolded flower cups – all disappeared under the feet of a detachment passing the edge of the forest. After the exhausted horses brought up the rear of the sub-machine unit, dragging the artillery, all that had been left in place of a living world was a downtrodden strip of earth dissected by gaping grooves.

Long after all these events, a scout-ant from the *Lasius flavus* shepherd tribe, who had survived by a complete miracle, hobbled around the now deserted former Eden, meeting neither friend nor foe, unable to guess his bearings, lost, miserable, a microscopic victim of the unfolding catastrophe of life on earth.

Following orders, the detachment spent the night in a small village. The dogs kept barking and retreating with a whimper; soldiers started drifting towards the river with their buckets and water flasks; a coarse voice issued words of command; the unsettled hens kept clucking, and then the night descended upon the earth, punctual to the second.

That was when the stars lit up in the sky, pouring forth the light that had been shining for billions of years.

THE PLANS

The agenda of the little swallow, the one that had flown to Sivtsev Vrazhek from Central Africa and settled underneath Tanyusha's window, was more or less fulfilled. The young had hatched, grown strong, learned how to fly and were ready for an independent existence. That meant that the remaining chores were few and easy, the appetite for life nowhere nearly as powerful, and the swallow's principal aims, those that she shared with her entire community, largely centred round a nourishing diet to ensure enough strength for the return passage. Only the young were genuinely intoxicated with life. Still strangers to passions but brimming with *joie de vivre*, they were happy to spend all their days snooping around and chasing flies, prattling atop the telegraph cables – only to stop suddenly and soar up high in pursuit of the rays of a departing sun – since the twilight was already creeping in down below.

The life programme adhered to by the disagreeably clever student, Ehrberg, was more complex. He was about to complete his studies at the university and expected to be offered tenure as per his degree (State Law), after which he planned to secure a marriage of convenience but based on passion. Since he was in no hurry whatsoever, he could comfortably take his time and have a good look around, prior to selecting a wife from among the young generation of the professorial circles. One of the candidates for such bliss was Tanyusha. That was why Ehrberg, the student, was a regular at the Sunday soirees in the old ornithologist's house; however, while keeping her in reserve, he continued his unhurried but comprehensive research, reasonably confident that he would form an adequate pool to select from.

War was declared in July. The disagreeably clever student, Ehrberg, having just completed his finals, turned out to be one of the half-a-billion people whose daily plans were thwarted and frustrated. Like all people of intellect, having partaken of the wisdom of political science, he believed that the war would last for no longer than two or three months, at the most. That was why, reluctant to undermine his career by securing a civilian vacancy on the home front, he enrolled into a school for junior officers. The uniform suited him; once he graduated to a full officer, the new uniform was guaranteed to prove even more becoming. An enforced vacation from intellectual activities was badly needed. Military drills were good for physical fitness. Ehrberg immediately mastered the art of thumping the ground with his boots, reporting for duty, keeping his belt tightened as per regulations, and leaving his clothes for the night in a neat and orderly pile. He was tall and so, during various drills, was invariably chosen as parade leader.

The person most ardently in love with him was the professor's maid, Dunyasha, whose brother had been at the front since the very early days of the war. Ehrberg, seeing as he was to become an officer, seemed to her a superior human being, utterly unattainable (which in her case was exactly what he was), and when helping him out of his cadet's coat, she blushed helplessly, huge red blotches spreading upwards from her chin and on to the tips of her ears. Dunyasha was the first to notice that Lenochka's gaze was constantly fixed on Ehrberg, her eyes round and full of amazement. And no wonder: he was handsome, imposing and able to discuss military operations with the same aplomb and confidence as he had previously shown in discourse on Stanislavsky's theatre or prominent issues of international law. Yet now, in this military uniform, he seemed even more lovable and endearing to the artless girl's heart.

Had Tanyusha guessed that she was among Ehrberg's favoured choices she would have feared him; but Ehrberg treated her like anyone else, only being particularly deferential and tenderly attentive towards the old lady, Aglaya Dmitriyevna. Tanyusha found this behaviour appealing and, as a result, she liked Ehrberg. She neither understood nor shared his interests. Still, it was commendable that, unlike some others, he didn't scurry off to this or that bolthole but opted for active combat and enrolled in the officer-training school. Every member of the professor's household approved, and Tanyusha was pleased that he was in her immediate circle. She had some vague inkling about Lena's feelings, but the times were such that no one thought of sharing or discussing issues of a personal nature, not even music: the war dominated everything and it felt bizarre to concentrate on anything else.

Ehrberg had a mother, a lady of a somewhat advanced age. He never introduced her to anyone; either the occasion never arrived or he saw no profit in doing so. His late father had been an ethnic German from Riga, while his mother was a Moscow commoner, totally insignificant. Ehrberg's mother, too, had plans: let everything in life be as desired by her wonderful son. Previously, everything had been to his father's liking, and nothing bad had come of it. Men knew more than women could guess. And so she wore a lace cap, ran the house, and made sure that the sturdy and durable white crocheted antimacassars on the backs of their armchairs stayed rigorously clean.

Ehrberg regularly kissed his mother's hand. Still, had she ever wanted to kiss his, it would have been equally easy and natural. When he was going out, she never questioned him about where he was off to or whether to expect him back. If necessary, he would let her know himself.

The swallow's plans included an anxious, rudderless migration; Ehrberg's plans were all stability and solid roots. When Ehrberg drank his tea, his hand, placing his glass in the middle of the saucer, looked steady, precise and beautiful.

TIME

In the basement area underneath the ornithologist's study, right where a girder supported the load-bearing wall, a fluff of white mould was spreading and masking a greenish stain. Over time, as the miniscule particles of wood and damp specks of plaster trickled down to the damp stones of the floor, a small mound was formed.

From the point of view of the mouse this stain was a sort of tapestry. The fungal design was intricate, subtle and multi-coloured. Thousands of generations had contributed their efforts towards its emergence. Exudation of the slake lime awakened the forms of life nestling within the cavities of the brickwork underneath the layer of plaster. Without any oversight or masterplan, the project of destruction was well underway. Microscopic organisms were at work, engaged in what they saw as love and nutrition, ploughing and fertilising the fungal field. They perished in their turn, exuding heat and stimulating the succulent mycelium that, in turn, was busy growing a dense forest of graceful palm trees, drooping willows and tenacious, extravagant vines.

The same continuous life and the unremitting effort that knew not an hour or a minute of relief kept the wooden girder warm. An infinitesimal grub, soft but steely-headed, drilled passages through the grains of wood; soon, exhausted, it would shroud itself in a cocoon, transform into a bug, lay an egg and die. The new grub would build a new tunnel and thus create, within the flesh of the wood, a sketch or a drawing. This was how the cold, dead wood that had, in times long past, greedily suckled the soil and unfurled its leaves so as to face the sun more efficiently, became warm again and imbibed the heat generated by millions of nests and workshops, and dreamed of returning to the soil and being resurrected by its life-giving juices.

The grey mouse was busy, straining his teeth and tiny claws to splinter the slivers off the thick floor boards, efficiently and steadfastly, the balls of his eyes glowing and the muscles of his tail engaged to the full. This was the project that had been started by his predecessors. The precise engineering assessment of distances and directions had already been carried out.

By now, the results of that assessment had been forgotten, but the traces left by the teeth and claws pointed him in the right direction. His hind legs braced against the unevenness of the wall and the friability of the stone chippings, the mouse was concurrently engaged in two projects: carrying on the cultural endeavour of preceding generations and filing down his teeth, which had been growing too fast.

An external noise spooked the industrious toiler underground. A wagon had rumbled by, bumping on the cobblestones of the Moscow side street. Several flakes drifted off the wall, the litter blocking the worm's passage. A decayed wood fibre had finally snapped. The professor's old house trembled and tilted by a few fractions of a millimetre, imperceptible even to a mouse's eye. A droplet of rain from the day before had slid between the pebble and the outside wall. A rusty nail snapped on the roof of the house, the very nail that had held the iron roof tile in place. The swallow flittered out of its nest underneath the window, hovered in the air, inspected the elements of its structure and returned to its abandoned eggs, reassured. Its new home was strong and sturdy.

The professor needed some reference data; he had been leafing through a voluminous German publication and then remembered that he had quoted these same figures in an earlier article. He pulled the box out of the filing cabinet, eased out the article and wondered at his previous conclusions; the new data called for new insights. The new manuscript was of the same size as the original one, but this one was recently conceived. The paper had been lined exactly as before, yet the old paper had turned yellow. What's more, the professor's handwriting, once bold and confident, was getting smaller and looked uneven, slanting to the right. The professor hadn't realised that was happening. His young wife, clad in a dress with puffed sleeves, her waist beautifully small, cast him a glance from the wall but he paid no heed, not even to her.

The old lady in the adjacent room retrieved her dentures out of the glass and wiped them dry. She put them in, masticated a bit, adjusted them and checked the result in the mirror: the depressions in her cheeks stretched out and looked smooth. She sighed and righted her bonnet.

Tanyusha was out. She sat in a large, half-empty classroom, listening intently to the lecture. The professor was cautious and wary of coming across as too radical; still, he was chipping away at the theory of directed evolution. His critical mind clamoured for a circular flow of history. Retreating through the centuries, he created a beautiful image of what used to be the culture of the Orient. An amazed Tanyusha, who had just finished her sixteenth spring and had been taught to admire Mediterranean culture ever since preparatory school, was suddenly made to realise that the cultures along the Mediterranean coast did nothing more than negate or restore cultures much more ancient, created by the peoples who had come into this world so much earlier.

From times long past a grandiose religious system emerged, its rigorous tenets all- encompassing and applicable to all aspects of life, permeating the interests of spirit and the trifles of the everyday, filling the entire human existence to the brim.

What was becoming perceptible from under the layers of Greek science and philosophy, unexpectedly stripped of their originality, was Babylon, and the sublime ideas generated in Egypt, Iran and India shone forth. The continuity of the historical process had been repeatedly severed by the fall of cultures and the completion of cycles.

All this filled the old professor with pessimism and bitterness, but the young were taking it in quite a different light; they were developing an admiration of the past, deference to their distant predecessors – not mere anthropoids but thinkers, poets and outstanding politicians.

Out of the ruins of the Ancient World, a new source of life was working its way through; thought was striving to find a new renaissance.

Yet both the old and the young were aware of this – the collapse of values supposed to be intrinsic, the tottering of the foundations of everyday life, the proximity of a storm gathering over the new Babylon.

Tanyusha listened to the professor and watched him closely, registering his gold pince-nez sliding off the tip of his nose, peeking into the past, developing a sense of the future. She was growing up. In her innocent mind, the records of infantile conclusions and straightforward beliefs were being struck out, the scribbles of childhood diaries were being overwritten with the stenography of a new lexicon; and so, the tar of thought was trickling into the honey of the heart.

Tanyusha was all ears, her mouth slightly open.

SOLDIERS

Dunyasha's brother, Andrei Kolchagin, a private in the infantry regiment, had very little to do with her masters' townhouse in Sivtsev Vrazhek.

Prior to his conscription, he had lived in the countryside, and the war broke out just as he was about to turn twenty-three. Before he knew it, he found himself in the trenches, and soon afterwards his regiment received the order to retreat.

For all that, Private Kolchagin didn't have the foggiest whether they were marching forwards or backwards. He hadn't had a chance to see the adversary at close quarters; he'd just heard something of them from a distance. He couldn't grasp why the war was necessary, but, whatever the orders, he carried them out diligently and promptly. He was resilient and usually content with the food rations. Being single and not yet in possession of a household, he missed the countryside less than the others. When exhausted, he slept; he would drink if it was appropriate, either if he could afford it or when on someone else's dime. He respected the officers that didn't make free with their fists, yet respected those of them who did resort to force even more, believing them to be the genuine article.

There were thousands, maybe millions of soldiers like him around – some older, some younger, some dimmer, some more quick-witted. *En masse*, they formed a formidable military resource, while individually, they were Ivans, Vasilys, Mikolais from, say, the village of Vytyazhki near the Krutoyar settlement. One or two thousand miles away from their little villages lay small towns with buildings of stone and access to rich supplies of manure – Blaukirche or Johanniswald. The soldiers coming from those townships wore copper helmets, were more literate and had a better understanding of things. They paraded more impressively, too. Yet they only formed a formidable force when together, whereas, viewed separately, they were Hanses or Wilhelms, petty farmers, seasonal farmhands, industrial workers. Further away still, once lived, but ended up being conscripted, certain Jeans and Basils, born in insignificant towns like Massy or Bièvres; in the south, women from a picturesque coastal Pieve di Castello or a mountainous Rocca di Sant' Antonio were seeing off their young Giovannis, Giuseppes and Basilios. The new recruits behaved dashingly and heroically, especially when the ladies were around; but what was really uppermost in their souls was the sense of absurdity thinly disguised as sheepish bewilderment. Still, a plethora of simple, easily pronounceable words had been dredged up, along with some beautiful figures of speech, nearly identical in all languages and utilised to replace and hollow out any critical thought. The introduction of those words had been the business of lawyers with little experience but a burning ambition to use journalism as a trampoline to give them a leg-up into parliament. Many decent, honourable and intelligent people were sincerely convinced that all of this was good, honourable and even intelligent, and that was what lent real gravitas to the notion of war and the idea of patriotism.

Sturdy waste pipes had been laid out underneath the edifices of diplomatic graveyards, and foul liquid streamed along those pipes towards the central cesspit, and then onto the irrigated fields, and the result was an incredible crop of cauliflower. That was how, having passed through the stage of diligent purification, bureaucratic dissimulation and filth were transformed into the beauty of bravery and genuine tears. As for the narrow-minded people, they talked about a straightforward deception, which was really unfair, since the deception had been complicated and grandiose. This was how low-brow people became defeatists while the wise retreated into their own shells, some for years, others for ever more.

In the meantime, the difference between these and the others, and the third group, and the fourth, and everyone else, was so infinitesimally small, so negligible, that fate decreed, for fear of a possible misinterpretation and not wishing to split hairs, to furnish them all with the same lot. Fate cracked its whip, and this whip left an angry red welt on the bodies of all and sundry.

So it went. However, there were things more pressing than these considerations, to name but one – the procurement of a shirt and some trousers. Somehow, from the start there was grief with the army-issue togs, while mobile baths were few and far between, or absent entirely. On the other hand, to possess your own hand-made shirt – that was something, it was not easy to explain why, but any fellow with a head on his shoulders would clock it straight away. If a bath was equal to the holy Easter, a shirt was tantamount to the day of resurrection, just like getting fresh air after having spent time suffocating in a dugout. That was why Andrei wrote Dunyasha a letter that passed the requisite censorship, reached the kitchen in Sivtsev Vrazhek and ended up in the professor's dining room.

It was Tanyusha who read the letter, and everyone joined in the discussion, while Dunyasha tried to work out how much it would cost to send a shirt to her brother, especially if she made it herself.

After lunch, Tanyusha came into the kitchen to give Dunyasha the money, a sum considerably larger than was necessary; large enough to buy two shirts at once, as well as the trousers. Tanyusha was embarrassed, while Dunyasha might have felt happy if only she could have worked out why her masters were giving her the money towards the needs of her brother. She had been a live-in maid for quite a few years now, and thought her employers were kind – they often gave her presents, which meant they had to be pleased with her service. Still, why they gave the money to buy Andrei a shirt was not at all clear. So Dunyasha accepted the gift as if it was for her own benefit.

It felt simpler that way. Dunyasha bought some durable fabric, spent a few evenings sewing, made the shirt, and sent it to the frontline. Tanyusha made enquiries about how to forward such a parcel, but it was Dunyasha herself who addressed the package. She also sent him a letter. She felt strange, did Dunyasha, to think the letter and the shirt would now go straight to the front line where Andrei was busy shooting the Germans.

Yet this is exactly what happened. Nearly a month passed and the postman delivered a reply from the soldier. Andrei had received the shirt, it fitted just fine; as for the enemy, *we will be done with 'em soon.* Hans was writing a similar letter to his wife in a tiny place called Blaukirche. But the best letter flew to Pieve di Castello, penned by the handsome Giovanni and addressed to his fiancée. He sent her *mille baci*, and at the very end he added: *'L'amor e invincibile, come la forza italiana.'*

It should be said that his unit was stationed, for now, on the outskirts of Verona. Still, that was not the issue. The card was nice, and in the upper left corner it carried the emblem of Savoy. Rosina showed the card to her best friend and both felt elated.

Going to bed, Rosina slid the letter underneath her pillow. She did go to sleep eventually, but first spent quite some time sighing. She was considered the most beautiful girl in her village.

TANYUSHA'S PARTY

On the day of Tanyusha's birthday (she had just turned seventeen!), music could be heard at Sivtsev Vrazhek well into the small hours of the morning, although performed not by Eduard Lvovich but by a hired ballroom pianist. For the first time ever, the professor's home, normally so civilian and proper, had opened its doors to young servicemen; quite a crowd in fact, including several officers, a number of cadets, and one volunteer, a certain Beloushin. Dunyasha's brother Andrei happened to be on short leave, recovering from a slight injury, and so gave Dunyasha a hand when attending to the guests. He would say to Dunyasha:

'Call that a tune? Our lads at the front could show them how it's done. And the music our boys play – that's real music! We've got the regimental band, see. This old racket, it's just not the same!'

While serving tea to the officers, Andrei would snap to attention; as for the cadets, he preferred to stand facing sideways, while the volunteer he ignored altogether.

The most dashing among the officers was Stolnikov, still quite young but already a full lieutenant, having received his promotion in the trenches. He was physically fit and well-built, tanned, a wit and a decent dancer. The only person who danced better was Ehrberg – still a cadet but on the cusp of graduation. If Lenochka's heart, as yet undecided, could ever be lured astray from her long-standing adoration of Ehrberg, the only person capable of this would have been Stolnikov. He was more direct and approachable, while Ehrberg's attraction lay in his gravitas and air of mystery. Lenochka was quite enjoying herself at the party, and her eyebrows were expressing less astonishment than usual.

Stolnikov was due to return to the trenches in a few days' time, and to tell the truth, he was rather looking forward to it. He was visiting Moscow on business, commissioned to procure some horses. By now, the front line was his home, whereas here, in Moscow, he was simply a guest. An artilleryman, he had been around the block, had things to say, had grown accustomed to his unit. He felt that real life happened out there, not in this place. Still, one could have a nice time here, too, especially when people didn't talk nonsense about a war of which they understood nothing.

Ehrberg, too, might soon be dispatched to the front. By now everybody was aware that the war was likely to drag on.

Among the guests there were also several students: a future doctor by the name of Mukhanov, the lawyers Mertvago and Trynkin, the naturalist Vasya Boltanovsky. The latter was Tanyusha's long-time friend, forever full of youthful enthusiasm, a believer, a theatre-goer, and a lover of music. According to Vasya, in whose company Tanyusha always felt uninhibited and free, the world had gone mad, but it was not something to worry about; on the contrary, it was all extremely interesting.

'We shall witness such phenomena, such events, things we cannot even conceive of at the present. Life is so fascinating, Tanyusha!'

Vasya Boltanovsky was the old ornithologist's favourite; besides, he still remembered Vasya's father as an equally passionate and cheerful student. Impeccably polite and somewhat old-fashionably well-mannered with everybody else, Vasya was the only one with whom the old professor allowed himself the familiar form of address. Sometimes he would affectionately tug on Vasya's forelock and pat him with a fatherly hand.

'Life is always interesting, my boy, and to be so, it does not need anything spectacular, actually the opposite is true. These events of yours only hamper our ability to read the book of nature with proper attention. You of all people, you read natural sciences and should know this better than anyone else. It is preferable to study wars through a microscope – it hardly makes any difference. As for life, it is always better in times of peace.'

Vasya tried to argue:

'All you can see through a microscope are specks, whereas here we are talking about people. And I don't mean only the war. The entire world, professor, is now topsy-turvy. Before the war is over there will be such goings-on, such happenings... It's awe-inspiring and joyous!'

'True enough, a lot of awe will be inspired. Not much joy is to be expected, though. If you get killed in action, Vasya, your mother is unlikely to be overjoyed. You mustn't talk like this! Think about the bloodshed. What a horrendous price to pay!'

Vasya added, pensively, 'True. That much is true. But as for the bloodshed...'

The future doctor, Mukhanov, who had not yet sat the exam on osteology, was quick to offer his own words of wisdom: 'Surgery means blood, professor...'

This earned him a dressing-down from the professor, who disliked medicine:

'I don't suppose you'd care to take into account that some operations don't involve blood. If, say, your jaw is dislocated, no one will be in a hurry to cut you open. But the essential point is this: the entire world of organisms survives without any operations; their existence is not at all inferior to ours, so there's no justification for your hubris. Nature does not tolerate forceful interventions into the global evolution. It provokes revenge, and brutal it is, too.'

Tanyusha thought that Grandpa was right inasmuch as he was a kindly man, and because killing a man was damnable. Still, did any war straightforwardly equal murder? Did the 'peaceful evolution' of nature even exist? Everywhere there were sudden leaps, wars, revolutions, conflict. Grandpa wanted things to be uncomplicated, tranquil and good. Yet reality was such that it simply wasn't always so. However, this gave rise to questions for which Tanyusha had no ready answers.

Dunyasha's brother Andrei also had an opinion on the subject of war. He expounded this opinion to Dunyasha in the kitchen, thus:

'I must've killed a man, sure; not with my own hands but with a bullet, of course. Still, if I have to, I won't shy away, I'll stick the bastards with my bayonet. Nothing to it, 'cause I'm not a murderer, but a warrior. As for why we are warring, Dunia, 'tis for reasons of state, not for our own sake. I don't give a damn about them Germans, seeing as I've got to hate 'em, don't I, 'cause it's them that made me take the oath, and it's them that's making me suffer. The officers give us an order and on we go, ready to be wounded or even killed. But do I want this war? Can't say I do; in fact I can say I don't want one, cross my heart. Then, the real issue is the lice. Why should I feed the little buggers? We still feed 'em, don't you know? And that's a thing to bear in mind.'

Asked, by the old professor, 'When will you beat the Germans?', Andrei came back all buoyant:

'Yes, sir, we'll finish the bastards soon, glory to the motherland. No doubt about it.'

Saying this, he glanced sideways at the young combat officer. The latter said, 'Well done, infantry!' and Andrei bellowed, 'Glad to be of service, your Excellency!'

There was general laughter, the cadets felt a prick of envy and Lenochka finally came to a conclusion that Stolnikov that day was definitely more exciting than Ehrberg.

On his way through the hallway Andrei pushed the volunteer aside with his elbow, as if by accident. Back in the kitchen he announced to Dunyasha:

'There's only one of them up there who's the real thing, just like me. The rest of 'em? Fancy boys, don't know their arse from their elbow.'

THE HIRED PIANIST

Eduard Lvovich, unintentionally forgotten by all and, surely, a most uninspiring person that day, was seated in the corner of the living room in a low armchair, his legs gracelessly drawn in, his shoulders heavily stooped. Listening to the hired pianist, he kept grimacing involuntarily as the pianist pounded the ivories; Eduard Lvovich's heart swelled in sympathy for the piano.

He couldn't, in all fairness, ignore the invitation to Tanyusha's party, a celebration to be held on such a momentous occasion (*she was turning seventeen!*). By now, though, it should have been quite possible to leave, without waiting for the dinner, but Eduard Lvovich did not dare to do so.

Glancing casually from his nook, he caught an occasional flash of Tanyusha's dress, her graceful head, very Russian, with her hair pulled back, tight and smooth. Tanya was promising to blossom into a veritable beauty. Hers was not just the charm of youth, she was genuinely lovely. She was as lovely as Eduard Lvovich himself was pathetic and homely. She was young, while Eduard Lvovich was quite advanced in years. He was talented, true, but this fact alone gave him no advantages over a single soul. Even Vasya Boltanovsky – the snub-nosed, dishevelled, funny Vasya – had a head start on Eduard Lvovich, by virtue of being young and daring. Vasya held Tanyusha in his arms and whirled her around on the dance floor. Tanyusha's breath was on Vasya's neck. The hired pianist kept bashing the piano keys, and it all felt nothing short of pure torture.

Just then Mertvago, the student, made his appearance in the living room – thin, with a shaved head, looking older than his years – along with his companion, a young girl whose surname was a mystery to Eduard Lvovich, as everyone else normally referred to her as Mertvago's fiancée. She was only a year Tanyusha's senior but already gave the impression of a young lady – calm, immaculately turned out, allegedly rich. Mertvago was due to graduate the following year. This meant that in only a year's time he would be wearing a tailcoat and addressing his audiences thus: 'Your Honour and gentlemen of the jury!' His evenings would be spent leafing through folders bearing the surname of his patron. For him, there would be no conscription – he was an only son. What a lucky fellow, this student Mertvago was!

Nevertheless, Eduard Lvovich did not feel envious of him, not really, and not even of Vasya – except when the boy danced with Tanyusha. But his envy of Ehrberg was much more persistent and truly intense. There was something a little frightening about Ehrberg. He was clever and crafty. How strange, though, that Ehrberg was about to become an officer and go to war. Was it possible that Ehrberg had miscalculated?

The professor sought out the composer.

'So nice when the young are having a good time! Are you not tempted to have a dance?'

Eduard Lvovich rubbed his hands together:

'Yes. Or rather no. I c-can't anymore. But I enjoy w-watching.'

'Our Tanyusha is all grown up, wouldn't you say?'

'Our' meant that Eduard Lvovich was now included in the family. Then again, why not? He was Tanyusha's mentor in music. Eduard Lvovich looked askance at the professor's beard and was met with his broad and happy smile. Immediately, he decided that he would leave right away. He sat there, fumbling for a suitable phrase and unsure whether the time was right to announce his intentions. And so, he simply rubbed his hands once more. Just at this instant the pianist hit on an indecently off-key cadence and brought the dance to an abrupt end.

The professor shifted his gaze to the future Mertvagos, came up to the fiancée, patted the student's shoulder but couldn't think of anything to say except, 'So, how is it going? Ah well, there, there!' and lumbered over to the dining room where Aglaya Dmitriyevna was critically inspecting the cutlery – was everything in its proper place? Had she counted right? Had Tanyusha remembered to place the name cards? Tanyusha's choice of neighbours was Vasya and Eduard Lvovich. The older couple were not dining with the others but the professor came up to the table, downed half a shot of vodka and chased it with a marinated mushroom. He felt immediately warm and cheerful. Slightly envious, he shot a glance at the made-up table, remembered his catarrh and said to his wife, 'Well, Grandma, you really have been busy!' He kissed her wrinkled hand and made to leave for his study. On the doorstep, however, he lingered and then came back. He approached the old lady once more:

'I have been watching our Tanyusha, Grandma. So grown up now, wouldn't you say?'

Aglaya Dmitriyevna looked at her husband, mentally counting how many forks she was short of. The professor stroked her cheek and she forgot her arithmetic. The professor reiterated:

'Quite a milestone, what? For our Tanyusha, this granddaughter of ours!'

Aglaya Dmitriyevna's kindly face beamed. Perhaps she recalled that once upon a time she had also been seventeen, or possibly she had finally worked out how many more forks were required. They stood there, looking at each other, so tenderly old. Suddenly, a teardrop rolled out of the professor's eye straight down onto his beard. Embarrassed, he turned away hastily and his button became entangled in the lace of the old lady's shawl. He offered: 'So that's the way it goes, right? Tell you what, I've just chased a nice little shot with a mushroom.'

And both of them, fragile and elderly, just stood there, wiping each other's eyes. Aglaya Dmitriyevna's small mouth puckered up, and the drop that had slid from the professor's beard ended up on his frockcoat – the old lady's hand got wet.

Stealthily making his way along the outer wall of the living room, Eduard Lvovich edged into the hallway. Once there, he spent a long time hunting down his cloak in the pile of military overcoats – his was reddish, with a checked lining. Then he tentatively opened the door into the kitchen and asked, sheepishly, 'Dunyasha, would you mind terribly locking the door after me?'

'Aren't you staying for supper, sir?'

'Yes. N-no, thank you very much.'

The whole way towards the turn-off, the energetic hired pianist continued punishing the ear of the timid composer.

VISIONS

Private Andrei Kolchagin, Dunyasha's brother, had been wounded in action but sustained nothing more than a minor injury. The bullet had grazed his head, ripped off a small patch of flaxen stubble and flown further on – it might have ended up deep in the ground or, perhaps, in someone's heart. At the time they were charging forward attempting to take an Austrian trench. Sure enough, they took it. Still, Andrei Kolchagin was picked up by the hospital orderlies as he had collapsed, either because of the blood loss or perhaps because he had suffered a concussion.

The wound healed in no time at all but even so Andrei was kept in the field hospital, mainly on account of unremitting headaches that gave him no respite. Sometimes he moaned, other times he could not even move. When the headaches had finally eased off, he was granted leave. Then, having properly rested in Moscow, he finally recovered fully. He had no permanent residence and slept in Dunyasha's kitchen while she took the bed in her room. His meals came courtesy of the professor's household, for which he was grateful. Where he could, he was glad to lend a hand, say, in running errands. He had been granted a month's leave.

The only reminder of his injury was troubled sleep, sometimes nightmares. Especially if he had drunk one too many. On the whole Andrei Kolchagin was not a heavy drinker – he drank mostly on high days and holidays. Besides, no wine was available in the shops, which meant if he did drink, it was only once in a while.

Andrei was woken up by the sound of his own voice; clearly and cheerfully he had exclaimed, 'Yes, sir!' And something in the left side of his body was pounding against the thin mattress on the floor, rather like a machine-gun – not faster, not slower, but just as loud. And straight away his dream evaporated.

By now, he was accustomed to this condition. Normally, he would lie there, lingering between a dream and wakefulness, thinking about something else. Back in the field hospital his bed had been next to a volunteer, a gentleman, and what fanciful things he had told Andrei! He had a good head on his shoulders and knew what was what – all about life, and the war, and that maybe the war had not been needed at all, and about all sorts of lies and deceptions. He talked about everything without restraint; he'd had his foot amputated and now he cared nothing for any of it, and, in any case, he had nothing to feel sorry about. To tell the truth, that was why Andrei didn't trust him all that much; not least because he was gentry, a former teacher. But listen he did.

Now, lying there all alone Andrei couldn't remember anything from those conversations, except this – that maybe there was no need for any war and that it was all a con. They were muddling the soldiers' minds. Still, no denying that the lice in the trenches were real pests. And yet, this was for the sake of the Fatherland[5]. But why there were no baths available? And when the machine-gun started to bark, just like now, in some place in the left side of his body – rat-a-tat, rat-a-tat...

After this Andrei started thinking about boots – boots in general, new ones, and especially fancy ones. He recalled all the types of boots that he had ever seen. To lay his hands

....

[5] In Russian, both 'Motherland' and 'Fatherland' are used, the former being more intimate, the latter – more official.

MIKHAIL OSORGIN

on a pair of officer's boots (so as to wear in civvy street, on special occasions), he would probably have sacrificed half of his leave. Still, those would have been no use in the trenches.

Then he switched over to thinking about the kitchen, but didn't linger there for too long – just that there were mice, that Dunyasha was wheezing in her sleep, that the kitchen smelled of fried onions and that he couldn't be bothered to get up and go out for a tinkle. Meanwhile the machine-gun in his side was still hammering on, and Andrei's forehead was doused in sweat. What sort of a disease was it, this one that just wouldn't go away?

For some reason his mind turned to his company commander – now, that was not someone beloved by his men! Other officers could be this or that, came in all shapes and sizes, whereas their commander was a beast, nothing human about him. He was brave in action, Andrei would give him that, he feared nothing, but, say, on a drill, or just on a regular day, he sure wasn't human, a fiend if Andrei ever saw one. The man had a lazy eye, roared at all and sundry, and was always free with his fists. There was nothing worse than an officer who bashed you for no reason, out of pure spite.

That was when a nightmare hit Andrei. It was as if the company officer started hitting Andrei and Andrei answered by hitting him back. But all he managed to hit was pure air, because he couldn't get purchase. Andrei was terrified but felt he could not stop, not now; he was a goner anyway, so at least it would be for a good reason. His breast felt ready to explode from anger, any minute now it could burst through his tunic. Andrei pushed his heart back in with his left hand, kept it firmly in, while his right hand pummelled the officer's ugly mug, straight between his piggish little eyes – and all in vain. It looked like he would perish for nothing, and that hurt Andrei most of all – now he would never get a chance to let it all out on the moustachioed mug of an officer! Meanwhile it looked like the cross-eyed bastard was sneering – he had never sneered before!

Andrei made an effort to wake up – thank the Lord! All had disappeared but still, Andrei was face to face with his company commander and the latter kept hammering him against his left side with a wooden spoon – left-two, one-right, left-two; the spoon was army-issue and so went straight through him. Andrei felt no pain, only hurt. So, his anger started growing again, and again his commander faced him, but the same nasty business repeated itself. Andrei grabbed him by the throat, just under his collar, and squeezed him hard but the officer's throat felt soft, like a clump of fabric, and nothing came out of it. The commander was rolling his eyes at the same time as his throat croaked: 'I'll have you shot, you bastard!' Then he snatched the spoon with his hand and yanked it out of Andrei, flesh and all. Andrei groaned and came to, covered in sweat all over again.

Andrei turned on his other side. His neighbour, the volunteer, squeezed one nostril, blew his nose and said, in that gentle voice of his, 'The war is senseless and now we shall tear your commander to shreds!' He pulled his bedsheet up as if it were the commander, and started ripping it and folding, ripping and folding. And Andrei thought: *There you go, you're a toff, it's all just a lark to you*! Something zinged nearby, and whz-z-z-z – grazed Andrei's head. He hollered a dirty word and woke up again, completely this time.

By now light was coming through the window. A large fly buzzed against the pane, and Andrei had a slight headache. He wet the back of his head with some cold water from the tap – just as the paramedic had advised him to, made a trip outside for his tinkle and noted that the alarm clock showed it was just after six in the morning. Andrei decided not to go back to bed – it would be time to get up soon, anyway. He pulled on his breeches, donned a tunic and went out of the gate where the caretaker was busy shovelling up some rubbish from the pavement and emptying his shovel in a large box. Andrei stood there watching him work, with no particular curiosity, perhaps even some sympathy. Much as he was a serviceman himself, he saw nothing humiliating in a job that involved cleaning the streets.

Afterwards they stood side by side, smoking. The caretaker said:

'Someone got up early today.'

'Can't sleep properly after the hospital.'

'Many days left?'

'Tomorrow's the start of the last week, and then it's off to feed the lice again.'

'You up to it?'

'Why not, there are decent folk out there too. Be nice to know, like, if maybe this war is for nothing, after all.'

The caretaker, who had been in his post for twenty years, mulled it over and offered, authoritatively:

'That, dear boy, is well above our station. It's not up to us to know such things. Then again, when a foe comes to Russia, we have to go to war.'

Andrei countered:

'It's our blood, though.'

'And what good is your blood? Or you, even? Off with you, onto a shovel and into a box. It'll all be sorted in the life beyond.'

Andrei's head was still aching but he went out to fetch an armful of firewood for Dunyasha's stove.

The day was Monday, a heavy start to the week. Sivtsev Vrazhek often struggled to wake up.

DE PROFUNDIS

Steel, copper, cast iron – that was its robust, well-groomed body. Its legs were rounded off into wheels, steam and oil ran through its veins while fire blazed in its heart. The colossus stood motionless.

Suddenly, there was a full-chested moan, then a series of abrupt coughs. The giant gave a shudder, and the entire chain of carriages came to life, shuddering, clanking and slowly juddering forth. A cloud of smoke billowed upwards, while deep in the giant's innards a soot-faced and oil-soaked stoker – its nanny, its parasite and caresser – kept pottering and bustling about. More food for the fire to help the giant breathe! And suddenly, it was far away.

Though huge, barrel-chested and powerful, in the distance it had turned into a crawling caterpillar. It had been tamed and now was busy tugging along all that had been entrusted to its great power. It groaned, whistled, sped forward, afraid of wasting even one minute; when encountering similar industrious toilers, hauling along their own cargo, it greeted them with a receding clamour. They all were enslaved by Man.

Private Kolchagin was being transported back to active service on board the giant's heated freight carriage, packed to overcapacity with live bodies. Now it also carried, in second class, young officers – among them the disagreeably clever Ehrberg, clad in a smart new uniform, solemn and forever enigmatic to every enamoured Lenochka. Ehrberg kept glancing at the hands of his watch and listening to the rattle of the train wheels.

Two minutes per verst[6] – too slow. The inscribed milestones floated by the windows. A large milestone, then four interim distance markers showing sazhens. Choo-choo, chooka-chooka, choo-choo, chooka-chooka. What if Ehrberg did not come back? Such a rational young man, do you really know your future? A bullet knows its trajectory but a man takes a step towards it, unaware of its flight. What if yesterday was the last time that he would ever see Moscow – the Kremlin turrets and Sivtsev Vrazhek? Choo-choo, chooka-chooka. How very strange! And yet quite possible. Ehrberg returned the watch to his pocket and buttoned up his field jacket.

A jolt. The tamed giant had come to a stop, hastily slurped some water, built a new fire, inhaled the steam. Soldiers hurriedly clambered back into their freight carriages and passenger compartments – kit bags with provisions on their backs, some carrying home-made biscuits, the lucky few even a leg of mutton. Why hurry, though? Seeing that people were being killed out there? Here was an officer, travelling second class; outside his window lay a field, and above it, the sky, and in that field was a body ruptured by a fragment of a shell. Earlier, this body had been travelling in a similar way, along the same route, and harbouring exactly the same hopes.

A soldier had hurled his kit bag into the freight car and proceeded to haul himself inside, trying to gain purchase with his left knee. His right leg still dangled free. How awkward he was; surely a commoner. Hey you, army boy, make sure not to be late returning after your short time at home! Hurry up, live out your final days. Here's your Order of St George for bravery, and a bucketful of lime over your puru-

....

[6]   A verst is an obsolete Russian unit of length defined as 500 sazhens. A verst is equivalent to 1.0668 kilometres.

lent wounds, so that you can choke on it, and not complain in the hereafter; also, here's a mound of soil thrown over you and a communal funeral service for the fallen privates. And the kit bag? What about it? Go on, munch away at your lamb shank – more fool you, with this sheep's brain of yours. On the other hand, an intelligent person, a coldly calculating gentleman would travel to the same destination as you, and this same steam train carries him, too! Maybe it is true that the world has gone mad? The train had pulled away again.

Having delivered this shipment, the locomotive returned with a tender cargo of mutilated human bodies. Fifteen legs to ten bodies – that would have to do! This one had a hole in his back, below the shoulder blade; the bullet went straight through and exited below the nipple. He was coughing, which meant he was alive. That one over there was blind, also alive, as if no fully-sighted ones had survived.

In came the ladies with red crosses, carrying tea, loose tobacco, and flowers. The wounded with the hole in his chest received a posy of wild bluebells, in recognition of his officer's rank, his youth and valour. Why didn't he pull himself up in one laborious movement, and then strangle, pummel someone, anyone, using his crutch as a wooden hammer with which to hit the red crosses and the healthy female breasts, to pound them flat – as thanks for the damn posy? But no, the injured kept smiling and the nurses' hearts were brimming with sweet emotion, their lips exuding honey. But they hadn't really tasted enough honey in their lives, those young warriors carried back by the steam train.

The train reached the terminus, got rid of this lot and rushed back, indefatigable. Now was the time to drag some substantial cargo: machine guns with which to kill and gas masks so as not to be killed, shells for killing and medications for surviving, howitzers for killing and wagons for the wounded. What else? How about a meatgrinder? Its iron sieve could come in handy when hacking, mincing and shredding the brains of Ivans and the hearts of Pyotrs into the same cauldron! Where was the tar and sulphur that would be so useful for making torches out of human carcasses, to light a path into the future? In addition, climbing irons for boots, made of steel and with curly claws – something to drive into the eye sockets and thus help to split the skulls into shards and fragments. Instead, there were bandages for dressing tiny scratches – oh, poor little soldier, he was splitting kindling wood and hurt his little pinkie; the splinter had been extracted, and his finger treated with iodine, wrapped with cotton, dressed with a bandage – such a darling little cocoon. And what if the soldier should start to murmur? Did you really think that the soldiers would stay at the front when the fresh winds started to blow? Yes! The world had lost its mind. The same mind that had earlier plunged it into bitter distress. But not everyone has to be guided by intellect – a fool, too, can set his sights on becoming a tsar.

This load was also delivered. Now the mail train was shuttling back with a letter from Nikolai to Daria, and with regards to all the neighbours, too. 'As for me, I am doing well, still in good health.' The letter still glided along the rail tracks as the one who had sent cried from the ground: 'Stop, wait, I am dead already!' Daria replied to Nikolai with a new instruction: 'May you live for years to come.' As for Nikolai, he did not get to live long, not at all – he had been buried before he turned twenty.

There were also two letters from Ehrberg – one to his mother, the second one addressed to Sivtsev Vrazhek. 'I haven't yet been in action, but on the whole, don't worry on my account. It is not as scary as it seems.'

And then to Tanyusha: 'My regards to you and your family. I often recollect your music soirées on Sundays. It all seems so far away. I hope to hear them many more times as…'

Hopeful? Oh, Ehrberg! Oh you, shrewd and practical Ehrberg, did you not hear the hissing ping – haven't you learned to recognise it yet? Oh, Ehrberg, duck to one side, run, Ehrberg! Throw yourself down on the ground, bury your head, deeper, deeper still! What are you afraid of, Ehrberg? That's what soldiers do. Your attitude might cost you your life, you who have always been so selfish and so scheming. It fell short of your position? Sure, but here it is again, this booming whoosh! Oh, Ehrberg!

That day at Sivtsev Vrazhek Eduard Lvovich was playing De Profundis.

THE DEPARTURE OF THE SWALLOWS

The swallows were ready to leave Russia for Central Africa, flying out in a compact cloud. All they wanted was to spend the winter over there, wait out the cold and then return.

Their homeland was Russia, which also happened to be the land they loved. Russia's fields and the little niches underneath her windows provided the best of everything – they offered food, shelter and love; foreign shores were just for resting on. However, in their motherland, sunshine in winter was sparse; it could easily turn the swallow's heart into a shard of ice. But then again, the summer sun in Central Africa was punishingly hot; its caresses could easily burn one alive. There must have been some other reasons urging the little white-breasted birds to be on their way but it wasn't in the man's gift to comprehend those, not even if this man was the old professor under whose window one of the swallows had left its sturdy little nest made out of Moscow clay.

Travelling at high altitudes, this is what the swallows saw: against the green background, the threads of rivers and cool stains of lakes; little piles of rubbish that were towns and settlements; the forests around them, threadbare; the green fields, scanty – as if nature shunned their smoke and filth and retreated further away.

What they also saw, flying low, was a steady ploughman with his quiet horse, and a trace of upturned earth in their wake.

They also saw the rapid progress of a train sliding along two threads of iron, and the advancement of a car along the grey compacted road; still, the swallows' flight was speedier.

They also saw how gigantic worms made up of armies of soldiers were crawling towards the same border from opposite sides, to the place where the earth had been blown up and where those worms melted down and disappeared.

It also happened, sometimes, that a bird of unheard-of proportions, its humming menacing but tiresome, would pitch up in the sky, encircled by bouncing balls of white and yellow. Several swallows flew into a yellow ball, when it ricocheted off the bizarre bird, and straightaway pulled in their wings as the tiny lumps of their bodies plummeted down to earth, and their immediate neighbours felt dizzy and woozy, hit by the poison that man sent into the sky.

But they kept flying fast and so all of this simply whisked by: viewed from above, the earth was as it had always been, and man was not all that visible upon it. All that changed was the straight lines and tiny squares that man had used to dissect the greenness of vegetation and greyness of fields.

The swallows flew above the sea and they could see, from up high, through the sea to its very bottom. Like tiny leaves propelled by gusts of wind across the pond, tiny vessels crisscrossed the sea, one after another, so dainty against the vast masses of water, speaking not of power but of the insignificance of man. Tired out, the little birds landed on board one of those ships. It was dark and their eyes could not see all that well.

When in the morning the swallows went back up into the air, ready to be on their way, a weird and awkward fish came up from the depth of the sea, approached the ship, emerged on the surface, spat something out and submerged again. The air trembled with such ferocity that it nearly shattered the wings of the tiny feathered travellers. The ship tilted to one side and began to sink silently until it had disappeared. The swallows saw it all but understood little; then again, they didn't really contemplate what business the fish had, sinking the ship with lots of people on board as it was peacefully chugging forward across the sea.

Next, the swallows flew over the sands, aware that their destination was within reach, and taking stock of their losses.

Their losses had been horrendous. Their leader, *en route*, had taken them to Sicily, for a spot of rest. When night fell, men took baskets, nets and sticks, came to the shore and set about thrashing the little birds. Many died that night. Limp and listless, their fragile bodies were shuffled off the beach in baskets; many were trampled underfoot and left to rot on the sand while the survivors picked themselves up and left at dawn.

The birds accepted people's gruesome deeds in the same way as they might accept a hurricane or the surreptitious approach of the murderous frost. Those who survived gave blessings to life and sang glory to the sun.

And then the trajectory of the swallows' flight took them to a spot from where they saw the glare of the first oasis, an event welcomed by their cheerful *chirps* and *whirrs*.

THE DEPARTURE OF A MAN

As the swallows flew away from the Sicilian coast, they had to leave behind many a member of their clan – some dead, others ground down into the dirt. One among other unfortunates could not follow the flock; her wing had been injured. The swallow kept thrashing the air with the healthy wing, momentarily forcing her tired body upwards as she tried to stretch her neck in the direction of her friends' departure. Her *chirp* was just an inaudible whisper and her suffering added nothing to the sum total of suffering in the world.

When the sun rose higher, the swallow curtained her eyes with a bluish sheath and started breathing in the hot air in rapid gasps. By the time the sun had started its new decline, the swallow was dead. It was the same bird that had spent three consecutive springs at Sivtsev Vrazhek, lining her old nest with the new fluff. The one that had seen the human maiden Tanyusha with a jug of water tilted over her naked shoulders, the one that had been chirruping for the old professor, and her song had rung sweeter than the cries of his beloved cuckoos. It was the same swallow that once picked up the grub that had been gnawing through the beam.

At the same time, in a small hollow, a short way from the woods flattened by shelling, some hundred versts from his country's border yet on foreign land (as if all land does not belong to everyone!) lay a grievously injured man in an ensign's uniform. There was a hole in his chest made by a fragment of shrapnel that, in its flight, had contaminated the wound with a scrap of paper, where the red had spread over the blue impression of a rubber stamp and this, now useless, word – 'Ehrberg'.

He was still alive, this man, so disagreeably clever and calculating in life. He was not shrewd anymore but approaching something akin to wisdom. His uninjured eye stared into the sky, which was inflamed and blurred by tears. The fingers of his undamaged hand kept scraping the roots of the grass. His ear picked out moans coming from somewhere nearby, familiar, his own. The moans were gradually replaced by wheezing; something in his chest burbled and this now alien body was enveloped, not for the first time, with cold. Whether or not his consciousness was still alive was something known only to him, the one whose name got stuck inside the oozing wound.

A mouse stuck its head out of the hole, twitched its whiskers and shot back, sensing danger. Trouble could take the shape of a bird of prey, or a hungry wolf. However, that day birds and wolves would have enough to eat.

A beetle with a gilded back, as if displaying the insignia of an officer, crawled past, sluggishly and aimlessly. It was on a lookout for a hiding place for the winter, hoping to survive, but its hours were numbered.

The sun rose up, reached its zenith, gloomily looked down and descended in a short, graceful arc, disappearing below the edge of the earth, leaving a red welt in its wake.

Ehrberg had a mother who lived in Moscow – a timid elderly lady. She didn't know that her motherhood would continue for barely another hour.

All this was simple, and ordinary; and necessary and unnecessary in equal measure. In the general count of the world's losses, it meant nothing at all; in the life of one person, it meant everything. Still, it was everything for only as long as a final breath still stirred the air above the dry, blueish lips.

Suddenly, from some hiding place where the still functioning consciousness tried to linger, reluctant to be extinguished, a thought winged its way skywards, fluttering like a swallow. The centre of the world stopped being its fulcrum, the universe lost its pivot, swerved around and swept off, following the thought. Simultaneously, all the threads of dreams, doubts and attachments that had filled a former life were severed with a slight crack like an electric spark, and all became clear, and all became easy, and the sheets of Bristol board[7] flew apart with a soft rustling sound as the house of cards collapsed.

The greatest human intellect would never have been able to dream up this state of extreme clarity and simplicity. All that was left was to peel away the membrane of human hubris, to throw some soil or cast a communal shroud over a body without a name, a wound without pain, a dark-brown scrap of paper without any real meaning.

Just then a star lit up in the sky, scanned the surface of the earth, spotted Ehrberg's motionless body and was reflected in his dead open eye – a reluctant pale image, as if paying a debt of duty and respect towards someone who had departed from life. Before long the star was obscured by a cloud, and it stayed hidden till the next day.

....

[7]   Bristol board (also referred to as Bristol paper or Super white paper) is an uncoated machine-finished paperboard. It is not named after the city of Bristol in the southwest of England but rather after Frederick Hervey, the Earl of Bristol. Bristol paper is used for printing documents, brochures, promotional materials, envelopes, watercolour painting, paperback books, file folders, tags, tickets and cards.

THE MOST UNREASONABLE CREATURE

It is conceivable that historians researching the various wars have established, or at least are capable of establishing, whose personal command, or whose slight movement of the finger, had sent the world's first ever shell to soar upwards and explode high in the sky.

It is possible that the first ever shot was discharged from a light rifle; equally possible that it had been an artillery salvo, and thus the identity of the first ever fratricide can never be attributed.

Who can tell whether the first ever bullet enjoyed a bath of fresh blood, or whether a fragment of the first ever shell splintered a bone; or whether, having completed the requisite trajectory, it timidly buried itself in the ground? What a priceless field for research! How much would an American collector be prepared to hand over for this pellet of lead or that shard of cast iron?

What was the name of the first bereaved mother? Is there a monument to her anywhere, complete with a fountain – a fountain of tears? Whose album proudly displays a stamp from the first ever letter posted by somebody's son from the frontline? And what was the first cry of pain ever recorded by a gramophone? Had it come from being strangled with a rope or crushed with a tombstone – and was this the first open word of condemnation, loud and vehement?

From now on and for many years to come nobody's inquisitive mind or vivid quill will ever be able to ignore the red poppies of war when ploughing the field or gathering its harvest.

The times of cornflowers and asters have receded into the distant past. The earth breathes anger and seeps with blood.

Where a red poppy won't grow, the ear of rye is also spurned and mushrooms are blazing red underneath a whispering aspen.[8] Vermilion is the colour of the sunset over the sea and incandescent streams trickle down the rays of the northern lights. And memories bind the evil conscience – not swarming like black flies but sticking to it like bed bugs engorged with blood.

Meanwhile, none of this is quite so dramatic, and nature has not changed at all. On the day when the European war broke out, not a single blade of grass and not one white flower, growing for reasons unknown, were overwhelmed with the grandeur of the moment; not a single mountainous rivulet accelerated its lucid course, not one little cloud shed one extra tear.

The storks had not found their nests atop the ruins of what used to be houses and so carried their promise of babies to the neighbouring villages. An apple had its cheek blushed by the sun, turned around and offered another. A mole stayed blind, a mouse remained agile and a hedgehog was as prickly as ever. We do not know why a bee is precisely aware of the shortest aerial route and why a beetle drones like a string on a bass instrument.

'What's happening to me?' asks a pea, swelling. 'Oh, that's hard!' says a young hunch-backed succulent sprout, pushing up a clump of soil. 'This is us, hello!' announces a mushroom washing itself in the rainwater. 'And us!' echoes a toadstool. And once, and for all times, the dome of the sky stays punctured with a gold drawing pin.

....

[8] Commonly referred to as 'aspen mushrooms', *Leccinum aurantiacum* is a species of fungus in the family of Boletaceae, found in forests of Europe, North America, and Asia; it has a large, characteristically red-capped fruiting body.

A chrysalis has burst and out crawls a tiny butterfly, its wings all rumpled.

In the same street, a man died, having declined to delay his death till the time when the outcome of grand events became clear, and a baby was born who wasn't frightened by the future. For their respective families, those events meant much more than any great war.

Something else happened. An old woman was pushing a huge quill along an enormous scroll – she was busy writing history, in a fluent semi-uncial script. When the first salvo rang out, the quill jolted and a drop of blood-red ink escaped off its tip. Like a tiny snake, a meandering wormling of ink slithered away from the drop; just then a tousled strand of the old woman's grey hair fell onto the parchment and smeared the drop over a whole cubit of the scroll.

When the old woman spotted the mess, she pulled up the wisp of hair, sucked it dry with her parched tongue and tucked it behind her ear. Still, the rivulet of ink trickled on, playing games, losing driblets to commas, sneaking underneath the lines, spreading parentheses over the semi-uncial script. It was busy telling lies, whitewashing sins, blackening heroic deeds, mocking the sacred, diluting the bile of words with crocodile tears. The devil behind the old woman's back kept snatching the upper tip of the quill, tickling the old woman's neck, whispering the words of youthful temptations into her ear while jeering at her childishly.

Mumbling with her toothless mouth, the old woman waved the devil off with her free hand and carried on writing, confident that she was scribbling true history. It may have been just like that. At dawn the cockerel began crowing and the devil vanished as the old woman fell asleep over her filthy red scroll of parchment.

The old woman's tabby cat had a sweet little kitten – a fruit of love consummated on the roof next door. When the old woman dozed off, the kitten leapt onto her lap and from there up onto the table. The oil lamp hadn't died out yet, atop a pile of papers yellowed with age. The kitten heard the old woman snoring, marvelled at it, tilted his little muzzle and pawed the old woman's moustachioed lip.

Just then the old woman was immersed in dreaming about a level road. At mid-point the road was blocked by barbed wire. The old woman hadn't spotted it in time and hit a barb at full speed with her upper lip. At that point she threw her arms up in the air, and the startled kitten jumped aside and overturned the lamp.

The oil spilled out; the parchment caught fire but didn't burn up completely. Wise people, learned people, each in his or her own individual, disparate way will later string the words together again, word by word, ember by ember. The only fragment of the scroll that was lost for all eternity was the top right corner, the place where the old woman had spelled out painstakingly, 'Who Is To Blame?' And this will be the subject of heated arguments for centuries to come.

As for the kitten, the fright made him peckish, so he rushed to his saucer and started lapping the milk, getting his muzzle wet all over. Having finished his meal he licked himself clean, sat down in the middle of the room and began thinking about how life could be really boring, even if one was young.

He was the most unreasonable creature on earth.

THE INCIDENT WITH THE CLOCK

Quite some time ago, a little screw in the professor's favourite old clock, the one that secured a lever controlling the winding spring, had come loose.

At two in the morning, as was his wont, the ornithologist pulled up both weights – dark-copper fir cones – and went to bed. The little screw inclined infinitesimally, still on stand-by.

By about three o'clock the barely perceptible rotary motion of the gear wheel tilted the screw to one side, and it fell out. The spring felt the unaccustomed freedom right away and started uncoiling, meeting with zero resistance from the wheel. The hands of the clock twitched, gained momentum and started frantically rotating around the face of the clock. As for the cuckoo, it never got a chance to open its mouth and so, frightened, fell abruptly silent.

While the entire household was asleep, time began its maniacal flight. The scales of plaster drifted off the walls in a whirlwind, the girders of the roof snapped, the grubs pupated and instantaneously transformed into beetles, dying, multiplying, gnawing at the beams. The cat grew old in his sleep and swallowed a hundred mice that had managed to create scores of new tunnels under the floor. The swallow – not the original bird, a new one – managed to visit Central Africa twice, all this without lifting its head from under its wing.

Right by the bed where Grandma Aglaya Dmitriyevna was asleep, a shadow emerged, clad in an old shroud and casting sidelong glances at the ornithologist's door. The breasts of the sleeping Tanyusha felt the influx of young blood.

On all fronts, the barrage of fire decimated the trenches and lives along with them. The ball of luck, courage and strategy kept bouncing back and forth between the enemy lines. Tears had no time to dry and converged instead, to form rivulets. Soldiers came down towards the confluences, flasks in hand. Mass graves piled up and became ramparts where one corpse rested dispassionately atop another, the very one that he had killed the day before – unknowingly, unthinkingly, taking no aim, just rotating the handle of his machine gun, and no more.

As the earth reverberated with the salvos, the bones of a Hans cuddled closer to the bones of an Ivan, and Hans's skull asked, all smiles, 'Tell me, are we safe, my foe Ivan? Surely, our shelter is the most secure?'

And Ivan answered, his teeth a-chatter: 'A man can die but once, my foe Hans!'

And both of them, cosy in their soggy grave, laughed at those nearby, still in their trenches, being unhurriedly consumed by the fat lice.

Those who had already exercised their right not to live felt serene and at ease. All the rest watched, with escalating horror, as the scarlet fog of the future descended to earth in the form of asphyxiant gases; and hurriedly and ruthlessly, lest they should be late, they elbowed their way out, ravenous for food and love; cuddled up to one another, and gave birth to their offspring – for whose sake this great human comedy was being played out.

Having exhausted the energy of its spring, the cuckoo clock stopped. Nevertheless, it was already too late – no one could return the past. The following day the old professor would get up more elderly and unable to explain his new feebleness – could it be an attack of catarrh? Aglaya Dmitriyevna wouldn't get up at her usual hour, and to her husband she would say, 'I rather fancy a lie-in today. I don't feel so good, my darling. Do send Tanyusha along.'

She would never leave her bed again, and would never again take her place by the samovar in the dining room. On Sundays, her bedroom door would be left ajar so that she could also listen to Eduard Lvovich play.

The two years that had evaporated so quickly and were lost by the grandmother had been gained by the granddaughter. And so, lifting the water jug over her naked shoulder, Tanyusha saw its healthy curvaceousness and cast a fleeting bashful glance towards the window – what if the swallows had seen it too? Rubbing herself dry with a new shaggy towel, she stretched out, tensed up and started involuntarily, suddenly aware of her novel sense of power and desire. The same non-committal mirror that had been examining every trait of Tanyusha-the-child and Tanyusha-the-young-girl registered in the stores of its reflecting memory, 'On such-and-such date the woman was born!'

Early in the morning Nikolai the yardman, a man with newly white sideburns, came out onto the street with his broom and shovel. He crossed himself, looked at the sky, all business-like, shifted his gaze to the pavement, gave a yawn, and diligently swept along the edge of the outside wall, brushing away the dust and the scales of the crumbling plaster.

All of them inside were still asleep, only he and the swallow working, although the greengrocer's cart could already be heard, rattling on its way towards Arbat Square.

UNCLE BORIS

Over the years of peace everyone had created a personal bolthole, become securely entrenched within its walls and put up a number outside, so that they could be identified with the help of this number. Every type of talent was displayed and assessed. A small group of the select few was thus singled out from the common crowd, to be treated with special veneration.

A poet was recognised by the touch of the muses, a scientist by the honours bestowed on him by the ignoramuses; and an artist was confirmed by the whispering crowd. An architect was superior to a carpenter by a substantial margin, a decorator seen as a pigmy before a painter. Once upon a time, there were two apples on the same apple tree, but the sun had lent a healthy glow to one while the other was corroded by worms. God had issued an order to His clerks to lay out the human wares along the counter of life and make sure they were shown to their best advantage: the better-quality merchandise on top, the more inferior underneath. Thenceforth, glory be to the sun, and indeed, to a dull half-melted candle.

Yet the war muddied all waters and everything changed. Who needed Eduard Lvovich's Cosmos now? Who cared what the old connoisseur of birds thought? The universe had teetered sideways. The birds had been dispelled by the roaring artillery. Who could deter the trajectory of a bullet by the power of intense and profound philosophical discourse? Who could disperse the choking gases with the purity of poetry? Cast iron and copper craved anonymous flesh; the time was wrong for the appreciation of brains. Blessed was he who was needed now, and only for the duration of now, by the new deity – the God of War. This was how Uncle Boris, the old professor's son, had suddenly become a man of importance and influence.

Uncle Boris, who couldn't tell his Chopin from his Scriabin, Uncle Boris, a tolerated nonentity, a rank-and-file mechanical engineer, not the sharpest knife in the box by far! Well then, the hour of Uncle Boris had come!

He would rise at the crack of dawn and already be at his factory by the second whistle. Where once buttons had been extruded, nowadays field telephones were manufactured. The steel he had smelted these days was different to what had once been needed for ploughshares. On the River Kama, upstream from the city of Perm, he supervised the building of an access road towards the plant that was to put out superphosphates – not for the benefit of agriculture, that would have to wait – but as an offering to the suffocating God of War. Spools for sewing machines had given way to barrels for machine guns.

Uncle Boris was multifaceted, he was everywhere, all over Russia, not to mention other countries, and wherever he went, he was the man of the hour. Greater demand existed only for a tall, thick-headed, hairy-chested and bull-necked general of the Prussian troops, along with a couple of experienced, long-since-implanted spies. And having said that, there was also a need for a doctor, a courageous young surgeon who knew how to chop off a leg when a foot had been blown away, up to the knee. However, this was purely to appease our conscience, for how could one live without any shame at all? Uncle Boris, just like the general, was needed for the main thing, he was needed for committing murder.

Uncle Boris had never killed anyone himself. In fact, the real Uncle Boris, Borya, Boris Ivanovich, the professor's son, was busy, humbly going about his business – managing a large industrial facility, coming to work early in the morning and leaving late in the evening, sometimes dropping by even on festive days and holidays. By now he had risen higher than those who had once listened to Eduard Lvovich's improvisations in the dimmed light. For some time to come, steel was going to be so superior to all of them put together that, by now, it didn't matter whether a straight line was the shortest distance between two points.

All of a sudden, people, only recently unknown to anyone and unrecognised by all, had come to the fore. They were not cannon fodder (even now, those were recognised only as statistics), but one level up. Much as they were also salt-of-the-earth, narrow-minded and unprepossessing – still, they were the doers. It was their time now; everyone had come to realise that they alone were the real thing.

These days, Uncle Boris, by now of a respectable age, wore a field jacket and looked younger. He had shaved off his beard but kept the grizzled moustache. Tanyusha would comment:

'Uncle Boris, you've become so handsome that I fear for Lenochka's heart!'

That would make Uncle Boris's wife frown but he himself looked pleased. He was even jolly. He no longer shied away from general conversation, didn't fade into insignificance. He would bide his time and then interpolate, and so everyone could see that he did not simply hold an opinion, but that he knew how things were. Previously it had been hard to find a topic for conversation with Uncle Boris, unless it was steam-boilers. So, something similar would have been chosen, something related to steam-boilers but more accessible and equally boring for everybody else.

Uncle Boris was needed by many and for many reasons. It was he who had arranged a vacancy for the newly-married Mertvago at the ZemGor[9]. Mertvago was now referred to as a

9   ZemGor – a joint committee between the zemstvo (local governments) Councils and the Municipal Council, set up in 1915. It operated exclusively on the home front and was created with a view to assisting the central government in supplying the Russian army. That

'zemhussar' on account of his uniform, which resembled those worn in the army. Uncle Boris rubbed shoulders with financial magnates; the latter might have been trying to find roundabout ways to use the prominent engineer for their ends; equally, they might have been talking about supplies or something of a similar nature. No one could doubt the probity of this Uncle Boris, the integrity of the old ornithologist's son and Tanyusha's uncle. Other Uncle Borises, while working for the common cause, never forgot their own interests. Such were the times that private interests often coincided with the interests of the state and the public at large. In times of peace, such a thing is much less common, though not impossible.

These days, when Eduard Lvovich played on a Sunday, Uncle Boris, beardless and clad in his field jacket, would install himself by Aglaya Dmitriyevna's lamp and sit there, illuminated, enjoying Scriabin, whom he was taking to be Chopin.

Once, when Eduard Lvovich had just finished his improvisation (one of those where the life of sounds would fade away as if of its own accord, and one could hear how the sounds waned) Uncle Boris was the first to loudly offer his appraisal: 'Marvellous! You're on top form today, Eduard Lvovich. Nice to hear. Still, I've got to be going – the factory awaits. We are now working Sundays, night shifts too. Going full steam!'

He said his goodbyes and left. And no one said anything else to Eduard Lvovich. So, that evening he didn't play anything else. Hence, the general chat continued about this and that, and the party broke up early.

Going to bed, Tanyusha turned her thoughts to Eduard Lvovich and it suddenly occurred to her, for the first time: *Did Eduard Lvovich ever love anyone? He never married, after all.*

....
is why the neologism 'zemhussar' (mentioned later) is used ironically.

She also thought: *How wretched he is!*

Above her large pillow Tanyusha had a smaller one, a cushion trimmed with lace. She placed her head on it, slightly to one side, so that her ear sank into the weightless down. And thus, she fell asleep.

THE SCRATCH

Tanyusha's childhood friend, and the ornithologist's favourite, Vasya Boltanovsky, graduated from university and, having passed his final exam, he popped home, splashed his face with water and examined himself in the mirror.

He'd lost weight during the exams but there still was laughter in his eyes. Now as before, he was mop-headed. The moustache was not bad, but his beard was hopeless, totally hopeless. The jacket was hopeless too, the only civilian outfit that he possessed. Still, the exams – hell's bells! – were over, along with the student life. That was splendid, indeed! Vasya tried to twirl his moustache but the mirror reflected some nonsense on a stick. He felt slightly embarrassed.

He had ab-so-lu-te-ly nothing to do. Somehow, all at once, nothing to do whatsoever. Vasya had been offered a job at his own university, which meant a lot of work ahead. But for now, there was decidedly nothing to do, would you believe it! Perhaps he should order some visiting cards? Or shave his beard off?

With his hand, Vasya covered the goatee up to his lip – it didn't look too bad. The exams had left a sense of some peculiar uncleanness, of book dust and ink. Perhaps, he should have a manicure? Well, that was total poppycock but as for the goatee...

The barber, having soaped Vasya's physiognomy, noted reasonably, 'True enough, given the quality of your face, the beard is good for nothing. As for your chin, it's a different story; there is also a dimple there, now we don't want to conceal an asset like that, do we, sir? Raise your head a touch for me, sir, just so. I hear they are reporting some advances at the front...'

Normally, Vasya lunched at the Troitskaya canteen, at end of Tverskoy Boulevard. He knew all the others who lunched there: the slightly hunched gentleman with the cap insignia; the Armenian girl from the conservatoire; the wretched married couple who would usually start rowing, in whispers, during their second course; the *privatdotsent*[10] with a tie *a la fantasie*. And of course, Anna Akimovna, seated by the window on the left, who would routinely consume ten slices of bread with her lunch.

Having finished his borsch, Vasya asked for some pork, but if possible, from the piglet's rump. He was served his hock, in aspic, along with horseradish sauce and soured cream. He also drank a little jug of kvass[11]. To top it all off, some kissel[12] with milk – the proper festive menu. Mopping his face with the serviette (bespoke, his initials in the corner) he remembered that his beard was gone. His face felt nice and smooth. And it felt fresh behind his ears – the barber had been diligent.

Vasya set off, on foot, towards Sivtsev Vrazhek. He kept swinging his thick cane freely and looked at the passers-by with a daring joy. The thing was, from that day onwards

....

[10]   *Privatdotsent* is an academic title conferred at some European universities to someone who holds certain formal qualifications that denote an ability (*facultas docendi*) and permission to teach a designated subject at the highest level. The title existed in the Russian Empire from 1843 to 1917.

[11]   Traditional Russian soft drink made with lightly fermented breadcrumbs.

[12]   Kissel or *kisel* is a viscous fruit (or milk) dish, popular as a dessert and as a drink in Central and Eastern Europe. It consists of the sweetened juice of berries, like *mors*, or milk, but it is thickened with corn starch, potato starch or arrowroot.

MIKHAIL OSORGIN

Vasya was a genuine adult, finally fully grown up. He felt warm compassion towards the students he saw on his way – so much hassle still ahead of them.

As he turned around the corner, a pleasant young girl, walking towards him, gifted him a glance. Vasya returned the gift and hurried on, impatient to see the professor and... Tanyusha. Come to think of it, the professor wouldn't be back home yet; he was still busy with the exams.

Here it was, the small, lovable house. Old, though, if it was anything! Vasya had never noticed it before but today, having shaved his beard off, he did. The professor's townhouse stood visibly straight but also, inclining ever so slightly. The gate was undoubtedly askew. And a lot of plaster had peeled off.

Tanyusha's upstairs window was open. So Vasya took a step backwards, towards the middle point of the road, and began to sing in a pathetic tenor voice, 'Quelle rose, quelle r-o-o-ose...'[13]

Tanyusha looked out of the window:

'Come on, Vasya, I'll let you in. Did you pass?'

'Passed the lot. A free citizen now.'

'What about the beard? What have you done?'

Vasya thought: *What do you mean, what I have done?* and came up to the porch. The door opened and Vasya immediately realised that, man and boy, he had been desperately and decidedly in love with Tanyusha, irrevocably, too, since there never ever had been or would be anyone better, sweeter, closer and more beautiful than her. Somehow it had never occurred to him before but now there could be no doubt. Should he drop to his knees and thus crawl upstairs after Tanyusha? Or do something of a similar nature, express him-

....

[13]   Reference to Monsieur Triquét's aria from Tchaikovsky's opera *Eugene Onegin*. The aria is performed at the party on occasion of the protagonist's saint's day. The protagonist is named Tatiana, hence Vasya's performance (we remember that Vasya loves opera).

self somehow. She looked so chaste, in that white blouse of hers with its dear little collar, so there he was, about to die from love.

When Tanyusha held out her hand and said, 'You know what, Vasya, it is really much more becoming!' Vasya felt completely overwhelmed, plonked down on a step and announced that he would not move an inch unless Tanyusha patted him on the head. Otherwise he would drop dead.

She didn't pat him, he didn't die, and both climbed the stairs to Tanyusha's room. Once there, he felt better. The mirror looked at Vasya minus his pitiable beard and thought: *My, my, he really is in love!*

'How's Grandma?'

'Better today, but overall, not good.'

'Professor not back yet?'

'Grandpa is at the exam board. You must wait for him; he was asking about you. Any plans for tonight?'

'Nothing much.'

'Will you stay? Do stay, I'm free today, too.'

The cat let herself in. Vasya grabbed her by the scruff of the neck and lifted her to his face, so the cat clawed his freshly-shaven chin. Vasya dropped the cat, wiped his chin with a handkerchief and said, 'Blasted beast! You know, Tanyusha, I love you, just like a dog...'

He blushed, justifiably convinced that he had said something absurd. He should have said 'I love you' but for some reason he had to drag a dog in.

Forever truthful, he corrected himself, 'Tanya, it's got nothing to do with any dog. Meanwhile I do, dogs or no dogs, hellishly...'

That turned out even worse. Still, had she chosen to understand him she would have. But she answered quietly, 'You'd better disinfect it with some cologne. Show me. Yes, she did give you quite a scratch! Well, you've only got yourself to blame.'

Had Vasya left his beard intact, the scratch wouldn't have shown. Immaculate timing as ever. It hurt, too. Vasya's love started waning.

They sat side by side on the couch and talked about how each would spend the summer. It looked like Tanyusha would have to stay in town, on account of Grandma's illness. They talked about people they both knew, those who were at the front. Ehrberg had died a long time ago, the first of the inner circle to have been killed. There were others, too. Even now, there were quite a few old friends still out there. Stolnikov wrote infrequently but he did write – what a decent chap he was, Stolnikov! Lenochka was a nurse, not at the front but here, in Moscow, so she wouldn't be going to the dacha in the summer either. Lenochka talked a lot about the wounded and was in love with several doctors. A white uniform with a red cross looked very becoming on her.

'You know, Vasya, I wouldn't be able to do it. That is, I would, of course, but it is... how shall I put it... It's somehow not for me... I don't know...'

Tanyusha was pensive today, and tired after her exams. They descended to the dining room. The professor was back and felt peckish; he put his arms round Vasya, congratulating him. While Grandpa ate his dinner, Tanyusha, at the request of the sick old lady who lay in her bedroom, played her favourite piece. Grandma continued slipping away without too much suffering, even without a particularly grievous disease, but somehow it was clear to all that her end was near. Her vitality had been exhausted and she was slowly fading away. Inasmuch as it was possible, they even became accustomed to the idea. During the months of her illness the professor started stooping noticeably but was still holding himself together.

In the evening Tanyusha's friend from the conservatoire dropped by. Vasya was telling the girls their fortunes.

'Upon your heart lies the eight of clubs, but soon you will get a letter of hearts.'

The conservatoire student was pleased – she had been expecting a letter. Afterwards he saw Tanyusha's friend home. When he was alone again, he couldn't quite choose whom he was in love with after all – Tanyusha or her friend? He decided it was with Tanyusha. But it felt bizarre – he had known her since childhood, they used to be just like a brother and a sister! Having made this decision he felt sorry again that he had dragged a dog in, Christ knew why – *must have been from embarrassment!*

He made it home, to Girshi. On the table sat a pile of books and a dirty cup. In the dregs of the weak tea floated several dead flies and a cigarette stub. Tomorrow he should send his laundry to the washerwoman. And in any case, he should go someplace for the summer. He decided to drop in to see his family the next day; it had to be done, after all.

Then all of a sudden, just like his love for Tanyusha in the afternoon, he was overwhelmed with the idea of life. His youth was over, he was embarking on a new and difficult path. Perhaps it was true that he would now need a life partner? Who, then? Tanyusha? His childhood friend? This time he thought about her with genuine tenderness. Just then he admitted to himself, in amazement, that he didn't know her at all. He had before, but he didn't anymore.

It felt like a revelation. How had it happened? Moreover, he was still a boy while she was a woman. That was what he had overlooked, buried in his books.

Embarrassed, he wanted to ruffle his beard, but his chin was smooth and on it there was a scratch.

He couldn't but love Tanyusha, but his must be this special sort of love; the love they portrayed in novels was something that he, Vasya Boltanovsky, couldn't do. How would that ever be possible? It even felt wrong, shameful.

It was truly sad. So, he picked up a book and sat there, reading, till he could barely keep his eyes open.

Vasya Boltanovsky possessed a lucky quality: he slept like a dormouse and would wake up fresh as a daisy. That was why he both loved life and knew nothing about it.

BEHIND THE CURTAINS

On the table by the door sat the cat who had, the previous day, clawed the freshly shaved chin of the new university employee. Served him right for grabbing her by the scruff of her neck! The cat was licking her whiskers, bored. At night, she had had a bit of a misadventure: the old rat, the famous resident of the underground, had escaped her claws.

The rat had scurried away considerably the worse for wear. It had been right in the cat's paws... How could it have possibly happened? The old rat wouldn't have been tasty at all; but that was not the point. But really, how on earth could it have happened? The cat's self-respect as a hunter was badly wounded. On such occasions she became bored, sat there yawning away, and her eyes went blank, although normally her eyes burned green in the dark.

Having found a comfortable position but keeping her front legs outstretched, so as to remain on red alert, the cat dozed off with only her ears awake. It wasn't going to get light for another two hours.

The old rat still kept trembling from the recently experienced horror. Holed up in the narrowest crack under the floor, he was busy licking his wounds. It wasn't so much the wounds that spelled danger, but the young rats getting wind of it. They would start watching him, tread on his heels, and eventually maul him to death. That was the principal hazard. They would show no pity on account of his grizzled hair and moulting back. What a damnable night it had proved to be!

A tall lanky figure in grey bent over Aglaya Dmitriyevna's bed. The figure extended its hand under the duvet and with a sharp nail pressed down on the nipple of a flabby breast. Grandma gave a soft gasp and groaned with pain.

Death lingered by the bed, listening to the old woman's moaning, and retreated into the corner. He had been keeping watch by the bed of Tanyusha's grandma for over a month now, shielding her from the temptations of life, preparing her for the acceptance of nothingness. If the night nurse nodded off, Death would give the old lady her water, smooth her duvet, all the while winking at her lovingly. And the dear old lady, failing to recognise Death, would say in a feeble voice, 'Thank you, dearie, thank you ever so much!'

When the old woman fell asleep, Death felt mischievous: now it would pull the duvet aside, now pinch the old lady on the hip, or cover her mouth with his knuckles so as to restrict her breathing. And then he would laugh, sniffling and baring his rotten teeth.

In the morning light Death would melt away, hiding in the folds of the blanket, the chest of drawers, the cracks in the window frame. Should someone yank the blanket away, or quickly pull out a drawer, there would be nothing to find inside, apart from a speck of dust or a dead fly. Death was not visible in daytime.

The old rat was surrounded by the youngsters: they stood there, watching him with their black beady eyes, listening to him squeaking. He tried baring his teeth, his long tail a-twitter. He would make a slight movement and the semicircle of young rats would widen out immediately; they were still wary of the old fellow since he did have some strength left in him. But their eyes stayed focused, glued to the licked-up fur with a stain of red upon it, and a drop seeping from the stain.

The cat also picked out the rat's yelping and her ear stirred. However, all was quiet in the house. The rats were scared, and would not venture out again tonight.

The old woman reached out to the nightstand, trying to pick up a glass containing a pleasant, slightly sour drink. The bony hand helped her and momentarily the two dry joints – the old woman's and that of her Death – made contact. Shivers crept up her arm.

'Oh, that will be the death of me!' moaned Aglaya Dmitriyevna.

'I'm here, calm down,' answered the angular form in grey. He added, reassuring the old lady, 'There's nothing out there, and so nothing to fear. You've had your life; you shouldn't usurp the years destined for someone else. When you were young, you were merry, danced a lot, wore beautiful dresses, the sun smiled on you. Haven't you had a good life? And your old man – haven't you been happy together? And your children – haven't they brought you joy?'

'But you claimed my son, Tanyusha's father, much too early!' complained Aglaya Dmitriyevna.

'So I did, it had to be done. But haven't I left you your granddaughter? Someone to give you, the old folk, happiness and comfort?'

'But how will she manage when we are gone? My old man, he is not immortal either!'

'Come on, the old man is still going strong, he will linger on for some time. Besides, she is all grown up now. She has a good head on her shoulders, she'll get by.'

'And what am I going to do without him in the afterlife? And what will happen to him if I'm not here? We've been together for so long!'

At this point Death burst out laughing, even started hiccupping with pleasure. However, his mirth was guileless:

'So that's what concerns you! What business is it of yours? You should just lie down in your grave, have a rest. They will survive without you, that's for sure. On the other hand, with you old and sick, how much pleasure is it for them? What are you if not a burden? You are talking nonsense!'

The cuckoo was heard crying four times in the study. The light was probably coming through the window already, but the window was draped with heavy curtains.

'Oh, it'll be the death of me!' moaned Aglaya Dmitriyevna.

'Let me straighten your pillow, it's all askew,' said the nurse. She arranged the pillows and returned to her slumber in the armchair by the bed.

The light seeped into the basement. The young rats dispersed to different nooks and crannies. The old injured rat dozed off too. The cat was busy, lazily chasing a large sleepy fly on the window. She would squeeze the fly lightly, then let go, and the fly would continue its crawl.

By the morning Tanyusha had her third dream; in it, again, was Stolnikov – laughing, cheerful and happy.

'Leave? For how long?'

Stolnikov answered gaily, 'Now it will be for ever!'

'How do you mean – for ever? Why?'

Stolnikov stretched out his arm, long and flat like a plank of wood; on his palm was an inscription in red: 'indefinite leave'.

Suddenly Tanyusha was overcome with fear: why 'indefinite'? Why, then, had he written shortly before to tell her that they were unlikely to meet up any time soon since, for the time being, he had refused to leave the front line on any procurement missions? 'I cannot leave the theatre of war at the moment; then again, I don't feel like leaving, the timing would be all wrong.'

Stolnikov wiped his hand clean with a handkerchief. The arm was now smaller and the red stayed on the cloth. Tanyusha woke up – what a weird dream!

It was only six in the morning. Tanyusha raised her arms above her head and fell asleep again. A trail of light coming from the gap in the curtains fell over the white sheet like a bright ribbon, coming to a stop as a little column on the wall above the bed. A stray hair rested separately on the pillow.

On Tanyusha's right shoulder, just below the collar bone, was a small birthmark. The girl's breathing raised the sheet rhythmically.

THE FIFTH CARD

Stolnikov probed around with his foot for the steps hewn in the ground, and descended into the communal officers' dug-out behind a makeshift machine-gun parapet. Inside the air was close and heavy with tobacco smoke. On a nearby bench sat the doctor and a young ensign, playing chess. A group of officers round the table were playing a game of cards, which had started well before lunch. Stolnikov came up to the table and wedged himself among the players.

'You'll have to miss two rounds, Sasha. Would you still like to play?'

'I know. I would.'

As his turn to play was getting closer, he felt for the banknotes in his pocket and said, 'That's all I've got left. How much is there?'

'For you, a hundred and thirty, with the card.'

'Deal.'

The eyes of all the players, as if following an order, shifted from the dealer to the card that he dealt to Stolnikov, who said, 'Go on, give us another card.'

'You get the hearts, and we get… also hearts. Two points.'

'Three,' said Stolnikov and reached out towards the stake.

It was the next player's turn to try his luck.

The war stopped. Everything and anything vanished, apart from the table surface, the money passing from hand to hand and the shabby brick of the pack. It was as if Stolnikov had never been a student, danced at Tanyusha's party, transformed from a fledgling officer into a veteran – the captain decorated with a St George; as if he had never been to the opera and would never return to civilian life. The curtain of tobacco smoke blocked off the rest of the world. He lit up, too.

'Your turn to deal, Sasha.'

'There we go, I stake all my winnings. To start with… the nine. No cut. The three for you, and for me… another nine. The stake is three hundred and sixty. Half goes to you, you get a hundred; you, Ignatov, get the rest. Damn it, if only I had another nine… Your win, here, take it.'

Stolnikov passed on the pack case, fashioned out of a box made for filter tubes, manufactured by the Katyk factory.[14] The number of the players was ten in total, so now he had to wait. Everyone's eyes were now on the hands of his neighbour to the left. All ears were listening.

'Nothing but bloody hearts. Damn it! Six each?'

'No, we only go seven each. I cut half. Don't risk your stake! I say, I haven't reached the third card once!'

'I didn't even get to the second one. Time to change my luck!'

They were changing their luck, cursing the 'rotten trick', trying to leave two stakes untouched and stuffing their field jackets with banknotes (to be on the safe side). If the fourth card were ever dealt, the player felt uplifted, felt more kind-hearted and generous, was agreeable to stake his card for the next trick. Then, after three long suits, his money would evaporate and he would sit there, nervously fingering a note stashed for an emergency.

The ensign at the end of the table wasted his stake and lost to the dealer. No one would even address him anymore.

....

[14] A popular pre-revolutionary brand of cigarettes and roll-ups established in 1891 by Abram and Joseph Katyks, natives of Crimea, born into a poor Karaim family. The factory quickly became the biggest in the Empire.

'Come to grief?'

'And then some.'

'Does happen, old chum. Just one of those days.'

'All my days are like this.'

Still, he didn't rise to leave; just sat there watching. As if luck could descend from the clouds onto someone who wasn't playing. Then again… perhaps, somebody would get rich and offer him a loan. He didn't feel like asking himself.

Stolnikov was in luck.

'I've been lucky two days running: yesterday in action, today in cards.'

The words 'action' momentarily brought them all round but it didn't last more than a mere minute and even then, it felt unpleasant. There was, and should be, no life apart from this one, around the table.

A private entered the dugout. 'Explosions, your Excellency.'

'Germans? Coming. Damn it, just before my turn to deal.'

'Show them what's what, Osipov!'

The artilleryman exited and no one followed him with a glance. When he was by the door one could discern the noise of the engine in the sky, to which they had long since become accustomed. Several moments later a cannon thundered.

'Osipov is trying his best. Why the hell do the Germans fly at night?'

There was a bang. It was retaliation from the German pilot. All the same, Osipov had already traced the enemy in the sky – one could hear the machine-guns crackling. The next bang was closer. All looked up from the table.

'Let him go hang himself. Give me a nice card. Seven. Sell the stake or you'll lose it after the seven. Well, then, give me a card…'

What followed was a deafening boom, right next to the dugout. The candle toppled over but didn't go out. The officers sprang to their feet, pocketing their money. Loose soil cascaded down through the beams in the ceiling.

'Damn it, he nearly hit us on the head. We should go out and check.'

Stolnikov exclaimed loudly, 'So it's my turn to deal, I've been cut short.'

The officers filed out outside. The searchlight illuminated the sky overhead, but the beam of light was already sliding to one side. The cannon rumbled while the machine-guns yattered incessantly. The slightly older officer said, 'Gentlemen, don't form a crowd, you mustn't.'

'He's left already.'

'He may return, though. And he will shatter all those glasses of yours.'

The hole made by the explosion was close by. Fortunately, there were no casualties – the German had wasted his attempt to intimidate them.

Stolnikov remembered that he was out of cigarettes and directed his steps towards his dugout. He reached it and stopped. The sky was amazingly clear. The beam of the searchlight continued sinking deep inside the darkness of the sky, guiding the enemy back – a barely visible pinpoint of light against the dark background. Another clap of thunder rumbled – a giant stomping his front cast-iron foot onto the ground. Somewhere nearby a shot rang out in reply, as if a glass had crashed.

Why am I not afraid? thought Stolnikov. *After all, he could easily kill me! When in action, yes, one is horrified but then again, there's no time for any of that. But these playthings in the sky...* Then he remembered: *It may well be so but it's my turn to deal. I beat four cards. I'll stake the lot. It would be nice to beat the fifth one. Could be a tidy sum!*

And he imagined himself revealing the nine. He smiled despite himself.

When the final German gift made impact, the officers instinctively dashed towards the dugout. They listened by the door to the receding noise of the engine and the dying down of the machine guns. Then all was quiet and they returned to the table. It looked like the German had happened onto the location of the reserve but had gambled to no good effect. All he had succeeded in doing was frightening the novices.

'Osipov will return. That birdie's proved too big for him.'

'He was flying too high.'

'Shall we sit down? Who's dealing?'

'Stolnikov. He's beaten four cards.'

'So, where's Stolnikov? Should we wait for him?'

'We should.'

Someone said, 'He went to fetch his smokes, should be back in a tick.'

An orderly came running in, hurrying towards the doctor, 'Your Excellency, captain Stolnikov's been hurt!'

And lowering his hand from the peak of his cap, he added, more softly, addressing the first person on his way out, 'His poor legs, nigh on blasted off, Your Excellency! One of them kraut bombs...'

THE MINUTE

The dark night encircled the house, pressing onto its old walls. It had seeped everywhere – the basement, under the roof, into the attic and into the big hall where the cat now lay in wait by the door. It had spread its semi-darkness into Grandma's room, which was now lit up only by the bedside lamp. Only Tanyusha's window, open and bright, scared the night off, dispelling its progress.

It was so quiet that one could hear the silence.

Tanyusha was perched in the armchair, wrapped in the travel rug, her legs tucked underneath her, her unseeing gaze not registering the lines in her book. Her face looked peaked; her eyes were directed straight ahead as if towards a film screen. Images of things that had or had not happened in the past kept flashing across the screen; people's faces looked fleetingly back at Tanyusha while an invisible hand scribbled the imperceptible characters of her thoughts.

Vasya Boltanovsky appeared for a moment, his scratch freshly healed; Eduard Lvovich had turned over a page of music; then there was Lenochka in her snow-white pinafore with a red cross on her breast, her amazed eyebrows arched below her headscarf. Then the front: a black line, overcoats, bayonets, inaudible shots. The hand on the screen kept drawing: there hadn't been any letters from Stolnikov for quite some time. Tanyusha herself crossed the screen, looking serious, unfamiliar.

Then the fog, again; it must just be tiredness. She closed her eyes and opened them again; all the objects around her moved in and took their habitual places. After minutes and hours of silence something new was sure to intrude. It could be the pit-a-pat of a horse carriage, might be a cry, or just the rustling sound made by a rat. Perhaps a front gate would bang in the lane below. And thus, the minute of deadly silence would be over.

On the screen Vasya appeared again, with his clean-shaven chin. He was crushing a matchbox and saying, 'Keeping in mind, Tanyusha, that you will marry anyway, I wonder if you would marry me? Since, devil take it, you do have to marry, come what may.'

Tiny splinters had fallen onto the floor and Vasya was busy picking them up, one by one, so as not to look up straightaway.

'Come on, Tanyusha, I mean it. It is madly interesting...'

Tanyusha answered gravely, 'No.'

She mulled it over and added, 'I think I won't.'

'So that's it, then?' said Vasya. 'All clear. A nice slap in the face, damn it! But why? I am tremendously curious.'

'Because... somehow... why marry you, Vasya? We know each other, that's all... and suddenly there is this talk of marriage.'

Vasya burst out laughing, not quite naturally, 'Would you rather marry someone you didn't know? That's rich.'

Vasya looked for something else to break. The matchbox had been reduced to bits of debris.

Tanyusha tried to explain, 'I think, to marry someone, it is when somebody appears... cometh... or when it becomes clear that you should never part with this person and can spend the rest of your life with him.'

Vasya tried to sound cynical, 'The rest of your life, my left foot. People make up, break up...'

'I know. But that only happens when they've made a mistake.'

The grim Vasya snapped a feather.

'All this is vanity of vanities. Mistaken, not mistaken. And in any case, to hell with it all. I for one am unlikely ever to marry. Freedom is sweeter.'

Tanyusha could clearly see that Vasya's feelings had been hurt. Still, she decidedly couldn't understand why. He was her best friend of all. And so reliable, if he was anything.

Vasya faded from the screen. The shadow of 'him who cometh' slipped through the fog but remained blurred. Then again, it would have been infinitely chilling if a real image had suddenly appeared on the screen – the eyes, the nose, perhaps even a moustache... and proved to be a total stranger.

Tanyusha suddenly closed her eyes and froze. Little chills ran up and down her entire body; her chest felt constricted, and her mouth quivered and fell slightly open. It lasted about a minute. Then Tanyusha felt blood rush to her cheeks and she tried to cool them with her still trembling hands.

Could it have been the draught from the window? What a strange, mysterious sensation! A mystery for the body and the soul.

The screen disappeared. It must be the intermission. Tanyusha tried to pick up her book: 'The quoted excerpt proves with sufficient expediency...'

What 'quoted excerpt'? From where?

Tanyusha turned back a page in order to try and find the initial quotation marks. She had no memory whatsoever whose words had been quoted by the author, and to what purpose.

The night nurse's steps on the staircase: 'Miss, would you mind coming down to your Grandma's room?'

DEATH

The underground world had been shaken by the monumental news: the old rat had failed to return! He might have been feeble but he still managed to squeeze his way nightly into the storeroom by means of the hole, the one gnawed through in the olden days by a generation of mice, who by now had disappeared from the underfloor realm.

In the storeroom resided a number of chests, as well as a perambulator, and stacks of old newspapers and magazines had been heaped up there, too – no pickings to talk of. However, next door, across the corridor, was the kitchen, and it wasn't all that hard to squeeze inside from underneath the door. As for the other rooms, especially that one, the big one, the rat never ventured there because he remembered only too well how he had once ended up in the cat's claws. The dawn came but the old rat, the veteran of the underground, didn't show up. The sensitive ears of the young had, however, heard him screaming during the night.

In the morning, heading towards the kitchen rubbish heap to throw out the old rat that had been bitten to death, Dunyasha heard the caretaker comment, 'Some rat she's defeated! Attagirl, our kitty! Must've been a hundred years old if he was a day.'

In terms of years, the rat was younger than a human adolescent. As for his real age, he had been stealing his years from the young.

No one came down for coffee. The professor was slumped in the armchair by Aglaya Dmitriyevna's bed. The nurse came up to the bed, twice, to smooth the folds. Tanyusha kept looking intently, her eyes big and wide open, at the wrinkles of the waxen Grandma, ironed out in death. The old lady's hands were folded one over the other in the shape of a cross, and her tiny fingers looked slender and pointed.

The nurse didn't know whether she should put the dentures in but didn't dare ask. The way it was, the chin had collapsed visibly. As for the dentures, they stayed in the glass of water and looked like the only live thing left of Grandma.

A tear ran down the professor's beard; then it poised on a curl of hair, wobbled and slid inside. Following the same route, but this time with no hesitation, ran another one. Then Grandpa gave a sob, and Tanyusha shifted her gaze towards him, blushed, and impulsively pressed herself close to his shoulder. She suddenly became a small unweaned baby, her tiny face upturned in search of the warm breast – this new world filled her with so much fear; she had never attended any lectures on history, and her thoughts were making their first tentative attempts to learn how to swim in the saline solution of tears. At the same time the old ornithologist was just a homunculus fighting off an evil rat with his tiny feet, his feelings wrongfully hurt, seeking protection from this young girl, his granddaughter, who was just as tiny but probably braver. And in their eyes, half the universe was now occupied by the gigantic bed on which an outwardly old woman lay, the wisest of all, who had broken off with them so abruptly. Just then, inside one soul the sun died out and disintegrated – as if a bridge between the eternities was collapsing, and the body, the only one, the immortal one, had suddenly become a site for some new, frenzied activity.

All that was left by Aglaya Dmitriyevna's bed were the two children, one very old, the other very young. The old one had lost everything, the young one had her life ahead of her. The cat by the window in the room next door licked her whiskers and watched, unimpressed, as the fly preened, rubbing its legs together, prior to taking off.

The only real event was in the process of unfolding in the bedroom of the professor's house in Sivtsev Vrazhek. In the rest of the world, everything was without incident, although lives went on, perpetually crossing paths, creatures were born, mountains kept on crumbling – and all of this continued happening with the usual social harmony. As for here and now, in this laboratory of grief, a murky tear mixed with the clear one.

This was the only genuine truth: Grandma had died loved.

'… For we, the mortal ones, have arisen from earth and shall succumb to common clay, as Thou hast commanded when Thou created us and said, "Ye are of the earth and so shall ye return to earth to which all shall so return, and make the final lament into a celebration – hallelujah, hallelujah, hallelujah!".'[15]

....

[15] A fragment of the solemn prayer for the dying 'For Thou art the one, true, immortal God, Thou who hast fashioned and created Man.' (Psalms, The Orthodox Church's canon read before a person's death, lament 6, Ikos).

THE NIGHT

A nocturnal bird had spread its wings over the house of the old widowed professor. And in doing so, it had occluded the shimmering of the stars and the moonlight. The wings were there to shield the professor from the world, to pay homage to the old man's profound sorrow.

Peace finally reigned everywhere, enveloping everything from the images of today to the outer boundaries of the universe, while in the comfortably broken-in armchair, the halo of his grey hair shaded by the lamp, sat an old man, thousands of years older now than his own self only the day before, when Tanya's Grandma, Aglaya Dmitriyevna, had still been breathing feebly and clinging on to life. Meanwhile, in the reception room, the candles by the coffin were reflected in the shining legs of the grand piano, and the nun spouted on, in an even and well-articulated voice, a burbling flow of words – dramatic but of no use to the silent listener resting under the dark brocade. The chin of the deceased was pushed upwards, right under her nose.

The professor was lost in reverie, consumed by the past. Looking deep inside himself, he was busy writing, mentally, page after page in his tiny penmanship. He would complete a page, put the manuscript aside, reread what he had written previously and then suture the pads together with a strong coarse thread – but still would be nowhere near the finale of his life's story, that new encounter. It goes without saying, he didn't believe in being reunited in the life after life, nor was such a union necessary to him. Then again, it could still happen when the final oblivion did arrive, sometime soon. Not many years, days and hours were still ahead, and the hours, and the days, and the years were rushing by. For 'dust thou art, and unto dust shalt thou return.'

The walls lined with books and the shelves crammed with written pages – he had loved it all, and it had all been the fruit of his labour. This too would pass when *she* called. And he pictured her as a young girl – a dimple showing in her cheek as she laughed and called to him over the strip of rye,

'Walk round, you mustn't trample it. It's no trouble, I'll wait!'

And they had set out together along the edge... only where and when did it all happen? And what did he best remember it for? Could it have been the sunlight?

They had been walking together, and had arrived together. Only this time she hadn't waited, she had left ahead of him. And he continued walking, again and again, round that strip of golden rye, shuffling his feet, an old man now...

In came Tanyusha, clad in a house coat and bedroom shoes. Tonight no one was going to sleep. The bird of the night hovered over the house, protecting the old man and his granddaughter from the rest of the world. The grief in their little world was completely awake.

'We'll go on living now without our Granny, Tanyusha. But we are used to living all together. It will be hard.'

Tanyusha stayed at his feet on the little foot stool, her head in Grandpa's lap, her soft plaits left unpinned, loose over her shoulders.

'Why was our Grandma so good? She was so good because she was kind to you and me. Our Grandma, our poor Granny!'

They stayed like that for a long time, tears already exhausted in the course of the day.

'Looks like you won't manage much sleep, will you, Tanyusha?'

'I feel like staying with you, Grandpa. You are awake, too. But if you were to put your feet up, say, here, on the sofa, I'd sit by your bedside anyway. Why don't you?'

'I shall… But for now, I feel like I've planted roots in this armchair; perhaps it's for the best.'

They fell silent again for a while. It wasn't something that could be expressed in words, but when they were together, they could share their thoughts. As the nun's burbling brook of words kept reaching their ears from behind the walls, they could see the coffin and the candles, and awaited further fatigue. Grandma had been so kind to both of them, and now she lay out there, in the reception hall, underneath the dark brocade, surrounded by the shimmering light of the candles.

We enter this world through a narrow door, crying in apprehension, desolate to be leaving the reassuring chaos of sounds, the straightforward and comfortable lack of understanding; we enter this world and stumble against the boulders of desire, and then proceed straight through, as if sleepwalking, towards another narrow door. Once by the exit, everyone struggles to explain that it is all is a mistake, that his trajectory was destined to reach new heights, not progress towards the horrible meatgrinder; that he hasn't yet had the time to look around properly. By the door – just a sarcastic grin, and the turnstile turns with a soft click.

And that's that.

Sleep eluded both of them but the images born of wakefulness were equally indistinct. Suspended between sleep and non-sleep, the old man could hear a young female voice calling from behind the final door, 'I'll wait for you here…'

He wished he could follow her but he wasn't allowed to trample the rye. And everything around them was bathed in sunlight. So the old man rushed along the narrow path by the edge to where she waited for him, stretching out her slender arms.

He opened his eyes and met with an inquiring gaze from Tanyusha's softly radiant eyes,

'Grandpa, you really ought to lie down and have some rest!'

THE TALL BOOTS

Nikolai the caretaker sat in his lodge, engrossed in a long, painstaking, profound contemplation of a pair of tall boots sitting in front of him on the bench.

What had happened was bizarre, almost beggaring belief. The boots hadn't been simply 'made' but rather constructed, quite some time ago, by the great architect of boots known as Roman Petrov[16] – an inveterate drunkard but also an un-rivalled artist of his trade, the likes of whom simply had not been around since that winter night when Roman had tumbled down the staircase, cracked his head and frozen to death, thereby returning his inebriated soul to where it belonged. Nikolai had known him personally, and severely disapproved of his drinking bouts, but, at the same time, was full of reverent amazement before his talent. And suddenly, would you believe it, Roman's craftsmanship was well and truly gone. Such boots were no more.

It wasn't that the ruination was totally unexpected, far from it. The signs of the impeding decline had already been showing, and on more than one occasion. Nikolai had to have three pairs of heels replaced, as well as having the boots resoled twice. Besides, there were patches on both of them – in the spot where a good old crooked little toe should by rights have a corn. One patch disguised the slash

....

16 Reference to Peter the Great (as the founding father of the Russian Empire) and the Romanovs, as its longest-ruling dynasty.

left by the wood chopper; that time Nikolai had narrowly missed chopping off half his toe but the sturdy leather had come to his rescue. Yet another patch covered the spot that had worn thin with age. Roman had replaced both the heels and the soles himself. The last time he had attached to Nikolai's heel a gigantic plate which guaranteed the heel's integrity for years to come. While he was at it, he had driven a dozen heavy-headed wrought-iron nails through both soles and fitted a cast iron strip apiece. The resulting footwear was incredibly heavy and noisy, but thereafter it never even occurred to Nikolai to worry about wear and tear.

Heaven knew how this had come to be, but one day the snow started thawing and Nikolai had to change out of his winter felt boots into Roman's pair. He pulled the boots out of the box by the Russian stove where they had been stored since the autumn, carefully treated with olive oil to prevent the leather cracking. Out they came, and suddenly Nikolai realised that both soles had come adrift – completely on one boot, and slightly less so on the other; also, that the leather in between the nails had rotted away, forming a gaping hole. Nikolai bent the sole – the hole spread further without squeaking. For the first time ever, he noticed that the bootleg was worn thin and had become almost transparent, so that prodding it with his finger resulted in a small protuberance that refused to stretch back out.

Nikolai took his boots to the cobbler, Roman's heir, who proved to be heir to the shop but not the talent. He inspected the boots, holding them up to the light, and announced, there and then, that there was nothing left to mend; the leather would not take it. Nikolai could see it all for himself, and so he hadn't harboured much hope.

'You mean, this is it?'

''Fraid so, take my word for it. Time to think about a new pair.'

Nikolai took his boots home, placed them on the bench and succumbed – not so much to sadness, but deep contemplation.

He thought about the boots in particular and the transience of all things mortal in general. If a pair like this had fallen apart, was there anything at all eternal? He considered the boots again from a distance; they looked like the same old pair, the one that would slide up his legs with customary efficiency. But those times were long gone – what was there wasn't boots anymore but a heap of rotten leather, of no use even for patches, let alone having to wear them on a caretaker's job. And to think that the heel plate didn't seem completely worn, and the nails looked intact – but all of it had been rusting from the inside.

What confounded Nikolai most of all, though, was the abruptness of the hopelessness that had engulfed him. While attaching his last ever patch, the bootmaker hadn't shaken his head, nor had he prophesied demise; he had simply run his finger from here to there, indicating the place for a patch, sewn it on and smoothed out the edges. It had been a case of simple mending, not a fight against destruction. Had there been a fight, the loss would have been less painful, whereas this sudden collapse had arrived unexpectedly.

'Looks like the decay started on the inside. The nails have rusted through and the leather has rotted away. Still, neat as you like. What matters is, it wasn't just any piece of craft, see, it was Roman's famous workmanship. No way they could sew like this nowadays.'

He was still deep in thought while adjusting the wick in his lamp – contemplating not so much the need to have a new pair made, but the transience of everything on earth. To an outsider's glance, things could seem like they would go on forever, and in good order. Yet the day would dawn, the wind would blow, the rain would fall – and nothing but rot would be left inside; some pair of boots it now was. It was the same with houses; they stood and stood, and then became unstable. Same with people.

The neighbours' caretaker dropped by in the evening – also quite advanced in years and beyond conscription age. Nikolai told him about his boots. They looked at them together, poked around: 'Nothing for it. You need some new 'uns. Kiss your money goodbye. Still, you ain't gonna get your hands on quality like this anymore.'

'That's that, then. It's not money I'm sorry about, but the craft. His skill was legendary.'

They lit up, and straight away the air in the caretaker's lodge turned smoky, tangy and homely.

'Then again,' said Fyodor, 'nothing's safe no more. What with the war, and all kind of trouble nowadays? Just the other day, the policeman was saying that there are some very strange goings-on! "Come tomorrow," he says, "they may do away with us, too. We won't go on the beat," he says, "we'll stay home and drink our tea."'

'I heard.'

'And as for Petrograd,[17] the things happening there – nothing like it used to be. They may even get rid of the tsar – would you believe it? But how can we go on, without a tsar? It's all clear as mud.'

'There's no way the tsar can be removed!' said Nikolai and cast another glance at his boots. 'Wasn't us who put 'im there in the first place.'

'Who can tell? The times we live in. it's all down to this war, all of it!'

....

[17]   The capital city of the Russian Empire, Saint Petersburg, was renamed to Petrograd in 1914, just after the outbreak of the First World War, for patriotic reasons. It was renamed yet again in 1924 as Leningrad to commemorate Lenin's memory in the year of his death. The original name of Saint Petersburg was reinstated in 1991.

On his way out of the lodge Fyodor dug his finger in the more deteriorated boot and shook his head,

'It's a goner alright!'

'I can see for myself,' said Nikolai gruffly.

After the neighbour had left, he threw the boots back into the box and heard glumly how the heel plate knocked against the wood. Luckily his felt boots were at least trimmed with leather. He picked up the shovel by the door and left for his evening shift.

'FIRE!'

Early in the morning, shortly after nine o'clock, Vasya Bol-tanovsky pressed the button by the entrance to the house in Sivtsev Vrazhek. Dunyasha answered the door, her skirt tucked up high, and said, 'The young lady and the master are in the dining room. Mind the bucket, sir, I'm washing the floors.'

Tanyusha greeted him, 'What's the matter, Vasya, why are you so early? Some coffee? Well, do tell us all!'

'A lot is the matter. How do you do, Professor. May I offer my congratulations: the revolution is here!'

The professor raised his head from his book: 'Have you learnt anything new, Vasya? No newspapers today either?'

Vasya did tell all. The newspapers hadn't come out because every editor was engrossed in bargaining with Mrozovsky[18]. Even *The Russian Gazette* – which was a pure disgrace. And in Petersburg there had been a coup d'état, all power was in the hands of the Duma,[19] a provisional government had

....

[18] Iosif Mrozovsky (1857–1934) was a Russian General of Artillery. On September 22, 1915, he was appointed commander of the troops of the Moscow military district, a position that he held until the February Revolution of 1917. Shortly before the outbreak of the revolution, in an attempt to normalise food supplies in the capital, he introduced bread rationing. Presumably, the editors were arguing over the coverage of this unpopular measure.

[19] After the abolition of autocracy and the overthrow of the tsar, the State Duma (founded in 1905 after the violence and upheaval in

been formed alongside it, and there was even talk of the tsar having allegedly abdicated.

'The revolution has succeeded, Professor. I have it on good authority. This time it's final.'

'Well, we'll see. It isn't that straightforward, Vasya.'

And the professor once again became absorbed in his book.

Tanyusha gladly agreed to go for a walk around Moscow. On days like these it felt wrong to stay at home. Despite the early hour, the streets heaved with people, clearly not engaged in any pressing business.

Tanyusha and Vasya walked down the boulevards towards Tverskaya Street, then descended to the State Duma. The square in front of the building was crowded, with small groups of people clustering together but leaving the traffic unaffected; in the crowd there were quite a few officers. Something was clearly underway inside the Duma. It turned out that admittance was unrestricted.

Inside, around the table in an oblong assembly hall, sat people obviously not local and not of the Duma. A pass was required at the entrance but since there was a shortage, visitors were vetted on the basis of simple verbal statements. Vasya introduced himself as 'a member of the press', and referring to Tanyusha, he simply muttered 'a secretary'. It was obvious that those around the table had been selected with equal randomness. Still, the question of 'who was deliberating' was answered by 'The Soviet of the Workers' Deputies'. The discussion wasn't too lively; a sense of confusion hindered the speeches. A more spirited contribution came from a soldier seated in the wings, who incidentally, was also referred to as 'a delegate'. The soldier boomed out angrily:

....

the Russian Revolution of 1905) was Russia's first elected parliament and as such, played a significant role of the events of the February Revolution of 1917.

MIKHAIL OSORGIN

'What's there to discuss? We should be acting, not talking! Let's proceed to the barracks, that's the long and the short of what I propose. You'll see, they'll join in. What are we waiting for? You on the home front do nothing but talk your heads off!'

They filed out in a small crowd but near the entrance they grew in size. Someone clambered to a higher point and from there tried to address the public but his words could be barely heard. The overall atmosphere was lacklustre, even pedestrian. The only encouraging sign was the presence of several soldiers and an officer with an empty sleeve sewn to his overcoat. A smallish group set out towards Theatre Square, followed by a crowd. At first, they glanced nervously around, lest the mounted police should appear, but not a single policeman was to be seen. The crowd kept growing, and after Lubyanka Square and further down the streets of Lubyanka and Sretenka, it was already easily several thousand strong. Here and there a voice would spontaneously strike up 'La Marseillaise'[20] and 'You Fell Victim to the Fateful Struggle'[21] but the resulting chorus sounded quite dissonant; the latest revolution didn't yet have an anthem of its own. They

....

[20]   'La Marseillaise' is the anthem of the French Revolution of 1789-1799 and now the national anthem of France. But in 1875 a Russian text (not a translation of the French one) was written by Peter Lavrov to the same melody and became one of the most popular revolutionary songs. After the February Revolution of 1917, it was used as the semi-official national anthem of the new Russian republic. Even after the October Revolution, it remained in use for a while alongside 'The Internationale'.

[21]   The revolutionary funeral march, first appearing during the Revolution of 1905:

> You fell victims to the fateful struggle
> Of unselfish love towards your people.
> You sacrificed whatever you had for it,
> For life, for honour, for freedom.

reached Sukharev Square, but when the Sukharev Barracks came into view the crowd thinned out again; some feared that the barracks would open fire.

Vasya and Tanyusha were among those in the vanguard; it felt both terrifying and fascinating.

'Are you afraid, Tanya?'

'I don't know. I don't think they'll fire. Those inside must know that the revolution in Petersburg has been victorious.'

'So why aren't they coming out, the soldiers?'

'Well, most likely they don't dare. Not yet. But now that they have seen the people, they will.'

The gates of the barracks remained locked but the doors in the gates were open. Clearly there was indecisiveness; it could well have been that an order had been issued against exciting the crowd. They spoke to the sentries. To the amazement of the those at the head of the crowd, the sentries let them through and a portion of the crowd, perhaps two hundred strong, let themselves into the courtyard. The rest sensibly stayed outside the gate.

Only a few barrack windows were open. In those windows were soldiers, in their overcoats, their faces agitated and curious – they had been locked in.

'Come out, comrades! The revolution is underway in Petersburg! The tsar has been dethroned!'

'Out! Come out!'

The visitors waved leaflets, trying to throw them as high as the windows. They vociferously insisted that the officers should be delegated to negotiate. While sending the soldiers friendly and cheerful smiles, they were not at all sure whether they addressed enemies or new friends. Apprehensive mistrust flitted around, in and out of the windows.

The barracks stayed silent.

The crowd came closer to the door. Without warning, the door flew open and the crowd recoiled, having come face to face with an officer in field uniform, with an entire platoon of soldiers at his back, bayonets at the ready, who could be seen occupying the staircase. The soldiers were ashen-faced; the officer stood as if carved from stone, ignoring the questions, uttering not a word.

It all felt bizarre and absurd. The boisterous crowd was allowed to roar in the barracks' courtyard, and in doing so, shout some frightening, new, mutinous and inviting words, yet the soldiers never appeared. At the windows some were yelling: 'We've been locked in! We can't get out!'

The other windows sounded sceptical: 'Shoot your mouths off, why don't you! Wait till the machine guns have a go at you lot, that'll be where yer revolution gets yer!'

As if in response to this, from the side door, at a brisk pace, one after another, darted a platoon of soldiers and took position, forming a line directly in front of the crowd, their rifles pointed forward. The commanding officer was incredibly young, his chin visibly trembling. The young amongst the soldiers looked pale and confused.

Virtually at once the command rang out: 'Fire!'

And then followed a volley.

Tanyusha and Vasya were at the head of the crowd, immediately opposite the muzzles of the rifles. Clasping each other's hands, they involuntarily sprang backward. The crowd began disintegrating on both flanks and sprinting back to the front gate. Those at the centre started retreating towards the wall, pressing against it.

'Fire! Fire!' – two more volleys.

In a feverish voice, almost crying, trembling with agitation, Vasya muttered something and tried to shield Tanyusha with his body: 'Tanyusha, dearest, they are shooting, they are shooting at us, at their own, it cannot be, Tanyusha!'

There was no escape route – short of a miracle, they were going to be shot.

As the volleys stopped Vasya looked around him – there were no moans, no injured, no dead. A moment of deadly silence ensued. From behind the gate came the cries of those dispersing in all directions.

Suddenly, a boy, one of those who at all times and in all places would be running ahead of the crowd, shrieked in a high-pitched voice: 'Blanks! They're firing blanks!'

And having leapt forward, the urchin started clowning around in front of the soldiers: 'Blanks! You're popping blanks!'

Immediately, several workers came running towards the soldiers; the workers grabbed their rifles, broke their line, and began yelling something, eager to convince the men. With difficulty, obeying the bark of the officer, the soldiers disentangled themselves from the crowd and vanished into the entrance.

A new wave of noise surged up, the windows started shouting again as the crowd reversed its flow and gushed back from the street and into the courtyard.

'Come out, comrades, come right out and join us!'

Tanyusha pressed herself tight against the barrack wall, her entire body shaking, her eyes brimming with tears. Vasya took her hand: 'Tanyusha, sweet Tanyusha, what on earth is all this? How awful! What utter nonsense! How can it be? To be shooting today, of all days! True, those were blank cartridges, but still, how is it possible? To aim at civilians! Tanyusha!'

Still trembling, she pulled on his sleeve: 'Vasya, let's get out of here. I'm cold.'

Hugging the wall, they rapidly left the barracks courtyard, bypassed the tumultuous crowd, in silence and arm in arm; they reached Sretenka Street and hired the first horse-cab they saw: 'To Sivtsev Vrazhek.'

Tanyusha pulled out a handkerchief, mopped her eyes and sent Vasya a guilty smile: 'Don't be cross with me, Vasya.'

'How could I possibly...'

'But, really, I got so agitated, Vasya. For the first time ever...'

'I pretty much went to pieces myself, Tanyusha.'

'You know, Vasya, for some reason I suddenly felt ever so sad. I wasn't frightened, even when they were firing. But they looked so miserable, the soldiers, that I felt sorry for the whole world. They weren't like beasts, nothing of the sort, just pathetic miserable people. And I am so ashamed...'

'They are not to blame, Tanya.'

'I am not saying they are, but it's all so... horrible, Vasya, when here is a crowd and over there – people with rifles. I used to think that revolution was something heroic. But what I saw today was that everyone was afraid and no one understood a thing...'

After a pause, she added, 'You know, Vasya, this revolution of yours, I don't like it.'

'A MIRACLE'

Its legs had been rounded off into wheels, its veins pumped steam and oil, and there was fire in its heart. Throughout all those years it had been working for the sake of bloodshed, nothing else but bloodshed, but it remained clean and sleek, for it had been taken care of – all its copper parts had been scoured to a high shine, as well as its number plate. Today it delivered the live remnants of someone who in a previous life had been a young officer called Stolnikov, the one who had failed to guess his fifth card right.

As before, the civilian nurses welcomed the injured at the railway station in Moscow but their erstwhile ardour had given way to a somewhat institutional attitude. It wasn't theatre anymore – just an everyday occurrence. They would come closer to strike up a conversation, mostly with the officers. But no one came up to Stolnikov; the person fussing over the dreadful human stump was his orderly Grigory who helped to arrange him on a stretcher.

The senior doctor said, addressing his younger colleague, 'It's a miracle that this… one is alive. Moreover, he'll live!'

The doctor meant to say 'this man' but cut himself short – a stump wasn't a man. The stump was a stump of a man.

Upon arrival, Grigory tried to pin the St George's Cross onto Stolnikov's chest. But Stolnikov shook his head and Grigory slipped the little cross back into the box, and the box inside his shirt. Neither family nor friends were there to meet him – they knew nothing of his arrival. Stolnikov hadn't warned a soul. Besides, he felt feeble, even if he was a 'miracle'. He had been kept for half a year in a hospital situated in some out-of-the-way little town, as transporting him was deemed dangerous. Now he would live.

He was taken to a hospital. The doctors there were equally amazed at 'the miracle'. Not one of them dared approach the officer without arms or legs and offer some words of comfort. The young doctors would come over to make sure that the bones in his knees had skinned over with bluish welts, and that what was left of the right shoulder could stir. They didn't understand the purpose of it but they still administered massages. Stolnikov observed their faces, their moustaches, their adroit hands. As they left, he would follow them with his eyes – there they were, walking on legs, like he used to do: one-two, one-two...

In his capacity as a miracle, he was assigned a separate cubicle. At all times Grigory was by his side, pensioned off from the army on account of having exceeded the age of conscription.

Of his contemporaries from his university days, two had come to visit; he was grateful to both but said that they shouldn't come back, since, for the time being, he was in no mood for visitors. They understood. Then again, they also found it hard – what on earth were they supposed to discuss with him? The joys and trials of life? The future? They brought him some flowers on Tanyusha's behalf. He said, 'Thank her for me. When I feel better, I'll send word to her. I'll be discharged from here soon, there's nothing to treat. I'm in good health. I'll find some lodgings... together with Grigory here. Then I'll make sure to ask her to drop by.'

He spent another three months at the hospital. He was 'fit' and had even put on some weight. The doctors kept reiterating: 'Pure miracle! See for yourself how well he looks. That's a formidable physique!'

And so Stolnikov was discharged. In the students' quarter, in a lane off Bronnaya Street, Grigory had rented two modest rooms – one for Stolnikov, the other for himself. He stayed on as Stolnikov's solicitous nurse.

What did they have in common? The helplessness of one and the homelessness of the other. They both had witnessed something out of the ordinary, this down-to-earth soldier and a stump of an officer. They spent their long evenings conversing. Or rather Stolnikov talked while Grigory listened. As darkness descended, he would strike a match, insert a cigarette into the Stump's mouth and place an impromptu ashtray – a saucer – by the side of his head. He didn't smoke himself. Sometimes Stolnikov would read to him, and Grigory, listening devoutly to the words from an incomprehensible book, would turn the pages at the sign. Little by little, Stolnikov learned how to do it himself, by taking his 'magic wand' – a pencil topped with an eraser – into his mouth. This way he had read to Grigory practically the complete works of Shakespeare. Grigory took it all in with puzzlement, wearing an air of importance – strange images, bewildering conversations. And Grigory was taking it all in in his own fashion.

Like a baby, the Stump was learning about life, his brain perennially engaged in this or that invention. He thought to install a little slanting ladder above his bedhead and so could get up by employing the muscles in his neck – otherwise his body would outweigh the residual limbs of his legs – although there was no special need for him to ever get up. With his mouth, he learned to pick up a cigarette from the shelf on the wall and, holding it between his teeth together with the 'magic wand', to press the button of a lighter affixed to the shelf, and so light up. It took him over a week to master this trick – once he nearly set himself ablaze in his bed – but eventually he did succeed.

Stolnikov had a meagre income, sufficient to provide for this sort of a life. He bought himself a chair on wheels and invented a motor that could be attached and he could control; still, he could only use it within the confines of the room; it was Grigory who took him out in this very chair for a spin around Tverskoy Boulevard and Patriarch's Ponds. Stolnikov got himself a typewriter and learned to type by clasping a curved stick topped with an eraser in his mouth, and pushing the carriage with the help of a lever attached to the chair by his left shoulder. He was upset that, for all that, the paper still had to be inserted by Grigory; he ordered him to glue long sheets of paper together, and took to writing with minimal space between lines. The entire surface of his desk was crammed with an assortment of bizarre implements, his own inventions, manufactured either by Grigory or a craftsman to order. Without a word of comment, Grigory would adjust a band fitted with a spoon and a fork on the Stump's head, and the Stump would spend hours learning how to operate this complex tool by wrinkling the skin on his forehead. He drank water and tea through a straw. At the sight of his exhausted impotence, Grigory often said:

'Do let me feed you, yer Excellency! What's the point in straining like that?'

'Wait! There is a point. Since I am alive, I've got to learn how to live. Do you see?'

Their business discussions were brief.

The Stump had no prostheses. The doctors pronounced them useless:

'Unless you want them for decorative purposes, otherwise… It is still possible to procure something from abroad, but even then, only for the right arm, there's some hope there…'

But decorative purposes could just as easily be served by putting on a field jacket with its sleeves filled out.

He thought of wearing it when he was expecting Tanyusha for the first time. But he changed his mind and received her, on that occasion, lying in bed.

And Tanyusha, aware precisely of the nature of Stolnikov's bad fortune, was amazed:

'He looks so healthy, even if he is motionless in his bed!'

On her visit Tanyusha was accompanied by the old ornithologist, also eager to say hello to the young man. They didn't stay long. On her way out Tanyusha promised to come again when he called.

Back home, casting her mind back to her visit, Tanyusha burst out crying, something she wasn't in the habit of doing. Stolnikov wasn't particularly important in her life – just a recent and casual acquaintance. But, without doubt, he was the most unfortunate person of anyone she knew or could imagine.

Before going to bed, she approached the mirror and watched her beautiful arms that flew effortlessly to pleat her hair in a thick braid. Her arms were full of life, and youth, and strength. What utter delight to be in possession of arms! Suddenly, at the mental image of the bluish scars above the sawn-off bone, Tanyusha gave a start, recoiled, threw herself headfirst into the pillows and sobbed from pity, and desperate compassion for this poor stump; something Stolnikov himself would never understand. It was worse than the sight of a dead person… a man squashed by life and still bustling about underneath.

'But of course, he hates me; he is sure to hate everyone…'

FROM THE FRONT

From the railway station, bypassing the Smolensk Market, along the Arbat, morning, noon and night, gushing forth in a huge stream and then splitting up into creeks and rivulets, straggled the ragtag shadows of soldiers, dragging along the filth of the trenches, bundles of unwashed laundry, kettles clanking against the butts of their rifles. They walked along pavements, in disarray, private citizens now, all thoughts of marching in formation forgotten. They were busy transporting the war from the front deep inland, but their thoughts were not about the war; all they could think about were their farms and villages.

There were no faces, only overcoats and rough boots. Their faces had disintegrated inside unshaven cheeks, sunk into the cavities of their eyes, insomnia, the deserter's conscience, the stubborn reluctance to look back. And thus they trudged on, never looking back, unaware of their bearings, unwilling to talk but keeping the back of the one ahead squarely in sight. They were stumbling from one landmark to another, moving as a herd – that is, until they got lost in the warren of side streets and lanes. Then the forwardmost soldier would ask directions from a timorous passer-by, and the rest would listlessly follow in his footsteps.

Eventually they would aggregate again, in some antechamber, a hall, on a platform at the railway station, just as they had in the trenches, accustomed to having to wait for a wordless command that would send them on a frontal attack against a train; long-distance, short-distance, commuter train – the destination was of no importance as long as it took them forward and homewards. Some adopted a laissez-faire attitude and allowed themselves to be sucked into the city, where they would set about propagating anxiety and trench lice.

Some carried rifles, whilst others had ditched or sold the irksome burden, leaving only a bayonet still dangling from the belt, seeing as it could come in handy in the household when they finally reached home. And if, while still in the city, they chanced on a young and fresh cadet, marching smartly down the street in his clean boots, the glance they cast him was brief and baffled, so that the torpid and tired brain was saved the effort of anything resembling mental reflection.

Without any goodbyes, a soldier turned right from the Arbat and into a side street, straightened the rifle on his back – barrel down, bayonet attached – adjusted his cap and picked up speed. It looked like he knew where he was headed. Further on, when already in Sivtsev Vrazhek, he regained a spring in his step – in contrast to the profound weariness on his unshaven and filthy face. He pushed the gate with his free hand only to find it bolted, and inside the dog started barking. There hadn't used to be a dog. He knocked hard with his fist, then spotted the bell and rang it. Either self-consciously or with affected audaciousness, he met the caretaker Nikolai's stern gaze with his swollen eyes:

'Whad'yer want?'

'To comrade Nikolai my regards. Don't you recognise me?'

'Dunyasha's brother ain'tcha?'

The caretaker's stare was mistrustful. Dusk already started gathering.

'The very same, private Kolchagin, a hero in grey, de-mobbed. Back to me billet at yer place.'

They exchanged hellos but Nikolai's attitude showed disapproval.

'How come yer quit warring?'

'War ain't forever.'

'Done a bunk?'

'Yessir. Never asked me seniors. What war we had – we're done with it now.'

'Is that right? Heading back to yer village then?'

'Sure enough, after some rest. I'm dog tired, a month on the road if it was a day.'

'R-i-i-ight...'

Dunyasha was both glad and frightened. After his travels her beloved brother did look a sight, so she remarked:

'Yer'll mess up my entire kitchen. And what's the rifle for? Isn't that army property?'

'Can't tell these days what's yours and what's theirs. Then again, Dunka, I could sure do with a bath.'

'We did heat up the bathhouse, as though we knew. D'yer have any clean linen?'

'I'll make do. I'll wash 'em meself, just show me the way to the bathhouse. Else I'll riddle yer with all kinds of creepy-crawlies.'

The old house had its own bathhouse adjacent to the main building, like any good old household should. And private Kolchagin didn't emerge from it till late at night. He washed himself, washed his clothes, dried the lot. He even took his kitbag in. He showed up for evening tea red-faced, glowing from the steam, in improved spirits, sporting a new tunic that was part of an officer's uniform.

'This tunic is truly top class. I got me hands on it when I was setting off. As for the pests, Dunya, I've killed the little buggers by steaming them off. A bath is just the ticket – could spend me entire life in it. 'Course, it belongs to them toffs who don't have it as rough as we do.'

He learned from Dunyasha about the old lady's death.

'Well, say what you may, she was getting long in the tooth. As for us lot, at the front, we was dying young, be it from the enemy or the sickness, only to profit capitalism.'

'Who's that then?'

'Take my word for it. We're done with all them lies.'

Nonetheless, he asked that his sister not blabber with the neighbours about his arrival and was vague when answering her questions.

'Why should I stick around over there, then? There's no war no more, is there.'

For the night, he settled on the bench and fell asleep straight away.

When she was clearing up, Dunyasha brushed the tap of the cooling samovar with her sleeve. A trickle of water streamed down to the floor, ran asunder in little streams, reached a gap among the floorboards, and disappeared.

The cat raised her head and watched, transfixed, as the water leaked from the tap, but having dampened her paw in the resulting puddle, she squeamishly shook it dry and retreated.

When Dunyasha returned to the kitchen from her room, the samovar was empty. The private deserter Kolchagin was heard snoring away in short heavy bursts.

BY THE MONUMENT

'Time for ye constitutional, ye honour, 'ere's hoping it don't rain.'

Before rolling the wheelchair from the passage into the street, Grigory threw a short cape over the Stump's shoulders.

'There's no need, Grigory, it's warm enough.'

'It's only because of the epaulettes, your honour – best to stay out of trouble.'

Those days epaulettes were being torn off from officers' shoulders. Would they really hurt a cripple? But lately the mood of the street crowds had been grim, folk not knowing left from right, and Grigory was anxious.

'There's no need, Grigory, leave it be.'

The invalid's chair rolled into the tree-lined alley on its large wheels. A crowd had gathered in a circle across from Bogoslovsky Lane, and in its midst a lean bespectacled gentleman with a pointed beard stood arguing with a soldier. In proving his point, the soldier was emphatic on the subject of lice in the trenches; the gentleman kept talking about France and England. Everyone around listened attentively.

A few cast a sideways glance at Stolnikov's wheelchair, followed his path with their eyes and went back to listening to the debate, stretching their necks through the gaps in the front row; faces inspired more trust than words alone. One listener observed under his breath:

'See, how many of those are around nowadays, invalids!'

A nanny pushed a child's pram towards the Stump, out of which stared a little blue-eyed girl in a white bonnet. When both sets of wheels aligned, the child's gaze met the adult's. But the Stump didn't smile.

The closer they came to the Pushkin monument, the bigger the clusters around the debaters grew. The topics ardently discussed were land, the Constituent Assembly, the parties, but before anything else –matters at the front line. Fragments of phrases could be overheard:

'… And as for those who got themselves a nice hideout in the rear…'

'… So who says I should spill my blood, eh?'

'… And how should I know what sort of a man you are? Anyone can get their hands on a soldier's uniform…'

'… Sure, you need scientists, too, for education and the like. But…'

The biggest crowd, as ever, was by the monument itself. The speaker was an officer, bandaged and leaning on a crutch. His military cap had been sent around the crowd, and everyone hastened trustingly to donate money for the invalids. To the side stood a small table, and the man sitting behind it kept tipping the banknotes into a jewellery box. People continued coming up to donate, not always aware of what the donation was towards, or who was collecting the money.

The crowd parted before the Stump's wheelchair, and Grigory pushed him right up to the monument. The speaker, already on the verge of losing his voice, pointed at the Stump for the benefit of the crowd and bellowed, wiping away the sweat:

'And for what did men like these – look, look at him! – spill their blood? To give Russia away to the Germans? No sir, we shall not allow it!'

The speaker's trouser leg gave away the fact that the limb beneath was bandaged. There was a fresh red scar on his left cheekbone, and when he opened his mouth, the skin over the scar would stretch and catch the light. When he finished speaking, he was replaced by a civilian in glasses, and the crowd shuffled forward with interest. A mere minute later it began to murmur in indignation, since the civilian started arguing against the war. Someone yelled out, 'Shame on you! See this officer over here – no arms, no legs!'

The civilian shouted back:

'And that is exactly why this is enough...'

He now faced intense resistance. Two sailors and a soldier shouted back at the crowd:

'He exercises his right to freedom of speech, comrades, you can't shout him down like that...'

The Stump turned his head, grasped an epaulette between his teeth, ripped it off and said to Grigory as the orderly bent down:

'Take it off. And the other one. Take off both of them. And throw them at him.'

'At whom, your honour?'

'At that dark man, the one who is speaking now. Throw them in his damned face!'

Grigory followed the order, and the epaulettes smacked against the chest of the speaker. The crowd started to howl, and the dark-haired man disappeared together with the soldier and the sailors.

Now the Stump's wheelchair was surrounded by people. There were yells of 'That's right!' Some grand lady shrieked incoherently and urged everyone to go smash the Germans. A curly-haired nurse stood next to Grigory, holding on to the handle of the wheelchair, and gesticulated to the crowd – her voice couldn't be heard – to take off their hats in honour of the crippled officer. Those at the front took them off, those at the back pushed to get closer. Someone piped up:

'Quiet everyone, he's about to speak!'

Sure enough, the crowd hushed down and the circle widened. Stolnikov looked around the crowd and, in the silence that had descended, said clearly and precisely:

'I have nothing to say to you. You are slaves, and that one, the dark-haired one, the one who was speaking against the war, he may be a scoundrel but he's right. To hell with this war of yours! Grigory, take me away from here!'

The front row parted. The nurse let go of the handle of the wheelchair. Those at the back didn't catch everything, but started yelling anyway: 'That's right, that's true, thank you, your honour!' A bearded gentleman explained to his wife: 'He's a very sick man, a cripple; of course, he's angry and bitter.'

And only one soldier, his military tunic unbuttoned, hollered, joyfully and breathlessly:

'How do you like it now, you bastards, huh? Now they get it, now that it's their legs being hacked off, too. Ha! Nice one!'

And, taking a handful of sunflower seeds out of his pocket, he set about nibbling them. A hastily rolled cigarette stuck out from behind his left ear.

The cheerful soldier's name was Andrey Kolchagin.

THE CARETAKER

There was no snow that October. At night it would freeze tentatively and then thaw out in the daytime. At the crack of dawn, the caretaker went out the gate of the professor's tiny courtyard with his shovel and his broom, carried slantwise. He took his time sweeping the pavement until it was completely clean, casting hostile glances at the unkempt stretch of pathway and the cobbled street in front of the neighbours' house. He was thinking that because of all these new freedoms people had grown work-shy. It was light already, so there was no good reason for the street to remain unswept.

The greengrocer stopped by for a quick chat, taking a short pause in his rounds – they were fellow country people who went back a long way. They rolled a cigarette each, shared a smoke. The horse kept looking askew at the windows.

'The old master, is he coping? Getting along?'

'Getting by. First off, he was mighty heart-broken, but he got used to it, you could say. It helps that the granddaughter is around. It would be real tough without her.'

The greengrocer knew the professor well, it must have been some twenty-odd years by now. It was he who had fixed them up with the caretaker, a fellow from his village.

'They gossip at the market,' said the greengrocer, looking aside. 'Especially this soldier who's not from round here. "Them rifles," he says, "no chance in hell they'll surrender 'em." – "And who yer going to shoot, then?" – "Whoever gets in the way, the toffs." – "And then?" – "Then we ditch this bloody war and start taking back the land." – "But yer finished yer war, and did a runner!" – "So what if I did," he says. "They pronounced freedom nowadays. Did I feed them lice for nothing?"'

'Folk don't know right from left,' said the caretaker.

'That's right. But I tell yer, there's power in 'em, look how many there are, trailing from the station. They just keep coming, day and night, lots of 'em. Must be no one's left over there at the front. It takes time to get back home, to the village, so they've got to get by somehow. That's when they egg 'em on.'

'Who's egging 'em on?'

'They have them orators. Meetings in every square. To do away with the bourgeois, so's to get all the power. And the soldiers are listening and taking good note.'

The horse gave another sidelong glance at the windows. The greengrocer jerked the rein.

'If you ask me, it ain't about to end peacefully. In the olden days, it was a different story, but now who's there to put it all to rights. Plus they have rifles now.'

'Not our business,' said the caretaker.

The greengrocer let it pass. They finished their roll-ups, and bid each other goodbye till better days. The barrow set off towards the Arbat Square.

The winter sun was on the point of peeping out but disappeared in the white milk. Several gates banged in Sivtsev Vrazhek and suddenly there was a smell of smoke. A man with a cardboard folder under his armpit, apparently a clerk, his chilled hands thrust deep into the pockets of a soldier's overcoat, scurried by, his heels clicking. The caretaker stared after him for some while, laboriously trying to decide who was more likely to come out on top eventually – the collective power of the masters or the mutinous soldiery. He passed through the gate and scrutinised it carefully – it needed mending but could last many more years as it was. He thought: *Must tell the master to get a dog, in case of thieves. Lots of them homeless folk hanging around, while the street is barely guarded. The watchman's[22] meant to be on duty but he is always either asleep or drunk. And no police. Life's not as it should be, nowadays, nothing but worry after worry.*

He retreated into his caretaker's lodge deep in thought, his face stern, almost monastic. The fire in his oven was now blazing up. The caretaker usually took his tea in the kitchen, at Dunyasha's.

His nail-rich imperishable boots clanked up the staircase in the service entrance.

He was single, well advanced in years, practically old. Sullen. Of a sound mind if slow on the uptake. On entering the kitchen, he would customarily cross himself in a sweeping gesture, utter some polite greeting and sit down to tea without further formalities, smoothing his moustache, so as not to be disturbed. He would gather the breadcrumbs into his palm and once there was a heap, toss them into his mouth.

'When the master is up, do call for me, Dunya. I want to talk to him about a dog.'

'What d'ye want a dog for? It'll need feeding...'

'A dog's role is to guard the house. Think of the times we live in.'

'But the gate's bolted!'

'The gate... That was good in the times gone by, nowadays you could simply scramble over. Lots of unknown folk around, yer could never tell who may break in. But if a dog starts barking, it's a warning of sorts. When he's up, do call for me.'

'Alright, I will.'

He finished his second cup, turned it upside down, wiped his moustache with a chequered handkerchief.

....

[22] This refers to the attempts to start some kind of a citizens' watch.

'Shall I bring some nice wood in?'

'Just for the two ovens. We don't heat up the one in the dining room, it's hot as it is.'

His new boots clanked again down the kitchen stairs.

'If only we had some snow. It's long since time.'

For a brief moment, a picture flashed through the caretaker's mind: the fields, the ploughland, the forest, and all of it deep in snow. The snow was pure, untrodden by sledge runners, with no admixture of ground or manure. Snow as a friend, not something daubed on.

The image lasted a minute and vanished, and in his soul, the dignified caretaker of the professor's old townhouse in Sivtsev Vrazhek felt like a city dweller all over again.

ENVY

'Why isn't he coming, Grigory?'

'He will, yer Excellency, it's still early.'

'But how will he make it? Will someone bring him here?'

'His Excellency will find his way 'imself. He lives only two porches along. He's used to dropping into the shop by himself, too.'

Ensign Kashtanov, who had lost his sight in the war, showed up only after it had struck eight. On hearing the footfall and his voice, Grigory came out and led the blind man to the Stump's desk.

'So, whereabouts are you, my friend Sasha?'

'I'm here, hello.'

After which Stolnikov added:

'You shouldn't hold out your hand again. I've got nothing to shake it with.'

'Alright. Some pair we make. One better than the other.'

Nevertheless, he reached out towards the source of the voice and patted Stolnikov on the shoulder.

To start with both were silent. They shared a smoke. Grigory served tea. Stolnikov was excited and hardly took his eyes off his friend – the person before him was, possibly, as miserable as himself (was it even conceivable?). This was a person who could not see the world, its colours, its enticing contours. Stolnikov could see the world but couldn't place his arms around it. Kashtanov could hug whatever he pleased but couldn't see whom and what it pleased him to hug. In this instant, to Stolnikov, the world felt like a woman.

In the beginning they talked about anything but themselves – about the various events and the shared friends in their unit. But after Grigory retired into his own room for the night, the conversation promptly shifted to their own misfortunes, and hurriedly, in a semi-whisper, embarrassed but cutting across each other, competing in the scope of their horrible grief, they poured out everything they had thought about, each locked in his own solitude, which had meant long, burdensome days for the one and the eternal night for the other.

Delivering his rapid-fire patter, clutching his temples and chaotically groping around with his hands, the blind Kashtanov whispered:

'Arms, legs, you say... but what good are they for me? Where should I go? What will I do with these hands? You know, Sasha, it's because there's nothing out there, just darkness, and the sounds out of the darkness, voices, noises, music, laughter... But none of it's there, just the dreams – but in reality, it's all non-existent. You, on the other hand, can see things at home and beyond the window, you get taken for rides outside, but for me – none of it is there but the endless night. You were saying you could sense your legs. But I also sense the light, the way it was when I could see it. In front of my eyes are houses, people, women, I feel like lurching forward towards them, but they aren't there, they've all drowned in the night. When I know it's dark, in the evening, it's easier. But when I feel the sun on my face, and it's warm – that's when it becomes intolerable, Sasha. The sun caresses me and I curse its impotence – why can't it dispel this never-ending darkness?'

Stolnikov interrupted, similarly in a whisper – as if sharing a secret – and crying:

'What you have, Kashtanov, is better. For example, you can't see and you say that there's nothing there. Meanwhile I can see and know it's there, but not for me. You can make your own way to the shop, and you have brought yourself here to visit me, while Grigory must wheel me around in a pram and feed me from a spoon. Simply consider this: am I truly a man? You feel everyone's equal, at least at night, but I – never. You can put your arms around a woman...'

'But she isn't real, Sasha, I won't see with my eyes what she's like...'

'I know you won't, but still, you can lock her in your embrace. But I, I can see and even fall in love, maybe I do love someone, Kashtanov, have loved her for a long time now, but I cannot touch her, cannot take her hand. I disgust her, Kashtanov, for I'm not a man, just a bluish stump, an offcut, a misunderstanding. I cannot piss without help, Devil take me... do take me, Devil... Here I am, weeping but unable even to wipe away my tears, so I have to shake them off my head. But the tears are running into my nose, damn it, damn it, damn...'

He sniffled and tossed his head about. At such moments Kashtanov got to his feet, pulled out a handkerchief, found Stolnikov's face and blotted his eyes.

'You should calm down, Sasha.'

They would fall silent. But not for long. As soon as another word was uttered, the passionate dispute would flare up yet again and Kashtanov would whisper loudly, choking on his delivery:

'It is so, Sasha, I know. But here's what I have to say to you, Sasha. At times I am ready to sacrifice not just my arms and legs, but all of myself, for the sake of just one little minute, to see things with my own eyes. You say you love someone, but do you know how much I've loved – and she's alive, she exists, she's even come round to see me once, and I heard her voice, I remember every little cadence of it. Her eyes, Sasha, they were... I say – they were... well, for me, they were and aren't any more, ever so blue, amazing eyes. So now, Sasha, they aren't there, not anymore, not for me. You say "to hug", but I need to hug with my eyes, to see her smile, otherwise every word rings false, and everything seems a lie and feels deceitful, and I have no need for anyone. Am I supposed to embrace the sun, or what? What's more, in this world, there exists the sea, the horizons, the forests, beauty, views, but where is all of it, Sasha? The Devil has devoured the lot. Look at it from my point of view. I've no need for arms, nor legs, what's the point? I feel sometimes like clawing deep into this veil and ripping it off...'

'You, Kashtanov, may still be cured. I read somewhere that there is this appliance, you attach it to your temples, it excites the ocular nerves...'

'Stop talking nonsense. Whatever are you saying that for? I've had both apples extracted, what's left is only two hollows.'

'Who can tell? They may still invent something.'

'Invent, my elbow. It'll rather be your prostheses.'

'So that means I'll be embracing with metal sticks? Caressing breasts with them? Is that it?'

And so, whatever was discussed afterwards, they invariably came to the same point – a woman whom one of them could not see while the other could not embrace. They were both young – the Stump and the blind man. And they kept talking until the tremulous anger rose in their souls, along with a mutual envy – anger of the blind man against the Stump, and envy of the Stump before the blind man. They were jealous of each other because of the woman who didn't exist, who didn't want to know either of them existed – a breath-taking beauty with blue eyes and velvety skin.

Grigory would return and see their distorted faces, hear their anguished speeches and try to pacify them:

'Yer Excellencies, the neighbours are asleep, they're sure to complain again. It's quite late, yer Excellencies...'

He would accompany Kashtanov home and, upon his return, put an exhausted and helpless Stolnikov to bed – a pathetic remainder of someone who had once been a handsome and courageous officer, a cordial friend and a passable dancer.

Only three years had elapsed since the day he had last merrily danced at Tanyusha's, on her special day, the day that had marked the beginning of her seventeenth spring.

OCTOBER[23]

On those days in October, white specks and white butterflies should have been flitting around and covering the road, layer upon layer. The children should have been having snowball fights until their tiny fingers became red and their necks became damp behind the collar; afterwards the little fur coats should have emitted a tangy aroma when Mama hung them up close to the oven to dry. Happy laughter should have leapt from their eyes onto their lips in response to the first fluffy snow, so clean, delicious, fussy and gentle.

But the snow never came. What now started flying over Moscow were leaden hornets – along the streets, above the rooftops, out of the windows and into the windows from

....

[23]   Much as the official name of the revolution that took place in 1917 was the Great October Socialist Revolution, it actually took place on November 6th – the date on which all the subsequent anniversary festivities were held. The reason for this discrepancy is that until February 1918 Russia had been using the Julian calendar (still adhered to by the Russian Orthodox Church). This calendar does not take into account the fact that it takes the Earth 365 days and 6 hours to complete its rotation around the Sun. Once every four years 6 hours make up for a full extra day which is accounted for in the introduction of leap years. Since the Julian calendar made no provisions for those extra days, over the course of several centuries the difference between the calendar used in Russia and the calendar used in the West (Gregorian) amounted to full two weeks. Hence, what is described in the book as the events taking place in October were, in fact, spread over the last past of October and the beginning of November.

outside. And the people hurtled horrendous little balls at each other and their explosions made the iron sheets on top of the little house in Sivtsev Vrazhek tremble.

The leaden snow first started on Tverskoy Boulevard. Having spent his morning at the university lab, Vasya Boltanovsky dropped at his usual hour into Troitskaya's canteen, the windows of which faced the boulevard. He took his habitual place by the window and placed a serviette inside its branded ring onto the table, next to his plate. His long-since-organised life had been running along smoothly as if it were a train on well-adjusted little wheels, and though the jellied piglet's rump had become way too expensive, on Sundays they still served pancakes with jam and cranberry kissel, its little islands turning lilac in the lake of milk. One felt anxious but life was stubbornly determined to go on.

After the soup with dumplings, some roast ham and mash. As Vasya Boltanovsky was busy mopping up the remains of the sauce with a crusty piece of bread, shooting broke out at the end of the boulevard, across the road from the mayor's house. Through his window Vasya could see the vista of the boulevard and figures running along the alley; whether those of uninvolved passers-by, the champions of the new order or the defendants of the old one he could not tell. The service in the canteen sped up. Vasya finished his bread kvass fermented from bread crumbs and went out onto the boulevard. The leaden hornets, now out of the nest, buzzed all around the boulevard, aimlessly and haphazardly. Soon the first of them reached their target and pinged against the window of the famous students' canteen.

As there was no snow in the boulevard's alley, it became dark especially rapidly. By now, the volleys fired by invisible rifles were sounding in different parts of the city. People continued shooting at each other, and undoubtedly, brother was now busy shooting brother. The rifles led the way, the machine guns followed after them, then the artillery. That evening and the entire night, and then for five days in a row, ordinary Muscovites shrank into themselves, trapped inside their rooms, and listened to the rumbling of cannons and the rat-a-tatting of machine guns. Leaden fear swept across the roofs, searching for an enemy, flying into the windows and pock-marking the outside walls of houses.

On the very first night a bright glow lit up the Nikitsky Gates: the house at the top of the boulevard caught fire and Troitskaya's canteen, where that very afternoon Vasya had been enjoying his ham and mash, burned right down. The napkin did not burn, but slowly smouldered to ashes while the wooden branded ring around it charred and split.

The house burned itself out, and the fire spread to another block, a monumental edifice at the internal passage of the boulevard, and instead of a place of residence, the pale morning was met with a blackened smoking coliseum which had not yet become an object of anybody's admiration.

Affluence fled from the burning houses, showered by bullets, privation bolted in horror, and both were caught in the submachine crossfire. Each shot brought the victory closer and ran down the number of enemies. Out of an un-prepossessing hotel, sharing an address with the canteen, hurried and scurried ten old women with their bundles; some escaped, shielding themselves against the leaden rain with their shawls; others died of fright; a few were riddled with bullets or burned alive – and the longed-for freedom came closer. A handful of young soldiers never stopped shooting from the corner house at a handful of young cadets across the road; some were killed, some managed to slip along the wall and disappear – and the coveted kingdom of fraternity and equality came a moment nearer.

His arms cast upwards and his rifle tossed aside, a dead soldier lay in the road, baring his teeth at the sky in a grin; he had never learned for the sake of whose truth he had died and which side would count him among their fallen heroes.

Meanwhile, screened by a ledge in the gate, a grey-faced boy in a sheepskin hat still coughed intermittently and spat blood, though earlier he had been firing his rifle, merrily and with gusto, taking aim here, there and everywhere: at the cadets, and any sweeping shadow, and his brother, and his grandmother – mostly wide of the mark, his bullets smacking into the whitewashed walls of the building – and now here he was, a bullet in his own lung, not long for this world – farewell, you poor silly boy! And freedom was closer by yet another step.

Behind the solid walls, in a room facing away from the street, certain civilians, who did not know how to pull a trigger or feed a belt into a machine gun, were busy conferring, discussing, reaching agreements, issuing orders and taking charge. But it wasn't they who exercised power, neither was any of this happening for their sake. What was destined to unfold was decided by chance, as well as by a carefree reckless bullet smuggled out by someone who had deserted the front-line. The Kremlin was still there, as was the Arsenal[24] and the Alexander II Military School, but also there was mayhem and squabbling among people who were always right, who were victorious only when they advanced without philosophising and without thinking. But that was exactly what was so frightening – that under the airborne swarm of bullets and

....

[24] The Arsenal building situated within the Kremlin walls and the nearby Horse-Riding School (Manezh) became two strongholds for cadets from the Alexander II Military School, a secondary military educational establishment for training infantry officer corps. In October 1917 they were fighting against the Red Guards.
The bloodshed of that autumn in Moscow shocked many people. 'One of the most macabre days of my life,' wrote Ivan Bunin about events of that day, considering the act of disarming the cadets the 'zenith of it all'. 'They have gutted Moscow, the cannibals!' The same events were also reflected in a well-known romance by the celebrated balladeer Alexander Vertinsky: 'I don't know who and why need this to be so...'

shrapnel, the very thought that had crept out of braincases only the day before was eddying, straying, and becoming muddled. This thought continued offering arguments, becoming confused, despairing, guessing and ending up tangled up in the cobwebs of alien concepts.

He who was used to not thinking things through, making no assessments, holding nothing in esteem and who had nothing to lose was destined to win. And win he did. The people in civilian clothes conferred and passed a resolution: 'It is we who have won.' Thus they drove the victor away and proceeded to occupy the command positions in the dead city.

All of this was right and proper; their civilian adversaries would have acted in exactly the same way.

Vasya Boltanovsky lived in Girshi Quarter, off Bronnaya Street, in Block 2 of the main house. Out of his window he could watch the fires blazing in the night and, like everybody else, Vasya did not sleep. At times it felt strange and unnatural that there he was, a young man, not a coward, not prone to passivity, yet staying at home and not joining either side. A minute later it seemed that there were no sides anymore, just a blind force of nature, a fire started from an accidental match. And nothing to fight this fire with. Go out unarmed into the street? What for? Procure a weapon and start firing? At whom? Aim at which of the two truths? But was it even possible that there existed two truths? And not even two but many – one truth governing nature, another pursued by man and radically opposed to natural order? And then yet another, totally different, believed in by someone else. Each was fighting his own corner, that was the essence of the fight for survival. But then a man would go and die for the sake of the others, contrary to his own interest. There was truth in both covetousness and self-sacrifice. So, whose side was he really on, this Vasya, a university research assistant and a friend of Tanyusha's? He wasn't siding with anyone who dreamed of power. His true goal was to be able to do serious work, and that Tanyusha should be happy. And that was the whole truth, emanating from his heart.

Shortly before dawn Vasya fell asleep but woke early, roused by shots coming from somewhere near his own house. It sounded rather like a desultory random fusillade; perhaps a pursuit or possibly just plain mischief. Why would anyone think of opening fire inside a peaceful students' quarter?

On such a day work was out of the question – unless he tried to make his way to the laboratory by a roundabout route through some back streets?

It was past eight o'clock when Vasya went out and bolted off towards the Nikitsky Gates, but gunfire made him turn back. He then set off towards Garden Street and took Skaryatinsky Lane to cross Bolshaya Nikitskaya. There wasn't a soul around Povarskaya Street and, his curiosity piqued, Vasya decided to stroll down to the Church of Saints Boris and Gleb, or even as far as Arbat Square. He was barely at the top of Borisoglebsky Lane when the air trembled from the blast of a projectile that knocked off a segment of the dome off the church. Vasya gasped and muttered, 'What on earth is all this? What's going on?' Then, he quickened his pace and he turned off into a side street. He had no idea what had just happened but he was thoroughly frightened. All was quiet in Sobachy Court,[25] and although gloomy, Khomyakov's House[26] looked dignified and respectable. One final option was to try and get to the university along the Arbat.

....

[25] Sobachy Court (The Dogs' Court) was a historical place, a square that existed at the intersection of several central streets and lanes near the Arbat. The area was completely reconstructed in 1962–1968 with the creation of the New Arbat, and the Court no longer exists.

[26] Khomyakov's House – a townhouse that belonged to the prominent Slavophile author Khomyakov. The house was in the Empire style. The house had been frequented by Khomyakov's friends and allies – the Aksakovs, the Kireeyvskys, et al.

Vasya made his way to the corner, stopped short and turned his curious gaze to the left, towards the source of rapid fire. Should he give it a go?

Only a blissfully ignorant research assistant, a civilian through and through, could have stood there like that, full of equanimity and unaware of the buzzing bullets. No one tried to stop Vasya and it didn't occur to him that he might be the target of the shooting from further down the street. Gripping his books under his elbow – a habit surviving from his student's days – he slowly crossed the Arbat. He didn't know that ordinary people, puzzled and scared, were watching his progress from behind lowered curtains; he didn't notice when a bullet squashed itself flat against a cobblestone just a couple of paces away. Even so, walking along the Arbat he felt a creeping horror, and apart from anything else, he had no way of knowing if there was still an open route across the square. The Alexander II Military School was just a stone's throw away, and by now, more than likely, the scene of heavy fighting. On second thoughts, a more usual and uncomplicated idea would be simply to walk round the church of St Nickolai in Plotniki towards the serene and welcoming Sivtsev Vrazhek and the professor's old townhouse where coffee was surely on offer, and if not, Dunyasha could heat some up anyway. There was nothing for it; he wouldn't make it to work today.

Clearly, the morning had been wasted. Still, he could redeem the time elsewhere. And besides, there were things to discuss with the old professor, who had surely decided to stay indoors. Besides, he wanted to share his impressions with Tanyusha, although his impressions weren't all that plentiful: vague nonsense, mainly.

Vasya rang the bell and, catching the sound of footsteps on the staircase, beamed in anticipation.

THE WALL BETWEEN THE WINDOWS

Rust kept slowly corroding the iron sheets of the roof, the grubs continued gnawing at the beams, the rats kept laying down new passages for their daring nocturnal expeditions; damp, mould, and billions of infinitesimally small invisible organisms were also involved, for the sake of love and propagation of the right to life, in the rocking of the foundations underneath the little townhouse in Sivtsev Vrazhek – and these days, their toil was greatly assisted by the tremors and vibrations sweeping over Moscow, the quivering of the air caused by little bullets and the shells that mocked cowardice. The window panes kept reverberating, thus causing the dried-up sealant to wobble; tiny nails continued to snap, the old paint never stopped flaking off, the brick continued losing particles of dirt and the soot that had been building up to the very top of the chimney and then dropping back into the oven in greasy lumps. These goings-on were invisible to all, save the minute creators and destroyers, still labouring incessantly and tirelessly.

A new fine line does not show on an old face. High above the roof a shell whooshed by, dissecting the air, propelled at random from the Sparrow Hills by some poor shot of a gunner – and the peaceful abode of the old professor bent down painfully, squinted breathlessly but bounced back – and thus another wrinkle was etched. But nobody could hear or see a thing, nothing but a barely audible rustling behind the wallpaper. It could have been a cockroach escaping from the kitchen.

The professor said, 'You mustn't go home, Vasya. We won't let you. Then again, we, too, feel safer with you around. Wait until they stop firing tomorrow, then go.'

'I'm not afraid, Professor.'

'As befits a young man. But taking unnecessary risks won't help anyone. Down there, by Nikitsky Gate, all hell's breaking loose. But, above all, you'll do us a favour. Besides, we could do with some company. Both me and Tanyusha.'

Lenochka telephoned from the Clear Ponds[27] where she lived:

'It's pure horror over here. They are firing at the post office. There's talk that the telephone exchange is also under siege.'

The young lady operating the telephones piped up:

'Which part of the city are you calling from?'

'Sivtsev Vrazhek. It's quiet here, what about you?'

'Terrible. Christ knows what next.' She put the call through.

But in quite a few districts telephones had already stopped working.

'Vasya, shall we go upstairs to my room? Grandpa will be working.'

The professor was a stickler for his well-established routine. Piles of atlases and index cards all around him, he would work well into the small hours, peering closely at the plumage of a turtle dove pictured on the art-paper, introducing corrections into the outdated classification. He would cut the pages of the English magazine with his ivory knife – a magazine that had made it, somehow, across the borders; he would lower his spectacles from his forehead, follow the lines with his nose and jot down some comments in the margins with his little pencil. It was all extremely

....

[27] The name of one of the boulevards.

164

MIKHAIL OSORGIN

important: migration, singing, tiny speckled grey eggs, a curved beak, a bright patch on the wings... It was ever so important; all of it was eternal and it served eternity.

Meanwhile a bullet softly thwacked against the roof – this one completely stray and drunk, set in flight from somewhere in the Arbat or perhaps the Smolensky Market.

'I'll be going to bed now but you, you youngsters, do stay up. Your bed, Vasya, will be made up in Grandma's room, or if you prefer, in the hall. Tanya will see to it.'

'I will, Grandpa, you go on. We'll stay in my room for a while longer.'

'All the same, Tanyusha, keep away from the windows. You never know. Better to sit in between the windows, against the walls.'

'Alright, Grandpa.'

They bade him goodnight and climbed the stairs. Up there was a good place to chat or simply to stay silent.

'How will it all end, Vasya?'

'Well, they'll never seize the Kremlin. After all, inside it is the Arsenal.'

'And if they do take it?'

They talked, going over the rumours. Tanyusha was thinking: *It's so strange. Vasya is not a coward but he definitely seems unaffected, as if he were an outsider. Someone else in his place...*

Who could that someone be? In her mind, she started briefly going over the names of people she knew, military men and civilians, living and dead. Would Ehrberg have joined the fray? Possibly. Whereas Stolnikov, had he... But of course! Poor man, the worries he must be suffering now! But her soul, as yet too inexperienced, couldn't even begin to imagine the poor man's ordeal in those days.

Vasya was sitting there smoking, so Tanyusha briefly opened the top part of the window. In came the rattling noise of shots fired somewhere nearby. Rat-a-tat... It sounded like a machine-gun.

They fell silent, listening intently, in close proximity on the sofa. Tanyusha kept thinking about the revolution. Vasya, for his part, was thinking: *I know I love her. And that she shows me affection, but only as a friend. Come what may, I love her terribly. So, will it always be just like that?*

This thought in mind, he raised his gaze and stared closely at Tanyusha.

'What is it, Vasya?'

'Nothing.'

Tanyusha got to her feet and pushed the window to.

'Goodness! How cold it is today.'

'It certainly is. And still no snow.'

The month of October was drawing to a close. What was being ushered in was the interminable, extraordinary and excruciating *October*.

Snow finally fell by the end of the fifth day of the riots in Moscow, when the leaden hornets had stopped flying around. Snow came on the morning of the sixth day – clumpy, scarce, self-conscious and yet needed by all. It painted white the pock-marked roofs, covered unremoved corpses with a white shroud, froze and powdered over the blood on cobblestones and in the courtyards.

And, straightaway, all was serene in Moscow. A common Muscovite peeped out tremulously, but curiosity got the better of him. Curiosity and scarcity, since by now the originally put-by reserves of bread, food, kerosene and wood had run out. One way or another, one had to go on living. A Muscovite sneaked inside the semi-open door of a shop, pushing his cautious way forward with his shoulder.

A passer-by would question an acquaintance he bumped into:

'But who won in the end?'

'They say it was them, the Bolsheviks.'

'So now what?'

'Now nothing. They won't survive long. The army will move in and restore law and order. How is it even possible to turn Moscow into a shooting gallery? It's a new low.'

'Is our bakery still open?'

'It is. You can enter from the backyard.'

Gazing around with wide open, puzzled eyes, pressing against the walls of the houses, scuttering across the street with shoulders stooped low, everyone continued going about their own business, prepared, at a moment's notice, to dive into an entrance, into a side street, behind the advertising rotunda.

And if there was anything at all that gladdened the eye, it was only the pure, still untrammelled, pleasantly chilling first snow that had fallen down on a frightened and exhausted Moscow and all its ordinary people.

THE BULLET

It had never occurred to Eduard Lvovich that it was possible to buy a new blanket, one that would reach as far as his chin and still fold onto itself underneath his feet.

He had always been aware of the discomfort of too short a blanket but only ever employed doubtful means of coping: he would cover his feet with an old coat, the one with a chequered lining. It wasn't because of miserliness, merely for lack of forethought. Eduard Lvovich did not suffer from poverty; he lived an unpretentious life and so could afford to spend significant sums on sheet music and books on musical theory and history. That said, he never stopped sending money to Riga, to his aunt whom he hadn't laid eyes on for twenty years; he continued making those transfers following tradition and from force of habit, since he had started doing it back when his mother was still alive.

The blanket did a poor job covering his feet, so he was forced to sleep on his side, doubled over. His one ear could hear the pulse resounding from the pillow while the other was picking up the rattling of a machine gun in the street: rat-a-tat… To Eduard Lvovich, the meaning of a firing machine gun was completely and decisively alien (it wasn't something that existed in his universe), although the rhythm was squarely within his sphere of competence. The blanket kept slowly sliding off his feet and the chill would interfere with his dream. Eduard Lvovich would then stir in his sleep and the tough bristles on his unshaven cheek would grate against the fabric of the pillow.

The rhythm of his pulse and that of the machine gun were in dissonance; it was necessary that they should be reconciled, arranged in order and placed within some sort of a system on manuscript paper. This was when an agonising incoherence would set in. Little black notes, betailed and big-headed, insisted on scattering all over the world. Some of them would settle on a hillock or on top of the roofs; they would paint the horizon black as alleys or telegraph posts. Another bunch was busy crawling up and down his blanket, grabbing hold of the threads on the manuscript paper and pulling on them as if they were strings, stealing their way into the wrong clef, thrashing around from major to minor. Eduard Lvovich tried to lure them closer and put on them a lid of legato,[28] but the black tadpoles simply kicked back with their tails and break loose and disperse anew – some back to their hillocks, the others to the folds of his blanket.

Eduard Lvovich knew perfectly well that hoping to reach a complete reconciliation between the notes on the horizon and those on the blanket was futile. Any sort of a harmony was out of the question. Very well, let there be disharmony; a musical idea could be predicated on dissonance, too; what had to be present, though, without fail, was some rationale, the law of harmony that was one and inalienable for all. But all he could hear in response was the rattling of the machine gun and the doleful pulse in the pillow.

But who was the culprit, causing all this trouble? Those on the hills were remarkably nonchalant and consistent. There was something cadaveric about them, just like in the cemeterial crosses looming against the background of the sky. The range was habitual, all tiny heads unidirectional; almost all of them were quarter-tones and quavers. It was a totally differ-

....

[28]   A musical term denoting a smooth, even style of performance, without any noticeable breaks between the notes.

ent story with those that had entrapped the pillow with their incessant disjointed tapping and defied accountability. Over there was the stability of everyday life, over here – confusion and agitation. Eduard Lvovich was on the point of catching one such escapee by its puny double tail but missed, and his hand became inordinately extended outwards. So, he raised himself, standing on tiptoe, his bare feet squarely planted on the snow-capped hill and started conducting a choir consisting of the tadpole-like notes – maybe they would give in?

To Eduard Lvovich's amazement, the choir turned out to be superb. With ease, Eduard Lvovich detached himself from the earth, and, smoothly waving his arms around, he found himself flying along the colossal self-perpetuating barricade of the notes, from one horizon to another, growing increasingly convinced that the dissonances were grating on the ear only if heard at close quarters, whereas heard from on high and from a distance, it all was part of an exquisite harmony, a marvellous choir and perfect music. Suddenly, he felt like enriching this choir with the most distant instruments, barely visible on the horizon. But he never managed to descend to them from his sublime altitude – something began ringing and the composer lost his balance.

Eduard Lvovich woke up and tried to pin down the sound that had interrupted his dream. Pulling his blanket towards his feet, he lay there, all ears: perhaps someone had rung the doorbell? But all was silent. Then again, the ringing sound had been rather similar to that made by a shattering glass. He recalled his dream – an amazing dream it had been. The most curious thing about it had been that merging and harmonising such apparently disparate rhythms was proving to be possible. It was revealing a sublime meaning. One's approach should be from afar and from on high. What had emerged was something like an idea for a bizarre new composition, arduous but possible. Arguably, he could grasp the meaning, imagine it – but what about recreating it?

170

A chilly draught wafted in. Eduard Lvovich straightened the coat over his feet, curled up, scraped the pillow with his cheek and tried to stay motionless in an attempt to get warm. The draught kept pouring in and the air felt even more chilly. The little notes disappeared along with the hillocks, but the rat-a-tat of the machine gun grew in frequency and was now more distinct. Nevertheless, by now his ear had grown accustomed to it. And Eduard Lvovich fell asleep.

As dawn crept in, tiny holes in a halo of radiating cracks became visible in the upper part of the window, in both panes. It got even lighter, and another tiny hole emerged in the wallpaper, on the wall opposite the window. The wallpaper around the hole was swollen from the pulverised whitewash.

No one had been aiming at the window. The October bullets were flying helter-skelter, not much bothered with hitting proper targets. For some odd reason, one of them, the most useless, though harmless, had flown into the composer's room and interrupted for a moment his nocturnal musical fantasy.

KOLCHAGIN'S CAREER

On the same day, the sixth of November, Andrei Kolchagin popped into the townhouse's kitchen. He was unshaven, red-faced and in high spirits, if somewhat jumpy – the last several days had taken their toll. He brought along a rifle and a stuffed bag. From inside his sack, he produced some sausage, a wheel of cheese and a sizeable lump of butter to which a scrap of newspaper was frozen solid. Some of the junk he didn't show to Dunyasha. On the other hand, he gave her an alarm clock and a barely used bottle of cologne, as well as a silk blouse with narrow sleeves and trimmed with lace.

'What's this? Where did ya get it from?'

'I found it. A box got smashed in the courtyard.'

'What good's it to me? It won't even fit. This stuff's for ladies.'

'Ladies, Dunyasha, nowadays, are no more. Ladies and their gents. Our power saw 'em all off.'

'And where ya been? You haven't been doing the shooting, have ya?'

'Sure was. I was in the thick of it. We took the telephone station.'

'Who's we?'

'Who d'ya think? We took it, the Bolsheviks.'

'Don't tell me you're with that lot!'

'Who else is there? We're with the people! Against them cadets and others from that bourgeoisie lot. It's curtains for them now, we're the winners!'

'I don't see the need for all this shootin'. It's nothin' but trouble.'

''Tis nothing for yer to understand. Better take this 'ere blouse and the cologne. We can have all this stuff now to our hearts' content.'

'Must be someone else's though?'

'Must be. Put a sock in it. Ya sure are simple, Dunka. A right yokel.'

For all that – he told her – it was better not to show any of it to the upstairs lot, seeing as it was none of their business. Those were his exact words – 'the upstairs lot'. No other words had been in circulation yet and he wasn't completely sure whether it was them, the bourgeoisie, residing in the townhouse whose kitchen had always welcomed him into its safe haven.

He took off shortly afterwards, not staying the night, and not even going to the bathhouse, though it was heated at the time. On his way out he picked up the rifle and tethered it around his shoulder, the barrel facing downwards. He fetched his bag too, now empty, as he had locked its contents into his storage chest.

Andrei Kolchagin set off down the street with a confident gait. A tuft of hair came loose from under his cap, Cossack style, even though he was infantry. Passers-by he met on his way sent him wary, unfriendly glances but he didn't even bother to look back. Andrei Kolchagin felt not like a rank-and-file individual, a lowly soldier, but a man of import, practically a hero, just as he had been in his village before they sent him to the front.

He took a shortcut towards the Soviet of Deputies' gate in Chernyshevsky Lane wherein a few soldiers were milling around without any clear purpose, on each shoulder a rifle facing downwards. Once there, he exchanged a few words with somebody, smoked a cigarette, asked around how to get through with his papers, and by which entrance. He bumped into some lads with whom he had taken the telephone station, but they had no papers. He elbowed his way through, waited in the queue, stuck to his guns and achieved what he was after. He conducted himself not as one of the boys but assertively, as an experienced fighter; the words he chose were the right ones.

At the table in a sour-smelling smoky room sat a man, scraggy, swarthy, in a suit coat but not timid, busy making notes and wielding a stamp. Off and on he yelled reprimands at the cannon fodder fussing around. Without looking at Kolchagin, he entered his name on a piece of paper, thwacked his stamp and said, 'Here we are, comrade, proceed to your destination.'

'Where's that, then?'

'It says here. You'll serve in Khamovniki. Next!'

In Khamovniki, in a big freshly-sequestered house, all was crush and confusion. It was impossible to tell who was in charge, who was the commander and, if so, what he was commanding. Soldiers sat in the armchairs, perched on the tables and window sills, and the parquet floor was bespattered with spittle and covered in cigarette ends. Anyone taking to bossing the others was obeyed.

Kolchagin scoured the rooms in an attempt to find out who he was supposed to present his new document to, but discovered nothing. There were several others like him, looking for the same thing. So Kolchagin collected their papers, checked them over and said offhandedly: 'Alright, all's in order, wait here.' After which he started asking every newcomer for papers. Suddenly, he felt like he was, somehow, in charge. There was no one in power, so authority had to be established. And Andrei Kolchagin set about forging the tools of power. And everyone realised that it was as it should be. From now on he was addressed with a degree of deference, as some kind of an elder. Shortly after, a civilian arrived in a rattling car, flew into the first room and yelled: 'Greetings comrades, everything will be alright now.' But no one replied to that. He started floundering around, shifting his briefcase from table to table, looking for an inkwell, clearly at a loss as to what to do next. And thus, forward came Andrei Kolchagin, composed, in a cap, a cigarette between his teeth: 'Mandates 'ave all been checked, comrade. Everything's in order. We're about to post guards, otherwise any Tom, Dick and Harry can barge in for no reason. The doors too, I'll have 'em bolted, no getting in without a special pass.'

The newcomer cheered up, didn't even try to put on airs or affect leadership. By now it was clear that the new authority had been born, as personified by Andrei Kolchagin.

Everyone was hungry. Kolchagin selected five soldiers and sent them out 'to procure'. He furnished them with a paper, sure; he wasn't much of a writer himself but somebody more literate had turned up, so Andrei appointed him a scribe on the spot. For all that, he signed the papers himself: 'Unit Commander Comrade Kolchagin'.

They made their procurement in an Arbat shop which had to be broken into to secure the welfare of the fighters, only there wasn't anyone to issue a receipt to, since the owner turned out to be absent from the premises. They lugged the loot back in sacks: a large wheel of cheese, whatever sausage they could find, a lot of butter, various boxes. Kolchagin received the delivery himself and decreed that it should be locked in a separate room. Afterwards he personally shared out the food. He stashed some into his own sack, in case of an emergency, as much as he could stuff in.

Some left, some stayed. They settled in for the night right where they were, without taking off their clothes, on the floor. Kolchagin was granted a sofa. It was right and proper – he was in charge; he had been toiling more than the others. Before going to bed Andrei first checked on the guards and appointed a shift to replace the earlier one.

The following day, early in the morning, some more organisers showed up, fussed around, went on about the typewriters, made some markings on the doors of the rooms, moved the tables around, disappeared, reappeared. Kolchagin was invariably on hand. He helped push the tables around, scribbled something on his own piece of paper and, once the others had gone, installed himself behind a desk in the front room, looked around long and hard, and uttered brusque commands to those at the entrance. Folks came and went, Kolchagin stayed on.

And the days started flitting by. By now, the room resonated with the scribbling of nibs. The waiting room had at first been thronged with common soldiers but soon rank-and-file citizens started showing up, too, frightened and hapless. Goods were delivered here too, from various sources; as well as persons under arrest; from here radiated, in all directions, instructions on behalf of the Khamovniki Soviet of Deputies – but nothing could happen unbeknownst to and unsanctioned by Andrei Kolchagin, who by now was referred to as the commandant. He had never been appointed, nor had he been elected or confirmed in the rank by a single living soul. Kolchagin was indispensable, natural, inevitable. And so, once an exasperated petitioner, having done a complete round of the rooms, would lose all hope, he would be advised:

'Comrade, you better appeal directly to Comrade Commandant.'

And the said petitioner would knock timidly on the 'Comrade Commandant's' door, behind which Comrade Kolchagin, well-known throughout the Khamovniki District, authoritative, business-like, unperturbed by doubts, would be having his tea with sugar and white bread. Kolchagin turned some supplicants away while sorting the problems of others personally – by issuing a signed paper endorsed with his personal commandant's stamp.

THE STUMP AT NIGHT

For the Stump, the nights were more harrowing than the days. During those terrible hours, in between sleep and wakefulness, he would frequently dream about a final revolt of the cripples and the grotesques.

On low trolleys fitted with wheels, each hand clutching a block of wood to pull the owner along the ground, the stumps and offcuts of war were flying forward, in a snail's whirlwind, towards a new war. And he, the stump *par excellence*, a miracle of surgery, by force of a similar miracle was leading the way in advance of the whole party, at full charge. Behind him hurried the blind, the contorted, those devoid of a face, the deaf, the dumb, the poisoned, the lethargic – whole platoons of St George's[29] monsters.

The Revolution started unfolding – a novel one, unprecedented, ultimate; all those who were still sound and in one piece ought to be hacked down and made hideous, with the same yardstick applied to one and all. The surviving arms must be gnawed off with teeth, the legs still capable of walking must be run over with a wheel, the seeing eyes must be pricked out, the breathing lungs must be poisoned, and the

....

[29]   The Order of Saint George is an order of chivalry of the Russian Empire founded in 1769 by Catherine the Great. The order was abolished after the revolution of 1917 although it was still awarded in the 'White' armies – the anti-revolutionary forces. The order was revived in the Russian Federation in 2000.

braincases must be shaken with a bolt of thunder. One measure ought to fit all!

Women, too! Give us female stumps, the same as us. For as long as their arms and legs are intact, their eyes fully-sighted and deceitful, they shall despise us and push us aside. Let them be stumps too, we shall leave them only their breasts. We shall slide down and merge without arms or legs. And let us breed children who will be just like us.

There must be a complete overhaul! Let the humans dress in sacks, and make them work with their teeth. Limbs should be allowed only on the blind and the mad, for they should be leading by hand or carrying other cripples. What difference does it make – weren't we guided by the blind and the insane before? If the deaf and the mute so wish, all healthy people ought to have their tongues ripped out and ears pierced through with a red-hot needle. No exception for the elderly, children or maidens.

Let there be silence in the world that had invented battle marches and anthems, the rolling of the drums and the rumbling of cannons.

What a veritable nightmare – bonfires built out of chopped-off legs and lit in public squares. Around those bonfires will fly the trolleys carrying people without legs, like a merry-go-round – a revolt of the legless, a coven of the freaks, while the insane will be throwing into the flames the things no longer needed: books, chairs, grand pianos, canvasses, footwear – above all, footwear, but also gloves, wedding bands – all this flotsam and jetsam only needed by the unharmed, since they won't be around, not now, not ever! Are you getting it now?

The acme of beauty will be welts and amputated limbs. The most mangled and lacerated will be the most beautiful of all. He who dares think otherwise should be burnt at the stake. Icons and pictures must be redacted, legs and arms should be blacked out, faces should be distorted so that the erstwhile beauty will be deleted even from memory. Inside the museums, ancient statues will be toppled over and shattered; all that should be left will be the marble torsos and the busts with broken-off noses. In all large squares there should be erected copies of the Herculean torso from the Vatican as the only worthy statue, an epitome of post-war beauty.

The world will be governed by a shiny blue residual limb. And if the world goes to pieces – good riddance.

Those horrible thoughts and nightmares made the Stump emit drawn-out and painful moans. Straining the muscles in his back, he was trying to turn over to one side. He knew how to do it using the momentum of an abrupt movement, butting his head against the pillow and helping himself along with his strong neck; sometimes, though, he would miscalculate the movement, flop on his belly, exhausted, and cry like a child. To rectify his position, he would rock himself back and forth for a while, tense his neck again and then scramble around in the pit of his soft mattress. Recovering his breath, he would shut his eyes, and the nightmare would start again at some point between the dreams and the reality of his agonising night.

To think about something else? Like what? Bring back to memory the past when he was able to stride around the world on those legs, and embrace and push away with those arms, when everything was accessible – a game or a fight, an outing or a waltz, a gesture or a task? When he could… when he could scratch his shoulder without resorting to laborious and exhausting manoeuvrings of the head in order to reach it, at least with his chin? It seemed to him that nobody's shoulder ever itched so badly, and he was thinking, in cold dismay: what if his flank or his chest started itching too, as had happened many times before? Should he call Grigory? Poor Grigory! What wouldn't he give, he, the Stump, to be as 'poor' – in possession of both arms and legs, even as an old semi-literate soldier? To be whomsoever, performing as filthy a job as was imaginable. A convict – yes, let it be a convict. Or even a spy! Any sort of life was better than his.

Suddenly there came to his mind his incessant, painful and futile debates with his neighbour, Kashtanov, the one who had lost his sight in the war. He was now finding thousands of new arguments and testimonies to the fact that the life of the blind was much easier, that it was still a life brimming with possibilities. At night, like now, in the darkness, Kashtanov is anybody's equal. He is lying down, cosy in his bed, he can get up, pour some water into his glass, drink it, stretch himself till his bones creak, fall asleep again. He can share his bed with somebody, and offer unseeing caresses. And this lucky scoundrel has the audacity to complain, he even dares make comparisons!

Propping his head against the pillow, the Stump raised his back, arched his body and started a slow and effortful descent, all the while letting out a constrained sound through his teeth, howling animal-like, like a wolf.

The bed squeaked in the next room and Grigory's bare feet padded across the floor.

'Are you unwell, sir? I heard you groaning. Could I be of assistance in any fashion, sir?'

He gave him some water, took a small flat bedpan out of the bedside table, fussed for a long while over his disabled charge as if over a baby, straightened the bedding, tucked him in, gave him a cigarette, moved closer a saucer for the ash – all this by the light of the night lamp. He sat next to him, on the bed, covering his yawns with his hand.

'So, what do you reckon, Grigory, is that what you are going to do forever – look after me?'

'What if I did? As if I'd ever leave you. My life is all good, as long as I can be of some comfort to you. You shouldn't take it into yer head, yer Excellency. Think less – sleep better.'

'Do you really believe in God, Grigory? Or is it just something you say for the sake of saying it? Perhaps you are only trying to believe?'

'I do believe, how can it be otherwise?'

'Is he kind, this God of yours?'

'He's got no business being kind. He's severe.'

'So why has he maimed me like this, your God?'

'Don't say that, yer Excellency! It's people who did it, not God.'

'And he allowed them.'

'Means he's got his own design, 'tis not ours to know. You, yer Excellency, must accept it. That's yer lot.'

'Alright, Grigory, I'll accept it. Go to bed.'

Grigory was yawning and crossing his mouth.[30]

'If yer need something else, be sure to call, don't torture yerself for nothing.'

'Thank you, Grigory, go now.'

He then thought about Grigory and his severe God with His own designs. And about those with belief, who could come to terms with any misfortune. Strange though it seemed, he felt no envy towards them. They were the only ones that he did not envy. At the same time, he was unable to find such faith in his own soul, or even look for it. It all was just a lie.

For all that, thinking about them did make him feel calmer, almost reconciled to his destiny, and allowed sleep to brush his eyes with its caressing touch. In his dream he saw himself healthy and in no hurry to use up his health – his uninjured arms and legs, his youth. He saw a woman; they were engaged in flirtatious chatter.

The Stump wasn't yet thirty. A man of his age had his whole life ahead of him. But the Stump wasn't a man…

....

[30] A good devout Christian, Grigory crosses his mouth when yawning to bar access to the forces of evil.

THE MONKEYS' VILLAGE

A moat had been dug out as a closed loop, and thus the outside wall had become a steep cliff. What was thus achieved was a little island with no way out.

In the middle of this island stood a tall dry tree with bare branches, well-suited for monkeys to practise gymnastics.

Underneath the tree was a scattering of tiny houses, with windows, attics and rooftops – very much like those for humans. A good swing. A pool with flowing water, and above it, on a crossbeam, a ring had been hung up, too. Everything that was needed for having fun.

A large family of grey monkeys led a carefree life there – they thrived and multiplied, gradually populating the little village.

The attendant of the zoological gardens had calculated correctly – the monkeys' village proved very popular with the zoogoers. The visitors would throw the monkeys nuts, bread and potatoes, they admired their tricks and laughed at their love lives and family feuds.

The attendant had decided to move a red-haired breed into the village too. Another little house had been added, this one with a somewhat stronger roof. The new residents were slightly larger, with stronger muscles and a more mischievous temper.

In the beginning, it all went well. There were a few scuffles, of course, but no strong community is ever possible without scuffles. Then the alignment of power had been established, which gave rise to the dominance of one species.

There was one individual among the redheads – a complete tearaway. Strong, agile, malicious, a leader among his own tribe, he turned into a veritable scourge of the grey monkeys. He never passed up on a chance to hurt, nip on the nape, scratch a leg.

At the beginning, he was wary of one new mother, whose dainty naked munchkin was always fidgeting nearby. But in the end, he sneaked in from behind, nipped the delicate baby with his sharp white teeth and then escaped the mother's fury by clambering up the tree.

The red-haired tribe appreciated the prank; they now felt newly empowered. It was then that the souls of the grey monkeys first filled with a sense of inevitability, of the impending unavoidable destruction of their patriarchal tribe.

And a grey sense of dread moved into the monkeys' village. Very soon their worst premonitions came to pass.

The red-haired bully felt bored; it was the same old story every time, not even a hint of any serious resistance. After once when he had driven a timid victim to the very tip of a branch, thus forcing him to jump down awkwardly and fracture a hind limb, no one dared climb the tree anymore. Raids on their food by now were boring too – for one thing, it was all beginning to feel rather repetitive, and besides, he had enough of his own treats. He simply had to come up with something special.

Boredom sent the red-haired abuser on strategic rounds, in the course of which he would spot a bunch of trembling monkeys, propel himself from the roof of a house straight into their midst, grab the first good victim by the scruff of the neck and install himself nearby, scratching his side and mocking the cowards with his white teeth, sneering at them. They would huddle together again, a little distance away, and sit there staring at him with their close-set little eyes, their teeth chattering. No matter which way he chose to spring, right on cue they all would spin round to face him, and watch closely his every move, readying themselves to leap aside should the need arise. When he ambled further away or was asleep at home, they could bring themselves to lick over their wounds, nibble a carrot, prune each other for fleas and love each other, hastily and half-heartedly. Much as life had become intolerable, it had to go on. But now it was the life of the doomed.

Once, when the redhead was out of his mind with lack of action, one of the grey monkeys risked having some fun. He leapt into the ring above the swimming pool and started swaying. The redhead noticed, quietly descended into the moat, went round the monkeys' estate along the bottom, took aim, unexpectedly sprang out by the pool, caught the grey monkey by the tail and yanked him into the water.

The grey monkey started swimming towards the edge but his enemy beat him to it. The grey swam in the opposite direction but did not manage to get out on that side, either. As soon as he reached the edge, the red-haired offender would smack him on the crown of his head with his strong arm, and dunk him back into the water.

At last the redhead had stumbled on a new and fulfilling pastime. The strength of the grey victim was waning, and every time he was submerged under the water, he sent bubbles to the surface. When the little wet head showed above the water for the last time, the redhead lightly flicked it back into the swimming pool, by now without much excitement, and kept him there for a short moment. All that floated upwards this time were bubbles. The trembling grey community watched from afar how the redhead was amusing himself, baring their teeth and tucking their tails between their legs.

The redhead waited, walked around the pool one more time, arched his back provocatively, then backed away, crouched, showed his teeth, shook his wet arm and, spotting a kidney bean, set about shelling it. The fun was over and he was bored again.

MIKHAIL OSORGIN

All in all, he liked the experience and the swimming pool became a routine magnet for his attentions. He now took to driving new victims there on his own initiative. If he managed to catch an off-guard grey monkey with his strong teeth, he would drag him to the swimming pool, fighting off the convulsive arms with his teeth, and swiftly throw him into the water. He took his time drowning them – he would allow short breathing respites, retreating coyly towards the edge but returning just in time to submerge the weakening swimmer's head. He was toying with them, amusing himself, leaping into the ring, swaying, but still getting back in the nick of time. When the drowning was done, he was bored again, and so he would stretch himself on the roof of his house, climb the tree and employ his powerful muscles to shake its dry branches.

The grey colony continued melting away. Dread mutated into hopelessness. The other redheads now followed the example set by their leader, launching surprise attacks on the emaciated, mangy, confused, shivering greys, breaking into their houses, driving them outside, snatching their food, gnawing at their arms, ripping out tufts of fur. The grey colony was being destroyed, while that of the redheads was propagating and prospering.

The attendant of the zoological gardens grew wise to the disappearance of the grey monkeys much too late – only after the water in the pool had been drained for maintenance. The keepers received severe reprimands. The surviving grey monkeys were rehomed from their free village into a special cage. They were fattened up again, and in front of their cage, a plaque with their name in Latin was put up. The wife of one of the keepers was allowed to set up a little stall next to the cage, offering a selection of little packages with kidney beans. This provided the keeper's wife with a small permanent income, especially on Sundays, and ensured that the zoological gardens saved on food supplies for the remains of the tribe.

Looking at the newly plump monkeys it was impossible to tell whether they ever indulged in recollecting their free village, their lost motherland. They stared at the visitors with their close-set little eyes, accepting the alms, baring their teeth and, uninhibited by any shame, they performed, in full public view, all those acts that were expected to be performed by such human likenesses.

THE INVALIDS

That day, from early morning onwards, visitors continued dropping in on Stolnikov: khaki trench coats with empty sleeves, clanking wooden legs and excited faces covered in horrific scars. All of a sudden, the Stump became their universally recognised leader, although they did have something like an association of their own – The Union of Invalids, and although of the two demands they had decided to come out with, the first – 'war to a successful conclusion' – did not meet with his approval. Their second demand concerned support for the invalids of the great war; however, that wasn't something on which Stolnikov had been dwelling too much, either. All he cared about was an open march of the people without arms or legs, and those otherwise deformed. They had been forgotten, but now they simply had to be heard. And the louder, the snappier, the more embittered and insistent the message, the better.

It had been decided that he, in his capacity of the ultimate invalid, would be carried at the front, seated in his chair, set on a tall litter. The procession would aim for the building housing the Council of Deputies, where speeches would be made.

By two o'clock they had assembled in small groups on Tverskoy Boulevard, perching on the benches and hanging around the monument to Pushkin, wandering all over the square. Once Stolnikov had been brought in, everybody gravitated towards him. There was only one banner – a red one, the colour of the Union of Invalids.

The resulting crowd was some three hundred people strong. The litter with his chair was being carried by three stronger fellows, Grigory being the fourth. Next to him walked those without arms or on crutches. Several blind fellows, Kashtanov among them, were led forward by the hand. In the midst of the crowd there was a predominance of white bandages.

Right along the pavement limped a horrifying little soldier who had no face: only the eyes, with no lashes or eyebrows, were prominent by their blackness against his shiny skin, the little holes of his nose flared too, and a tiny wisp of mottled beard hung to one side.

When the procession drew level with the Council of Soviets, five people came out onto its balcony. One of them, a fair-haired bearded fellow resembling a cultured young merchant, corpulent and confident, leaned his well-fed body over the banisters of the balcony and started waving his hand. The other four, elbows on the railing, were observing the crowd of little ugly people without any special curiosity. This tableau was hardly new.

From the crowd of invalids, various voices started yelling in a discordant choir. A few phrases could be made out: 'until complete victory', 'disgrace', 'we demand'. Some participants were waving leaflets – but it was evident that the crowd was lacking in organisation, its members at variance with one another over their wishes.

The blond man on the balcony gave another wave of his hand and started talking. His voice was hoarse, evidently overstrained by incessant speeches. It was his sixth speech that day from that balcony, to the sixth crowd dressed in soldiers' overcoats. His speech had been memorised, one size fitted all, the only variation being the form of address. In this instant his appeal was addressed to 'comrades invalids of the imperialist bloodbath'. The words boomed, bouncing off the monument to Skobelev[31] from which the bronze figures had been only recently removed, carrying on further and disappearing into the low vaults of the nearby guardroom. Passers-by didn't linger for long – rallies in front of the Council had long become a habitual phenomenon, and the words radiating from the balcony were long familiar. The only thing attracting attention was the Stump's chair, dominating the crowd.

Stolnikov, teetering from the awkward manoeuvrings of the litter, was all eyes, staring at the healthy, bi-armed and bi-legged speaker. Strapped into his chair, he was washed over by a particularly acute realisation of his own helplessness, his inability to make a gesture that would have been appropriate just at this minute.

By mid-speech, dissenting shouts were already cutting across the orator's delivery; by the end, the din of voices drowned his words completely. Those closest to the Stump's litter started rolling up their sleeves and thrusting their blueish truncated limbs in the direction of the balcony; others waved their crutches and yelled with raw emotion. The blind also bellowed something incomprehensible. The soldier without a face came forward, too, and was howling wordlessly – he was mute.

The orator chanted out his concluding words, pointing his arm to some point afar and above, wiped his lips with a handkerchief and back-tracked towards the door. The others did likewise.

The situation called for something, but no one knew for certain what it was. The delegates with the list of demands

....

[31]   The monument to Skobelev was an equestrian statue to the popular hero of the Turkestan campaigns and the Russo-Turkish war of 1877–1878. Mikhail Skobelev (1843–1882) was an infantry general. The monument was designed by Pyotr Samonov in 1912 and dismantled on the eve of 1 May 1918. Nowadays in its place is a monument to the founder of Moscow, Yury Dolgoruky.

came back: someone had accepted their list but they themselves were barred from entering the Council. Young soldiers with rifles were keeping guard by the entrance, and more of them were spread along the pavement, shooing away the pedestrians who were slow to leave. A young man in military dress flew out of the front door. His uniform was cleaner than that of the others and more dashingly belted with a sash – evidently, he was a commanding officer. He crossed the pavement at a trot, and, keeping his distance from the top of the procession, cried out:

'Do move along, comrades, break it up, that's enough. You mustn't block the square.'

He retraced his steps but returned with a detail which then promptly occupied the entirety of the pavement in front of the building.

The crowd of invalids shuffled around indecisively, but the ones at the flanks and in better health had already started backing away. The banner-carriers set off towards the street.

At this moment, roaring above the hubbub of voices, rang out a shrill and feral, almost inhuman cry that broke into a shriek:

'Thieving scum! Thie-e-eves!'

The litter tilted. Swiftly, with his free arm Grigory swooped up the Stump's body, which had shattered the light cross-bar keeping it in place and was already sliding off the chair. Someone rushed forward from the crowd to give a hand. The commander of the guards, together with two soldiers, ran up close to them, almost face to face:

'Out of here! Get him out of the way, if you know what's good for you! Comrades, you've heard the order – disperse immediately!'

The Stump was unconscious. Grigory passed along his corner of the litter, busy securing the arms of the chair with a length of rope, winding the same rope around the Stump's chest and the back of the litter, snapping thickly:

MIKHAIL OSORGIN

'Come on, swing the edge over. This is no time for messing around!'

The crowd fell silent and rapidly moved on. Only a proportion followed Stolnikov, while the others, overtaking the folded-up banner, scattered in the opposite direction towards Tverskaya Street.

'You can never be too careful,' said an invalid striding next to Grigory. 'They'll show no mercy, old man; so what if he has no arms or legs. The main thing is, he's an officer. Fancy throwing words like that in their faces!'

'What can they take from 'im, eh?' Grigory answered gruffly. 'It's all been taken already.'

And, urging the bearers on, he forced the on-comers and the gawkers, by the sheer intensity of his stern gloomy gaze, to give way to the bizarre procession.

The Stump came to, found Grigory with his eyes, dropped his head again and didn't look up the entire way home. And only occasionally, if the litter suddenly and clumsily jerked, would he grimace in pain.

THE NOOSE TIGHTENS

That day Dunyasha heated the oven in the living room where the grand piano now resided, occupying half the available space. The hall and the dining room stood locked. Tanyusha had moved into Grandma's chamber, next to Grandpa's bedroom.

The first floor wasn't heated anymore, as wood was hard to come by. Nikolai and Dunyasha had gone together on their most recent wood-procuring expedition, the greengrocer having lent them his wagon. They brought back chopped birch logs, dry and beautiful, but as for where those came from – that was Nikolai's secret, with no need for idle chatter about it. On the way, some individuals had tried to sequester the wagon but Nikolai stood his ground:

'I am taking it home for meself, to keep me old bones warm. Plunder others if you must, but not a common worker like me. I am a Sovdep[32] too, you know?'

And that was that; they let him through.

Eduard Lvovich was playing Chopin. He played calmly; he wasn't highly strung, for once. Tanyusha, the lady of the manor, served tea. The ornithologist took the deep armchair, not the sofa. Poplavsky was also there, skeletally thin – his life was extremely hard. Of course, Vasya Boltanovsky was there

....

[32] An acronym born in the revolutionary days, standing for Soviet (Council) of Deputies. As with many other such abbreviations introduced by the new officialdom, it gradually took on a pejorative connotation.

too, a daily visitor by now, or not even a visitor but rather a family member. As for the new acquisitions, along came Alexei Dmitriyevich Astafyev, a specialist in philosophy, *privatdotsent*. Tanya had met him through Vasya, although the old professor had tangentially known Astafyev from the university and approved of him. The guests were all men. Even Lenochka wasn't there – shortly before the revolution she had married a doctor.

They drank genuine tea, saved from the old days; the bread was white, baked from the flour that Dunyasha had been sent from the country. The sugar was from the ration, still occasionally available.

The professor was thinking that there was no longer a lamp in the corner, the one that had cast light over Grandma's grey hair, her bonnet and her handiwork. He shifted his gaze to Tanyusha and noted that this granddaughter, in her grandma's place by the samovar, now appeared completely grown up. Confident, caring, contemplative – perhaps too much so; one could be a touch more light-hearted at her age, then again, not in times such as these, when no one was light-hearted anymore. *Vasya here hardly ever takes his eyes off her. He's a nice boy, Vasya. Still, Tanyusha is unlikely to single him out in a special way; much as he is a nice character, he's no match for Tanyusha. She needs someone entirely different.*

Poplavsky said:

'Your house is so nice and warm. And cosy, even cosier than before. My home is simply arctic; I live only in one room, and there are stalactites hanging down from the dining-room ceiling; our water pipe burst.'

Eduard Lvovich rubbed his hands and recalled that his home was icy, too. True, he had a small wood stove, but it was tricky to keep it going, even if he did have some wood chopped into small blocks and piled up nearby. The thought crossed Eduard Lvovich's mind, but he said nothing; this was a conversation out of his sphere. The important thing was that he had his grand piano. Some had had theirs confiscated. He shivered and rubbed his hands.

Tanyusha asked Astafyev:

'Where do you live, Alexei Dmitriyevich?'

'In Vladimiro-Dolgorukovskaya. Our house has been given over to the workers. I am the only remaining bourgeois element there. For the time being they are letting me be, but, most likely, they will force me out, too. It is noisy where we live, but curious, too.'

Vasya snorted:

'What's so curious about having everything taken away?'

'What does it matter? Then again, they haven't taken everything. I still have books.'

'But no shelves?'

'A few. But I burned them myself. It was somewhat cold there.'

'They'll seize the books, too.'

'Quite likely. I won't be all that upset.'

'But how will you work?'

Astafyev smiled and took his time answering.

'Work… It will, of course, be impossible to work like I used to, but then again, nowadays it won't be allowed. Still… I'm not sure I should.'

Tanyusha was now looking at him directly, so he carried on:

'Philosophy has obviously become a luxury. Just like any science. For my own part – yes, and for the others – I'm not sure. What can you teach others when life is a better teacher than any philosopher?'

Tanyusha thought: *What's he doing? Is he being ironic, or trying to show off with his paradoxes?*

This exchange plunged Poplavsky into melancholy while the old ornithologist became anxious:

'So now what? What should we occupy ourselves with – sweeping the streets? Wisdom that has been accumulated over the course of many centuries cannot become superfluous overnight.'

Astafyev really didn't feel like arguing. Or even talking at all. It felt so cosy in this old house, so warm and old-fashioned. It felt so good, listening to Eduard Lvovich's music and drinking tea, poured by Tanyusha's hand. But an answer was expected.

'You see, Professor, your area, natural sciences, it is so... how shall I put it? It is so error-free. Meanwhile, philosophy isn't even a science, much as it is referred to as the science of sciences. It is bred from the luxury of life... or from being tired of life. It is a gateau. And a sneer. And a detachment. But life nowadays is such that if you leave it for a minute, it will leave you for days. He who wants to survive must hold onto it tightly, clamber upwards, push the others off the footplate – just like in a tram.'

'This, too, is philosophy,' said the professor. 'A sad one, of course.'

'Not at all, whyever sad? It is just that we have come closer to nature. Daily life has become coarser and more primitive; so, the spiritual life should be adapted commensurately.'

Poplavsky interposed:

'Come now, the spirit cannot become coarser. It is the other way around: consciousness becomes subtler. Our feelings now are more acute. Daily existence carries on regardless, while the spiritual life...'

'You believe it evolves towards complexity? I don't think so. Weariness turns the common man into something like a philosopher – and a philosopher into a common man; both are cynics. The Spirit does not benefit from any of this. But the main thing is that none of it is needed as it was needed previously. It is much more important now to keep and develop one's musculature, whereas books... What are they good for? Unless they are popular booklets, manuals, possibly, fairy tales – for recreation.'

Astafyev smiled such a smile that one could interpret his words as a joke, but it was equally possible to take it all seriously.

Eduard Lvovich looked around them all with his myopic eyes and offered in an unusually confident voice, still unable to speak without a stutter:

'Would you like me to p-perform s-something c-classical?'

While he played, Astafyev was observing Tanyusha, busy washing up the teacups and trying not to clank a teaspoon. Astafyev thought: *Who is she? Her facial features are those of a child, yet she is a grown woman.*

By now Tanyusha was in her twenty-first year. She was svelte and beautiful, with a face that was stern, almost cold, although very Russian, too. Her smile, on the other hand, was wholesome, unreserved, heart-warming. When a smile disappeared from Tanyusha's face, it would leave her face flushed for a moment longer, and her eyes beamed tenderly. And then Diana would be born again. In the evening Tanyusha's grey eyes seemed dark blue. Her hair was combed back tightly, away from her high forehead. Tanyusha belonged to a special breed of unfashionable women, incapable of an ungraceful gesture, those who never had to premeditate the position of their arms or the incline of their head. That was her public persona. Alone, she was different: her eyes would open wider, a light fold would form in her forehead and suddenly she would be transformed into a vulnerable, frightened little girl who didn't know where she should go, or whose door to knock on; a girl with no one in this whole world capable of showing the way or offering advice. Tanyusha would cast a glance through the window but see only a grey sky; she would pick up a book and find no answers in its pages. She would let out a sigh and her blouse would suddenly feel tight. Her heavy hair was weighing on her head. Every object in her room, infinitely familiar, stared at her with indifference and excessive logicality. In such moments she would seek out her grandpa and huddle up to his rough cheek. Grandpa would stroke her and think: *What's going to happen to my Tanyusha?*

Tonight, Eduard Lvovich's performance brimmed with special confidence and, as he was playing, he knew that everyone was at a loss, while the superior truth was known only to him, to Eduard Lvovich. He was the only one in possession of something incontrovertible. No one could take the incontrovertible away. The incontrovertible consisted of music, the world of sounds, the power of sounds, composition. He would strike a key with his finger and the key would respond in a way determined and demanded by him.

It was snowing outside. Neither a horse nor a passer-by could be seen in Sivtsev Vrazhek.

In Khamovniki, in a big building with brightly lit windows, people in military tunics, leather jackets and soldiers' overcoats bustled about. They were constantly going out in groups, taking their seats in automobiles and revving away faster than was advisable. As Eduard Lvovich played, a clumsy soldier's finger started painstakingly tracing out the letters of his surname and applying a stamp. Music and composition were undeniable and inalienable. But a grand piano was an object that could be alienated with ease. In fact, nowadays it was easier than taking somebody's life. Besides, a grand piano was absolutely necessary for a workers' club.

Having entered the composer's name into the blank mandate, the same finger, now much less constrained and more confident, even somewhat frivolous, entered its owner's name below, finishing with a red flourish: 'Andrei Kolchagin'.

A THING

The apartment door blew shut with a bang but voices could still be heard from the stairs, and each time the stops and starts resulted in a jolt the strings of the grand piano protested in an astonished mellow bass.

The room faced the inner courtyard, so Eduard Lvovich couldn't see the grand piano being loaded onto a dray.

However, one member of the requisition crew came back, knocked, let himself in, and repeated to Eduard Lvovich in a placatory tone:

'Now listen here, citizen, don't get yourself all upset. If it turns out that your exclusive right is confirmed by the music institution you will get it back; if not the very same one, then another. Thing is, we can't go against a decree, and workers' clubs need them pianos as a matter of greatest priority, so we can't let just anyone keep 'em. Stands to reason. As for you, you shouldn't worry about nothing, no one will hurt you, and everything is being channelled to meet the necessary needs of our country. You, as a person of education, should even be glad. Or if not, put in a complaint if you wish.'

And with this he left.

Although Eduard Lvovich did eat, drink and sleep like everyone else, he was different to everyone else inasmuch as he hardly ever registered what he was eating or drinking, and he would only ever go to bed because he couldn't play at night – the others were asleep. To top it all, the others had additional interests – something that puzzled Eduard Lvovich – related to their families, business, politics. From the sheet music of their lives, people kept performing their opuses, extremely alien to the composer and somehow in conflict with the theory of counterpoint. In all probability, it was all necessary, but in any case, one could easily do without it all, subject to the existence of that all-embracing and comprehensive phenomenon that was music.

Experience proved the same thing. By now, Eduard Lvovich was on the wrong side of fifty, he had never had a family or any other attachments, and even if something of the kind had happened in his youth, it had all long since been transformed into sounds and comfortably fitted into the five lines on the manuscript paper. And sure enough, Eduard Lvovich had not noticed how instead of somebody as regular as the chromatic scale – albeit with a perfect-pitch ear – he had now become a 'citizen'.

After the man who had called Eduard Lvovich a citizen had departed, on the floor, where previously the legs of the grand piano had stood, there remained tiny spots of dust, and from those spots, towards the door, ran three faint narrow ribbons, like tracks in the floor boards. And on the stack of shelves sat the sheets of music, suddenly redundant, especially the hand-written ones, stored inside a massive old folder.

Also left behind in the room was an old second-hand thing, of no use to anyone in the whole world – Eduard Lvovich himself. The thing lingered in the middle of the room, touching the thinning hair on its temples with its hand, then sat itself on a chair by the wall. As for the round piano stool with a raised back – it stood vacant in the middle, and it would be somewhat strange to sit on it now – heaven knew which way to face; it was all the same, really.

For some half an hour the thing just sat there, sufficiently aware of the enormity of what had just happened (although somewhat vague on the details), but mostly unable to understand what to do next. There was even an instant when the thing smiled and thought: *But this cannot possibly be! Most likely*

it is something out of that life, their life, that has nothing to do...
Surely one cannot suppose that suddenly someone really could, for
some reason, take away and move out... well, nearly... that is, not
nearly but certainly... one's soul – just grab it and take it away on
a dray? But without an instrument it is impossible not just to ar-
range, but even to roughly to conceive a symphony, or even a dainty
romance, and in general – one cannot live in this world without an
instrument – how is it even conceivable? What is left in such a case?

It was all so absurd, so much resembling a bad joke, and
felt so utterly improbable that the thing seated on the chair
by the wall tried to smile; then it closed its eyes for a brief
minute. Right away, the three faint narrow ribbons on the
floor disappeared, the legs of the grand piano reinstalled
themselves on the spots of dust and everything came back
to normal. But when the thing opened its eyes again, it saw
both the spots and the tracks running to the door.

At this point, out of the distant corner of memory, from
an old music book where all entries had turned yellow and
faded, a sudden thought burst forth like a little semi-forgot-
ten tune – something like this had once happened before.
The details: an object had once been carried out, too, looking
more like a box, and then a gaping emptiness had remained
in its place. The box had been somewhat smaller, and lighter,
and narrower. The box had been a coffin inside which had
lain Eduard Lvovich's mother, the companion of his entire
life, almost till the age when his own hair turned grey.

Still, there was a difference. What had this difference
been?

Firstly, on that occasion, Eduard Lvovich had followed the
box out of the room and walked in its wake along the street,
up to the graveyard. The box had been lifted down into the
earth. Then... Then Eduard Lvovich returned home, and to
him the apartment (in those days, he had his own apartment
that wasn't contested by anybody) had seemed empty. And
that was when... something happened that helped comfort

him, reconcile… but of course! He had sat down at the piano and started playing. And kept going till dusk. And when he was playing, he forgot his loss. And so, every time that emptiness encroached on his life, he would fill it with the sounds of the grand piano.

And now? At this point the thought was becoming painfully confused and losing direction. The rational Eduard Lvovich was dissolving and what was sitting on the chair in his place was this unwanted thing, aged and faded, referred to as a citizen.

The little potbelly stove[33] died out and Eduard Lvovich's legs felt chilly. To start with, he wanted to make a fire but he realised that now there was absolutely no point. Instead, he put on his shabby rust-coloured fur coat, felt boots and hat, and carefully, lest he should step on a ribbon on the parquet floor, went out.

A dim light in his memory was leading him after… after that box containing the essence of his entire life. He had to follow it, as that would give him a chance to complain. But where should he follow it to? Along what street? In which direction?

The last time, the box had been carried towards Dorogomilovskaya Square. Then along a road, through a gate, and on further down and to the left, towards a small grave inside a wrought-iron fence, and a little bench by its side.

Eduard Lvovich felt very tired but easily found the grave – the grave was familiar to him. The graves next to it were familiar, too. It felt so nice to meet again, to be surrounded by such accessible, serene and agreeable… really, they were like good friends. Since that time, it had been… Eduard Lvovich made a

....

[33] A potbelly stove is a cast-iron wood-burning stove, round with a bulge in the middle. The name is derived from the resemblance of the stove to a fat man's pot belly. It first came into use to replace fireplaces but disappeared after the introduction of central heating.

quick calculation… how many years?… it must have been fifteen or sixteen. What a cosy grave, his mother's grave, although so plain. He lowered himself onto the bench.

His mother had died a very old lady. Actually, he was nearly an old man himself. He had little hair, and what remaining hair he did have was grey. When he had had more of it and it wasn't yet grey, now and then it would happen… little tunes started wafting again, gingerly, from the old music book… from time to time he would have things to complain about to his mother – his early failures, the indifference of the public, the lack of understanding from the critics – his grievances then had been varied, and important, too… but of course nothing like this one, nothing like this had ever happened before. So, if now… if, let's say, he now complained again to his own mother (because he had been hurt in a new, intolerable way), she would at least understand him; the others, the rest of them, perhaps wouldn't understand but his mother was an old friend. She was sure to understand!

Clad in down-at-heel felt boots, heels patched with leather, in a shaggy old fur coat, having taken off his hat, not looking like a citizen but very much like an unwanted second-hand thing, the grey-haired little man, now, as then, of no use to anyone, slid off the bench to his knees, and, kneeling in the snow, burning his bald top against the iron of the fence, burst out crying, sniffling like a child. In a cemetery one ought to be crying about others, but he cried over himself because his feelings had been badly hurt; they had taken away the only plaything of his entire life. He was such a wretched little thing, just like a baby, even if he was nearly an old man himself. And just like a little boy, he forgot his words, and all he could remember and repeat over and over was the short word 'Mama'; he had no others. He wiped his nose on his sleeve as his abundant tears drilled holes in the snow and froze into a lucid icicle on the curlicue of the fence. Through the mist of his tears he saw the little holes and the icicle, but at the same time he kept translating his sniffling into notes, inserting an appoggiatura,[34] separating it with a dash, noting a three-four metre with a rest.

When he had no more tears left, he got up, looked around, gave an embarrassed smile, bowed politely towards the grave, shifted his feet as if lingering in someone's hallway before leaving a party, and set off towards the exit, sinking into the snowdrifts of the cemetery, these days unkempt.

He walked towards his home, slowly dragging himself along the streets, shuffling his felt boots, giving way to passers-by, trying to protect his face against the cold by burying it in the hide shreds of his fur collar.

At home he was welcomed by a cold room, the stove unheated. By now it was dark, and neither the dust spots nor the strips were noticeable on the parquet floor. The thing cautiously opened the door a few inches, let itself in, groped around in the dark till it found the chair, and sat itself down.

....

[34] A musical term denoting a musical ornament that consists of an added non-chord note in a melody that is resolved to the regular note of the chord.

A LITTLE BRONZE BALL

Tanyusha came over to see Stolnikov. This time he received her seated in an armchair. He was dressed in a field jacket with superfluous sleeves. Next to the armchair stood a desk on which his 'inventions' had been arranged – and in the middle was a little bronze ball, lying on a sheet of dark green paper.

As soon as she entered the room, Tanyusha was overwhelmed with the same sense of embarrassment that had kept her from visiting him again. It felt bizarre – to enter a room and not be able to offer her hand. Perhaps she should bow. And, of course, there should be no theatrics, her gaze must be friendly and cheerful. That meant arranging her face, which was the most difficult of all. And thus she blushed when she was still on the doorstep.

Tanyusha knew perfectly well that she shouldn't ask about his health, nor 'how he was', that she should unselfconsciously lead the conversation, talk about something, someone, narrate, entertain. But it was so hard, and she brightened up when Stolnikov was the first to speak. He said:

'I'm glad, I am ever so glad to see you, Tanyusha. I am calling you Tanyusha, as before, although you are now quite grown-up; me, on the other hand, I am now something like an old man, although Grigory does call me a baby-in-arms. How are your studies, Tanyusha?'

She started telling him, but noticed that he was barely listening, immersed in his own thoughts. She asked:

'Is there something you need? Can I be helpful in any way?'

'I rather feel like smoking. Pick up a cigarette and stick it straight into my mouth, without any ceremony. That's it, thank you. As for the ashtray, Grigory puts it right in front of me.'

'What's this ball over there?'

'The ball... Yes, it's quite a remarkable ball.'

Suddenly his face fell and he started talking in a rapid whisper:

'This ball, Tanyusha, is capable of changing everything, turning everything upside down and bringing everything back... You don't believe in miracles? But I do, for they say I am a miracle myself – a miracle of surgery and stamina. So, I am watching this ball and waiting – it must start moving. And it will, Tanyusha, I will make it move, I will force it with my stare.'

She didn't understand, but Stolnikov wasn't looking at her anyway.

'There must exist this force, you see, a force that must be developed. To start with – a trifle, to make the ball roll; and if this happens, then – do you see? – everything will become possible, all it takes is to train your willpower. If I succeed, I will have no need for arms or legs; even without them I'll be more powerful than most, than everyone, you see.'

His facial muscles strained, and he swayed gently back and forth while staring intently at the ball, as if pushing it forward with the power of his thought. The cigarette fell into the prepared ashtray. Tanyusha stared at him just as intently, wide-eyed, brimming with compassion and dismay and thinking in alarm: *What should I do? Oh my God, what should I do? He is out of his mind; he is completely ill.*

Stolnikov allowed his eyes to rest for a moment, and all at once calmed down, smiled at Tanyusha once again, just as he used to, looked directly at her, and said:

'No, Tanyusha, you shouldn't think like that. I am not mad. That's not it at all. This is my only way out, my only salvation. My life, as you can imagine, is hardly a bed of roses. But since I've got to live, it is important to make this life tolerable, whereas the life I live now is intolerable. To live like this is unbearable for me, Tanyusha. Either I believe or I don't. My little ball isn't really insanity. People who have no arms write with their legs, those without legs propel themselves with the help of their arms, the deaf can hear through an ear trumpet, the blind can learn to see by employing various instruments. All these cases are miracles, tantamount to the miracle that I am waiting for. After all, I have achieved a lot: I can eat my soup with a spoon and light up in bed without anyone's help. There's no limit to what can be achieved. It is quite easy to write with your mouth. But I've set my heart on something infinitely greater because my misfortune is, likewise, infinitely greater. There are some spheres of the spirit little known to us, but nevertheless they are real, not speculative. It is possible to detonate explosives from a distance, without recourse to wires. It is possible to be in Europe and hear a voice from America. They say it will be possible to fly an aeroplane without a pilot. All these are miracles, of course. They exist in the sphere of engineering, but there must be things even more miraculous inside our psyche. Not all fakirs are charlatans. And these are not the miracles I am after. I don't want to move a cliff, only a light ball. A man is a source of gigantic power; it is imperative to research and guide that power. No, Tanyusha, I am completely sane.'

'I never thought…'

'But of course, you did, I know. I am now generally more sensitive than other… than those who are whole. But that isn't the point. The point is… There, there… would you look at me, Tanyusha?'

She raised her eyes and met his gaze, which had changed yet again, and now was at once sharp, distant and otherworldly. And once more, deep in the Stump's big dark eyes,

206   MIKHAIL OSORGIN

somewhere in the irises, flickered a spark of something that Tanyusha believed to be insanity.

'Fear not, keep looking. Now shift your focus over here, towards the ball, and concentrate, harder, that's it… that's it…'

Tanyusha froze. And then something incomprehensible happened, strange in its simplicity and suddenness: the bronze ball wobbled, rolled towards Tanyusha, reached the edge of the desk and fell with a thud at her feet. Tanyusha cried out, recoiled, jumped up and ran off towards the door.

Regaining control, she looked back and saw the Stump's head, tilted backwards. His eyes were semi-closed and seemed white. Grigory came into the room.

'What's wrong, miss? Is his Excellency unwell?'

Registering the state of the Stump, Grigory shook his head:

'It happens to 'im sometimes. His Excellency must've been playing with this 'ere ball again. If only you knew, miss, what an unfortunate man he is. Languishing like that, day and night. You go, miss, I'll cope on me own, he'll come to, soon. He'll soon recover, I know, we should give 'im time. But it'll be awkward for you to be 'ere.'

Tanyusha left, barely able to walk on her trembling legs. What had happened was so bizarre and so horrible. Did she imagine it, or had it truly taken place? What if he had pushed the table? How pale he was, and how delirious his eyes were! It was more horrific than anything Tanyusha had ever seen in her life.

The frosty air outside invigorated her. Bypassing Bronnaya Street, Tanyusha hastily walked towards the conservatoire. Had she bumped into anyone she knew, she would not have recognised them.

A VISIT

They came to Stolnikov's in the early hours of the morning and raised Grigory by their knock on the door.

'Who are you, citizen?'

Grigory understood it all perfectly well but answered with a gruff question of his own:

'And who are you, then? Whaddya want?'

Four of them stood around with their rifles; it was the fifth who did the asking – a fellow in a leather jacket with a red bow that looked fresh from a theatre's prop room. He waved his Nagant revolver in front of Grigory's nose:

'That's who we are. Officer Stolnikov, which one is he?'

'Whaddya need 'im for? His Excellency is asleep. No need to bother 'im.'

'So, you are what, his orderly?'

'I am.'

'We'll take you away, too, then. Orderlies are no more, brother, if you haven't caught on yet. C'mon, snap to it.'

And they barged into Stolnikov's bedroom.

Grigory's face clouded over. One thing he wasn't, and that was afraid – he'd seen his share of things.

The Stump was lying under a blanket, facing the visitors. The knock had woken him up too. He got the message and was silently examining the callers, his brows knitted, a derisive sneer glowing in his eyes.

'Officer Stolnikov, is that you? Now then, get up, don't be shy, there aren't any lasses around.'

A grim Grigory cut in, enunciating clearly:

'Yer should first ask if his Excellency is capable of getting up. Yer don't, do yer, have a clue what yer about. Is it a done thing now, to harass invalids?'

The Black Jacket snapped:

'You, comrade orderly, keep your mouth shut; we'll take you too, we don't even need an order for that. Raise your master. We've got a mandate. Stop blabbering, citizens, and present your papers.'

Stolnikov spoke softly:

'Give them the papers, Grigory.'

'What are you, an invalid?' asked the Black Jacket.

Stolnikov didn't respond, but stared scornfully into the Black one's eyes.

'When I ask a question, you must answer. And why are you lazing in bed? Our order is to deliver you. Someone in charge will figure out what's wrong with you. It's not for us to decide.'

The soldiers watched with curiosity. The voice and the face of the recumbent officer were out of the ordinary. They could see that the commander of their detail was embarrassed, much as he was trying to behave in a superior manner.

Handing the papers over, Grigory added quietly:

'His Excellency has neither legs nor arms. He's of no interest to ya.'

The commandant growled:

'It ain't my place to make decisions. I've got an order to bring him in for questioning. And I don't want any back chat here. Can he walk, at least?'

'Well, if I tell ya he ain't got any legs or arms…'

'All the same to me, even if he's got no head. The order is clear so there's nothing to discuss. Watch it, or we'll arrest you, too.'

'You can't do this, I'm his minder.'

'You mean, his nanny? Some soldier you are, then.'

'What's it to you? I never asked yer permission.'

'Hold your tongue, comrade, or we'll bring you to justice. Well then, raise your master.'

'What about you, you scum, did you even fight in the war? Or are you only good for fighting officers?'

Black Jacket was incandescent:

'Take him away, lads, as he is, that's enough of this rubbish!'

Not a single soldier budged. So the Black one came up to Stolnikov's bed, holding out his revolver, and barked:

'Up with you!'

He was met with a sarcastic stare. Stolnikov didn't stir.

Enraged, Black Jacket snatched a corner of the blanket and whipped it off the figure underneath. From a slit in the shirt peeped the shiny weal of the shoulder; the other sleeve was tucked underneath his back, and the shirt itself was folded under the hips. Not twitching a muscle on his face, the Stump fixed his stare on the Black Jacket's face.

Grigory interceded:

'What on earth is this, lads! How can you do this?'

One of the soldiers banged the butt of his rifle on the floor and grumbled:

'Oi, leave 'im in 'is bed, let 'im be. He ain't doing any harm.'

Another one piped up in support:

'What the heck's he good for? See for yourself, he's a total invalid.'

Grigory came up to the bed, pushed Black Jacket aside with his shoulder and covered the officer with the blanket. The Stump was lying with his eyes shut. His left cheek was jerking, his jaw firmly set.

The Black one, not knowing what to do, started yelling at Grigory:

'You, comrade, gather your junk together and get ready. Go on, move it. What's that machine here? Pick up the machine, lads, it's required for the secretariat. We'll draw up a report and be done with it. You, citizen invalid, shall stay at home, under house arrest, pending investigation. That's no business of mine, the mandate has been duly issued. And you, orderly, pack up. They'll teach you over there how to tuck an officer in.'

Grigory cut him off decisively:

'I won't go. Drag me away by force, if you've no fear of God. Tin soldiers!'

The Black one raised his revolver and aimed it at Grigory:

'Seen this? Shut your trap!'

But his hand was sharply pushed away by another hand. A young soldier, blushing up to the line of his pale blond hair, muttered bluntly:

'Leave it. I said, 'ands off. Take the machine, if you must but leave 'im alone. We've come to the wrong address. One of 'em's been hacked up in the war, the other takes care of 'im. We're not animals, are we? Go on, let's get going.'

The Black one, now visibly deflated, tucked his revolver away.

'It's not your decision, comrades. I am in charge here, and you must do as you're told.'

'Pack it in, will you! In charge or not in charge – don't push it. Take the machine and that's that.'

The others sided with him, too:

'That's right, it's a special case here, comrade. Gotta have some sense, ain't we…'

The Black one, now totally subdued, stuck his revolver into its holster and turned towards the door:

'Right then, so, one of you, fetch the machine.'

'All right.'

The four of them swung round to face Stolnikov, and casting sideways glances, one after the other, saluted him:

'All the best, then!'

The young one lingered behind the others, approached the typing machine, touched it and his face went red again:

'Ah, to hell with it. What's the bloody use in it? Keep the damn thing.'

He spoke to Grigory:

'Have no fear, comrade. After all, we're people, too.'

He turned to address the Stump, with due frontline formality:

'Goodbye and good luck, your Excellency!'

And then he left, his jackboots making a rock-crushing sound.

THE CONCERT

There they were – Dunyasha, wearing felt boots and a warm shawl wrapped over her cardigan, Tanyusha in her old ankle boots and a grey fur hat. The freezing temperatures were still holding. The city stood frozen over. If only they could make it till springtime, surely it would be easier after that.

The Sovdep's door was plastered over with a multitude of announcements, knocked out on faulty Remington typewriters. No ribbons were available, so carbon paper had been used instead.

The stamps on the announcements were huge, endorsed with reddish signatures in a mixture of various inks. What sort of position was 'a commander'? Underneath there was a signature in a large chicken scratch, and out leapt the name – 'Kolchagin'. Followed by a flourish, scrawled by a rusty nib.

'Who do you want to see?'

They let them through. Still, they kept them waiting. Luckily, he came out himself, spotted them and said, 'Come in, I won't be a minute.' Then he snapped at somebody sternly:

'You're wasting yer time, citizen, you've had our final word.'

Even Dunyasha was on the back foot. Tanyusha's curiosity was excited: here he was, someone who had camped in their kitchen but was now a big boss. He held Eduard Lvovich's destiny in his hand and, most likely, the fate of many other people.

In his 'office' Kolchagin changed his tune. He greeted them timidly; he must have been nervous.

'Do forgive me for the wait. You must have some problem that needs my attention? You see, Tatyana Mikhailovna,[35] we happen to meet again. Of course, it's a sign of the times. We are introducing new rules. Do sit down; perhaps you'd like some tea? You, Dunya, sit down too, I haven't seen you for a while. I'll call for some tea.'

'No, thank you, we are here on business; there must be other visitors waiting.'

'Let them wait, it don't matter. They are mostly here for useless reasons. Still, we do have to see to it all, of course.'

Dunyasha's brother wasn't sure how to behave. He was fussing about but nonetheless was eager to demonstrate his importance. Tanyusha, meanwhile, was uncertain how to address him. Previously he had been called Andrei. Dunyasha came to help.

'Andryusha, why's it that they snatched the piano from Eduard Lvovich, the teacher of my mistress here?'

Tanyusha explained. Although Andrei had signed the papers himself, he had no idea to whom they were referring.

'Would it be possible to give it back to him? He is a composer and a professor at the conservatoire. He cannot exist without his instrument. What should he do otherwise?'

It was all coming back to Andrei:

'Which one, the squint-eyed fellow, the one who used to play at your place?'

'Well, yes, him.'

'But who took it away?'

He made inquiries and learned that it had been done for the benefit of a workers' club. But the grand piano hadn't

....

[35] Clearly, Tanyusha's father – who is absent from the narrative, having only been mentioned once as one of the three children of the old ornithologist and his wife, now deceased – had been named Mikhail, thus making Tanyusha's patronymic (father's name used as a polite, or official, form of address), Mikhailovna – daughter of Mikhail.

been forwarded yet and the club hadn't been opened. He summoned somebody over the phone, to demonstrate his efficiency, yelled for a bit into the receiver, furrowed his brow, and left the room.

'I'll find out now, and give orders.'

Most likely, he was glad that he was capable of getting things done on his authority and quickly. He disappeared somewhere for about a quarter of an hour, bustled around, came back.

'It's possible to reinstate it. It's a special case, of course, if it concerns a musician. It was a misunderstanding.'

Dunyasha, keen to firm up on their progress, said:

'Do try your best, Andryusha, for Tatyana Mikhailovna's sake. She sent you shirts to the frontline.'

'I'm all for it, by all means. I'll go to the warehouse with you m'self. It's a special case, a mistake – you can't oversee everything. The times have changed, of course, but we have nothing against the citizens, we know who's who. Don't worry, Tatyana Mikhailovna, and if you have any trouble at home – say, they pay you a visit, or try to requisition something, come see me, by all means, and don't worry.'

He went out again, wrote out a paper, applied stamps. An order, in brief.

'Here we are then, let's go to the warehouse. I'll come with you, just to be sure.'

They went out. By the gate an automobile was already waiting – a noisy, beat-up, revving thing. Kolchagin, stern and important, told the driver abruptly:

'Let's go, comrade, to the warehouse, same as last night.'

The warehouse, situated in a shed formerly owned by a trading company, was piled ceiling-high with furniture, rugs, pictures in broken frames, desks, pianos, mirrors – all of it scratched and ruined as a result of hasty delivery. Of the two grand pianos present, it wasn't hard at all to recognise the familiar one belonging to Eduard Lvovich. But God almighty, the state it was in: dusty, filthy, its lid scuffed and scarred. Still, Tanya's spirit soared as though she had seen a long-lost relation.

'That's the one, Andrei, this one! What do we do now, how do we take it out?'

Kolchagin decided to act magnanimously and imperiously till the very end:

'We'll deliver it, I'll give an order to that effect.'

'Will you really? When might that happen?'

'I'll order a lorry. Don't worry. If not today, then tomorrow. Don't forget to leave us the address.'

Tanyusha caressed the grand piano's polished surface, raised the lid – it wasn't locked. But hadn't it been damaged in transit? She perched herself on an upturned box and ran both hands up and down the keys.

Dear Eduard Lvovich, how happy he was going to be!

Attracted by the sound of the grand piano, two soldiers and a man in a civilian suit peeped into the shed. Kolchagin was standing there, a holster on his belt, grand and self-satisfied.

'Perhaps you'll play us something?'

Tanyusha looked around in astonishment.

'Here?'

'What of it? Here's as good as anywhere. We'd listen. Although, true enough – some audience we are.'

Tanyusha was suddenly brimming with delight. Play for them? If it helped to secure the return of the grand piano, she would do whatever it took. Her hands were cold, though... She looked round again and realised that a little gaggle of curious onlookers had congregated at the door of the shed. Would she play for them, perhaps? Oh yes, she would.

Dunyasha, meanwhile, dug out a stool, wiped it clean and put it by the piano. Tanyusha warmed her hands with her breath, gave a happy smile (it was so strange to play here!) and burst forth with the first piece that came to mind.

The keys were black and white icicles, and the needles of frost pricked her fingers. But the sounds she made were warm and resonated with Tanyusha's deep joy: she was playing for her teacher, for the lonely unwanted Eduard Lvovich, an abused old child. For the first time, she could express her gratitude to him for the gift of music, for the years of his rigorous attention to her and her achievements – for everything. She was ready to play for as long as her fingers would obey, for as long as Dunyasha's brother and the people by the door demanded it. It made no difference, whether it was a frozen shed or a hall illuminated with chandeliers, whether she was playing for connoisseurs or soldiers. How strange it felt, and how exquisite!

She was tense when playing, because her fingers kept slipping up and down the keys covered with hoarfrost. Through her old boots she felt her toes turning into blocks of ice on the pedals. And yet, she played on.

She finished the piece, and wasn't sure whether she should play something else. Her fingers were frozen stiff and she could no longer warm them up by breathing on them... She swivelled round with a guilty smile and saw that they all were looking at her, in silence, with kindly, amused, stunned eyes. By now a veritable crowd had accumulated by the door, and those at the front shifted forward, not saying a word, waiting. It now looked as if she should play for them some more. Her fingers were so rigid with cold that it was bringing tears to her eyes. But if she had to...

'Huge thanks to you, comrade Tatyana Mikhailovna. Don't you play beautifully! Of course, this is no place...'

The others chipped in:

'Thank you kindly. That was the real music, that.'

Dunyasha helped her out:

'Your hands must be frozen solid. It's ever so frosty here. My feet have gone numb in my felt boots.'

A man in a leather coat came closer:

'We would like to ask you, comrade, to oblige us, and play in our club. We are opening the club and will provide the instrument. We insist. We'll thank you as best we can, some rationed stuff, the proper way.'

'Yes, yes, of course, I will play,' Tanyusha answered distractedly. 'As much as you wish. If only I could make sure that this grand piano was delivered.'

Kolchagin came back, authority personified:

'I told yer. Either today, or tomorrow, once we've got a lorry available. The order's been issued, it's a matter of the dray. Since I've given the order, there's no need for you to worry.'

The three of them left the shed together. By the gate everyone was trying to bid Tanyusha a personal farewell, thanking her over and over again, and she was thinking: *How nice they all are. It seems to me I played poorly. But they are so nice. They were an amazing audience. And overall, things are good. If only they give it back, if only they do...*

The commandant's automobile swerved towards the little house in Sivtsev Vrazhek, rakishly rumbling on the snow. Tanyusha and Dunyasha stepped out.

'Do see to it, Andryusha, won't you?'

'I gave my word, that means it'll get done. Keep well, Tatyana Mikhailovna. If anything is amiss, come straight to me!'

The caretaker emerged from the gate, so Kolchagin saluted him, as a well-disposed person of significance:

'To comrade Nikolai our respect!'

And then to the driver:

'Let's go back to the Sovdep.'

Caretaker Nikolai followed the departing car with his eyes, shook his head and muttered under his breath:

'Here we are, the new authorities. Dunka's brother, the deserter. Whatever next?'

A FIRST KISS

'Has anyone called, Dunyasha?'

'Just this one comrade, came asking for ya.'

'Which comrade?'

'A soldier. Kinda elderly. He told me to say – Grigory, from Bronnaya Street. So that you'd go over.'

Tanyusha hadn't visited Stolnikov in quite a while. She would have done, but she felt that her visits brought the Stump no joy – quite the opposite; he had been strangely flustered. Equally, she hadn't forgotten – he was sure to remember, too – the episode with the little bronze ball. Poor thing, it must be painful for him to look at her, a healthy young girl with whom he had once danced. After that bizarre episode she had visited Stolnikov several times, but always accompanied by someone else, most often Vasya Boltanovsky, who had a special gift for coming across as unpretentious, affable and even joyful. His company had made things easier.

This time Tanyusha went alone. Perhaps something had happened to the patient, prompting Grigory to come looking for her?

It turned out the initiative had come from Stolnikov himself, who had sent Grigory to Tanyusha's and asked her to come by.

Today he appeared approachable, if somewhat ill at ease.

'I've been missing you so much, so I've decided to trouble you. I am starved for company.'

'But of course, Alexander Ignatievich. I would have come of my own volition but I wasn't sure if you wanted to see me...'

Stolnikov's eyes filled with laughter:

'It's always good to see you, Tanyusha. It's my body that isn't always in a sufficiently good state to receive visitors. But I feel fine today, I can breathe.'

Still, she didn't know what to talk about.

'Would you like me to give you some books? I've brought several but I'm not sure if they are of interest.'

He thanked her and said:

'You shouldn't be engaging me in a conversation, Tanyusha. I only wanted to have a good look at you. What a beauty you are growing into, so lovely. It's just that the times are so hard.'

She shared with him all kinds of domestic worries, told him how Eduard Lvovich, who had had his grand piano confiscated, had nearly lost his mind, poor thing; how she, together with Dunyasha, had been to the Sovdep where Dunyasha's brother was now serving as a commandant. She was trying to maintain the thread of her narrative while being aware, all the time, of Stolnikov's eyes, so artless and gentle today, never leaving her face. She started actually to enjoy telling him her stories.

Grigory popped in and out, also looking at her affectionately. He had long since approved of her – she visited the invalid regularly and brought him some comfort, at least. A genuine and good young lady.

After a short silence Stolnikov said:

'I have written you a letter, Tanyusha, rather a long one. I haven't had it posted because now there is no need. In this letter I have told you more about myself. I must tell someone, but whom? You are easy to turn to, and you would understand me better.'

Tanyusha remained silent.

'I have described my impressions in that letter. These days I see the world in a very special way, unlike anyone else. As if it were an alien world. At times I am full of rancour, but then I reconcile myself to it. Otherwise it would be completely, totally impossible to go on living. So that's why I turned to you on paper. I wrote about myself – that's out of weakness, of course – and about you. As if blessing you to have a good life. That isn't wrong, is it, Tanyusha?'

'My God, of course not.'

'So there. Don't be embarrassed, I'll tell you... I love you very much, in such a way, you know, in a good way. After all, even a tiny insect, even – how shall I put it? – even such a... well, somebody who's not quite a full man, like me, for example, also needs to have feelings, to caress something in its heart. I am caressing your name, Tanyusha. Do forgive me. This is me inventing little hooks to cling on to life.'

They both fell silent, and then he continued:

'Yes... Steeped in old recollections. On the whole, I am not immune to recollections. The fragments of the past can, at times, furnish one with a reason to live.'

How exceptional Stolnikov is today. And how can he speak in such simple words? How strange it all is.

'There we are. And you know, Tanyusha... you've got such a sweet name... you know, perhaps, the entire human world, various events, and personal reasons to rejoice, and grievances of all sorts – all this is completely overestimated, whereas, in fact, it all boils down to a very few essentials. Sleep, for example. To be able to sleep is to be happy, and sleep is available to everybody, equally. Or, say, a joyous moment of complete liberation – death.'

'Alexander Ignatievich, don't.'

'Oh no, Tanyusha, I am not talking about sad things. This is an aside, something inspired by philosophy. Please don't think that I'm trying to bemoan my lot... truly ill-starred though it may be. My point is totally different, much as it is hard to explain.'

He took his time searching for the right words. Then he shifted the gaze of his large eyes to Tanyusha and said, bashful as a young boy, in a studied jocular voice:

'There we go, then. And so, I've made up my mind to seek your help for my thoughts on an unpleasant matter; or to be more precise, your help for keeping me going, since I am alive, of course. Will you do it?'

'Just say the word, I'll do whatever it takes, although, of course, I don't know...'

'Tanyusha, that's the thing... on the whole, it's not difficult, if only a touch unorthodox... Damn it, I'm rambling because of my embarrassment... Fine. You will probably go home now; I guess, it is time. The thing is, as you are leaving, will you... *kiss* me?'

And then he added, trembling:

'This will be your sacrifice. For everything that I've been through.'

Tanyusha's heart missed a beat, frozen. For an instant she felt insufferable fear, worse than the time with the little bronze ball. The Stump was sitting there, his eyes closed and his head thrown back.

She got to her feet, came up to him, and, filled with a mixture of terror and infinite pity, she put her arm round Stolnikov's head, bent down and brought her lips close to his. He opened his eyes, which, in this proximity, became huge. And then, shaking with nerves, she kissed the Stump's hot dry lips with her cold ones. He was holding his breath and did not respond with even the slightest twitch. He was completely still, his face otherworldly.

Tanyusha took a step back, then retreated towards the door and uttered a barely audible 'goodbye'.

He didn't stir, didn't open his eyes, made no answer. Tanyusha let herself out.

It was Tanyusha's first ever kiss, and her first kiss had been given to a man who most wouldn't even describe as either a man or a human being.

IRA CIGARETTES

Grigory left early in the morning to take his place in the queue for grains. The Stump was seated in his moveable chair by the desk. In the middle of the desk, as per usual, lay his little bronze ball. The window was open, letting in the clamour of wheels and a shrill woman's voice:

'I've been queueing 'ere since dawn but when I got near the top – they shut down. That's it, they said, nothing left, don't expect anything till tomorrow.'

Another voice answered:

'Christ almighty, for crying out loud!'

Stolnikov's room was on the first floor. When taking the Stump for a ride, Grigory would usually first bring down the chair, then climb back up the stairs, fetch the Stump, and descend with Stolnikov in his arms as if he were a child.

It was spring outside. Still, if anyone felt carefree it was the swallows and the sparrows – and even that was probably for show.

The bronze ball just sat there, motionless. Just as motionless were the Stump's eyes, directed towards it – grey eyes of steel.

The bronze ball itself was tiny and insignificant. However, it radiated ripples, with the first circle enveloping the Stump's existence, his sorrowful and inhuman daily life. But the circles kept spreading further out and becoming wider all the time. One of them came to encapsulate the whole of Moscow, another swallowed the entirety of Russia, then the Earth, and eventually the whole of infinity. Within the scope of eternity, the Stump's presence was insignificant, unobservable, non-existent – like a point in mathematics; yet his existence was the centre, the radiant point, the thing that blinded the eye; it sent out rays and illuminated the world with meaning and significance.

The Stump snapped the thread that was his stare and flung his head back. Above him was not the sky but the dirty ceiling with a yellowish patch of damp over the window. His soul felt stripped of stars, completely void – it wasn't something that could be fed with lies. There was no hand which could swept away the moisture clouding his eyes. What was the purpose for the sake of which he was going through all of this? Which dream could fill the life of this remnant of a man? Where could he find strength? And for what?

Gritting his teeth, he started mumbling:

'Kill me, Grigory! Slave, kill thy master!'

Grigory, meanwhile, was stuck in the queue for the sake of a handful of grain and six lumps of sugar.

With the remainder of his leg, the Stump thrust his weight onto the flat lever that he had invented himself. The chair rolled slightly backwards. That was it, the limit of what was accessible to him. The bronze ball looked distant and lacklustre. The circle had dwindled to the confines of the Stump's personal life, the life that was of no use to anyone. The woman in the street shrieked:

'The trouble they've made! Now what – if there ain't any bread?'

A gruff voice retorted:

'Shut up, you'll live. And if not – good riddance.'

The Stump leaned on the lever again, with all his might, and propelled the chair towards the window. His chest was level with the windowsill. In the house facing his, all the windows were open; in one of them there was a pile of pillows and blankets, badly stained, a long while since they were last washed.

All he could see was a strip of the sky obstructed by the high rising storeys of the house. A cloud drifted across the sky whose profundity was bright blue and beautiful. The spring outside was necessary for someone, and tender towards somebody, too. A swallow cut through the sky at a sharp angle, and swooped into its nest.

He planted the stump of his arm onto the windowsill, flexed his muscles and lifted himself off the chair. He felt like a child eager to clamber up a tall stool. Out there, outside the window, there was much more space. He propped his chin against the cold plank, raised his body with the help of his strong neck, and froze. If the chair rolled back, he would simply flop down onto the floor. But the chair sat askance, sturdy.

And this way, helping himself along with his jaw, he reached the bar that locked the frame, and sank his teeth into it. All the Stump needed to do was position his chest onto the windowsill. The ridge of the windowsill pressed painfully against his chest, but he braved it out and heaved his entire body onto the plank. The momentum of this movement sent the chair rolling back, and the travel rug Grigory had wrapped around the remnants of the Stump's legs dropped down onto the floor.

He was now on the windowsill, barely covered with a long shirt, exhausted from the excessive effort, weak and enfeebled. He turned his head towards the street and lay face down. He could now see even more of the sky.

What's going on, down there, on the ground?

Supporting himself with his chin, he worked his way towards the edge of the windowsill and hung his head over. Down below was the poorly swept expanse of stone, and right under his window lay an empty box of *Ira* cigarettes. That was the brand he smoked himself; it might even be his own pack.

The windowsill chilled his body. A pedestrian walked the length of the street, peeked upwards, spotted the gazing head and went on. The street was now empty.

The Stump inched closer to the edge, fastened his gaze for another moment on the pack of *Iras*, then raised his head and realised that the cloud was about to slide behind the roof. The sky was spotlessly clean. Somewhere in a field, in the countryside, one could breathe easily now, freely receive a lungful of air. However, that was only for those who had a fulcrum and a purpose in life, who found their future worth fighting for, who clung on to their existence. He felt no rancour towards them. Or anyone else, for that matter. But neither did he feel love for anyone. Or anything at all. Above him was the fathomless sky, below – an empty cigarette pack on the grimy slabs of the pavement.

A figure appeared in the window across the road, the one with the pillows piled high. Spotting the Stump, she gasped and called to someone behind her in the room:

'Nastasya, Nastasya…'

The Stump made an abrupt move, freed his chest, arched his neck upwards and pointed his head down. His body teetered, stilled and slowly slumped back onto the windowsill. With a childish grunt of vexation, he fiercely repeated the movement. The ugly clump that was his body swayed again, stayed motionless for a fraction of a second and began to tilt. Next thing, the pack with the lettering saying *Ira* was suddenly flying towards him, then darting skywards, then growing again – now to a gigantic size.

MIKHAIL OSORGIN

'ATTENTION!'

Grigory, grave and dignified in his neatly mended soldier's uniform and grey puttees, walked slowly along Bolshaya Nikitskaya Street, peeking into the dirty windows of empty shops boarded up with planks. He had a vague sense that he had recently spotted in passing what he needed now, someplace across the road from the church.

True enough, in the window stood a massive, expensive, ornate coffin on little legs, though it was shrouded in dust. Perhaps they would have something simpler to offer. On the door hung a padlock and a little plaque sealed with wax. Grigory went into the courtyard to make enquiries.

He addressed a woman he bumped into by the gate. First, she couldn't make sense of what he was on about, but then she answered him, nervously:

'I've no idea, gracious comrade. None at all. The undertaker's shop's been boarded up. Mind you, he himself never lived here, anyways. Ask around at the house committee, since you have a need.'

At the house committee they told him the same thing – the shop had been requisitioned, while the former owner had moved out and left no forwarding address. Might have done a bunk.

Grigory frowned.

'So what do I do now, if I have to bury some'un?'

'It's the Sovdep you need, or the precinct. They're the ones what distribute coffins nowadays. There's folk dying left and right, so coffins are scarce. You have to queue. Or else, go to a carpenter you know, if you know one. Only you'll have a hard time finding some proper planks. The dead nowadays ain't no better off than the living. Was it your wife that died or what?'

Grigory left without bothering to answer.

However, he didn't go to the Sovdep, having learned from a neighbour that the coffins were being issued only on loan – to enable a delivery to the cemetery – after which the coffin had to be vacated and returned to the issuer. Truth be told, not just anybody was supplied with one, most had to wait. It felt like a better idea to craft something by his own devices, whatever the result. These days it was more common to bury people without coffins.

Grigory made a detour on his way home; he dropped into Arbat Square where, according to rumours, the church shop still had some candles. The folk at the shop acted wary but still came up with the necessary. He paid out of his large leather pouch, but opening it he made sure to block their view with his back because, hiding inside this pouch, underneath the contemporary sham money, was a gold ten-rouble coin[36] sewn into a clean piece of cloth, along with about five roubles' worth of silver.

Back home, he placed the candles by the body of the deceased, lit them, crossed himself, and left again to attend to other errands. He had spotted a tiny store nearby where, sometimes, the light would be on in the evening. He dropped in to ask whether, by any chance at all, they had any empty boxes available. First, he was told: 'No, we've burned the lot for firewood.' Later, however, they agreed to barter five pounds of flour for a large, sturdy empty box that had been

....

[36] Between 1898 and 1911, under the last Russian emperor Nicholas II, 900 samples of gold alloy coins were minted with values of 5, 7.5, 10 and 15 roubles. The content of pure gold in the 10-ruble coin was 1 spool and 78.24 shares (7.74235 g). The total weight of the coin was 8.6 g.

MIKHAIL OSORGIN

used for storing tableware and was reinforced around the edges with metal clamps. The box carried a clear message, printed in large letters – 'Attention! This side up!'

The rest of the day Grigory spent labouring in the shed belonging to their building. He sawed and shaved, and affixed little legs. The box became shallower, although the base remained square. The inscription 'This side up' disappeared, and all that remained was the word 'Attention!'.

Despite his heartache over the absence of a proper coffin, as befitted a proper Christian, he nonetheless brought the box inside, and placed it on the table, lined its interior with a blanket and a white sheet, and a cushion for resting the wretched broken head.

He managed it all by himself. There was no help to be expected from the blind Kashtanov, who was seated on a chair in the corner, listening intently to Grigory's movements. Not a single neighbour looked in. They knew about their plight but had more than enough of their own sorrows to cope with. A militiaman came over, made a note, and said, 'A doctor will be sent over to certify the death.' But no one had put in an appearance till the evening.

The situation with the priest turned out to be awkward as well. The old man from the church of St John the Evangelist refused to perform the rites over a suicide. Somebody recommended reciting the burial service once they were at the cemetery. In the morning Grigory went to the Dorogomilovo cemetery and spent a long time there haggling. They weren't interested in charging him for the plot, but the sum they demanded for digging the grave was astronomical. Grigory felt there was nothing for it but to promise a top-up in silver over the payment in banknotes, since he'd used all the flour he had left to procure the coffin.

There was no point even dreaming of a dray or a cart. These days, the poor were laid to rest by home-spun means: on a small sled in the winter, in a wheelbarrow in the summer, and, if bearers were available, the body would be heaved onto their shoulders.

The Stump had no friends except the blind Kashtanov. His nurse, his only friend and whole family had been Grigory. And so it followed that it fell to him to see the deceased to his place of eternal rest.

The caretaker had lent his barrow but was adamant that it be returned, without fail, by six in the evening. The barrow was needed for distributing the rations of bread among the tenants.

Kashtanov couldn't see Grigory placing the white cross of St George over the white sheet on the officer's chest. However, he did hear the hammer banging in the nails, and on hearing this he got up and stood crossing himself till the last nail had been driven home. He came closer, groped for the box, tried to control a twitch in his cheek and stumbled towards the door. He wouldn't be accompanying his wretched friend on his last journey. No tears could be forced from his absent eyes.

At three o'clock Grigory twisted the sheet into a rope, hitched it over the square box and effortlessly brought it down into the courtyard. No one could possibly recognise the square box as a coffin, despite the little legs that had been carefully attached to it. Grigory hoisted it onto the barrow and set off towards Dorogomilovo.

None of the oncoming people crossed themselves. Grigory's hat was perched on top of the dreadful box while the inscription on its side was clearly legible, black on white: 'Attention!'.

AXIOS[37]

The catalogue of sorrows had received a new entry – although most coveted and fair one: death as a liberator.

Cowering in the corner of the sofa, shrinking herself into a tiny ball, Tanyusha looked deep into her heart. On the shelves of her soul stood little tomes bound in black – the opening volumes of her life's archive.

There was a thin booklet with a cover that was cool to the touch, bearing the name of Ehrberg on its spine. She had barely known him and didn't think about him often. His life had started cleverly, calculated for a long time ahead; the life of numbers, geometric figures and sensible aphorisms. And suddenly – an error in calculation. The first from the inner circle to go had been Ehrberg, so young and yet, from his very youth, coming across as a mature adult. Such a no-nonsense logical foreword, and yet cut short after only the first couple of chapters.

A pleasantly plump, ancient volume, lovingly leafed through time and again, perfumed with sweet lavender – the volume bearing Grandma's sacred name, inscribed on the opening page in an old-fashioned and very familiar hand. Darling exhausted Grandma had gone to sleep well loved, having used up a lifetime of affection, care and serene vener-

....

[37]   *Axios* is a word in Classical Greek meaning 'worthy, deserving, distinguished'.

ation. The nuptial candle interwoven with a yellowed moiré ribbon had burnt itself out.

The book of death. And now there was this new demise, entered into a black book, as yet unread by anyone. Who would dare turn over the pages of torturous thoughts, passionate pursuits, delusions, suppressed outbursts of envy towards everything alive, the morbid struggle between the mind and a belief in the reality of miracles, the visceral impetus to leave this life behind? What a macabre book! It had been written by the ultimate martyr, whose lifeless lips Tanyusha, horrified and compassionate, had gifted with her first ever kiss.

And now the same feeling, suddenly revitalised, made her cringe in the corner of the sofa. How horrifying it had been! How full of horrors life is!

Spring had been so carefree. At seventeen years of age – how beautiful the sun had been! How easily arising questions aligned themselves into orderly sequences, how omnipotent was science, how harmonious was music. Where had it all sunk to, what had happened?

Why is it that death and more deaths had to be the predecessors of life? The road starts from funereal crosses, the ode to joy is preceded by liturgical chants. And then what?

Should she ask Grandpa? But Grandpa was quite old himself; what answer could he possibly give? *It won't do to frighten him with questions of this kind. Vasya? Vasya is so loyal and considerate, a truly good friend. He may even find words, only not the right ones. He will be concerned and try to entertain and distract me, but that's not what's needed, not at all. He will tell a funny story, and if that doesn't work, he will ruffle the unruly locks of hair on his temples, install himself in a corner and start ripping apart a box of matches. No, Vasya is no good; he himself has no answers. Still, why hasn't he, Vasya, come along today? One way or the other, it feels good and safe when he's around.*

Riffling through the names of the few close people who were left nowadays, she thought of Astafyev. If only he would agree to answer – but how should she pose the question? Was it even something one asked about? When it came to Astafyev, though, Tanyusha felt more confident. Of all those who visited the old townhouse these days, he was the most unfamiliar and unconventional. It would be good to see more of him, and to learn something about his life, about the sort of a person he was. She should ask Vasya, who saw him much more frequently.

Twilight was falling over the spring day, and the window was open. Tanyusha got up and looked at the street outside. All was quiet, hardly any passers-by. She sat down at the grand piano, lifted its lid, and placed her fingers over the keys. But her head, fair-haired and exhausted by all this thinking, sank into her hands.

She stayed like that for a long time, not moving a muscle.

When she finally got to her feet, the tears in her eyes began to dry up – the accidental, unexpected tears of a young girl. It was possible that it was the tears that had lifted her fatigue – to be able to weep must have been important.

She stretched, straightened the shawl over her shoulders and, all of a sudden, her body registered a new sense of lightness.

It felt chilly in the room, with the evening gathering outside. So, what was happening? Were the many deaths casting their influence over everything? Why this sensation of lightness and the desire to do something, to know new things, to meet people and to look among them for somebody who was more knowledgeable and would be able to give her a better answer?

Tanyusha was conscious of how amazingly easy it became to breathe, how the sense of being alive was clearly triumphing over her thoughts about the numerous deaths and death itself. She had to go somewhere, do something – and as soon as possible. To see someone. And sometimes, if only once in a while, to laugh and not think about sad things, not to juxtapose the black and the white, for the white should come out on top. The black volumes sat on the shelf, but the white sheets of paper hadn't been written on yet. So that meant that she should start filling them without delay.

She thought: *I am already twenty years old.*

Again: *Does complete, unspoiled joy even exist anywhere in the world? Where, then? Where is it to be found? And ultimately, what is happiness? Wherein lies the key? And where are the doors opening into the large world, boundless, unrestricted by the walls of the old townhouse?*

She threw her hands behind her head, straightened up, and said out loud:

'I want to live! I want to *live!*'

She didn't see the tall straight girlish figure, arms raised, reflected in the dim lustre of the large mirror; she didn't hear the strings of the grand piano echoing her words with humming sounds of amusement; didn't register that a heedful evening was taking in the profound tenderness and simplicity of her words; that the walls of the little villa were standing motionless and puzzled – the same walls that had seen Tanyusha as a child, had heard her babyish babble, played silent witnesses to her development, assiduous guardians of the cherished secrets of her heart.

The walls whispered, the strings communicated the sounds to the spring ether – and the darkening sky sent forth the first star as an envoy of the decision passed by the council of celestial bodies:

Axios! – Worthy!

DEPARTURE

With a measured gait, putting one foot in front of the other, pulling his boots out of the mud that swamped the road, a satchel thrown over his back, a kettle dangling off the satchel, and with a soul brimful of brooding thoughts, the old soldier Grigory headed for Kiev.[38]

He had chosen Kiev because he no longer had anybody or anything left for him in the whole world – not a friend, not a son or a daughter, not even a patch of land. All that he had left was his firm belief in the inclement God, the God who

....

[38] An attentive reader may notice that we have used two forms of the Ukrainian capital's name: *Kiev* in the text of the novel proper and *Kyiv* in the footnotes and additional comments. This is due to the fact that the former was the standardised (and internationally accepted) Russified spelling from as early as the mid-17th century – in the days of the Russian Empire, then the Soviet Union, and all the way up until the dissolution of the USSR in 1991. On gaining independence, the Ukrainian government mandated the Ukrainian transliteration (*Kyiv*) to be the norm, although it did not catch on internationally. However, following the outbreak of the Russo-Ukrainian War in 2014, the city's name (again, previously spelled *Kiev* in English), lost favour with many Western media and has now been firmly replaced with *Kyiv* – the official Ukrainian name for the city. This spelling is now used for legislative and official acts. The narrative, however, takes place in the early days of the Revolution of 1917. To insist that Grigory set off for *Kyiv* would be an anachronism, tantamount to claiming that Pushkin's Yevgeny Onegin or Tolstoy's Anna Karenina lived in Leningrad.

had abandoned Moscow for the mother of Russian cities,[39] or perhaps even more distant lands.

He had been told he wouldn't make it on foot. But he who had nothing to save or to lose had become a free pioneer. The vast expanse of Rus[40] – or Russia – had always been roamed over by wayfarers, by wretched souls, by those seeking the truth or alms, by the lesser brotherhood of the dirt-poor, by wandering minstrels – and no one could bypass Kiev. Being sound of body, strong in his faith, neither blind nor squalid, and not bereft of reason, the old soldier Grigory was certain he would make it.

The road became a mire. He pulled off his boots, bound them together by running a narrow belt through their tabs, and thus secured, flung them over his shoulder and carried on, kneading the mud with his bare feet. He would make it. One village at a time.

The countryside lay low, in wait, trying to make sense of it all. The haste with which so many trees had been felled could have been gratuitous. New house frames sat around unwanted, serving no purpose, their timber rotting. Thrift-boxes were stuffed full of useless pieces of paper – what could one possibly buy with those? Folk flooded in from the cities in search of bread, dragging along their wares of bright chintz, or even silk, as well as blouses trimmed with lace, all types of junk, useful and useless – anything to barter for a handful of grain. But the grain was being hidden deeper, further and further away, since for all their newly acquired riches, the peasants were increasingly fearful of depriving themselves, of being doomed to hunger. The womenfolk were glad of the

....

[39] Ancient chronicles called Kyiv the 'mother of Russian cities' highlighting its pre-eminence over other population centres in ancient Kyivan Rus. One may only assume that Grigory chose Kyiv as his destination because of all he had been through in the by then 'Godless' Moscow.

[40] Rus is the ancient name of Russia.

new outfits, of course, and took to wearing flimsy seamed stockings and collarless blouses. All that was very well, but a husbanding owner had to think ahead.

The countryside waited, skimping, ducking and weaving, hiding its fear: *newly arrived strangers from the city looked suspicious, light-fingered, envious. What if they brought soldiers in their wake?*

Grigory followed public roads so as to save his strength. If he was certain of his route, he would use shortcuts. He didn't sell anything, nor buy, nor did he beg. His demeanour was solemn, his beard had grown back, his eyes looked honest and grave. On entering a peasant's dwelling, he would usually cross himself and be offered, either out of destitution or affluence, both shelter and a slice of bread, and following the old tradition, would not be asked for money. He wasn't garrulous, but would answer questions curtly, avoiding hollow phrases, displaying sound judgement and wisdom.

He shared the roads with many others who were in flight from Moscow, who were now walking, riding, picking out their way, hunched up, weasel-like, their gait fearful, erring, hesitant. Those aiming south shunned the new for the sake of the coveted old, eager to restore their hopes – natives of that Russia that had disappeared forever. Their roads overlapped but Grigory walked alone. He wasn't propelled by fear, old soldier that he was, but by a sense of being orphaned, and the monastic severity of his thoughts.

On his strong shoulders Grigory carried his old faith, his ideas of fairness and humanity, leaving behind the land of debauchery and heading towards the saints of Kiev[41] or even

....

[41]   Kyiv is home to the Holy Dormition Kyiv-Caves ('Kiev-Pechersk') Lavra, one of the first and most ancient monasteries in the former Russian Empire and contemporary Ukraine. This burial place for numerous sacred relics is considered a shrine and a place of pilgrimage for the entire Orthodox Church.

further – wherever a direct way could lead a straightforward person of unshakeable faith. He wasn't a fugitive, or
a traitor to his country, or a coward, but someone who had
shaken off the dust of falsehoods and brazen shamelessness.

At the borders[42] he witnessed chaos and fires, and of borders there was a multitude: today the frontier could run here,
tomorrow a hundred-odd versts away; now behind his back,
then ahead of him. A thunderstorm could strike in a similar
way, afflicting cattle and houses. Impossible to see through
it all. All those ragged heroes: today the Whites, tomorrow
the Reds, grave upon grave. What were they battering each
other for? There was no making sense of any of it.

Accompanied by the rattle of machine guns, a wave of
hatred and death gushed forth, or sometimes simple mischief and profanity. And it was all in the name of freedom,
everything for the sake of freedom, but what did freedom
even mean? Some were afraid, some were ramping up the
fear, and they all rushed forward to grab fearfully onto each
other. If they could be seated round the same table and made
to share a communal pot of cabbage soup, they would all be
similar in their thoughts, desires and appearance. So why
were some of them on this side and the others on the other?
How could they tell themselves apart? Could they? Why was
Ivan turning against Ivan? The same grass would shoot up
from their gravesides. The same sun shone on them, and one

....

[42]   It may seem strange that there were shifting borders within the
country, but after the Treaty of Brest-Litovsk (March 1918), Russia
was out of the World War I, albeit with serious territorial losses. The
newly independent state of Ukraine, of which Kiev was capital, was,
for several years, the target of quite a few invasion campaigns: Germany, Austro-Hungary, Romania and France were present in different parts of Ukraine with the result that newly introduced borders
were everywhere, constantly changing. Also, attempts to form 'states
within states' were made by various political factions: the Reds, the
Whites, and the Greens – the anarchists.

single rain fell on their heads. Incomprehensible. It simply baffled comprehension, and all it spelled was trouble and sin.

Grigory's eyes were overhung by thick grizzled eyebrows, and the satchel behind his shoulders was sturdy, if sparse in its contents. Nobody in the countryside caused Grigory any trouble.

At times Grigory would switch to country roads. He walked along ploughland and the boundless expanse of young winter crops, and as he travelled the rye became taller and taller, already forming ears. The fields ran from one edge of the sky to the other, from the clear horizon into the hazy distance – and all this was Russia, baptised in its toil and a vainglorious sneer at human labour, caressed by the harrow and stomped underfoot by the jackboots of a reluctant warrior, the land celebrated and then scorned.

When the soil had dried out, Grigory fixed himself a pair of *lapti*,[43] so as to save his jackboots from excessive wear, and to go easy on his feet. His light birch bark shoes fluffed up the dust in the road, leaving behind nothing apart from a miniscule circle imprinted by the traveller's staff, and even that not for long, as the first breeze would blow it away. A man could pass by and not a trace would be left behind, just as there were no traces of those who had taken the same road before.

As a rule, he would walk from dawn till noon and eat his midday meal somewhere off the road, under a shady tree, on the grass. He would take his afternoon break in a similar spot, listening as a lark trilled away to its heart's content, thrusting itself into the celestial firmament like a tiny vociferous rivet. And underneath Grigory's ear, tickling his fist, the young cool grass whispered constantly to the puny ants.

....

[43] *Lapti* were shoes pleated from stripped-off lengths of birch tree bark, commonly worn by the lowest and poorest classes.

And thus, unhurriedly, persistently, step by step, Grigory was taking his old Rus further and further away, towards a holy place of eternal rest. His way was not one of hooting and cursing, much though it was for others; he didn't carry it stuffed in bags and suitcases, secured by bayonets, like those doomed never to come back. Rather, he followed the age-old way of pilgrims and wayfarers, bearers of the artless down-to-earth truth, seekers of the truth everlasting.

Whether or not the old soldier Grigory made it to Kiev, whether he found what he was looking for or turned around and headed north, towards the Perm hermitages,[44] or whether he took a sea crossing to Bari[45] and Jerusalem, whether he kept his beliefs or jettisoned them somewhere on the way along with his depleted and worn-out satchel – this is something that no one will ever be able to tell.

....

[44] After the reforms in the Russian Orthodox church implemented by Patriarch Nikon in the 17th century, many adherents of the Old Church fled religious persecution and resettled in Siberia, where they formed numerous monasteries and hermitages. Perm is the name of one of the regional centres in Western Siberia.

[45] Bari is the capital city of the Metropolitan City of Bari and of the Apulia region, on the Adriatic Sea, in southern Italy.

PART TWO

SPRING

Spring had arrived, longed-for, snail-paced and sluggish. It spread itself around Moscow in muddy rivulets, through the fetid odours of unkempt courtyards and infectious diseases. Even the professor's little villa had taken a turn for the worse because the snow hadn't been swept off its roof at the right time. Meanwhile, in other houses ceilings started leaking; water and filth from the pipes that had burst in the winter now seeped through the walls, and the remaining yellowish chunks of ice melted, at last, in flooded basements.

On the other hand, it was now possible to put away the makeshift ovens, discard the waterlogged felt boots, and even unbolt the street-entrance doors that had been nailed shut in the winter to keep out the frost and the fear.

Nature itself took part in the great spring clean of the city. People tried to assist nature's efforts – they could clearly see that life had to go on, however full it was of hunger and hardships.

In the courtyard of a big building in Dolgorukovskaya Street, where nearly all the flats had now been given over to the families of workers, the clean-up and sweeping were well underway in the communal areas, as decreed by the house committee. Spades were available in abundance; wheelbarrows were somewhat scarce, and only one cart was available – but no horse. Snow and rubbish were taken out into the street, where the residents would aim to get rid of it all by tipping the barrows into the streams flowing down the gutter. Committee Chairman Denisov, previously an assistant in the grocery shop situated in the same house but which was nowadays boarded up, personally supervised the proceedings.

Work progressed torpidly, without spirit, for appearances' sake and under the threat of a penalty or perhaps even detention. Most of those labouring were women. As for men, resident Astafyev, the last remaining member of the intelligentsia and the bourgeoisie in the entire house, appeared to be the more forthright and efficient figure. Chairman Denisov approached him personally.

'Are you getting used to it, comrade Astafyev? After all, the work is hard and unpleasant.'

'I have no intention of getting used to it, but since it's necessary, I am doing it. It would have made more sense to chip the ice back in the winter and taken it all out then.'

'We didn't get round to it in the winter. Of course, you, a learned man, cannot possibly find work enjoyable. Still, it's a case of needs must, comrade Astafyev. Previously we were working for you, now it's your turn. Such are the times we live in.'

Astafyev smirked.

'I am working as hard as the next man. Not a problem. I cannot recall, though, when it was that you, Denisov, have ever worked for me. After all, you used to spend most of your working life behind the counter.'

'It's not about your former occupation. It's about how you responded to the revolution.'

Astafyev lifted a heavy spadeful, tipped it over into the barrow, forcibly patted the load down, and said:

'Each one of us responded in the way that was to his advantage. You did your thing, I did mine. No point in settling old scores.'

Denisov went away and Astafyev thought to himself: *He will probably have a go at having me evicted. And he will succeed, of course. I'll get by somehow, no matter.*

He wheeled the full barrow out, dumped its contents by the edge of the ditch, although the ditch was clogged and the water couldn't pass through. So that was that, then. Splashing across the spreading slush with his boots, he pushed the newly empty barrow back inside. On his way he met a woman, pushing a barrow and looking unwell and frail. He very nearly offered to help her but changed his mind: *No matter, let her get on with it.*

He pulled out his pipe. Astafyev smoked shag now as no other tobacco was available. It must be said, though, that he found the shag healthy and aromatic – once you got used to it. And he got used to it with the same ease as he had taught himself to like Havanas when travelling abroad.

According to the workplan, Astafyev had been allocated a significant portion of the courtyard. He did his quota in good time; the chairman wouldn't have any grounds to cavil. When he was finished, he took his barrow to a lean-to, left the spade in the same place, wiped his boots on a newspaper kicking around on the stairs, and set off home.

Previously, Astafyev had lived here in a flat; nowadays he retained two rooms while the third had been assigned to a worker – a single man, shy and browbeaten. Normally the man would get home by the end of the day and go straight to bed, so Astafyev hardly ever saw him.

There had been designs to requisition Astafyev's second room, the one where he kept his library – but for the time being he was able to win that battle thanks to a protective certificate issued on account of his professorship. The room was cold and uninhabitable in winter but he hoped that in the summer he would be able to work and receive visitors there, provided there were visitors to receive and ideas to work on.

Back home, he changed, filled a new pipe, and picked up a book.

Spring air wafted in through the window, mixed with the odours of manure and excrement. He really didn't feel like reading. Perhaps it would be better to do something practical. And there was a lot to attend to: he could mend the frayed hem of his trousers, wash the handkerchiefs with the clay soap, feed kerosene into the lamp fashioned out of a little bottle, needed in case the electricity was cut off yet again. Today was Saturday. Tomorrow it would be possible to go over to Sivtsev Vrazhek to pay a visit to the ornithologist. What sort of a girl was she, his granddaughter? Not like all the others, not that easy to read. For all that, she seemed nice enough.

The tenant knocked on his door. Astafyev thought, with a lack of interest: *Who could this be?* In came a man, humble but strong and well-muscled, dressed in a worn jacket and faded down-at-heel boots. No shirt was visible under his waistcoat.

'Sorry to bother you, Alexei Dmitriyevich. I am not even sure how to ask this.'

'Just go ahead and ask.'

'Of course, I should just go ahead and ask, only these days everyone keeps everything close to their chest. So, I thought, what if you could spare me some old book? Something easy. I'd be glad to read it.'

'I've got lots of books, choose any one you like. Only I'm not sure which one will do you any good. What's that you would like to learn about?'

'Don't know, something about the workings of life. I'd like to learn the ropes.'

'So, you are what, off-duty today, Zavalishin[46]?'

....

[46] This character will appear many times in the narrative, so it's important to realise that he has a 'telling' name. *Zavalit* (the infinitive) means, in Russian, to 'bring down' (as a wall), or 'to kill' (as a bear). In the 20th century it became a slang word for 'murder'. Combined with

'Yes sir, no work today. The factory is out of supplies, so we're on a pause. Still, the wages get paid, so 'tis okay.'

'I can give you a book, no problem, but what do you expect to find there? You reckon it may teach you how to live a good life? That it will explain things? Do sit down, Zavalishin, let's have a proper chat. So, it's like I said, a book will be of no use to you. Why are you asking, anyway, is your life that tough?'

'Tough or not, I'd like to get a grasp of things.'

'And what's that that you are failing to grasp?'

Zavalishin looked confused and faltered, searching for the right words:

'I am looking round and – what's the word? It's as if everything is false nowadays.'

Although his language was clunky, he did manage to explain himself. In the old days he had thought that all there was to it was simply living and waiting, and in the end, it would all arrange itself somehow. But now they should go about things in a new way, should apply themselves. What new way? New was bad. All this fuss, and in the end nothing to show for it. And yet, was it possible that everything was in vain?

'Why rush, Zavalishin? You need to wait.'

'Waiting is okay. We did a lot of it before. Would be good, though, to know what's all this waiting for.'

Astafyev thought to himself: *This is it, the slushy nature of their praised working class – a perfect match for our intelligentsia. The shop-assistant Denisov, scoundrel that he is, is worlds better: at least he is trying to build something…* And he said:

'I understand you, Zavalishin. You are miserable because the very ground under your feet trembles. Life before could be nasty, too, yet it was stable. Nowadays everything is falling apart, the new is yet unattainable, whilst you're sick and tired of the same old grind. You have no real strength, Zavalishin.'

....
the tender suffix of 'shin', it makes for a particularly grotesque name.

'True enough – about strength; I don't have enough of it. It's also true, Alexei Dmitriyevich, that I'm bored out of my head. The key is to somehow make sense of it all.'

'Why the hell should you be bored? You are single, in good health, and still get paid, for now. Why care at all? Do you drink?'

'Don't mind if I do, if it's available. Don't go on binges, though. I'm not a heavy drinker.'

'You should drink more, Zavalishin. Wait till I get my hands on some booze, we'll share it. You'll never find any answers if you are completely sober.'

'You are making fun of me, Alexei Dmitriyevich!'

'Not at all. I am getting straight to the point – you are not suited to life. What life can you possibly build for yourself? You don't have genuine faith, you are not insolent, you don't know how to steal – you'll get pecked to death and discarded. On top if it all, your head is full of diverse thoughts. It's better simply to take to the bottle. A drunk person is wise.'

'Heavy drinking is wrong. You're really not helping here, Alexei Dmitriyevich. I'm turning to you for advice, seeing as you're a learned man.'

'Better take yourself off to the country, Zavalishin. Any family there?'

'Nah, I'm a city boy, me. No village for me.'

'That's bad. Look here, Zavalishin, I don't know whether you are sensitive or not. On the other hand, none of my business, I don't really care. Would you like me to be totally honest? Take me, for example – a learned man. I've read many books – you wouldn't be able even to read and understand their titles. And yet, those books are no use, not for understanding life; things would be exactly the same without any of those. Like you, I get bored at times. And I'm equally unsuited to this life, even if I am probably stronger than you. So far so good. Do you want to carve a niche for yourself? So, become a bastard and stop snivelling. We live in treacherous times;

honour will take you nowhere. But if you are reluctant to do it, as I said, better drown all your thoughts in wine. Or take to methylated spirit; works a treat. You are no warrior. No one is afraid of you, which means no one respects you. You are a timid person and, nowadays, people like you are finished. Somebody like Denisov, our house committee's chairman, a charlatan and a lout, will bring you down without even trying, though you look stronger. So, he will be the survivor. Then again, it's up to you.'

For a while they sat in silence, then Zavalishin got to his feet:

'Well, Alexei Dmitriyevich, thank you kindly just the same. You clearly are not interested in talking to me. I'm only a humble man.'

'Come on, Zavalishin, it's no good you playing the fool. I am humble myself, perhaps even humbler than you. Do drop in tonight, we'll share a drink at least.'

He turned to face Zavalishin with a kindly smile:

'I mean it, no offence. I am only talking like this because my life isn't exactly all roses either.'

'Sure, Alexei Dmitriyevich. I don't mind, really.'

When the tenant had gone, Astafyev thought: *Perhaps I laid it on too thick. The main thing is that I could be mistaken. He is diffident and spineless, no doubt about that, but his eyes did flare up with real anger. I hurt his feelings. It's good that he is still capable of feeling furious. This way he may even survive. It's rather curious!*

He chuckled: *He turned to me for help, eager to read books. So that eventually he could blame me and my books for his misfortune, and have a good reason to hate someone.*

In the evening Astafyev walked briskly home along Dolgorukovskaya Street, carrying under his coat a bottle of alcohol and some lousy grub to chase it with. Would he drop by? Zavalishin did. This time his knock on the door was more confident.

'Are you busy, Alexei Dmitriyevich?'

'Let's attend to this business together.'

By nightfall Zavalishin was blind drunk and Astafyev excited and brimming with curiosity. He was examining his client through a microscope, amazed: *My my, there's more to him than meets the eye. He may well prove himself, become an impressive villain. He's got heavy fists, which is the main thing.*

Shifting his torpid eyes from one empty plate to another, the worker was mumbling in a slurred voice:

'Granted I'm drunk. But I can still understand what's what. Thank you for your lessons but we've no desire to be discarded. None whatsoever. And we could have our own... wass it... them plans. Thank you humbly for the meal, and that you deigned... a man of learning...'

Astafyev knitted his brow:

'That's it, go sleep... you drunken scum.'

Zavalishin, momentarily rendered speechless, squinted out of one eye:

'Whazzat?'

'I said, go to bed. I'm tired of you. If you sleep it off and become a scoundrel, consider yourself lucky. But if you remain a piece of slime, come back for more carousing.'

His strong arms grabbed Zavalishin by his collar and pushed him towards the door.

THE BOOKS

The old ornithologist spent a long time leafing through the book, looking closely at the illustrations. Before putting it into his briefcase, stuffed full as it was, he inspected the spine of the book, moistened his finger with saliva and pasted back the protruding edge of the coloured paper of the binding.

The book was good, and in good condition.

Suddenly, he remembered something that got him flustered, so he pulled the book out again, perched himself on a chair by the table and, letter knife in hand, carefully scraped off his own name from the author's inscription: *To my highly esteemed teacher... from the author.*

He put on his coat, which was hanging right there, as well as his hat, ancient by now, adjusted the briefcase more comfortably under his armpit and went out, locking the door with an American key.[47]

By now the little villa's dining room was occupied by strangers, who had moved in under the Compacted Accommodation Decree. Dunyasha lived in a small room upstairs, next door to the room that had once been Tanyusha's; while Tanyusha's room was now home to Andrei Kolchagin – only he was hardly ever home, mostly spending the nights at the

....

[47] Presumably, supplies became available through the American Relief Administration (ARA) – an American relief mission to Europe and later post-revolutionary Russia after World War I. Herbert Hoover, future president of the United States, was the programme director.

Sovdep, where he could always doss down on the sofa in his own office.

On occasion Dunyasha would lend Tanyusha a hand running the house, just for friendship's sake; she wasn't a servant anymore but a tenant.

The professor was still relatively sprightly. On his way to Leontyevsky Lane[48] he rested briefly on the boulevard benches just three times, and even that was mostly because of the weight of the briefcase weighing down his arms. These breaks were not lengthy, and while resting, he would reflect on the frequency of his visits to the bookshop in Leontyevsky and try to imagine how much longer his reserves of books would last.

It just so happened that, once, they found themselves with no money at all. Bread, horrible though it was, was issued against the ration cards but Dunyasha, who, back then, still considered herself a servant and lived next door to the kitchen, announced that she didn't have any more potatoes, or gruel, or any other provisions left, and so there was nothing to cook.

Tanyusha thought that she should turn to Grandpa for a top-up and was very embarrassed to learn that he had no money, either. At which point she borrowed just a tiny sum from Vasya Boltanovsky.

Tanyusha and Vasya had spent that evening conferring over various domestic problems, and the following morning

....

[48] The Writers' Bookshop in Leontyevsky Lane was opened in September 1918. Mikhail Osorgin was instrumental in its creation. The shop provided invaluable support to members of the artistic and academic community, helping them survive during the years dominated by the paralysis of trade and the collapse of the economy. It became a cultural centre of sorts. Among those who were able to sell their books were prominent writers such as Mikhail Osorgin, Boris Zaitsev, poet Vladislav Khodasevich, Professor Berdyayev, et al.

Tanyusha disappeared till lunch time, and upon her return explained, excited if a little self-conscious, that she had received an offer to perform a series of concerts in the district workers' clubs.

'It's so interesting, Grandpa. Besides, I'll be paid in groceries.'

That same day Poplavsky dropped in and spread the word about the amazing antique books that he had happened to glimpse in the Writers' Bookshop in Leontyevsky Lane. In recent days the books, previously impossible to find, had suddenly appeared on the market.

'I've spotted a complete set of Lavoisier[49] in the original French; it's exceptionally rare for Moscow. I also saw a curious little book, probably the first ever Russian publication on mathematics, printed in church script and dated 1682. The title looked remarkable, too: *A Convenient Reckoning Helpful to Every Man, Whether Buying or Selling, When He Strives to Easily Find the Number of Any Thing*. They also have logarithmical tables available, dating back to the days of Peter the Great.'[50]

'So, did you buy anything?'

'Me? No, Professor, it was the other way round. I was selling my own stuff. You can make a really good sale there, or you can place your books on commission.'

....

[49] Antoine-Laurent de Lavoisier, also Antoine Lavoisier after the French Revolution (1743–1794), was a French nobleman and chemist who was central to the 18th century chemical revolution and who had a big influence on the history of both chemistry and biology.

[50] Peter the Great or Peter I (1672–1725) ruled the Tsardom of Russia and later the Russian Empire from 1682 until his death in 1725. Through a number of successful wars, he expanded the Tsardom into a much larger empire that became a major European power. Peter also laid the groundwork for the Imperial Russian Navy. He led a cultural revolution that replaced some of the traditionalist and medieval social and political systems with others that were modern, scientific, Westernised, and based on the Enlightenment.

On the lower shelves of the big bookcase in his study there lived numerous author's copies of the professor's scientific treatises. Getting ready for his morning walk, he fetched several copies. In the Leontyevsky bookshop he met with a friendly and respectful reception; among those behind the counter he saw some familiar faces – young lecturers from the university. They accepted his books, paid the price, and told him that merchandise of this nature was in huge demand; the books were routinely requested by the new public libraries in the provinces and by the new university libraries. They asked for more. And no one was astonished that here he was, a famous scientist, personally delivering, by hand, his own books for sale.

Himself an ardent lover of books, the old ornithologist rummaged through the bookshelves, mostly out of curiosity. He was overjoyed when in the pile of junk he managed to spot an extremely rare publication – *Description of a Chicken with a Human Profile*, complete with three illustrations. He leafed through the brochure lovingly and, spluttering with a happy old man's laughter, read the inscriptions under the drawings:

The presentation of the chicken's profile is fairly accurate and depicts the old lady the way she is. The second figure is the image of the head, face-forward, and represents a real Satyr. The third figure shows her yawning while simultaneously exposing her tongue.

He fiddled with it, enquired about the price. Those days, old and rare books had no value.

'Nowadays, Professor, we are selling editions from the times of Peter the First or Catherine the Great[51] at a lower price than fresh-from-the-press poetry by the Imaginists[52].

....

[51]   Catherine II, most commonly known as Catherine the Great, was Empress of Russia from 1762 until 1796 – the country's longest-ruling female leader.

[52]   Imaginism was a Russian avant-garde poetic movement that

And we are not buying them ourselves, either; this one ended up here completely by chance, as part of a collection we'd purchased earlier. How about we do it this way: we will present this brochure to you and you will undertake to bring more of your books to sell on commission.'

'But this is an unheard-of rarity, even if the publication isn't that old!'

'So much the better. Take it, Professor, for safekeeping.'

The professor returned home in the best of spirits. In the evening, over tea, Vasya Boltanovsky read the book out loud and the old professor was as thrilled as a child, drinking in every word. So the following morning he stuffed the briefcase full of his 'superfluous' copies and took them to the familiar shop where he had been welcomed with such kindness.

'Tanyusha, I've got some money, you shouldn't worry.'

However, by then, single roubles had long since become hundreds, and millions were already in the offing. The 'author's copies' didn't last long. The professor went through his shelves and discovered new commercial assets there: first, a number of duplicates, then popular literature – not required for scientific pursuits, even if they were valuable as part of a collection; then atlases and tables which one could, more or less, do without, and finally books with autographs, gifts from the authors. The shelves in the professor's study were gradually growing empty – but Tanyusha looked so pale, and was so tired from her concerts in the working districts… The ornithologist believed that she was unaware of his frequent visits to the Writers' Bookshop and felt happy that he, a useless old man, was not a burden on his sweet granddaughter, that he could help. He himself didn't know that Tanyusha's

....

began after the Revolution of 1917 and tried to distance itself from the Futurists. It was founded in 1918 in Moscow by a group of poets including Anatoly Marienhof, Vadim Shershnevich, and Sergei Yesenin.

children's books, previously kept in her own bookcase, had long since been sold to the same bookshop, and for a good price, too, since books of this type were always popular.

The silver lining was in the fact that Grandpa's breakfast had never, not once, included horse meat, and Tanyusha was able to slip real sugar into his glass of tea[53] while surreptitiously adding a pastille of saccharine into her own cup.

'Say, Tanyusha, I guess sugar is hugely expensive nowadays?'

'How would I know, Grandpa? I am issued it free of charge.'

....

[53] A very traditional Russian way to drink tea out of glasses in ornate glass holders.

MIKHAIL OSORGIN

A STRANGER

Tanyusha wasn't home. She was out, moonlighting some-where in the workers' district, in a club named after Lenin.

In Tanyusha's room, on her desk, an old photo album lay open. In the album's clear little windows were photos of Grandpa and Grandma, both still young. Grandpa was wear-ing a frock coat fitted at the waist while Grandma, laced up tight in her stays, had her hands resting on her hoop skirt. Grandpa's spectacles had flared into the lens and so one of his eyes was just a white spot. The photo was badly faded.

On the right-hand side was a photo of Tanyusha's mother in an outfit fashionable in the nineties.

The room was empty, with only Time bending its sil-ver-haired head over the album. Time regarded the photo and whispered under its breath: *She was just like Tanyusha: the eyes, the hair, the mouth, the earnestness. She had been full of the same appetite for life, and equally unaware of how it would all turn out.*

Time continued flipping through the album.

Two students, one somewhat older, sporting a goatee, wearing a technology student's uniform – Uncle Boris. The other one, good-looking, with his trim moustache and a high forehead, a university student – Tanyusha's father.

The girl and the student had spotted each other across the album's cardboard, peeking out of one window into an-other; they fell in love and got married. And right away the album presented an infant with a big head and milky eyes, an amazed eyebrow, a fluffy halo of hair, in an ill-fitting dress that had ridden up her back right up to the back of her head. That was the first photograph of Tanyusha herself.

Everybody had a mother and a father who were older, sometimes really old. Tanyusha, however, had never had old parents; at the age captured in the pictures they could have been her contemporaries and friends. Both had died very young, never having had the time to offer their girl any advice on what she should do to be happy. So, back when she was still very little, her grandpa and grandma had replaced her own parents. Her mother had only succeeded in passing on her own grey eyes, her golden plaits and her intense pensiveness. Her eyes seemed inquisitive, but who would answer their silent question – and how?

As for her father, he was both close and remote, and a stranger, all at once. Tanyusha had no real memories of him, as he had died before she had turned two. Tanyusha had a very peculiar feeling of being the daughter of a young student who never became a real adult. The fact that her mother had also been almost a girl was somehow easier to understand. She had very vague recollections of her, as if based on stories she had been told, but mostly according to an inner sense, the need to know one's own mother.

Mother seemed to be Tanyusha herself, except that she had lived in the past. Her name had also been Tatyana. Thumbing through the pages of the old album, Tanyusha would rest her curious eyes on her father's features. Sometimes it would cross her mind that maybe one day she would also meet a similar man, as her mother had done; surely, he existed, someone destined for her? It was really hard to imagine anyone else who could possibly be her intended. And thanks to the old photograph, Tanyusha was a tiny bit in love with her father; on opening the album she would seek him out.

Grey wisps of hair overhanging the page, Time continued leafing through the album. The little girl Tanyusha was growing, shooting upwards, and lo and behold, here she was, wearing the white pinafore of a gymnasium pupil.[54] That moment was the starting point of that part of her history of which the dates were still firmly remembered. Her fifth grade was the recent past. The old album became fresher and its pages would have taken us to the present day, had they not stopped abruptly with the pages filled up.

Its last page showed a male image, a contemporary portrait of a man who would be normally be referred to as 'someone familiar, really nice... what was his name?' For some unknown reason the portrait had been inserted into the final window by an unknown hand, and that was where it stayed – as a first link to the world of strangers. Had someone taken the picture out of its frame (it was a family album after all), the aperture would remain vacant. And thus, completely by chance, a stranger had established a permanent presence in the family.

That was when Time smiled: *But surely, Grandma and Grandpa, as well as her mother and father, were also total strangers once, completely unknown to each other? The same with Tanyusha – someone who she would meet eventually, sooner or later, mustn't he be a stranger now?*

Time sprinkled dust over the album pages, applied a yellow tinge to the photograph of Tanyusha's mother, lightly frayed the corners of the leather binding, and left the album as it was, open on the same page.

Tanyusha was out. Today she was playing Bach on an inferior instrument that was out of tune.

Before her performance, Comrade Braude had climbed onto the podium and delivered a speech outlining the current international situation. What followed were humorous

....

[54] The school uniform for girls in pre-revolutionary Russia, carried over to Soviet schools, was a chocolate-coloured dress and a pinafore – black for every day, white for special occasions.

stories and couplets presented by the darling of the workers' clubs, Comrade Smekhachev[55] – a stage name adopted by *privatdotsent* of philosophy Alexei Dmitriyevich Astafyev.

Astafyev stood in the wings, listening to Tanyusha play. He was clothed in a ruptured top hat, his cheeks rubbed with chalk, a touch of red applied to his nose, his very appearance calculated in such a way as to cause immediate laughter. More often than not, he would have to take several encores.

Tanyusha also used a stage name. Based on her mother's maiden name (the name of the lovable girl from the album), the name that advertised her performances in the clubs' programmes was Tatyana Goryayeva,[56] a professional entertainer.

His eyes following Tanyusha's white nimble fingers, Astafyev thought: *How serious she looks, as if it were a real concert. And they are snacking on sunflower seeds and spitting the husks on the floor. For the sake of a ration I am fooling around and satisfying my spite, whereas the same portion of herrings[57] induce her to come here and make a gift of her soul. She really is special.*

....

[55] A tell-tale name – *smekh* in Russian means laughter.

[56] *Goret* in Russian, means to burn, to be inspired.

[57] A typical ration during those days.

THE TWILIGHT

As was his wont, Vasya Boltanovsky dropped in on Tanyusha today, too, but left early, before nightfall. He was busy, systematically and painstakingly arranging a food-hunting expedition to Tula Province and selecting the wares with which to barter. He had high hopes for Tanyusha's silk blouse, while the professor had dug out a pair of old but excellent hunter's boots – exceptional merchandise.

Vasya appeared with a posy of field flowers – scrawny but fragrant.

'This is for you, Tanyusha. Guess where I picked up these flowers.'

'You've been out of town?'

'No.'

'Well, I don't know, in a garden somewhere?'

'You'll never guess. This one is a buttercup, and that's a bluebell. And this one here is an ear of rye. And I assembled the entire bouquet on the streets of Moscow! I even gathered some grass by your fence. There are places out there where the entire pavement is overgrown.'

The ornithologist carefully inspected each flower, and fingered the grass.

'I would suggest, Vasya, that the posy be dried and pressed. It is history personified, so make sure it's well-preserved. It should go to a museum.'

'I'll get another one, Professor; the outskirts are good enough for plaiting wreaths. In some places the pavement is completely overgrown, whereas this one is from the city centre. I didn't even have to go outside the Garden Ring.[58] This one is specially for Tanyusha from her faithful knight.'

While Tanyusha was putting the flowers in water and Vasya was watching her hands, the professor's affectionate eyes lingered on Vasya's face. Vasya met the professor's gaze.

'Why are you looking at me like that, Professor?'

'I just am. Come here.'

When Vasya Boltanovsky came nearer, the professor, still seated, put his arms round Vasya's waist.

'Do bend down towards the old man, I wish to kiss you. You told the truth, Vasya, you are a faithful knight. I loved your father and now I love you too.'

After Vasya left, Tanyusha picked up her book and snuggled in her usual place in the corner of the sofa. The ornithologist bestowed on his beloved granddaughter a similarly long stare.

'Tanyusha.'

'Yes, Grandpa?'

'He won't do, this knight of ours, Vasya?'

'How do you mean, he won't do?'

'Well, as a husband, or something like that. I can see that he just doesn't fit. More's the pity. I'm sorry for him and for you, too. He does love you very much. You are aware of it, aren't you?'

Tanyusha put her book aside.

'I am, Grandpa. I like him, really. Vasya's a beautiful person and we're very good friends. But as for marrying him, like you suggest, I don't believe I would, Grandpa.'

'I see.'

'Would you rather I got married, Grandpa?'

After a slight pause, the old man said:

....

[58] The Garden Ring is a circular ring road avenue around the centre of Moscow.

MIKHAIL OSORGIN

'Sooner or later you will anyway. It's probably not a good idea to marry too soon. Then again, Vasya is possibly too young for you. You are nearly the same age, am I right?'

'I don't want to get married, Grandpa. I prefer to live here, with you.'

'Is that so? Well, I suppose we'll wait and see.'

The windows were open, the air fresh, and Sivtsev Vrazhek was enveloped in silence. The deep comfortable armchair in which for many years Aglaya Dmitriyevna liked to rest at twilight was now occupied by the old ornithologist, dozing peacefully, his grey beard like an ornament on his chest. Tanyusha wasn't turning the pages over or running her eyes along the lines – she was simply sitting there, deep in thought, listening to the silence.

All was quiet upstairs where Sovdep's commandant Kolchagin now resided together with his sister, and behind the wall, in the rooms occupied by total strangers, and in the basement where a family of rats were making arrangements for the upcoming nocturnal raid. The entire townhouse of the old professor was plunged into slumber, recollecting the past, second-guessing the future. The professor's favourite clock – the one on the wall with a cuckoo inside – was ticking and tocking.

In the unswept and neglected cobbled streets of Moscow, young green grass was pushing up – first as tremulous little green protuberances, then becoming bolder; it grew more confidently in the shallow ditches and along the lengthy wooden fences, the nettles outsmarted by yellow splashes of budding flowers. If it had not been for this dogged creature, this savage dreamer – man – who was also striving to stay alive at any price and grow as some pathetic excrescence over the urban cobbled pavements, the grass would have triumphed over the stone and broken through and adorned it; it would have made living everyday things history and obscured its very pages with a greenish sheen and the kindness of a fairy tale.

During the hour of falling twilight, the turbulent life of the houses came to a standstill, and the sparrows and swallows slept in their nests and the gaps in the attics. Their sharp eyes were now curtained by their bluish, secure inner eyelids.

Over the last dreadful year, the professor's villa had grown greyish, and become older and faded. It was still putting on a brave façade during the daytime, but by nightfall it would sag heavily, stoop down, and utter brief sorrowful moans which emanated from the clamps on the beams and the whitewash on the walls.

Poor old thing. Previously it had been cosy, quietly joyful in its years-old contentment. On the other hand, old things always got tired, they needed peace and retirement into eternity. Pickaxes and machines would clear the space amongst the boulders, the land would have asphalt poured all over it, and in the place of the dead and demolished little colonnaded houses, the ancient nests guarded by kindly home spirits, the old walls that had been witness to the days gone by, they would erect the walls of great new edifices, complete with the comforts of modernity. The grass would retreat into the fields for years to come – waiting it out until this page, too, was turned over, until the varnish, so fresh today, started peeling off; until the thought passed its prime and disintegrated, and ashes and moisture appeared all anew in the crevices of a stone city, good enough to support a dogged field cowslip. Maybe then the grass of oblivion would triumph, just as it had triumphed over the Acropolis, and the Roman Forum, which it had beaten and buried, along with memories, the multitude of things unknown to archaeologists that now would never be discovered. However, it was equally possible that man would proclaim his own victory from the rooftops – yet again, and for an infinitesimally brief time in history.

'Grandpa? Are you asleep, Grandpa?'

MIKHAIL OSORGIN

The twilight became evening and the air turned chilly. Tanyusha switched on the lamp.

'Were you sleeping, Grandpa?'

'I believe I nodded off, Tanyusha.'

'Shall we have some tea?'

The professor got up from his armchair, propping himself up with both hands.

'Well then, Tanyusha, I would be sincerely glad of some nice tea.'

THE WHITE DRESS

The time had been shifted forward by three hours[59] and Moscow woke up incredibly early.

First it came to life in Presnya, Blagusha, Sokolniki,[60] as well as all the railways stations. Then, still yawning, the Trans-Moskva part of town woke up, Zamoskvorechye, along with Rogozhskaya, Sukharevka and the Smolensky Market.

A lorry rattled down Sadovo-Chernogryazskaya Street, a policeman on the beat in Pokrovka hooted at a mangy bony dog, two women rushed down Sretenka Boulevard towards Trubnaya Square, chattering excitedly – most likely in a hurry to take their place in a queue for sunflower oil.

And finally, all at once, as if obeying an inaudible command, out of all Moscow's houses, banging their doors, clattering their heels, sneezing at the rays of the sun, scrambled the shabby, sleepy, earthen-faced figures of the Soviet public servants: typists, heads of sections, committee chairmen, comrade couriers, employees of transport departments, ex-

....

[59]   Daylight Saving Time (DST) was first introduced in Russia by the Provisional Government's Decree of 27th June 1917 for the period from 1st July (one hour forward) till 31st August 1917. In 1918–1921 DST was applied without any coherent system and only in selected parts of the country. In 1918–1919 summer time in Moscow and in certain areas of European Russia was ahead of the average local summer time by two hours.

[60]   Boroughs in central Moscow.

perts, executives. Most of them, mistrustful of the tram, set off towards their place of work on foot while the tram juddered over the overgrown rails in Bolshaya Nikitskaya, its wheels screeching at the corner of Lubyanskaya Square and attempting to squeeze through the narrow opening of the Red Gate.[61] The tram was a rarity; few people ever succeeded in getting a ride and, once onboard, would elbow their way in, angrily snapping at each other and casting unfriendly sidelong glances at the ticket lady.

The professor's little townhouse on Sivtsev Vrazhek, too, shook off the remnants of its sleep early, and, as in the blissful carefree Moscow of old, a swallow had built a nest under the eaves of the roof and was now busy rearing her young.

The windows were open and a tea spoon jingled occasionally against the rim of the ornithologist's favourite cup.

'Will you stay home, Grandpa?'

'I will. I'll do some writing till lunchtime. But it would be a good idea if you went for a walk, Tanyusha. It's a glorious day out there.'

'I will. I've some business to attend to, only it's rather far, near the Red Gate. I should be back by about two, Grandpa, but not before.'

Tanyusha cleared away the cups, rinsed them in the kitchen, and, suddenly overwhelmed with a particular sense of freshness and pleasantly cool cleanliness, put on her white dress with loose short sleeves, ironed the day before, fitted around the waist with a narrow elastic belt. It would have been nice to complete the outfit with a pair of white shoes, but these days non-essential footwear was an unaffordable

....

[61]   The Red Gate (Krasnyye Vorota) was an architectural monument situated at the crossroads between Novo-Basmannaya and Sado-vo-Chernogryazskaya Streets. It was built in 1753–1757 by a prominent exponent of the Russian baroque, Dmitry Ukhtomsky. The gate was demolished in 1928.

luxury. She did have a straw hat, though, fashioned out of an old one, cleaned with lemon powder and adorned with a multi-coloured ribbon from their old reserves.

A familiar girl in white smiled at Tanyusha from the mirror and smoothed her hair under the hat with both hands. The girl became serious, had another close look – eye to eye – turned to one side, smoothed down the dress, bid Tanyusha farewell, and retreated back into the frame of the mirror.

Moscow on a summer morning – an impoverished, dirty, injured Moscow – was gorgeous despite everything, still a chaotically beautiful, beloved Russian city. Its streets, crooked and covered with cobblestones, with their evocative names – Plyuschikha, Ostozhenka, Povarskaya, Spiridonovka, Ordynka; its lanes – Skaterny, Zachatyevsky, Nikolopeskovsky, Chernyshevsky, Kiselny; its squares – Trubnaya, Krasnaya, Lubyanskaya, Voskresenskaya,[62] despite all sorrows and oppression, destitution and fear, were now bathed in sunlight, radiating a generous rose glow onto the walls, gleaming on rooftops and cupolas, outlining lilac shadows with a golden trim. Just as before, the Moskva River's busy waters flowed under the Stone Bridge,[63] and as it has done since time immemorial, the Yauza[64] was disguising its impurity with a luminous rainbow.

....

[62] Many of those are 'telling names' in Russian, harking back to medieval times when certain quarters of the city had been the settlements of various professional guilds, for example, table-cloth makers (Skaterny), confectioners (Kiselny), cooks (Povarskaya), trumpet-makers (Trubnaya); some have religious connotations – Conception (Zachatyevsky), Resurrection (Voskresenskaya).

[63] One of several bridges across the Moskva River by the Kremlin, connecting the historical centre with the Trans-Moskva part of the city.

[64] The largest tributary of the Moskva River, which also flows through Moscow, predominantly its working districts.

In the Arbat, all the shop windows were boarded up with planks and strewn with dust; there were no more displays inside the windows, shop signs were few and far between, and any that were still there meant very little. At street corners and crossroads cowered boys selling cigarettes, ready to take to their heels at the first hint of trouble.

A woman in Arbat Square had the bright idea of putting out a small bucket filled with bouquets of field flowers: white, yellow, forget-me-nots, pansies. Tanyusha stopped by, had a good look, asked about the price, and moved on. She wished she could carry a posy in her hand, smell it, or pin it onto her breast or belt, on such a wonderful morning.

The boulevards were green with the curly foliage of the trees. The straight alleyway was like life itself, enticing her with tremulous sunlight, amazing with its shadows, receding into the distance like a narrow road. It felt easy and pleasant to be walking down the boulevards, although, at times, it meant adding distance to her journey. It felt as though nothing out of the ordinary had ever taken place here, not really. The houses became much greyer, dirtier, seedier but within the boulevards all was well, just like before, maybe even better – perhaps due to the greenery being thicker since it hadn't been cut back.

Two young men in army uniform shirts sat on a bench, wearing khaki puttees but civilian cloth caps. They followed Tanyusha's passage with an indecent word and then broke out guffawing. Tanyusha paid no heed, lost in her private reverie. Her eyelids, not overshadowed by the brim of her hat, were caressed by the dappling sunlight, blinding but tender, and her gait was light.

She walked up to Strastnoy Boulevard, veered off diagonally towards Tverskaya Street, crossed Soviet Square[65] in

....

[65] The square in front of the erstwhile City Duma, at the time of the

which, just at this moment, the monument to Skobelev was being replaced with a temporary obelisk.[66] She passed by Petrovka and Neglinnaya and crossed Kuznetsky Bridge.[67] She wasn't tired, but that was where the street began leading steeply uphill.

The street, once central, handsome and commercial, by now had lost its erstwhile buoyant pride. The windows of the central arcade were clogged with forgotten rubbish, there was an abundance of signs advertising various new establishments with long clumsy names, and the passers-by she was seeing didn't look like they belonged in this once rich Moscow trading thoroughfare. The closer to Lubyanka she came, the more people in the street looked like members of military institutions, sporting new trench coats with uncomfortable, badly-fitting collars, oversized jodhpurs and, at times, leather jackets – all this despite the summer weather. Many of them carried briefcases. Rare were the passers-by in the street who refrained from casting an eye at the girl in the white dress; some of them visibly tried to preen themselves, stick out their chests, stomp their feet cadet-style, whilst stealing a peek under her hat. On such a luminous day Tanyusha wasn't put out by any of it – let them.

What couldn't she forgive on such a day, what wouldn't she respond to with a smile? So why was she alone today?

....

narrative a Mosdep (Soviet of Moscow Deputies), used to be called Skobelevskaya.

[66] In April 1918 the Bolsheviks demolished the monument to Skobelev, and replaced it, to mark the first anniversary of the revolution, with Dmitry Osipov's Monument to the Soviet Constitution. The monument was a three-faceted pillar with copper plates welded to its pediment. In 1919 a sculpture was added to the monument and Skobelevskaya Square was renamed Soviet Square.

[67] It was a bridge until the 15th century. Now, as then, it is a street in the centre of Moscow.

Among all those people, dressed with a certain degree of so-phistication or flaunting their poverty and filth: the dashing, the browbeaten, the self-satisfied, the worried, the carousing, the hurried, handsome and ugly, there wasn't a single one she could identify with, not one who would be thinking not about himself but about her, a slightly tired Tanyusha drunk on sunlight. If only there were just one such person!

Why did one have to live in such times – in expiation of what sins? Would it last long? But it had been different once, it had!

She crossed the street, and looked back. Here it was, Kuznetsky Bridge towards which she used to gravitate in the past to buy sheet music. It felt different now, and yet unchanged: the same contours, the same capricious and con-fident backward turn in the street, the same Church of the Presentation of the Virgin in the Temple[68] at the corner. No, Moscow was not to be subdued!

In Myasnitskaya she bumped into Uncle Boris – by the very entrance to his office, the Department of Science and Technology. He rejoiced at seeing her, pumped her hand, and asked about her grandpa's (his father's) health – the thing was, he could rarely drop in to visit him now, what with being busy at the office and having to hunt for food. He said:

'You're looking really pretty. You look positively bour-geois in that white dress.'

He walked her to the corner, and then became all flus-tered:

'Well then, must run or I'll miss the hand out. They are issuing meat in our office today, it's no joking matter. So long, my dear niece.'

....

[68]   The Presentation of the Blessed Virgin Mary, also known as The Entry of the Most Holy Theotokos into the Temple, is a liturgical feast celebrated by the Catholic and Orthodox churches, and some Anglo-Catholic Churches.

And she walked on again, alone.

By the Central Post Office, she thought: why not turn right, towards the Clear Ponds? She could make her way home from there by a back street; the detour wasn't significant.

Once she entered the alleyway, she felt the fatigue lifting off once more. What's more, it was quiet there, and one could unquestionably hear birds.

She reached the pond. Its banks were trodden down, its fence pilfered for firewood, the water by the shoreline strewn with sheets of newspaper, egg shells, rotten burlap mats. But just as before, bushes and trees peeped into its water, and the coolness was still nice, just like the subtle ripples on the water's surface. No boats – hidden away or burnt for wood in the winter? Then again, who would think of hiring a boat now anyway?

Tanyusha remembered that she used to visit a friend from her gymnasium who lived nearby, and the two of them would come to the ponds to skate. They would skate from after lunch until the evening, and by seven o'clock Tanyusha, her cheeks pink from the frosty air, her breath light, nicely tired all over, would make her way home to Sivtsev Vrazhek, to the protection of Grandma's wing and Grandpa's affection, to sweet biscuits with tea. That was something that, probably, was never coming back.

Hearing somebody's footfall behind her, she turned and spotted a man in a soldier's uniform, his narrow eyes squinting, full of fear:

'Would you like to buy some pork belly fat, citizen? The genuine product, from Kiev.[69] I could give you a good price – do buy some, citizen.'

He was half-way through pulling a dirty package from inside his breast pocket when Tanyusha said: 'No, I'm not interested.'

....

[69]   Ukrainian national delicacy.

MIKHAIL OSORGIN

For a brief moment the sun slid behind a cloud, the pond grew dark, and Tanyusha took a step aside.

Could it possibly be that the boat, the skates, and the erst-while levity – none of it would ever come back?

She left the boulevard by the side exit, crossed the street, and picked up speed on the shady side of Kharitonyevsky Lane – preoccupied, in her white fitted dress, alone on such a wondrous summer day.

So when she entered Sadovaya Street and saw a house with a green front garden, the Red Gate, and in the distance, small in the vista of the street, the Sukharev Tower, she stopped again, despite herself, and thought: *Come what may, Moscow is beautiful, just plain beautiful. Moscow, dear lovable Moscow! It's still the same, still as it ever was. It is people that change, Moscow is immutable. It's become somewhat sadder, and is as awkward and slovenly as it's ever been, but still dear, sweet and forever my own.*

A DECLARATION

The lorry couldn't drive everyone involved in the show to their homes. Tanyusha and Astafyev had to get off in Strastnaya Square.

Both carried small parcels with their earnings paid in provisions: a little sugar, five pounds of flour, a pound of groats, some fruit butter and two herrings apiece. This particular district club was rich and generous. Astafyev's tattered top hat, his large paper collar and bright tie – accessories of his buffoonish outfit – were packed in the same bundle. He had washed off the chalk and paint from his face the best he could, backstage at the club.

'Well, you should stay on Malaya Dmitrovka and I'll head off into the back streets.'

'Out of the question,' Astafyev replied. 'We'll go together and I'll see you home.'

'No need, Alexei Dmitriyevich, I'm not afraid.'

'But I fear for you. Besides, your bundle alone is a lure. It's past midnight already.'

Tanyusha was aware of the enormity of such a sacrifice from somebody so tired, who had, just like her, put in performances in two different clubs that day. But she was dreading having to walk home on her own, and Astafyev wouldn't hear of it anyway. Poor thing, it would be quite a step for him to get back home to Dolgorukovskaya.

She was grateful – he really was a genuine friend. For all that, she didn't allow him to give her a hand with her package, determined to carry the hard-earned treasure herself. It wasn't a burden, but pure joy. The main component in it was sugar for Grandpa.

The lorry had been bouncing and jolting, so talking had been out of the question. As a result, they had initially set off on foot in silence. Then Tanyusha had said:

'Do you find it hard, Alexei Dmitriyevich, to take on such a role?'

Astafyev laughed softly:

'What else could I do? Offer lectures on philosophy? I did deliver them, for as long as I could, until they stripped me of my professorship. The way I hit upon the idea was simple. In the past I used to appear on stage telling short stories – it goes without saying that these were usually amateur concerts and various charity events. As for clowning around, I had done some impromptu numbers in student clubs, and actually, wasn't half bad at it. So after I'd been forced to switch jobs I remembered those experiences. To be an actor is quite profitable – after all, you can get your hands on some nice flour and herrings. That's how I've became Comrade Smekhachev with the powdered physiognomy. As you can see, I'm making a good go of it.'

'But it's hard for you?'

'It's hard for you too, and for everyone. But you, Tatyana Mikhailovna, labour over your music in earnest while I see it as an outlet of sorts. It allows me to poke fun at them, at the people I'm entertaining, at each and every guffawing imbecile.'

'Why do you want to poke fun at them, the working people, Alexei Dmitriyevich? I don't like that about you.'

'You are kind and I am not, not really. I don't like people *en masse*; I can only love a specific person, somebody I know, value, respect, someone who is dear to me for whatever reason. As for the crowd – no. So here I am, a professor and philosopher, powdering my face with flour, rouging my nose with a beetroot and putting on an act for the benefit of a victorious crowd that pays me in herrings. And cheap jam that's gone off. And the vapider and clumsier the stories I deliver, the riskier the witticisms I dish out, the happier they are, the louder they laugh. It often makes me rather dejected.'

He paused to control his temper, then continued.

'You do know me a little, Tatyana Mikhailovna. And you must understand that I find it hard to put together and then spout all those vulgar platitudes. And yet compose them I do, and then bawl it all out. And the more fatuous the result, the happier I feel. It's possible that what I also feel is a kind of joy from my revenge – against them, our current lords and masters, and against my superfluous knowledge, and my wasted intellect.'

'Why should it be wasted?'

'It gets in my way, impedes my new career. Well, not mine, though, rather Comrade Smekhachev's. Philosopher Astafyev keeps trying to put words of real satire into Comrade Smekhchev's mouth, some genuine wit, some artistic integrity. He, Astafyev, is ashamed of Smekhachev, but that's completely unnecessary; all it proves is that Astafyev himself, a professor and philosopher, hasn't yet reached the true heights of philosophy, hasn't yet shaken off the academic coquettishness, is still so stolid, though not yet a stoic – forgive this feeble attempt at a pun from a sworn buffoon. It is, probably, incredibly hard. To be a Diogenes and to live in a barrel is easy, but to shed the pauper's coquettishness is hard. The phrase 'stand aside, stop blocking the sun', a phrase reverberating through the centuries, if you think about, is nothing more than cheap frivolity. A real Cynic should have come straight to the point: 'Get lost', or, even better, not answered at all, given a yawn, fallen asleep, scratched his back – damn this Alexander the Great popping up here when I am bored stiff as it is, and when even without this blasted visitor there's a crowd of idiots gathered around my barrel, gawking at it and its resident. Instead, Diogenes blurts out a historical phrase and is very pleased with himself, and everyone around him is pleased too. This philosophical gaudiness is attractive to middlebrows.'

'Stop it, Alexei Dmitriyevich.'

'But why, aren't I telling the truth?'

'You may well be right but your truth is really unpleasant. It gives no joy. You yourself are not consoled by it. And it's distasteful to me.'

Astafyev fell silent. Underneath a street lamp in the corner of the Arbat, Tanyusha turned her face towards him and looked into his eyes. Astafyev's face was ashen-coloured and haggard, his eyes full of anguish.

'Have I offended you?'

He was searching for words. He wasn't offended, that was not the word. But he felt sorry for himself. A simple 'no' wouldn't have been the proper answer.

'You are partly right, Tatyana Mikhailovna, whereas I am somewhat confused and showing off my intelligence. It's also unintentional coquettishness, really.'

When they got close to her house, she said to him:

'You know, I used to be afraid of you. You're fiercely intelligent and unconventional, different from the others. Now I'm not as afraid; probably not afraid at all.'

He was listening closely.

'I'm not afraid because I've understood many things since I've started to live for my work, coming into contact with many people, some of them totally new to me. It did occur to me once that we are all just frightened children – you, me, Grandpa, the workers, Comrade Braude – all of us. We are talking and thinking about bizarre trifles – herrings, the revolution, the international situation. Meanwhile, what's important is not any of this, none of it. I am not sure what is, but not this. What is important for you, Alexei Dmitriyevich?'

'Let me see. For me. It's important… It's important and essential to see you from time to time, Tatyana Mikhailovna, and talk to you like we are talking now. Also, that you should be beating me in such a conversation as this one. And what's important to you?'

'To me? I do believe that the most important thing to me would be to see by my side, if only occasionally, an ordinary man, somebody mentally healthy, and if possible, someone who's neither a philosopher nor a buffoon.'

'Aren't you being too bitter, Tatyana Mikhailovna?'

'No. I am generally not bitter; you've admitted as much just now. But I am gagging for air, not some pitch-dark prison that lures you all and where you would like to lock me in, too.'

'Who's trying to…'

But Tanyusha interrupted him:

'I'm twenty years old, Alexei Dmitriyevich. Do you think I like it that all I ever hear is funereal wailing and angry words? But the main thing is that it's all about the dear self, everything is around the self and for oneself, and everyone is like that, even the best of us. Grandpa, to be fair, thinks about me but it's the same as thinking about himself. Take you, Alexei Dmitriyevich, do you even consider anyone apart from yourself?'

Astafyev's torpid face lit up with his intelligent smile:

'Amazing,' he said, 'how a superfluity of words warps original thought. You cut short my torrent of verbosity with an excellent aside and immediately knocked me from my entrenched position. But then you got carried away with the coquetry of thoughts and words, and here I am again, saved. At least I don't feel embarrassed anymore. It's so absurd, this intelligent language of ours. What are you trying to say, in essence? What are you asking me about? Does anything apart from myself even exist to me? I can offer you a simple answer: yes, you exist too. I wouldn't be taking you home otherwise, and wouldn't be frightened for you. There we are; you are not completely right.'

'I am grateful to you, Alexei Dmitriyevich.'

'Don't mention it.'

Astafyev picked up the thread of his thought, and enunciating clearly, as was his wont when he found the going hard or when he wasn't all that confident of his words, said:

'All these conversations, they're about relatively trivial stuff. What is not trivial, though, is that I... that you are becoming too real for me. Yes, it is exactly what you've just thought – a feeble attempt at some sort of a declaration. The continuation of such a declaration is impossible today: firstly, because we've practically arrived, and secondly, because I'm still somewhat annoyed with you. Perhaps you've bruised my male pride. Anyway, take care, best regards to the Professor.'

He shook Tanyusha's hand, waited till her ringing of the bell was answered with a banging of the door at the caretaker's lodge, and, turning sharply, started walking up Sivtsev Vrazhek.

Tanyusha rested her forehead against the chilly frame of the main gate and thought: *Can a declaration ever be so cold? And why am I not thrilled?*

DEEP INTO THE WOODS

At seven in the morning the loyal knight was already pressing the bell at the entrance to the house in Sivtsev Vrazhek.

An excited Tanyusha glanced out of the window and called to him:

'I'm ready, Vasya. Would you like to come in? Would you like some tea?'

'I've had some already, and we're really pressed for time. You better come now, Tanyusha. Don't forget the baskets. I have a large sack and enough bread to last us the day.'

'What do you need a sack for?'

'What do you mean, what for? For the pine cones, of course. We'll gather some pine cones as kindling. And it might come in useful in other ways.'

What a glorious day it was. A slanting ray of sun swept over Tanyusha, who was standing in the frame of the window – so fair, so luminous and open. How good it felt to live… at times.

'You are quite stylish today, Vasya.'

Vasya Boltanovsky's elegance consisted, mainly, of a pair of relatively new sandals worn over his bare feet, and a Russian folk shirt, untucked and belted with a leather belt. Vasya wouldn't wear a hat, both for reasons of hygiene (the hair had to breathe freely!) but also because his old hat had been soiled with grease and badly worn out, and a new one, nowadays, was impossible to find or afford.

These days you were elegant if your underwear was clean and your dress was neatly darned; who cared if the overall effect of your outfit was outlandish. For lack of fabric, buttons and piping, the erstwhile sharp dressers were finding a way to fashion new ensembles out of curtains. The underwear might be made out of tablecloths whilst the ladies sported hats constructed of green and red baize ripped off the surfaces of card tables and writing desks in Soviet offices. Attempts had been made to treat it as a punishable offence but the initiative was short-lived; it was very hard to prove criminal intent. Nowadays, a pair of trousers with a sharply pressed crease represented not only a bourgeois prejudice but a certain defiance in the face of the new ideology.

To the most exacting eye they looked like a sufficiently elegant young couple: he in his Russian shirt with its embroidered collar fastened to one side, and in his sandals; she in her clean and freshly ironed old white dress fitted at the waist; both hatless and barelegged. Baskets in their hands and an empty cloth sack over Vasya's shoulder did nothing to ruin the impression – whoever would venture out of his home now without a sack?

The morning sun was gentle. They were both young and fancy free. They had a whole day ahead of them.

The houses in Sivtsev Vrazhek, both big and small, followed them with a smile. Even the professor's little villa, tarnished by its age, glowed in the day's sun and put on a brave façade. Today Tanyusha, normally so serious and business-like, was laughing readily in response to all of Vasya's flummery, while he himself felt like a young boy of gymnasium age. Their legs were breaking into a trot of their own accord, and they had to curb the urge. If this wasn't happiness, whatever on earth was?

The train was made up mainly of heated freight cars, and the bulk of the passengers were milk maids returning home with their empty churns. On the line connecting the city to the dachas,[70] only four trains had survived the cull – two in

....

[70] The *dacha* is a great Russian institution. Most families, starting

the morning and two in the evening. The advantage, though, was that one didn't have to obtain a special pass for the journey – that was only required for travelling on a long-distance train.

It took the juddering train almost an hour to cover ten versts; it remained stuck at three stations for a very long time without any obvious reason. Tanyusha and Vasya got off at a station called Nemchinov Post.

'Here we are, we have reached our destination. Where should we aim for, Tanyusha?'

'Some woods, and as quickly as possible.'

'There is a little wood nearby. However, if we go straight ahead through the fields for about half an hour, we will enter an incredible forest that stretches all the way towards the Moskva River. Are you up for it?'

Their legs walked as if independent of their bodies and needed no encouragement. They passed by a dacha village, now semi-derelict and deserted. The dachas were registered with a local Sovdep. One could only get one after a lot of fuss and bother, petitions and subterfuges, and only in the name of an organisation; but if you had a personal connection, you could easily make up something that would do. The previous winter, many little huts had been pilfered for firewood, despite the woods being right there, in close proximity.

They emerged into fields trimmed with scarce ears of rye trodden in by the road side. Still, a golden wave rippled through the field, the blue eyes of cornflowers were peeping out of the bread crops, and an invisible lark was singing

....

from aristocratic times, would strive to spend the summer months in the country, living in *dachas*, no longer the svelte country houses of the past, but any wooden makeshift structure. The tradition is still alive today and train timetables feature designated trains connecting the city with the dacha villages.

MIKHAIL OSORGIN

high in the sky. Nature was stubborn: it was alive, and urged them to go on living.

Tanyusha took off her shoes and walked barefoot between the two grooves in the road. Now and again her feet felt the green grass, nicely cool on her heels, slide between her toes and out again. Vasya undid the collar of his shirt and sang the whole time, in an unskilful voice and incredibly out of tune; he was renowned for being totally tone-deaf and it took a fair morning like today for musically gifted Tanyusha not to suffer from a performance like this. She would merely block her ears at Vasya's most daring roulades and then cry at him, laughingly:

'Vasya, have pity on me. You'll frighten all the birds away.'

'But when we retrace our steps in the evening, the frogs will be ecstatic. My singing is very much to their taste.'

They were fooling around like children, racing each other, adorning themselves with wreathes pleated from cornflower; they munched on unripe grains of rye and sweet blades of grass. By ten o'clock they had finally left the fields behind and, having made it across a deep ravine, reached the forest road.

The forest immediately moved in to encircle them with its young: the new oaks, silver birches, and hazel bushes. Then it enveloped them with the freshness of the old birch trees, aspens, firs, and pines. A crooked, barely-trodden path ran through the forest, its grooves bypassing young bushes and running over frayed roots, with russula mushrooms,[71] their caps a variety of pink and green, poking up between the ruts and along the edge of the road.

On their way, they barely met a soul, and those they did meet were on foot. The village on the steep edge of the Moskva River's bank was about four versts away across the

....

[71]   This type of mushroom is very common in the mushroom-hunting nation of Russia, brightly coloured and not very well respected, mostly picked up to make up the volume rather than taste.

forest. The berries here were scarce – either heavily picked or simply because this was not a good place for berries. But nuts were already making sure that the milky kernels in their chiselled green bonnets were growing fuller and firmer.

By noon they had left the scattered houses and the dacha huts of the village behind and reached the river. En route, Vasya had procured some milk, and so they stopped for a picnic at the top of the steep bank.

The greyish glutenous ration bread with coarse salt had never tasted so good. Tanyusha was amazed at the laboratory assistant's gift of domesticity: his basket had produced not only a bottle for the milk, but also two sturdy glasses.

'Take this glass, Tanyusha, I only ever use it for drinking.'

'And the other one?'

'The other one is for shaving, naturally. But I've washed it thoroughly. And I can tell them apart from this bubble in the glass; see for yourself.'

'Vasya, you are so funny, an absolute darling. Let's clink our glasses.'

Vasya, for his part, blushed and gasped when he realised that Tanyusha's basket contained two large cutlets.

'My God, the audacity!... It is pure extravagance. It's a repast fit for a royal!'

'Do not think for a second that this is horsemeat, Vasya. It's genuine meat, and I fried them myself in real cow's butter.'

They split one cutlet between the two of them, and saved the other for lunch. They ate in silence, as if following a ritual, momentarily lost in serious thoughts.

After they had seen away the baked potatoes, the basket of provisions became noticeably lighter.

'It's berries for dessert.'

'If we pick enough. We must gather some for Grandpa, too.'

'There are masses of bilberries and cowberries in that woodland over there.'

They were seated above a sheer drop, admiring the astonishing view of the river's sloping banks. Down below was another little village, Archangelskoye,[72] barely visible in the distance.

'What beauty!'

'Beauty?'

'Are you content, Tanyusha?'

'And happy, too. How about you, Vasya?'

'This means I'm double that.'

'Why double and why does that mean anything?'

'I am happy with my happiness, and also yours.'

Tanyusha looked at Vasya with gentle and contemplative eyes.

'Sweet Vasya, thank you for everything.'

'What's that for?'

'For everything. For your caring and loyal friendship.'

'Hmm, my friendship – that's right. And to you, Tanyusha, thank you for existing. For my love for you. It's no bother to you but, thanks to it, I find it more bearable to live. I love you so much, Tanyusha, oh, that...'

Vasya tumbled sideways onto the grass and started pummelling it with his tight fist:

'Okay, consider it silly but so be it. Don't listen to me, Tanyusha, it's the wonderful sun that's driving me insane. Oh my, what a total fool I am today, my, my, my... So foolish, it's even agreeable.'

They sat like this, for a while, faces in the grass, with Tanyusha gazing pensively at the green beyond. When Vasya raised his head, she simply said:

....

[72] Arkhangelskoye is a historical estate located some 20 km west of Moscow. The estate, built in the neoclassical style, used to be home to several aristocratic families: the Golitsyns and the Yusupovs. Nowadays Arkhangelskoye is a popular tourist attraction, and is often visited by Muscovites on short trips. Important cultural events such as music festivals take place at the estate.

'Shall we go into the forest now?'

'Yes. Let's. Let's go to the forest.'

He sprang to his feet.

'Let's go. Right, the old forest starts here, the real maze. Some of the pines out there remember the times of Tsar Alexei Mikhailovich.[73] You'll see for yourself. True, we're sure to graze and scratch our legs, but it is miraculous there, Tanyusha. I've been there many times and know the terrain well.'

The tall grass lashed at their legs. The pathways petered out. They entered the enchanted woods as if it were a grotto, pushing aside the straggling branches of bushes. Despite the hot summer noon, they suddenly found themselves in a place that was cool and damp.

The tree tops had interwoven to form hundreds of dark vaults, and the entire expanse of the forest floor, despite lying in the shade cast by the trees, was thickly overgrown with grass and caressingly cool. The forest floor was soft and spongy and it must have taken the whitish blades of grass a long time to pierce its surface and break free, to eventually become green.

Deeper into the woods there was no sign of any paths; all around was a green wall of bushes and the looming posts of centennial black trunks. In one place there lay a pine, its timber much rotted, that had fallen many years before, with only its bark leaving a trace among the shrubbery and the young trees, while its top was lost in the dark mist ahead. The fallen pine was as thick across as a man would be tall, so they had to make their way around as if a wall had suddenly emerged.

....

[73]   Alexei Mikhailovich was the Tsar of Russia from 1645 until his death in 1676. His reign saw wars with Poland and Sweden, schism in the Russian Orthodox Church, and the major Cossack revolt of Stenka Razin. Nevertheless, at the time of his death Russia spanned almost 2,000,000,000 acres. He was the father of Peter the Great.

MIKHAIL OSORGIN

'Where are you, Vasya?'

'Right here next to you. I've got myself into such a jungle that I can't work my way out.'

'It's wonderful here, Vasya. What a forest! What a marvellous forest! Can you see me?'

'Your dress flickers occasionally but I cannot see your face.'

'I'd like to live here, Vasya.'

'You'd get bored. You'd be longing for the world outside.'

'The world outside, Vasya, is no picnic.'

'That will pass. It'll get better.'

'Do you really believe that?'

'How can I not? Look at the riches that we possess. This forest alone is something in itself. And in the north... ouch, I've got caught on a twig.'

'What were you saying about the north?'

'I was saying that in the north, where I lived when I was little, the forests are even better. They are coniferous and stretch for thousands of versts. I only have to remember those forests to realise that people, and all politics, and problems with accommodation, and those decrees and what not, are nothing but ridiculous.'

'Do you love life, Vasya? Aren't you afraid to be alive?'

Vasya's shirt emerged from the thicket.

'Well, Tanyusha, I'm completely stuck here. It's all because of the basket – something snags it all the time. As for life – how is it possible not to love it? I do love it. But I love you more, Tanyusha.'

'Don't start.'

'But I'm telling the truth. I can even put it this way. Wait, Tanyusha, don't move. I'll help you out of there in a moment. Listen to me for once. I swear on this forest, Tanyusha, I'm not asking anything of you but, if need be, I'll give my life for you. Just wait a minute, let me get it off my chest. I swear on this forest, if you ever need my help, well... whatever happens, do remember, Tanyusha, that I am your loyal friend, a friend forever, and that I will put up with anything for you, even death, Tanyusha, and even gladly. There. I really mean all of it, and I won't speak of it again.'

The branches stopped cracking and no birdsong could be heard.

'Vasya.'

'What?'

'Vasya, where are you?'

'I told you, I'm stuck.'

'Come closer.'

'I can't. The branches are all tangled, and something is pricking me.'

'Well, stretch out your hand.'

There was more cracking and then Vasya's large arm appeared out of the jumble of branches.

'Oh, Vasya, your hand is badly grazed.'

'It doesn't matter.'

'You poor thing. There, hold onto my hand.'

Tanyusha leaned against the shrubbery and reached Vasya's fingers with her hand.

'Got it?'

'Got it.'

'Don't pull or I'll tumble down. Vasya, dear Vasya, I've listened to everything you said and value it all a lot. It's myself I don't know yet. I feel good, here with you, but when we are back home in the city, I am always anxious. There are many things that I cannot grasp, things about myself. Don't judge me, Vasya.'

'How could I ever...'

'It's so hard, Vasya, so hard.'

'Oh yes, that is something I do understand.'

'Vasya, darling, you are my only real friend. So there. Now let go of my hand. We should find our way back out of this maze.'

The branches parted and Vasya, with his rucked-up tufts of hair, reached the tip of Tanyusha's finger with his lips.

'We'll find a way, Tanyusha. I did promise to help. We'll soon find a path through the forest. I will get you out, Tany-usha, never you fear.'

CONVERSATION NUMBER TWO

Astafyev warmed some water on his makeshift stove and cleaned the remainder of the flour and paint from his face. The mirror reflected a gap in the door, and in the gap, the swollen face of his neighbour, the proletarian Zavalishin.

'Stop snooping, Zavalishin, do come in.'

'Making yourself presentable?'

'I'm washing the flour off my mug.'

'Made yourself dirty?'

'Evidently. How's life?'

Zavalishin came in, warmed his hands by the stove, and said, clearly and confidently:

'Life's good. I'm raking it in.'

'At the same old factory?'

'Not the bloody factory. Nowadays, I'm in a totally different line of business. According to your advice and direct instruction, Comrade Astafyev.'

'I can't really recall giving you any advice. So, what is it, then?'

'Your instruction was to fight back, and even not to shy away from back-stabbing. "Otherwise, you'll perish, Zavalishin," you said, "they'll eat you alive." And so now, we fight.'

Astafyev looked at his neighbour with new curiosity.

'So how goes it, is it working for you?'

'Can't complain, things are getting better. I've even come over to offer you a treat, Comrade Astafyev, a thank you of sorts for your spread the other day. Unless, of course, you're too proud. Not moonshine, either, but genuine cognac, from before the war, two bottles.'

'So, you got it by villainy, you say?'

'Yes, sir. Human nastiness of the purest kind. Don't shun the offering, if you please.'

'How curious.'

'Don't you get more curious than that. Would you happen to have a couple of glasses to hand? I'll bring food to eat with it, smoked bacon and some other stuff, too.'

Astafyev looked at his neighbour with interest. The change in him was obvious. He was better, no, positively well-dressed, his former look of servile humility was gone, and yet he didn't quite give an impression of real confidence. He was putting up a front and throwing his weight around.

Zavalishin brought the cognac, of an inferior brand, but genuine stuff, distilled before the war. Out of his pack he pulled bacon, caviar and some dubious whiteish rusks. All of it an unquestionable luxury for the times. They moved the table closer to the stove.

Zavalishin filled their glasses half way.

'To your health, comrade scientist. My humble thanks to you for everything, for your guidance, for your advice – you did help this fool to see sense.'

'Still, Zavalishin, what is it you do nowadays? Do you go round stealing? Have you joined the holdup fraternity?'

'Goodness gracious me, of course not! I'm getting my wages for the dutiful discharge of my responsibilities.'

'Which is what?'

'Well, that is a secret matter, Comrade Astafyev. In a nutshell, it's work, the real thing. The job is mighty important, in the service of this Republic. But I can't be doing with idle chit-chat about it.'

'Oh, what the hell, just drink up then.'

They drank in silence, following their drinks with caviar and thick slices of bacon. Astafyev was hungry – a strong person needed a lot of food. Cognac warmed him up and shored up his strength. Zavalishin, on the other hand, quickly fell into a torpid state, but kept drinking, lapping up the alcohol. His face turned red from a rush of blood, the little eyes got even narrower and stared vacantly into his glass.

The moist timber crackled inside the little stove.

Sunk in his armchair, Astafyev forgot about his guest. His thoughts meandered: he was thinking about Tanyusha and their last conversation, but his train of thought was constantly being mixed up with stand-up witticisms, the vulgar verses with which he had been entertaining the crowd that day. He could also hear the piano: Tanyusha was playing Bach.

Astafyev gave a start at the sound of his neighbour slamming the table with his fist.

'Halt – don't move, you bastard...'

'What's wrong? Have you had one too many?'

Zavalishin raised his drunken stare.

'I don't... I don't want 'im to move.'

'Who?'

'I... just don't w-want...'

He giggled:

'That's just... no reason. You, c-comrade, don't worry. I can do anything, comrade.'

'Oh no, Zavalishin, far from it. Besides, you are weak, even if you seem a man of muscle.'

'Me, weak? It's me who's weak? I can kill someone easily, that's how weak I am.'

'Fancy that, to kill a person – a child could do it, especially when armed with a revolver. It takes no strength. As for you, that's your limit, you are not capable of more.'

'But what more is there?'

'To create something. Make something with your own hands. A cigarette lighter, for example.'

'I'm not a turner.'

'Well, plough a field.'

'No need. The peasants do all the ploughing.'

'And you, a proletarian, are now a master. Peasants do the ploughing and you eat the bread. You, Zavalishin, are good for nothing – you don't even know how to drink your cognac in the proper style – you are guzzling it like some cheap ethanol, and you get drunk as a fiddler after the first glass.'

'We chug it down the way we know how, Mister Astafyev. We never studied at your universities and never had no time for sipping. We just gulp it down. So there!'

He filled his glass up and downed it in one go but choked, and with shaking hands set about slicing up some food to follow it with.

Astafyev finished his glass and filled another, keeping pace with his neighbour, and lost himself in thought. His head was spinning pleasantly.

He was distracted by Zavalishin muttering.

Supporting himself with his arms against the table and resting his drunken head on his hands, Zavalishin was staring at his drinking companion with his little blinking red eyes.

'For such words we could send you down for good. For what you said about me being a machine. And peasants. Send you down or even mark you as redundant material.'

Astafyev screwed up his face in disgust:

'Chekist![74] If you are drunk, Zavalishin, take yourself off to bed. We'll finish tomorrow.'

'Tomorrow? Tomorrow I've got a day off. Something… something like a holiday. No urgent material for tomorrow.'

He started shaking again with drunk and apprehensive giggles.

....

[74] The All-Russian Extraordinary Commission, commonly known as Cheka, was the first of a succession of Soviet secret police organizations.

'Tomorrow no material, and whatever there was today, we did away with the lot. I, Zavalishin, was doing it. Bam – it's done and dusted.'

And then, banging the table once more with his fist he shrieked:

'I said stop pumping me. It's none of your business.'

He filled his glass with a trembling hand and downed it in one. The cognac burnt his throat. Zavalishin's eyes popped, and he gasped and tried to reach for something to eat, but suddenly collapsed and rammed his forehead against the table.

Astafyev got up, grabbed his guest by the collar, gave him a shake, tilted his face upwards and saw a pale face contorted with drunken horror. Zavalishin's teeth were chattering but his tongue was trying to speak. Astafyev picked him up firmly by the collar, propped him up, and hauled him towards the door.

'What a lump! Off you go now, you great hero!'

He dragged him as far as his room, hurled him onto his bed, lifted up his legs and arranged them. The drunken man was burbling something. Astafyev bent over and briefly listened:

'Oh my. Goodness gracious, where to... where are you taking me...'

Astafyev returned to his room, gathered the remainder of the food, an empty and a half-empty bottle, and took the lot into Zavalishin's room. Returning to his quarter, he opened the window, aired the room, and collapsed into his bed with the first book that came to hand.

THE PROFITEER

The carriages bumped against each other with a heavy ker-thud, and the train came to a halt. A route that previously never took more than twenty-four hours now claimed the best part of a week.

The train would linger at small stations and railways halts for hours or even days; the passengers would be driven into the woods to gather fuel for the locomotive; sometimes the carriages would be uncoupled and the passengers would be forced to change trains; at such times an entire crowd of grey people with sacks would rush clomping over the carriage roofs, thronging the platforms and, grunting and cursing, rush forward to take over new seats. One of those elbowing his way through the crush, struggling to drag his little case and sack full of shoddy wares, fighting over a place and hastily edging through, was Vasya Boltanovsky, an assistant at the university laboratory, the loyal knight of the house at Sivtsev Vrazhek.

He completely forgot when he had last washed himself. Like everyone around him, he would reach deep inside his shirt with his open hand to scratch his chest, shoulders and back – anywhere his fingers could reach – till they bled. He had only travelled on top of the carriage roof once; he usually managed to win a baggage shelf inside and then stared triumphantly from above at the jumble of human bodies below, at the travellers bonded together by their sleepless nights, the filth and the sweat, by abuse and witticisms about their own fate. The lucky ones slept on the floor – in the aisles and under the benches; the losers had to nap standing, shuddering at the jolts.

Closer to their terminus the carriages grew less crowded and the roofs cleared. Most of those with sacks got off and dispersed around the neighbouring villages. Vasya travelled further than most, reasoning he would get a better deal for his goods if he made it to more distant places. On the road he had made several friends among the more experienced peddlers for whom it was a second or even a third chaotic foray to procure bread and gruel.

Leaving the train behind, they broke into small groups, waited for the stragglers, smoothed down their clothes, arranged their sacks more comfortably, and set off in different directions.

Vasya's companions were two battle-seasoned women, both Moscow commoners, and a 'former engineer', as he introduced himself, dressed in a pair of good boots and semi-military khakis; the only defect was a ginger-coloured flat cap instead of a proper peaked one. He was often taken for a soldier and addressed as 'comrade'. Vasya felt particularly close to this man, readily admitting his authority and experience. The engineer's name was Pyotr Pavlovich Protasov. Despite being shabby, unshaven and half-asleep like the rest of them, he nevertheless had an amazing capacity for keeping his spirits up. He would engage in light-hearted badinage and tell everyone stories about his previous 'campaigns'; he knew where to find boiling water, how to appease the bickering, barter salt for tobacco; he would yield his place on a bench, temporarily, to those more tired than him and to women; and, during one lengthy stop he lent a hand to a novice stoker, thus helping resurrect the locomotive. He acted as an unofficial leader of the carriage, and treated Vasya, whom he called 'professor', with special tenderness and attention.

Engineer Protasov was about thirty-five years old. He was broad-shouldered, sturdy, healthy, friendly and gallant. He could find words to talk to anyone in a language that would be understandable to his interlocutor, and about things that they would find accessible. Passengers getting off the train always made sure that they would say goodbye to him; novices would fall under his patronage.

The little group made its way out of the station, and set off.

'Well, we've made it this far, but how will we manage on the way back, bulging sacks and all?'

'We'll think of something. Folks manage.'

'It's not too hard to make a trip one way – the trick is to make it back.'

'And breaking through the cordons[75] is no mean feat.'

'We'll work our way around them. It's too early to think about that. The first thing is to find some worthwhile trade.'

'My legs can't carry me anymore.'

'Don't worry, they will. We'll rest up in the forest.'

'Which means in the pouring rain.'

'We'll find a dry spot. Or perhaps someone will let us into their *izba*[76].'

'What sort of a life is this?'

'Still, it's better here than on board the train.'

It was true. They were taking in the fresh air, leaving the stifling fug of the carriage behind.

Along the muddy autumnal roads running by the water-logged fields they reached a small village where dogs and people alike met the intruders with suspicion. It was clear that this was no place for trading; but perhaps they could somehow manage to dry their clothes, warm up and do some asking around.

....

[75] Anti-profiteering cordons were military units brought in for spot checks in an attempt to stop the spontaneous forays of city dwellers into the country, ostensibly under the slogan of fighting profiteering.

[76] A traditional wooden hut in Russian villages.

Nevertheless, they did manage to gain entrance to an *izba*. Learning that the unexpected visitors were in possession of some tea, the owners became visibly more agreeable and, from their side, contributed a jug of milk and a generous hunk of bread. The bread was the real thing – tasty, filling, nothing like the stuff issued against ration coupons in Moscow. Several pinches of tea bought them a heated bathhouse and a promise of shelter for the night. They were in luck, as a good wash was essential.

For the first time that week, Vasya Boltanovsky could strip himself naked and, under the guidance of his experienced companion, spend a long time steaming the lice from his clothes and underwear. They put back on their clean garments and enjoyed a proper rest that night, oblivious to the bites of the bedbugs, which were by now seen as harmless and acceptable.

At the break of dawn they set off again, along the roads and overland, in search of some richer and thriftier peasants.

In the very first village, their female companions fell behind – having either succeeded in finding a good bargain or simply having decided that travelling in a group of four was not very profitable. Vasya fared well and got the ball rolling by bartering an old dress and a summer blouse of Tanyusha's for a small fortune – half a *pood*[77] of buckwheat! Protasov was quite complimentary about the deal. Tying his sack up, Vasya watched in horror as a young farm girl thrust her coarse red labourer's arms into the sleeves of Tanyusha's blouse, trying it on over her own old and filthy garment and pushing up her breasts with her clenched fists. Nevertheless, it was a start, and a good one at that – for Tanyusha's sake.

The men looked at the outsiders glumly but, even so, they started haggling over the engineer's boots, though he had

....

[77] The old Russian measure of weight equalling 16.8 kg.

no intention of selling them. They offered a pittance for the scythe and the whetstones – the haymaking season was still too far away. Vasya was curious about the provenance of a new unwhetted scythe in the engineer's possession. It turned out that he had obtained it through an institution where the rations often included various strange and unexpected items; still, the staff were quite happy to accept them – hoping for an opportunity to barter.

They decided to not stray too far away from the railway tracks. The biggest challenge was to find shelter for the nights, the locals being quite reluctant to take them in, forever mistrustful of strangers from the city. However, if someone did agree to accommodate them, the guests would be bombarded with questions – about Moscow, and the Germans, and prices, and what was going to happen now. The villagers had heard that the war had been aborted; but as for who was ruling over Russia now, whether it was true that the tsar had been taken away, and what it was that the Bolsheviks wanted – their ideas were quite vague and often far-fetched. Rumours about taxes excited more interest than politics, as well as whether there were any plans in place to requisition grain from the peasants, and whether the landlords[78] were going to be reinstated. They would listen to the answers with bated breath, but evidently did not put too much credence in the word of people from other parts, and so tended to interpret the strangers' words in their own way.

By the end of the fifth day the itinerant traders had their sacks full, having parted with blouses, stockings, chintz, carrot tea[79] and flake tobacco. In the last village Vasya sold the ornithologist's waders for a *pood* of white flour and a *pood* of

....

[78]   One of the very first decrees of the newly-victorious Soviet power abolished the private ownership of land.

[79]   For lack of any normal merchandise, tea was made out of whatever came to hand, even carrots.

millet – a transaction of which the engineer was sceptical and which he pronounced unprofitable. By now he himself was also laden with provisions. They decided to hire a dray that was heading towards the nearest station and pay their fare with paper money. This, too, worked in their favour – luck was on their side for this expedition.

When they made it out of the village, the dray's owner turned round to face his passengers, gave them a good once-over, ran a mental appraisal, and said to Vasya:

'The way I see it, you ain't fancy enough to be a toff but you don't look like a comrade, neither. So I'll call you "mister".'

Protasov asked him:

'And who do I look like?'

The peasant was reluctant:

'How should I know? You ain't from around here, you're a stranger. I guess you belong to the military estate.'

The cart was all the more appreciated because Vasya Boltanovsky, unaccustomed as he was to adventures of this kind, felt washed out; he'd even had a slight fever the night before.

The most difficult part was to load themselves and their sackloads of goods onto a train because it was, as had become usual, packed to bursting. They spent the first night inside the train station; the following day they were in luck, yet again – it took some doing but they did find a place, first on the coupling above the brakes and then on the platform between the carriages. At the station after that they were pushed deeper into the carriage by a new wave of sack people who had fought their way towards the gangway and even occupied the roof. Inside, it was hard to breathe and they were forced to travel standing. Still, since, against all odds, they had managed to get on board, they were thanking their lucky stars for that, too.

This time the train was going faster with no lengthy delays, and before the third day was out they were already in close proximity to Moscow – having successfully passed through the first cordon, and got off with only a tiny bribe. Vasya couldn't wait to be back home – he knew his strength was waning. To make breathing easier, the windows in the carriage were kept open, and Vasya was shivering, his entire body shuddering. By nightfall the shivering gave way to a fever, and, looking at his young companion, the engineer kept asking in a doubtful voice:

'What's wrong? You coming down with something? Maybe you caught some nasty bug or other?'

'It's nothing. If only we could get home sooner.'

In the immediate vicinity of Moscow, they ran into yet another anti-profiteer squad. Some blanks were fired, forcing everyone off the roof. The passengers in the front carriages were kicked outside and had all their sacks confiscated. However it appeared that having exhausted themselves with the initial effort, the squad decided to call it quits and let the others be. But the apprehended peddlers were determined to defend their goods by hook or by crook – they refused to let the sacks go, they shouted obscenities, they oscillated between flattery and bribery, they tried to huddle together and block access to the inside of the carriages, and hectically stashed their wares underneath the benches, under skirts, inside shirts. Vasya and his companion were fortunate yet again – they were travelling in the last carriage and the squad ran out of the time and energy required for a thorough search. After two-odd hours of delay the train finally moved on. Moscow, by now, was some five hours away. The major hazard – losing what had been procured, and at such cost – was behind them. Protasov was dispensing advice:

'When you get home, first of all, wash yourself properly, pick out the lice, drink as much hot tea as you can manage and then get straight off to bed. Better still, call a doctor, if you know one.'

Vasya felt really very ill. The stress of having to deal with the anti-profiteering force had left him incredibly weak. He slumped on his sack, looking like a sack himself. The throbbing in his temples was so loud that at times he didn't even hear the clanking of the wheels. His body, crawling with lice, was drenched in cold sweat.

'Everything I look at keeps sliding together and swirling around.'

'I bet it does,' the engineer was casting his fellow traveller compassionate glances. 'It looks serious, old boy. Good thing we're practically back in Moscow. We'll manage the sacks somehow, maybe we'll be fortunate enough to get a cheap carter.'

Rumbling at switches, whooshing at turning points, sluggishly, as if determined to waste time deliberately, heavily, weightily, spitefully, the train crept on towards Moscow.

Trying to warm himself up and look more buoyant despite the burning in his head, Vasya was thinking: *It doesn't look good for me, not at all. Still, what I'm carrying is a lot of good stuff. Tanyusha and the professor will now have it a bit easier.*

And he was also thinking, smiling a sickly smile: *I'll see her shortly, her... Tanyusha.*

THE 'STIFFS'

In the evening, Committee Chairman Denisov had warned the residents that those not in possession of a document confirming their employment with a Soviet organisation should present themselves at the militia station at three in the morning, and make sure to bring their own spades.

'You will be sent to public works.'

Nearly everybody had the requisite papers, and the industrial workers were exempt in any case. The Chairman dismissed two of those without proof of employment on his own authority: one for reasons of health (he was dying from typhus) and the other for reasons of a very advanced age. There were only seven of them left – three women and four men, one of the men being *privatdotsent* of philosophy Astafyev.

'As you know, I serve as a performer in workers' district clubs.'

But Denisov was obviously pleased by Astafyev's evident lack of prudence.

'Since you don't have the right papers, Comrade Astafyev, you must show up without fail.'

'But I only finish work late in the evening.'

'It's no concern of mine. If you refuse, it's my duty to report you, and you will be escorted there by force, and perhaps not allowed to come back; that will make it all the worse for you. Nowadays, Comrade Astafyev, no one treats the bourgeoisie with kid gloves. Be so kind as to show up by 3 a.m.; here's your assignment slip issued by the House Management Committee. You should get it signed once you report for duty and then return the slip to me. We will provide you with a spade. I am very sorry, Comrade Astafyev, but it seems you aren't the only one who's trying to shirk this duty.'

Astafyev knew that, had he really wanted to, he could wriggle out of it – Denisov didn't exactly enjoy a reputation for incorruptibility. But, having thought it over, he gave up on the idea: *I should go through this, too; after all, perhaps it's only fair.*

At three in the morning, the gate of the militia station remained firmly locked and by half past there was a large, motley crowd consisting of resigned men and women – most of them without spades. It wasn't easy to make out who all these people were, dressed in shabby mismatched clothes, but judging by their appearance, the majority were the designated bourgeoisie and intelligentsia. Two older men sported officers' overcoats, although misshapen, mangy and with civilian buttons. All in all, the crowd was dominated by senior citizens.

The gate opened at four. The functionaries let the crowd in, took away their assignment slips and entered their names on a list, grumbling somewhat that the number of spades brought along was clearly insufficient. Four guards were detailed to lead the crowd of about sixty.

At first they walked in order, passing along the unilluminated, unkempt, and still sleeping streets; later on they just plodded on in straggling groups. One couldn't just go and leave – their signed papers were to be returned to them only at their destination. When asked about the nature of the work, their guards, bleary and bad-tempered, snapped back that they didn't know themselves. Their orders were to deliver the crowd to the second verst beyond the outpost, to the roadside where the guards were to be replaced.

'Last night we took some folk to the Nicholas railway line.[80] They were assigned to clean the rails and sleepers. Today our order is to bring you somewhere else.'

A young woman, vivacious and jaunty – a commoner, judging by her accent – was garrulously telling all and sundry that this wasn't her first time on public duty, far from it, and that she was doing it of her own free will, covering for a friend practically for free. And today, most likely, they were not being taken to clean and repair the road but to bury the stiffs. The work itself, although disgusting, wasn't hard, and what you got paid for it in bread was quite reasonable, sometimes a whole pound in one go, and the bread was good, of the sort they would issue to soldiers.

Astafyev wasn't quite sure of the exact meaning of the word 'stiffs'.

After more than an hour they finally reached their destination where another detail of guards was waiting for them. It turned out that the place of work was right there, close by. They were told that there was no time for a respite – the lorries were on their way. A break would be announced later, once the bread had been distributed.

The crowd was lined up in the wasteland and told to dig a large hole. Those without spades were told to wait their turn and then replace the first shift.

Astafyev soon learned the meaning of the word 'stiffs', or rather worked it out for himself: it referred to cadavers. Answering their questions, the guards explained that they had to inter those who had died from typhus, as well as the dead arriving from various hospitals and railway stations.

Spring moistened the soil, and so they were making good progress, much as the diggers weren't really accus-

....

[80] Nikolayevskaya Railway Line was among the first lines in Russia, opened in 1851 and connecting Moscow and St Petersburg. The project was supervised by Emperor Nicholas I personally.

tomed to digging. The hole was not supposed to be very deep; the most important thing was for it to be quite wide. From among their own numbers there had emerged a few leaders who now took charge, snapping at others and even showing off their experience and the ability to boss everyone around.

By about six in the morning the first lorry had arrived; it slowly snored its way across the mud and finally came to a stop, practically flush with the edge. The first pit had by then been completed; another one was being dug nearby. Against the background of a pale, rainy dawn, four newly-arrived figures in aprons set about pulling out and tossing their horrendous cargo down into the pit –stiffs haphazardly covered with rags, or even completely naked 'stiffs'. Astafyev stood next to the pit, aware that it was becoming more and more difficult to breathe, and that the drizzle now felt neither fresh nor pure.

Another two lorries arrived after that. All in all, Astafyev estimated the total number of corpses to be about forty. The order was to cover each consignment sparsely with loose soil but to save the rest of the space for later. However, the first pit had by now been filled, so they had to erect a mound of sorts over it.

The old-timers were swapping opinions: 'A good rain will wash it all away.'

The diggers stared morbidly, frowning and avoiding eye contact; the women were coping better than the men, and whispered more among themselves. Only the fussy young woman, street-wise and practical, betrayed neither fear nor revulsion; she welcomed each successive lorry with a particularly lively interest, trying to get a peek inside it, getting in the way of those working, exclaiming in amazement and eager to explain:

'This lot is from the hospital again, or could be the railway station, the ones that come in carriages. Look, they're all naked, every single one of them! Their boots always get taken, even though they've died from typhus!'

The latest lorry never made it to the pit itself because its wheels became stuck in the churned mud. This one was accompanied by two guards in military helmets, the red stars on them prominent and trimmed with a black cord. Volunteers were called forth to unload it and promised an additional pound of bread.

'Otherwise we'll pick some folk out ourselves!'

Astafyev cast his gaze around the crowd, registered the distress on the darkened faces, and stepped forward first. The garrulous young woman was already bustling about by the lorry. Another two, dressed in altered military overcoats, were summoned by the guards:

'Don't be shy, these ones here aren't infectious, fresh as can be!'

The new stiffs presented a more horrible sight than the previous ones. Nearly all of them were fully clothed, although they wore no shoes, and their clothes were amply drenched in clotted blood. The command was to pull them off the lorry by their feet, and to be quick about it:

'Nothing to gawp at! A corpse is a corpse!'

Gritting his teeth, trying to avoid looking at the faces, Astafyev touched the first body. Through the grimy underwear his hands inadvertently came into contact with the slimy cold of death. He summoned all his masculine will, but his lips refused to arrange themselves into the habitual sceptical smile. He just couldn't shun the thought that this dreadful stiff had been a person, a healthy individual, possibly only an hour previously. He felt that he had known this man, couldn't help knowing him, that this pre-dawn victim of the great terror had belonged to his own circle, perhaps a university friend or an officer with whom he had been familiar.

As if in response to this thought, one guard remarked to another:

'These ones are mostly thugs.'

Suddenly, Astafyev became aware that his co-worker, the fussy young woman, was hoisting the dead body up by the shoulders while adroitly groping around, her hand thrust deep inside his tattered collar. Making out that it was too heavy for her to support, she lowered the body down for a moment, and inside her clutched fist glistened a gold chain with a cross. Fidgety, she lifted the body up again by its shoulders, whispered something, apprehensively searching Astafyev's eyes, and broke into a smile, as if he were her accomplice.

The guard cried out:

'You, over there, stop dawdling! You volunteered, so get going!'

And added a soft aside:

'Some lass. It's all the same to her, as if she's shoving bread inside an oven. She's even amused by it!'

Astafyev worked like an automaton; he dulled all his thoughts and all sense of time, no longer aware of either horror or revulsion. Hauling yet another stiff off the lorry, he mechanically kept count: 'three, five, six…' There were twenty-odd corpses, those underneath more gruesome than the ones on top, saturated in blood – their own and that of the others.

Astafyev's gait, as he walked from the pit towards the lorry, was sturdy and confident, his head raised high, his gaze directed straight ahead of him. The guards watched him with curiosity – a tall man, dressed better than most, belted at the waist, his pale clean-shaven face as if carved from stone. To the luck and good fortune of his fussy assistant, he served as a good distraction, diverting the guards' attention from her deft rummaging hands.

They were ordered to cover the pit with earth. Astafyev went back to fetch his spade, but as soon as he touched it he realised that his wrists and cuffs were sticky to the touch and burgundy-red in colour. He left the spade, stepped to one side, dropped to his haunches and, still overcome with the same dull indifference, started rubbing his hands clean against the soil and the sprouting young grass.

The world still existed. But the world was void, dead and senseless.

Astafyev wiped his hands dry on his handkerchief, tossed it aside, and went straight towards the road, bypassing by the guards and the lorry. As he walked past, the soldiers fell silent and stepped back. One at the flank did try to snarl, 'Where do you think you're going?' but never repeated his question. Another soldier interpolated: 'Leave it. It's knocking-off time, anyway.'

Astafyev reached the road and set off towards the city, never looking back. After about half a verst, he felt tired and slumped by the wall of a derelict little house that stood near the road.

An empty lorry puffed by with two soldiers onboard, soon followed by the labouring 'bourgeoisie', who by now were walking unguarded, in groups and alone, their steps heavy but hurried. Many of them were munching, as they walked, the recently handed out bread.

The brassy girl wasn't there among them. Astafyev spotted her in the distance, lagging behind by a long margin. She was walking by herself, hauling a spade over her shoulder.

And my spade was left back there, thought Astafyev.

He got up and walked towards the young woman. When they drew level, she felt visibly alarmed and tried to dodge him.

Astafyev came up close, grabbed her by the front of her vaguely masculine coat's collar with a strong arm, and hissed:

'Give it back. Give all those crosses back.'

The girl ducked and attempted to wriggle free but her eyes, much as she was trying to smile, were full of feral horror. She wheezed out in a shrieky whisper:

'What are you doing, my love? I ain't got nothing.'

'Do it,' repeated Astafyev. 'Or I'll do you in.'

With shaking fidgety hands, the woman started riffling through her pockets and pulled out four crosses, two of them on ruptured gold chains, and a ring.

Without a word, Astafyev frisked her pockets himself, shook out a kerchief, found two more crosses that had been worn next to the skin of their previous owners, hurled the ring back at her and, ignoring her wheezing lamentations, strode back, under the drizzle, towards the worksite.

The site was by now deserted; all that was left were the lengthy clay mounds and the shiny grooves left by the lorry tyres.

'And my spade has been nicked, too,' muttered Astafyev.

He came right up to the second filled-in hole and threw in the crosses that he had reclaimed. Then he thought a moment longer, and climbed on top of the mound, stomped the crosses deep into the ground with the heel of his boot, and with his hand raked fresh soil on top of them.

A non-believer, he didn't cross himself, didn't bless the grave, didn't bid them farewell. He turned around sharply and, watching his step, set off by the same road back towards Moscow.

'I KNOW'

The ornithologist was plainly missing Vasya Boltanovsky, who had gone on a food-finding mission more than a week earlier but hadn't been seen or heard of since.

'He ought to be back by now, don't you think, Tanyusha?'

'You know, Grandpa, you love Vasya more than me.'

'I don't know whether it's more or less but I do love him. He has a heart of gold, our Vasya, he really does. He is kind.'

Along came Poplavsky, a warm knitted cardigan peeping from underneath his old black frockcoat, his sodden galoshes left outside the door.

'I'll leave footprints all over your floor otherwise; my galoshes are leaking – I must get hold of some rubber glue from somewhere. What do you reckon, Professor, is anyone likely to pinch them from outside your door? You do have tenants, after all.'

Poplavsky, who used to stick to the subjects of physics or chemistry, nowadays didn't even brighten up on hearing the name of Einstein and his book, the rumours of which had just reached Moscow. They were discussing the theory of relativity behind the counter at the Writers' Bookshop, a provisional cultural centre for Moscow which the ornithologist had been frequenting in connection with his own trading affairs; a mathematical formula for Doomsday was pinned with a tack to the counter, in jest. Poplavsky himself was aware, of course, that the idea of 'luminiferous ether' had been discredited, but the thoughts of this as yet young professor were firmly occupied with matters totally disconnected from all of this. He, just like numerous others, was concentrating on sugar, saccharine, molasses and the insufficiency of fats. And on something else, too – the nightmare of terror that had already been unleashed.

'Haven't you heard? They shot another forty people yesterday!'

The pained ornithologist shook his head and tried to steer the conversation away from the subject of multiple deaths. The little villa in Sivtsev Vrazhek was protecting itself against the outside world, eager to live its life peacefully, just as it had been before.

At eight in the evening Eduard Lvovich came over, punctual as ever, although visibly emaciated and aged. His lopsided pince-nez kept sliding down his nose, adorned with a length of common twine that had come to replace the frayed black string.

At the next knock on the door (the bell, as everywhere else, was not working) Tanyusha sprang to her feet more hurriedly than usual and rushed to answer it. She returned animated, followed by Astafyev.

Over the course of several days recently, he had taken to calling frequently and staying for hours. At times, he would even outlast the ornithologist, who would retire to his quarters in good time and stay up reading in bed.

With Astafyev's assistance Tanyusha put on the samovar while the professor's teaspoon was already jingling inside his large cup. The old man loved it when his hearth attracted bright people whose company and conversation made the evening warm and cosy.

'Science must be protected. Generations will disappear but the light of science will stay. Science makes us proud.'

Poplavsky drank his tea silently and munched on rye croutons; he was starving. The conversation was being kept alive by Astafyev.

'Proud how, Professor? On account of our logic? Meanwhile, there are times when I believe that our studies, especially in the field of natural sciences, have led us astray – that is to say, veered us off the true path, the way of thinking in images. Primitive man thought pre-logically; in his perception, objects were part of each other, and that is why his world brimmed with mystery and beauty. We, on the other hand, have come up with *la loi de participation*, and the world has faded, has been stripped of its vibrancy and wonder. It goes without saying, this has been to our detriment.'

As was his wont, Astafyev continued stirring his unadorned tea with a spoon but when Tanya moved closer a little saucer piled with sugar, he replied:

'No, thanks, I've got my own.'

After which he pulled a tiny box out of his waistcoat pocket, and slipped a pastille of saccharine into his cup.

'Why do you refuse? We've got some.'

But Astafyev resolutely pushed the saucer back:

'Tatyana Mikhailovna, let us observe the good rules of economy, they are well-known by now.'

The professor said:

'It's imperative to synergise logical thinking with thinking in images.'

'No, Professor, it's impossible. The synthesis is missing. Let me refer, say, to Eduard Lvovich. He, for one, lives in the world of musical images; how can he possibly accept the logic of our modern times? It would be tantamount to reneging on art.'

Eduard Lvovich blushed, fidgeted a little on his chair, and murmured:

'I must admit I haven't q-quite understood you. Music hath its own laws, and its own logic, but it's not quite the l-logic you're t-talking about. Although I find it very hard to explain myself.'

The ornithologist gave Eduard Lvovich an approving nod and added:

'Me neither. Alexei Dmitriyevich, for some reason, I am also finding it hard to understand you. I can follow your argument, but as for you, somehow, I fail to grasp the essence of you. On the surface it should be easier for you – compared to anyone else – to accept and justify contemporary developments. Here you are, negating science and advocating savagery, a pre-logical way of thinking. Although, with you, it's all coming from the head, not from the heart. Our modern times, the times we live in, reject all that – culture and logic; as for modernity itself, it's nothing if not completely devoid of logic.'

'Quite the contrary, Professor, our modernity is nothing else but our stripped-down construct, pure mathematics, a learned puzzle. Logic and technology are the new gods that are replacing the ones that have been dethroned. And if they have no power to help us, it's not their fault; it doesn't obviate their sanctity.'

Tanyusha was listening to Astafyev and remembering, despite herself, other words, also spoken by him. Astafyev was contradiction personified. Why was he talking like this? For the sake of a paradox? Would he say something else entirely tomorrow? Why? And still, he seemed sincere. Or was it all an act? Why was he doing this… Out of despair?

She was listening only to Astafyev's words, not even trying to fathom their meaning. Enunciating loudly and distinctly, clearly speaking for speaking's sake, Astafyev carried on, reluctantly:

'The people I hate the most are pilots, drivers, and meter readers for gas and electricity. They totally disregard the fact that I find the noise of their propellers unsettling, much like the preposterous racket made by an engine that cannot be justified by any reason whatsoever. They burst into our lives uninvited, and all the time they consider themselves to be not simply within their rights but almost superior to the rest of us.'

'The people of the future.'

'Yes, they are branded with this horrifying mark – the people of the future. Overall, as we are talking about un-savoury characters, I prefer footballers. They are, at least, unquestionably cretinous and are aware of the fact. As for pilots and engineers, you can glimpse some intellect there, even if it has been maimed.'

Tanyusha shifted her gaze to Grandpa. The old man was listening to Astafyev with obvious displeasure, trying to sup-press the feeling of mistrust and dislike. It was nothing more than idle chitchat, and not even witty at that. It was nothing more than ill-judged tomfoolery, even if the conversation was touching on serious matters.

Why is he doing it? thought Tanyusha, vexed.

That night, Eduard Lvovich did not play, and left early. The ornithologist took Poplavsky to his room, eager to seek his opinion on the books culled for selling. Astafyev stayed on, now alone with Tanyusha.

'Why are you talking like this, Alexei Dmitriyevich? You go on, yet you do not believe any of it yourself.'

'It's because I believe neither myself nor anyone else any-more. You're probably right, talking is worthless. Although you do exaggerate somewhat; I am right about certain things.'

After a pause he added:

'Yes, it's silly. It looks like I've offended the Professor with my schoolboy arguments. All in all, I am bored both of think-ing and of talking. Besides, I've no idea what it is that I want.'

'I thought you were stronger than that.'

'Used to be. Not anymore.'

'Why is that?'

'It looks like I've miscalculated badly. It seems to me that you are partially to blame, too.'

'Me? Why me?'

Astafyev reached out of the armchair where he was seated and placed his hand on the sofa, next to Tanyusha's. Tanyusha threw a cursory glance at his large hand and involuntarily shifted away, just an inch.

'You do understand why, Tatyana Mikhailovna. At least, you should. I am not good at hiding my feelings, but then I'm not really trying to, although perhaps it's not very befitting. The main thing is, I don't have the words, I cannot even pronounce them properly... For example, don't you have a sense that I've fallen in love with you?'

It wasn't his first declaration. The first one had been back there by the gate. And it had been just as cold. Tanyusha answered quietly:

'I don't. Probably, you find me attractive and you are inclined to think this way. And yet it doesn't look like love.'

Astafyev smiled unpleasantly:

'What do you know about love, Tanya?'

Nobody ever called Tanyusha 'Tanya', and she didn't like this version of her name. Why was he...

Tanyusha raised her eyes and fixed Astafyev with a direct stare:

'Me? But I do know!'

It came out artlessly, just like that. And Astafyev felt that she was telling the truth – she did know. And that she knew much more than he, who, in his lifetime, had seen, loved and learned so much.

'I know,' repeated Tanyusha, 'and that is why I can comfort you; you don't really love me. Most likely, you don't love anyone. You simply can't. That's the way you are.'

'And you, Tanya?'

'I am different from you. I am both capable and willing. More's the pity that I don't have anyone to love. You? Perhaps I could. In the past, I could have. But when I'm with you I feel cold... frightfully so. There were moments, before, when it seemed to me... when it felt good. But these were just moments. After all, you yourself aren't always like this.'

'That's more or less what I thought,' said Astafyev. He slowly moved his hand off the sofa. The world had contracted, became drearier, and now Astafyev was genuinely miserable. He stayed silent.

Tanyusha added, as if speaking to herself, earnest and with not a hint of affectation:

'There was a time when I thought that I loved you. I was amazed by you, then. Nowadays I don't think so. Once you start thinking about it, it means – no. If I didn't have to think…'

Astafyev remained mute. Most likely, Grandpa and Poplavsky were about to return to the room. So Tanyusha asked loudly:

'Alexei Dmitriyevich, when do you have a concert in Basmanny District? Is it Wednesday or Thursday?'

Astafyev replied firmly:

'Thursday. It's always Thursdays with them.'

When the ornithologist returned, Astafyev got to his feet and bid his goodbyes.

On her way to bed, Tanyusha thought about many things: that she was about to run out of sugar for Grandpa, that she was free that Wednesday, that Eduard Lvovich looked peaky. She also thought about Vasya, since it was high time he should be back. She then thought that Astafyev was right, that logic was killing things: beauty, mystery, the fairy-tale-quality of things. She then took a look at herself in the mirror – dressed all in white, her arms bare, the plait of her fair hair let loose over her shoulders, her eyes tired and not loving anyone apart from her grandpa, and she buried her face in her pillow, so that dearest Grandpa wouldn't hear if, for some reason, she burst out crying.

THE MAN IN THE YELLOW SPATS[81]

As he drew level with Astafyev, the man in the yellow spats glanced fleetingly at his face, lingered for a moment and then quickened his step and swerved over into the first side street.

Whether it was his gait or his eyes, Astafyev had a feeling he looked familiar. On the other hand, these days there were a lot of faces just like that around; outfits, too – a cross between an army uniform and a civilian suit.

Once home, Astafyev set about attending to the business at hand: he had to clean his tiny wood stove – an efficient contraption that was flat, had a corrugated bottom and, whilst producing good heat, required little fuel; he also had to inspect the iron pipe threaded through the upper section of the window pane for taking off the smoke; then attach empty condensed milk cans underneath the fastenings and gener-

....

[81]   Reference to Boris Savinkov (1879–1925) – a Russian writer and revolutionary. As one of the leaders of the Fighting Organisation of the Socialist Revolutionaries (SRs), he became involved in the assassinations of several high-ranking imperial officials in 1904 and 1905. After the Bolsheviks disbanded the Constituent Assembly that had been instituted to introduce a multi-party government in the wake of the October Revolution of 1917, he declared his resolute intention to fight Bolshevism. During the period described in the novel, Savinkov was frequently seen in Moscow – in disguise or without it, and often recognised, and therefore numerous rumours circulated in connection with political assassinations that he was believed to be plotting. The yellow spats, as is explained later, could be one such attempt to distract attention from his face.

ally start getting ready for the winter – it would get bitterly cold very soon. He had no firewood as yet, but was certain it would materialise from somewhere; if push came to shove, he might turn to his neighbour Zavalishin for help – he was a scoundrel, of course, and a Chekist, but what the hell.

Someone knocked at the front door. With his soot-smeared fingers Astafyev unfastened the door chain and turned the key in its lock. All those complicated locking and bolting devices had been installed by Zavalishin who had recently turned into an obvious coward, possibly fearing for the safety of his provisions and bottles.

'Comrade Astafyev?'

'Yes, that's me,' replied Astafyev. The man on his doorstep was the same one, the one in the yellow spats.

'May I talk to you... for a minute?'

Despite himself, Astafyev took a step back.

'You may, of course, but... pardon me... aren't you really... who are you?'

'Let's move into your room, Alexei Dmitriyevich,' said the newcomer under his breath. 'Well, how are you? Which door is yours? This one?'

'Yes, this one.'

Astafyev showed his guest inside, but even before any formal greetings had been exchanged, he went back into the corridor, approached Zavalishin's door, and listened carefully. He gave the door a gentle rap and, in the absence of an answer, pushed his neighbour's door open a crack. Zavalishin was out. Astafyev shook his head.

'Well, that's lucky. One can never be too careful.'

His guest was waiting patiently, still wearing his coat, and still on his feet.

'Have you recognised me at last?'

'I have, of course, although you're... an astonishing actor. You may speak freely, no one else is home and the door's chained. Why these odd-looking spats? They do catch the eye.'

'That's why I am wearing them – so that it's the spats that attract attention, not the face. The more something is obvious, the less it is noticeable.'

'So you simply roam around Moscow, just like that? Practically without make-up? You'll get caught, my dear fellow.'

Although they were alone, he kept navigating around his guest's real name.

'Sooner or later I shall. Preferably later. Look here, Alexei Dmitriyevich, you're not a timid sort, tell me straight up: can you put me up until tomorrow morning?'

'It's that bad, is it?'

'It is. Nowhere else to turn.'

'In which case, I can. That's why I'm asking if it's an absolute emergency – my apartment isn't a perfect choice for you. I'm the only bourgeois element in the entire house and my tenant is a Chekist of sorts, although he's mainly a drunk. Come to think of it, he's rarely home during the day, and not always at night, either. Do you think it's an acceptable arrangement?'

'Not at all, but if you consent, I'll still stay the night, seeing as I've got no choice. It would be good to make sure that your Chekist never claps eyes on me.'

'I won't let him in. Besides, he doesn't strike me as a curious type, and as I have said, he's a confirmed alcoholic. As for his evil doings, he is my disciple and even argues that it was me who set him on the wrong path.'

'But could anyone search your place? Everywhere you look, they are doing mass searches, entire houses at times.'

'Hardly. Our house is mostly populated by working-class families. Although anything is possible.'

'Definitely. So, I've got your consent?'

'Take off your coat. My daily bread is of questionable quality but will do as a chaser for a drink or two.'

'Sure, that's always important.'

318

They cooked together, working as a team. The man in the yellow spats produced a hunk of pork fat, Astafyev unearthed some groats. The resulting dinner was quite delightful.

'When he comes home, this Chekist of yours, it would be better if we didn't talk at all. I'll go to bed; I'm devilishly starved of sleep.'

'Well, this would be rather excessive. I do get visitors. Speaking of which, did you bump into anyone in the courtyard?'

'There was this one man, with his moustache curled up, and a smarmy mug of a salesman.'

'An upturned moustache? That will be Denisov, the Committee's chairman. Not so good. On the other hand, it's too soon to worry: how would he know who you are?'

'Well, let's hope so. You know, Astafyev, I'm indebted to you. You're a good sort, that's why I've sought you out. But didn't you recognise me in the street?'

'I paid no attention. I did spot you, though, as you overtook me.'

'I was reluctant to go in at the same time as you. I walked up and down the street three times, in the hope of meeting you.'

'Why?'

'No reason, for good luck.'

'Are you always in luck?'

'Not so much these days, Astafyev. Not really. But it does look as though our luck will turn soon.'

Astafyev smirked:

'If you mention luck, it probably means its echo will be resounding all over Moscow, or even Russia. But what of it? I'm not nosy.'

They had a bite to eat, and then spent another half an hour chatting, remembering their earlier encounters both in Russia and abroad, as well as the friends they had shared back in the days before the first revolution.[82] By now, very few of them were still alive or not on the run.

'You have immersed yourself in science, haven't you, Astafyev? A total departure from the past.'

'Yes, it's impossible to stay a militant if you don't believe in anything.'

The eyes of the man in the yellow spats receded deep underneath his eyebrows, and he said, slowly and deliberately:

'Well, there are few real believers among us nowadays, and those who are tend to be half-wits and simpletons. That's not the point, Astafyev. It's imperative to have something to live for, and to be able to die for it: you can't live for the sake of a bowl of fetid cabbage soup, drag your feet and console yourself with verbosity. If you've got to perish, let it be at least… You know what, I'm ready for bed. Where would you like me to bed down? Wherever it is, I'm not taking my clothes off.'

At the crack of dawn Astafyev, who had been sleeping in the armchair extended with two additional chairs – he had yielded his bed to the guest – was woken by footsteps echoing against the asphalt of the courtyard. He got up, went to the window and realised that the apartment in front of his was brightly lit, with silhouettes of soldiers with rifles dawdling downstairs. It looked like a search. A shadow in a peaked cap flashed across one of the windows, then another

....

[82]   The Revolution of 1905, also known as the First Russian Revolution, was a wave of mass political and social unrest that spread through vast areas of the Russian Empire. It included worker strikes, peasant unrest, and military mutinies. It led to constitutional reform, including the establishment of the State Duma (the lower house of parliament), a multi-party system, and the Russian Constitution of 1906. Some historians contend that the 1905 revolution set the stage for the Revolution of 1917, and enabled Bolshevism to emerge as a distinct political movement in Russia whilst still a minority.

MIKHAIL OSORGIN

silhouette appeared, this one belted with a sash. Yes, it was definitely a search.

Looks like he's finally run out of luck completely, thought Astafyev.

He was thinking this with his usual sneer, but soon found himself inadvertently trembling with nerves. Then it occurred to him: *We will both be held responsible. Even so, it might still be a random search in that apartment alone.*

Against the illuminated frame of the window, figures kept popping up and disappearing. Astafyev sat for a long time, watching; lighting a cigarette, he tried to make himself return to his armchair, but the window drew him to it. Another half an hour later the windows on the floor above flared up, and Astafyev felt his feet turning cold: *Looks like it's a full-blown raid. Which means I'm done for.*

His apartment was upstairs but the communal entrance led into this courtyard. However, as far as one could see without throwing the window fully open, guards had been placed in all passages and by all entrances.

Shall I wake him up? Or let him sleep some more?

It didn't look like such a good idea to wake him; there was little point in getting all steamed up in unison. There was no way to get out of the apartment, in any case. Perhaps the raid would be aborted before they got to them.

Quietly pushing his armchair towards the window Astafyev watched intently as the third floor, the last one, lit up too. He recalled: *No one lives on the ground floor, and that's why it's in darkness; most likely they came in and then went straight out again as there was nothing to look for. So now they'll go to a different entrance. Which one?*

The search on the top floor was dragging on and on. By now it was completely light outside and the shadows in the courtyard had assumed the tangible forms of soldiers in khaki overcoats. They were sitting around, slumped on the entrance steps and directly on the asphalt, by all evidence completely exhausted.

They are taking their time looking, which means they are after supplies, not people. A regular house-to-house raid. However, they are guaranteed to take away a person without a residence permit... along with the room owner. Does he have any kind of papers? Still, once they lay their mitts on him, they'll identify him straight away. What a tasty morsel for the Cheka!

Boots started stamping in the courtyard and a small crowd of leather jackets emerged from the entrance. It was a horrifying moment and Astafyev's heart flew into his mouth.

The group of people milled about briefly, then moved to another entrance, in front of Astafyev's window.

A new reprieve. This time, the final one.

In the second entrance the windows were lit up on two floors at once, then on the third floor, and nearly straight away on the fourth. It looked like the search party had split in two and was making better progress. The soldiers in the courtyard were dozing where they sat, their rifles parked in their laps.

Astafyev stopped counting the minutes and half-hours. Tense anxiety had replaced itself with exhaustion: *It's all the same now. The only thing left is to wait.*

He smoked continuously, his eyes shut and his eyelids only fluttering upwards at the sound of steps in the courtyard and fragments of the soldiers' loud exchanges. By now, the morning light was merging with the blaze of the lit-up windows. The sky was turning pink. The cigarette was finished and Astafyev began drifting off. It had been about three hours since the first alarm, or possibly more. However, wasn't it all the same?

Yet again, the stomping of feet downstairs made him jump up and come to the window. From behind the curtain he spotted the same group of people, now in the centre of the courtyard. The group was joined by the previously dozing soldiers. It wasn't possible to make out the subject of the conversation but it was obvious that some sort of conference was taking place. Presently a group set off towards Astafyev's entrance, while some of the soldiers retreated, gesticulating with their hands in a disappointed fashion.

There immediately followed the booming sound of steps climbing the staircase.

Looks like it's time to wake him up.

Astafyev went into his second room, its corners all filled to overflowing with books, for that was where his guest was sleeping.

'I say, time to get up!'

He tried his shoulder to shake him into wakefulness. His guest was fast asleep, worn out by too many sleepless nights. All he did in response was mumble. Astafyev thought: *Come to think of it, what's the use? He's got nowhere to flee. I'll wake him when there's a knock on the door. For now, they're one floor below and we're on the third.*

He was now completely in control, overcome with a peculiar tragic calm. Once again, he wasn't a petty townie but a philosopher. With a crooked sneer he glanced at the pallid face of the sleeping man in the yellow spats, whipped around, saw his own face reflected in the dull mirror, smoothed his hair, lit another cigarette, and went out into the hallway.

He didn't have to wait for long. There was another burst of heels clomping against the steps and the sound of people climbing up, chattering loudly.

Hearing a fist drumming on the door of his flat, Astafyev did not flinch. He took a deep drag on his cigarette and remained where he was, by the door.

Behind the door was a hubbub of voices. Astafyev could discern them clearly:

'It can't go on like this, comrade. The men are falling off their feet. Besides, it's daytime already.'

'Fine, this is the last one and then we'll call it a day.'

Another raucous bout of banging, and then another voice:

'Dead to the world, aren't they? Cannon shots won't raise 'em.'

They are about to kick the door down, thought Astafyev. *I've got to wake him up.*

Behind the door several more voices piped out, now louder than before:

'Enough, comrade, it's a job for another day. Two nights running… that's no way to… it ain't human.'

Astafyev hurled the cigarette butt away and put his ear to the door. The murmur behind was growing in volume. Finally, somebody's voice, harsh and shrill, snapped irritably:

'Fine, devil take you. About face! You can't even do one entrance thoroughly. You've gone all limp on me, like little old ladies, the bloody lot of you. There'll be nothing for us here tomorrow, it will all have been tidied up.'

Back came the retort: 'We're not work horses, you try working like that, why don't you…'

But heavy heels were already thundering downwards. And just when Astafyev was about to take his ear away from the door, he was nearly rendered deaf by a new blow of a fist against the door. And the same shrill voice hollered peevishly:

'Hey you, take this one for the road. Asleep, aren't they? Bloody bourgeoisie!'

Pulling a new cigarette out of the box with trembling hands, Astafyev listened to the echo of running boots dying away down the stairs. Slowly turning round, he locked eyes with the man in the yellow spats:

'It looks like there has been some unpleasantness, Alexei Dmitriyevich?'

Astafyev blew out a ring of smoke:

'Quite the contrary, everything's safe and sound. Did you have a good sleep?'

'A perfect sleep. You, however, are not a bad actor yourself.'

'That seems to be my current profession. I believe they've now left for good.'

The man in the yellow spats reciprocated:

'Let's hope so. By the way, yesterday I forgot to forewarn you, Astafyev: I won't surrender myself without a fight, nor will they take me alive. It makes no sense.'

'I do understand,' said Astafyev. 'And I see how it is. But for now, you can put your plaything back into your pocket.'

He added, bursting into laughter, sincere and light-hearted:

'Still, it's worked out a treat! You're definitely in luck. What would you say to a cup of carrot coffee? It's not a good idea for you to leave here, not just yet. Do you know how to start a kerosene stove?'

THE LOYAL KNIGHT

Answering the knock, Tanyusha opened the door and saw a stranger with two large sacks, the sacks hooked together with a belt slung over his shoulder. The visitor was wearing a paramilitary uniform and a *pince-nez* – a typical member of the intelligentsia, now leading a much more down-to-earth existence.

'Well,' he said, 'I think there can't be any doubt. You must be Tatyana Mikhailovna.'

'Yes, that's me.'

'Here you go then, I've got a parcel for you: some flour, groats, a bit of this and that. This is the first consignment; I'll bring the rest later – too heavy to do it all at once. I've been instructed to deliver it all to your place.'

'Who was it that instructed you?'

'I've been told to say, "This is from the loyal knight".'

Tanyusha brightened up and immediately became concerned:

'From Vasya? Where is he, Vasya? Is he back?'

'He's back alright, we arrived together, only he didn't have such a good journey. He's ill. If you ask me, seriously so. Must have caught something on the way.'

Sweet Vasya, her best friend and knight was ill!

Tanyusha invited Vasya's companion in.

The visitor swung the sacks down off his shoulders, and introduced himself as Pyotr Pavlovich Protasov. Then he added:

'I used to be an engineer. But nowadays I rather seem to specialise in barter.'

He explained how Vasya had held it together until the very last moment, but as soon as they reached the railway station in Moscow, he had gone to pieces, not only unable to drag his sacks towards their hired cart, but barely able to make it there himself. Protasov had taken him home, made him undress and wash, after a fashion, and taken away his clothes to steam and clean them.

'There's a good oven in my apartment, one that's fitted with a boiler. A nice stash of firewood, too. Everything's to hand. I live like a bourgeois.'

'So where is Vasya now?'

'At home. He told me to bring you these bags. I have inspected the bags, of course, lest there should be some nasty infection left on them.'

'Do you believe he has typhus?'

'To be quite frank with you, yes, I'm afraid so. He needs a doctor. I am counting on you, Tatyana Mikhailovna – that is, if you're not afraid of infection. Camp fever isn't transferred by air, of course, but still.'

The engineer was watching Tanyusha with a confident smile on his face – this sort of girl wouldn't be afraid.

'Goodness gracious, but of course I'll go over to his place, straight away. And I know a doctor who lives nearby, here, in the Arbat. I'll take him to Vasya's. He has always treated Grandpa.'

'Perfect. So you make haste and I will go home.'

They agreed that Vasya's companion would drop by in a day or two, by all means, say, tomorrow evening. And great thanks for the sacks.

'As I said, I'll bring the rest tomorrow.'

'You must be tired after your travels?'

'A bit. But I'm like a cart horse. I'm used to it all, I don't tire easily.'

They were chatting as though they had known each other for ages. Protasov must have been about thirty-five; he hadn't shaved for some time and looked frayed around the edges, although he must have had time to change. His animated face was radiating kindness. He addressed Tanyusha as if he were talking to someone much younger, but still, there was a chivalrous respect.

'I recognised you as soon as I saw you.'

'How's that?'

'He told me, "Go there and knock on the door, she will most likely answer the door herself – Tanyusha, Tatyana Mikhailovna."'

'In which case, it wasn't all that hard.'

'But he also added, "She is an amazing girl, one of a kind." And that's how I recognised you straight away.'

Tanyusha felt embarrassed.

'That's Vasya for you. Such an eccentric.'

All the same, it gave Tanyusha pleasure to hear these words uttered by a total stranger, especially offered without affectation, easily, with a kind smile.

'You've become friends, travelling together?'

'We have. He's a nice fellow, a really good sort. He's quite an idealist but that's good.'

'Vasya is a wonderful friend. You must be a good friend yourself; look how much you've helped him.'

The engineer answered simply:

'It's really not a burden. I'm durable, and I've been around the block.'

They parted company at the Arbat by the doctor's house. Tanyusha insisted that Protasov should come along the very next evening, right after dinner.

'Grandpa will be very happy to see you. He loves Vasya very much and has been missing him dreadfully. You'll tell him all about your adventures.'

After they had gone their separate ways, Tanyusha thought: *What a pleasant person! Exceptionally so. Such a gentle smile, so tactful and so full of life... As if nothing has happened. And he has taken such good care of Vasya!*

The engineer strode homewards, rubbing shoulders that were tense from the weighty bags. He was thinking about his own affairs and obligations... But a smile lingered on his lips, a reminder of an affable encounter.

Vasya Boltanovsky stayed in bed.

His room, once so familiar in all its outlines, had now lost its former sharpness: the angles were washed out and filled with an oscillating mist, the window kept jerking and burning his eyes with excessive brightness, the etching on the wall facing the bed floated around, suspended in space.

Especially awkward and vexatious was his pillow; Vasya's head just couldn't find a comfortable position. The pillow pressed on the back of his head like a stone, and it kept settling itself at a wrong angle, sliding down. The pillow would suddenly upend itself and tickle him with its corner, creep over his head and make it difficult to breathe, steal underneath his shoulder and project his whole body upwards. The blanket was too thick but nevertheless failed to keep his feet warm, and Vasya, suffocating from the heat and stuffiness, endlessly tried to grope for its edge with chilled and shaky feet and snuggle underneath. The room was filled with a din reminiscence of the clamour of train wheels, and each stroke painfully echoed in his temples and the left side of his body. He was desperately thirsty but the carafe of water Protasov had left on a little bedside table had shifted back unattainably and was teasing him from afar, bouncing back even further from his outstretched hand.

Closing his eyes, Vasya felt his chest rise up to the very ceiling and slide down, swinging gently around as if carried by waves, making things murky and causing nausea. That was why he couldn't sleep. Also, he was bothered by a crowd of outsiders thronging the bench on which he was trying to settle, along with his sacks, even if the bench was too narrow and short for him. It was weird that the train kept switching from one set of tracks to another, although Vasya remembered perfectly well that he had already arrived at the Moscow station and had had time to take his clothes off. He tried in vain to force his way through a crowd of people with sacks; he was looking for a bag of groats, an object of exceptional value since it had been procured in exchange for the professor's waders. The ornithologist was irate and stamping his feet – Vasya had never seen him like this. It became clear that Vasya was now wearing the waders himself, and that was why his feet felt so horribly cold; the waders were proving impossible to pull off; then again, there was no time: all vacant seats in the carriage must have been taken by now, and Protasov would leave without him. *The good thing is*, thought Vasya, *that at least I've asked him to deliver the bags to Tanyusha's; otherwise, I'd have to wait till someone drops in and makes a telephone call to her. If what I've got is typhus, I think I should have my hair shaved off.*

These words had unexpectedly reached Vasya's ears, and he guessed: *I'm delirious! It was me who said this just now. This must mean I'm really very ill.*

Opening his eyes, Vasya realised that it had grown dark. However, the room boomed just as it had done earlier, though perhaps that was an automobile going down the street. With an enormous effort, Vasya raised himself, finally reached the carafe of water and started drinking in huge gulps, his teeth chattering against the glass. The water made him bitterly cold, as if his chest and stomach had been wrapped with an ice compress, but his feet became somewhat warmer, and his head cleared up a touch. The bottom of the carafe forcibly hit the wooden plank of the table, and Vasya's head lolled back onto the pillow.

'Yes, I'm very ill. Very, very ill. Someone should help me.'

'Someone' could only be Tanyusha. No one else cared about Vasya one little bit – neither the other tenants, nor the landlady, nor his friends. Besides, all of them would be afraid of contagion.

The shivers caused Vasya feverishly to try to wrap himself in the blanket. His temples began thudding again, and the headache by now was pure torture. His dense and implacable pillow started its restless prancing all over again.

And so it felt really pleasant when his forehead was touched by a cold hand, and an unknown male voice spoke:

'Of course, he's got a burning fever. No doubt about that. He should be taken to a hospital but where could one send him nowadays? They're all packed to the gills.'

The words failed to register in Vasya's consciousness, but there came another voice, now beautifully familiar, no doubt belonging to Tanyusha, that momentarily soothed him and filled him with joy.

'What should we do then, doctor? Can't he stay here, at home?'

'He'll have to, of course. But who will look after him?'

'I could.'

Surely, surely, it was her voice! Vasya lay still, as if smothered with caresses. In an instant he forgot about the knobbly pillow; his body became warmer and the headache receded. For all that, he did not care to open his eyes – let the dream last awhile.

'Well,' said the doctor. 'How will you cope? What's needed is a professional nurse. Typhus is no joking matter.'

'I'll cover the days, and we'll find a night nurse somewhere.'

'I could probably find you a nurse but what about paying her? You could pay her in groceries, perhaps– some nice flour or whatever. I know this one lady, she's experienced, used to be on the hospital staff, her husband was a doctor. Only we should examine him, and give the room a proper going-over. Did you say he had recently returned from travelling?'

'He arrived back just this morning.'

'That's the point – there's hardly been time to prepare the room properly. We must be careful. So, what, you'll stay on for now?'

'I will. Tell me, doctor, what should I be doing?'

'Doing? I'll have to find what's needed. The pharmacies have got zilch to offer, but they won't sell anything to a private individual anyway. I'll get what's needed myself and bring it over. You'll have to spend a couple of hours alone with him.'

'I'll stay for however long it takes.'

Vasya heard their voices, aware that they were discussing him, and that Tanyusha was one of them. He knew it all and felt ill and happy. There really was no need for Vasya to know and understand anything else.

'Vasya, are you in pain?'

He opened his eyes briefly and saw the familiar sweet shadow; he smiled, and, all over again, sank into longed-for oblivion and tranquillity. The loyal knight felt content; Vasya was asleep. But for his face flushed with fever, Vasya might be taken for a healthy and gratified person, peacefully asleep.

And thus, a minute passed, or possibly an hour, or an eternity, until Vasya's sleep was frustrated, all anew, by his hard and misbehaving pillow.

But this time somebody's strong arm was there, curbing and suppressing the pillow's mischief. And there was a voice, whispering:

'Vasya! My poor knight! My poor, poor Vasya!'

CONVERSATIONS

A manhunt was announced in Moscow. They were trying to track down that inveterate member of the Socialist Revolutionaries, the old terrorist. He was, undoubtedly, somewhere nearby. It was established that he wasn't simply visiting his acquaintances but had audaciously delivered a lecture on the situation in the south[83] in front of a group of intelligentsia. At the gathering in question, the old militant had worn yellow spats.

A certain individual, who might possibly be an Armenian, in a round astrakhan hat and a brightly-coloured vest underneath his wide-open overcoat, was holding a quiet conversation with a swarthy girl in a kerchief; they were standing by a parapet on the embankment of the Moskva River.

'I am well informed about all of this, of course; that's exactly why I've converted myself into a humble Armenian. They are all chatter-boxes, those fellows. Would you like to know what happened to my spats? I personally sold them in Smolensky Market. I badly needed the money and spats are always in demand.'

As they parted, the Armenian gave the girl's little hand a firm shake.

....

[83]   The Civil War was raging all over the country, and in various areas, particularly in the south – in Crimea and around the city of Odesa – various foreign powers were alternating in gaining and losing control over various provinces. On recapturing temporarily annexed territories, the Soviet state subjected them to mass terror.

'Well, my dear, farewell. Or perhaps we'll see each other again some time. Miracles do happen. Let me kiss you. Now, go and don't look back.'

She was about to move off when he stopped her again.

'Wait a minute, my friend. In case of misfortune, or if something out of the ordinary should happen – you do remember the address? That's where you should deliver a note.'

'Yes, I remember everything.'

'Do you believe in God? Me neither, but in my own way I'll pray for you. For our success!'

When she had disappeared around the corner, the Armenian pulled down his hat, buttoned up his coat and set off towards the Trans-Moskva District.

The rumour of the attempted assassination swept round Moscow like bush fire, igniting fear and hope in its wake. No one had any doubts that this whole affair had been instigated by the man in the yellow spats. And equally no one had any illusions that many people would now be held to account for the attempt; those who had nothing to do with this conspiracy, not even remotely.

The whispers had it that when the soldiers had lined up in a shed and aimed their guns at the breast of a certain slender Jewish girl, one of them had collapsed in a fit of hysterics, causing them all to misfire, and the wounded prisoner had been finished off by a shot to the head from a Colt, fired by a former factory worker currently employed at the Lubyanka, a confirmed alcoholic and a dependable operator. Such rumours abounded – grotesque, anxious, true and whimsical – and Moscow had shrunk into itself and was lying low, waiting for even more terrible things to come.

It did not have to wait for long.

The greengrocer, who was friends with the ex-caretaker Nikolai (caretakers had ceased to exist), found his situation was slowly improving. Clearly, there wasn't even the remotest chance of being able to bring a barrowful of produce fresh from the gardens around Moscow directly to the market in the Arbat Square, as he used to in the old days. These days, one had to trade covertly, on the sly, perpetually glancing over one's shoulder. However, carrots, cabbages and turnips weren't something that could be requisitioned, dumped into a God-forsaken shed and then distributed, little by little, against ration cards on behalf of the entire nation. This particular trade required skills and expediency. That was why the suburban gardens were flourishing while some of the most enterprising elements had even taken spades to their orchards. It was hard to keep track of all these goings-on, however, since folks nowadays were all guided by degraded morals.

The greengrocer was narrating all this in the minutest detail to Nikolai in the course of a conversation that was taking place in the caretaker's lodge by the townhouse in Sivtsev Vrazhek.

Nikolai was in agreement:

'Folks nowadays are nothing but thieves and knaves. Take a dog, say – even a dog knows what's what, what can or shouldn't be done. But nowadays people are eager to nick whatever's going, as soon as you take yer eyes off it. Or even if you've got your eyes on it.'

'All that started in the war.'

They proceeded to discussing politics and voicing their hearty condemnation of shag tobacco:

'It's like wood shavings these days.'

'Hear, hear.'

'No real kick to it.'

The air in the lodge was heavy, thick, flavoursome and cosy.

The greengrocer, Fyodor Ignatich, in his capacity as one who was streetwise and well-informed, described the current goings-on.

'Word is that, yet again, Christ knows how many folks have been shot. Some, maybe, for a reason – thieves, or, say, burglars, or bandits. But many got shot for nothing at all, except to give us the shivers, to chill the spine.'

Nikolai concurred grimly:

'One shouldn't kill nobody. If there's a need, drag 'im to trial. And then let some go, and send the others off to do hard labour, for the purpose of moral correction. Thou shalt not kill.'

'Just like I'm saying, if, for example, it's for a good reason. But here they've just nicked 'em, kept 'em inside for a while, and then gone and shot the lot as a warning to everyone else. If, say, some of 'em were old fellows, what 'ave they done wrong? Or a boy, for example, what good did that do? And one size fits all. And this little kid here could've become a man, and a damn good man at that, better than most.'

'It's the worst thing of all, to kill a child. You don't get forgiveness for that.'

'Just what I'm saying. There's this lady, I used to deliver cabbages to her. Her son was taken away and finished off; the lad wasn't even seventeen. There were those lists, and folks got taken away according to the lists. But it looks like they didn't do nothing wrong.'

'What animals,' Nikolai said darkly.

'Worse, seeing as there's no use in 'em.'

'What use can a murderer be? He who lives by the sword shall perish by the sword.'

'And they can't organise a thing. Say you need to buy somethin'; where can you go, nowadays? But Moscow used to be nothing if not rich!'

'Plundered the lot.'

'Just what I'm saying. Look who's in charge now? This soldier of yours, Dunyasha's brother, Andrei the deserter.'

'Andrei is no more.'

'Got 'imself kicked out?'

'Did a runner. Someone came over, asking for 'im. Got caught doing something he shouldn't have done, hands in the till, something like that. Been living well, affluent like, better than them masters. The old master 'imself's got nothing left, his granddaughter lives on herrings – and Andrei and Dunyasha always used to 'ave Landrine sweets for tea. They used to treat me to nice things, too: they'd say, "We've got as much as we like." And meat every day, if you please.'

'Has he done a bunk then?'

'Left for good, and said nothing, even to Dunyasha. Must be back in the countryside, to be with his own kind. Might 'ave been taken, come to think of it. What do we know? Fact is, the commandant is no more, much as 'e was top brass.'

'So that's how it is. They go after their own, too, then. He must have rubbed 'em up the wrong way somehow.'

After this, Nikolai turned to his own plans. He wasn't a demanding sort but still, a quarter of a loaf of bread a day wasn't much to go on. The young miss, Tatyana Mikhailovna, was offering him herrings, she said, they had enough. But how? Where from? Dunyasha was helping, too. Still, with Andrei now on the run, she didn't have much to eat herself. She had volunteered back into service for the young miss, but the latter had nothing to feed her with. Besides, who needs a servant if they are now squeezed into two rooms? So, she was considering going back to the countryside herself. Andrei had been giving her some money, so she'd saved a bit, but money was cheap nowadays... Might buy her passage, though. Of course, she's from a place not far from here, in Tula Province. But me, I'm from far away. And they don't let ride you anywhere for free.'

'It's tough alright, can't deny it.'

That was the conclusion they came to, that it was tough, and there wasn't anything else to add. The greengrocer got to his feet, ready to head home, and Nikolai stepped out of his lodge, too, to get some fresh air.

'Looks like the frost's coming soon.'

"Course it will. Ain't gonna wait. No decree can stop it.'

They bade their farewells by the gate. Following the habit of years, Nikolai swept his worn-out broom over the pavement. Then he looked up at the sky, righted his broom by banging it twice against the slabs, and set off back, in contemplation: *Things were bad before, and they're bad now. There used to be hangings and floggings, sure, but nothing good came out of it. They're all the same, the lot of 'em.*

The warmth and the smell of tobacco were pleasing, but Nikolai nevertheless briefly left the door of his lodge ajar. *The shag they've got nowadays, it'll like as not get you poisoned if you fall asleep. And what is it made of? It's all nothing but a lie.*

SISTER ALYONA

Present by Vasya's bed were the doctor and the nursing sister. The doctor's name was Kuporosov, a former seminarian, well advanced in years, slightly rough around the edges and very sympathetic. The only doctor in whom the ornithologist had any faith.

'He's someone you can trust. He understands that medicine isn't really a precise science. A kind word works better with the sick. He's a good man, is Kuporosov! Where on earth did he get himself a name like that, though?[84] He really is a pillar, a man of substance.'

Kuporosov had always treated Aglaya Dmitriyevna, as well as the old professor, and Tanyusha too, back when she had scarlet fever. Nevertheless, he had never set foot in Sivtsev Vrazhek without an invitation; generally, he always had more than enough to keep him busy at his own surgery, mostly treating people of humble means.

It was the doctor himself who had brought along the nursing sister Yelena Ivanovna to look after Vasya – a woman still very young but already a widow. Her husband, a doctor, had died from typhus. Doctor Kuporosov had been very fond of his young colleague, and so after his death he continued supporting his widow, finding her jobs,

....

[84] *Kuporos* is the Russian for vitriol; however, it means that the doctor was of humble origin – the son of a country teacher, or a priest, since it was the children of those lower classes that had formed the nascent professional classes of Russia in the late 19th century.

instructing her in the intricacies of nursing, and generally treating her as his own daughter. He called her by the name Alyona – a tender version of Yelena, but for all that he remained, as was his wont, very demanding and uncompromising when it came to caring for someone grievously ill.

'What's at stake here, Alyona dear, is human life. There simply can't be any lapses. The most important things are that everything be spotlessly clean and there be an abundance of fresh air. And – this might be a surprise – medications are no help with any of this. Our fellow here is young; it must be possible to put him back on his feet. You do understand all of this, Alyona?'

Alyona, Yelena Ivanovna, was a short plump woman, glowing with health, snub-nosed and in possession of enormous blue eyes, unquestionably ordinary but very pretty. Back in the gymnasium, she had been referred to as a 'dumpling' and pinched by fellow students during lessons, in response to which she would merely shriek feebly, as the thing she feared above all else was being tickled.

The most engaging thing about her was her laughter. She was incapable of repressing her giggles, and would break out as if in a tinkle of clear little bells and eventually, abruptly, erupt in a bizarre deep gurgle – similar to a piglet's snort. Her girlfriends were totally fascinated by it, while her own snort would always startle Alyona and make her instantly eager to look serious. To her, this tiny shortcoming had been a source of profound distress, and she simply couldn't see a way of getting rid of it.

Subsequently however, she had decided that it wasn't really something to get all worked up over: her fiancé, a young doctor, had declared to her that what had really won him over was this laughter of hers. After they were married, when he was feeling particularly tender, he would address her as his dear piggie.

MIKHAIL OSORGIN

Alyona could have been happy with him, but they were only married for a short time, just about half a year. He was sent to the front, to curb the outbreak of typhus, and soon enough Alyona received a letter in which he complained about feeling unwell. That was the last letter he ever wrote.

For a long time afterwards Alyona was unable to laugh her infectious laugh and, having failed to become a lady, she became a daughter and protégée of doctor Kuporosov's. It had been his idea to start employing her to care for the sick.

'Alyona my dear, I will go on my rounds, since I've got to attend to other patients as well, but I'll be home by seven. If the patient takes a turn for the worse, contact me immediately – either yourself, or better still, get somebody to come over. Let him drink to his heart's content and keep replacing the vinegar compress when it gets too warm. The rest, Alyona, is as per usual – you do know the drill by now.'

'I do, doctor.'

'There you are. Then I can rely on you. Don't let anyone in, apart from the young lady you saw here, and his friend, the one who has also visited. They're good people who will be of help to you, and in an emergency they'll give you a break.'

'Alright, doctor. So who is she?'

'The girl? She is the granddaughter of a certain professor, my old patient. She's called Tanyusha; her patronymic escapes me. She's a lovely young lady, excellent at playing some instrument, I seem to recall. Perhaps at something else.'

'How beautiful she is!'

'What? Beautiful? May well be, I couldn't possibly say.'

Doctor Kuporosov was no connoisseur of female beauty. Perhaps Alyona was a beauty, too; but then again, she might be ugly. Let others sort out all this stuff.

After Kuporosov left, Alyona looked round, pulled the heavy armchair closer to the bed, and lamented the absence of a soft cushion on it. Out of her little basket she pulled what she had brought along – a little yellowed book by Knut

Hamsun, *Victoria*. She had read this novel already but liked it so much that she decided to read it again – although, it wasn't as if she had a choice. Snuggling up in the armchair, all nice and comfortable and prepared to spend a long time there, she switched her gaze to the face of her sleeping patient and started investigating it, curiosity personified.

Vasya Boltanovsky's sleep was ragged, his head lolling back and forth over the pillow. The thing to do was constantly to rectify his pillow and replace the vinegar-soaked cloth on his forehead. His chin hadn't been shaved in a long time while his face, aglow with fever, was beset with dark shadows. Still, one could clearly see a dimple in his chin and, for some reason, it immediately endeared him to Alyona.

'Poor duckling, he's got such a pleasant face!'

Vasya's room had been thoroughly cleaned – thanks to the efforts put in by Tanyusha and the engineer. The bedside table was covered with a clean handkerchief, one of Vasya's, with a clearly visible 'V' embroidered in a cross-stitch in the corner.

Vasya's forelock, the eternal object of Vasya's concern and anxiety, rested limply on top of the compress, wet and tangled. Alyona brushed it aside, closer to the pillow.

'I think I'll need to cut his hair.'

And then Knut Hamsun started to tell his soothing story of love. Alyona's idea of love fitted perfectly the one offered by Knut Hamsun. Love is a hectic thing, and the novel in no way suffered from the fact that, from time to time, Alyona had to put the book aside: now to rectify the compress, now to bring some pleasantly tangy drink closer to Vasya's dry and burning lips, or even to send the patient a warm smile that he was in no state to either register or appreciate, seeing as Vasya Boltanovsky was rarely conscious.

There was an alarm clock on his little table, and the hours started ticking along. This looked set to be a sleepless night – perhaps Alyona would only manage a brief kip in her armchair.

She would be replaced in the morning, either by that beautiful girl, the professor's granddaughter, or perhaps by the gentleman who had also come to visit but then left at the same time as her. Perhaps they were engaged? Or perhaps this patient here was her fiancé?

Yet again, Knut Hamsun spun his tale of love. How wonderful his description of it was!

When darkness descended, Alyona switched on the table lamp, erected a screen around it so as not to hurt the patient's eyes, pulled a slice of ration bread and a little jar of something edible out of her basket, as well as salt in a paper cone and an apple. She had her meal at Vasya's desk, her Knut Hamsun propped up against the inkwell, she herself immersed in the book. When she had finished her meal, she wiped her hands on a piece of paper, brushed the crumbs into a neat pile, put the little jar with the remainder of the edible stuff back into her basket and decided that her apple, a big and pink-cheeked specimen, should be saved for later, when she was able to read again. And finally, before settling back into her armchair, she came up to the mirror to correct her head kerchief.

Looking at herself in the mirror, Alyona would usually tilt her head downwards so that her nose didn't look quite so upturned.

Vasya said softly, half-asleep:

'So what, then? What must we do? Is it about to depart?'

And then he shouted loudly:

'Wait for me, at least. It's not that I can, just like that...'

Alyona came up to him, squeezed the cloth on his forehead dry with her plump hand, and replaced it. Vasya suddenly opened his eyes and asked her in amazement:

'So, who are you, then?'

'Calm down.'

'But who are you?'

'I'm a nurse. Are you feeling better?'

Vasya shut his eyes for a moment and then said, very clearly:

'I'm terribly thirsty.'

Alyona picked up the glass and helped him drink, after which Vasya once again fixed her with a stare from his swollen and attentive eyes:

'And what's your name?'

'My name's Yelena Ivanovna. You shouldn't talk, better try to have a nice kip.'

Vasya gave a pained smile and mumbled: 'I'll try,' and indeed, fell asleep promptly, while Alyona thought: *He's got such a nice smile! Poor, poor little thing, he's suffering so very much!*

The landlady knocked on the door, extremely ruffled owing to her tenant's illness. Alyona went out to talk to her and straightaway concluded a peace treaty, having put the lady's mind to rest on account of trench fever's lack of contagiousness – that is, as long as everything was kept spotlessly clean. They discussed the essentials and came to an agreement. The landlady offered to boil some water, should the need arise. Vasya had been her tenant for a long while, and a preferred one at that. As she was taking her leave, she complimented Alyona:

'Aren't you young and rosy-cheeked? Anyone would get better with you around. Such a nice young girl. You can't possibly be married?'

'I'm a widow.'

This new morsel of information melted the landlady's heart completely:

'If you need to pop out for a while, let me know and I'll stay with him. And how will you sleep, then?'

'It's okay, I'm used to sleeping in an armchair.'

The landlady brought over a little cushion, to make Alyona more comfortable while she sat, as well as a big soft pillow designed to make her sleep in the armchair more bearable.

'At least it's warm here, thank the Lord. You won't freeze. We've got firewood and I'm heating my stove every second day, the one right behind this wall. It's even the source of some envy around here. That's why it's warm in this room, too.'

Later in the evening Dr Kuporosov dropped in for a short while, felt the patient's pulse, told Alyona to record the temperature on a piece of paper, approved of everything she'd done, and kissed her on the forehead.

'Well, I'm off. And you, my dear, should get some shut-eye, if only in this armchair. See you tomorrow, then. I'll come round after eight.'

Knut Hamsun picked up his narrative, and it was amazing that Alyona could picture his character's love and tribulations with such amazing clarity!

THE FIFTH STATION OF THE TRUTH

From the days of Boyar Kuchka[85] to our times, five stations of the truth, as it applies in Moscow, have been identified.

The first station was where the truth would be forced out of the defendant under the lash. This would take place in a city granary, by the Kaluga Gates,[86] inside the hut housing the Office for Investigative Affairs.[87] In the course of the recovery of a debt by torture, an executioner would deftly extract the truth wielding whips and ropes, whilst hoisting the naked body over the rack. An office scribe, meanwhile, would produce records, created line after line in tiny cramped

....

[85] The legend about the creation of the city of Moscow insists that in 1157, Prince Yury Dolgoruky (the Long-Armed one, on account of his expansionist policies), halting on the high bank of the River Moskva on his way from Kyiv to Vladimir in search of a strategically advantageous position for a city, killed the local Boyar Kuchka who 'did not show the Grand Prince due respect'. Then the prince was said to have ordered the building here of 'a fortress with wooden walls, and to call it Moscow, from the name of the river that flows by it.'

[86] One of several gates in the medieval rampart built around the historic centre of Moscow as part of its defence system.

[87] The service founded in 1619 on the initiative of Peter the Great. The Detective Order was engaged in investigating fugitive people all over the country. It was intended for restoring the normal functioning of the cities following the destruction brought about by the Polish invasion of the late 17th century, for examination of complaints from persons of different estates on oppressions and offenses, for the solution of land disputes and questions of changes in the land relations.

handwriting, at all times armed with a goose quill and seated by the table.

The second station would arrive with the help of a person's nails: his hands would be harnessed into a clamp, and the fingers would be held by pliers, while wooden pegs would be hammered underneath the nails. 'You have kept the truth back from the whip, you'll reveal it all on parting with your nails.'

The third station was to be found at the Peter and Paul Fortress,[88] under the auspices of the Government Office in Preobrazhensky village, managed by the Almighty Prince Fyodor Romodanovsky[89] – 'a man of particular temperament who looked like a monster and behaved like a wicked tyrant, a great unwisher of good unto anyone.' The things he had inflicted on his charges 'made the Devil pull his hair out'.

There had been a glimpse of the fourth station, the one that had started emerging near the Church of the Resurrection in Kadashi,[90] in the district on the other side of the Moskva River, where a famous merchant had resided in the fifties of the nineteenth century – City Mayor Shestov, defender of the interests of the Moscow underclass. But such a station was a false harbinger since the truth it ushered in had no chance of surviving for long.

Thereafter the count had been lost of how many more stations still remained in and around Moscow. The proverbs

....

[88] Peter and Paul Fortress – a fortress in St Petersburg founded by Peter the Great and used from its early days as a political prison.

[89] Prince Fyodor Yuryevich Romodanovsky (c. 1640–1717) was one of Peter the Great's foremost assistants in the task of modernising Russia. He served as the country's first head of secret police, operating the Government Office of Transfiguration (Preobrazhensky Prikaz) from 1686 to his death.

[90] A major Baroque church in Moscow, formerly the tallest building in the Trans-Moskva District. It may still be seen from Red Square.

stopped mentioning them separately – neither the one in Butyrka,[91] nor in Taganka,[92] nor Gnezdikovskaya[93]. The populace had grown wise, and in its new wisdom summarised it all thus: 'The truth existed once but has fled into the woods.' Or even thus: 'I'm telling the truth, you're telling the truth, the truth is all around but it doesn't exist.'

And so it was that the fifth station was invented in our days at the Lubyanka.

The truth teased out of him through torture, a man would be of no further use, and so be shortened by 'a quarter and a half'. Quite a few sites in Moscow had proved useful in this respect, and had been immortalised in popular memory. In Red Square alone, in the stretch between Nikolskaya Street and Our Saviour's Gate, a cluster of little churches had sprung up 'on bones and blood', and one more 'over the ravine'. Ivan the Terrible cut people short within the confines of the square in the vicinity of the Church of the Most Holy Mother of God, in front of the Holy Ivan's[94] Bell Tower – the same Ivan that later came to be known as the Great. 'And the severed heads would then be swept away, towards Mstislavsky[95] Court, so that devildom had something to use as bowling balls for their amusement'.

....

[91] A prison.

[92] A prison.

[93] Formerly, the address of the criminal investigation department.

[94] Ivan the Terrible.

[95] A member of the princely family of Gedimind origin who, prior to their move to Russia, ruled the principality of Mstislavl. The Mstislavsky family subsequently produced several notable military commanders, such as Ivan Mstislavsky who fought in the Livonian War. His son, Fyodor Mstislavsky was one of the Russian magnates during the Time of Troubles and the leader of the Seven Boyars who temporarily ruled the country. Their 'court' (chambers) was located inside the Kremlin, next to Ivanovskaya Square.

Similar sites had also existed by the Serpukhov Gates, and in the Trans-Moskva area by the swamps, and by the Church of the Great Martyr Barbara, and on the corner between Myasnitskaya Street and Furmanny Lane and, in winter, even on the ice of the Moskva River itself.

There had been a veritable plethora of places in Moscow where rams had had their horns straightened, tongues had been sewn below the level of the heels, folks had been hoisted *on the strength of their bones*, and had their flanks welded together, spared no soaked birch twigs, as well as twisted till they made a gag of their own mouth and finally beaten till the blood would dry and could run no more.

Russian life is rich, as is reflected in the language: beautiful and sonorous and capable of cataloguing various names for torture; and it will get richer still.

When the fifth station of the truth – the one in the Lubyanka – came into existence, they began kicking people out into the streets with all their earthly possessions, eliminating them, putting them up against the wall to be shot, and generally doing away with them in every other way imaginable. Thus new places sprang up in Moscow, such as Petrovsky Park, the Lubyanka basements, the Anchor[96] Association, the garage in Varsonofyevsky Lane, and wherever else proved expedient...

....

[96]   The building originally belonging, in the 19th century, to the merchant Likhamov was later taken over by the insurance association Yakor (Anchor) with its basement converted into a kind of a hold. According to the legend, the Cheka's founder Dzerzhinsky had his office here, on the second floor, prior to moving the organisations' headquarters into Lubyanka. The sealed basement and the proximity of a garage made this building in Moscow's Varsonofyevsky Lane an ideal place for mass executions. It has now been proved beyond doubt that over 15,000 people were executed in the basements of the Varsonofyevsky complex.

In the old days the neighbourhood had mostly been populated by men of commerce, and eight or ten-percent interest rates were the dominant forces. The gap between eight and ten had been huge – eight spelled common affluence whereas ten meant being relatively rich. But all of this had now disappeared. The new people weren't looking too far ahead and knew for certain that life was only for today, and that even a hundred percent was a trifle, that they were either to seize the entire world, or, equally probably, and no later than tomorrow – face an ignominious end.

The new people shunned faith, or least they thought they did. Undoubtedly, that was what they thought. A kind of faith was still alive though, a faith of the most naïve kind – they believed in the overwhelming power of a Browning, Nagant or Colt, the power of rapid action. How could they possibly know that the grass was growing according to its own inalienable laws, that human thought wasn't to be twisted concomitantly with the human neck, that a bullet was powerless to penetrate either faith or faithlessness?

A huge courtyard, with old buildings, the entrance doors plastered over with a multitude of papers announcing various decrees. This was a place ruled and steered by force and unthinking action. This was the street where meek locals would enter the premises trembling, present their requests stammering, take their leave awash with tears, all their timid attempts at deceit pathetically transparent. Meanwhile power was dressed in a military overcoat or a leather jacket, with all its hooks buttoned up to the very collar.

If you turned left by the entrance and crossed the two inner courtyards, you would reach a narrow passage, and after that there was a big warehouse, nowadays a pit, a well-lit underground room that only yesterday had smelled of trade ledgers and the recent mustiness of trade samples, but nowadays was the Ship of Death. The floor was laid out in decorative ceramic tiles.

There was a balcony by the entrance on which guards were posted – young Red Army soldiers seconded to the special operations unit – barefaced, ignorant, infected with military discipline and the fear of being punished. The balcony ran around the 'pit', accessible through a spiral staircase, in which seventy people, flat on their backs, on the stacked plank beds, on the floor, atop the big burnished table – and two of them even within it – awaited their destiny.

Two tiny cells had been additionally constructed out of freshly shaved planks, a little window in each door, for the condemned. A small anthill for the idle ants.

The walls of the cells were covered with graffiti executed by the sentenced in pencil:

'My life was cut shooort.'

'Me spring did me in, and now I die for nuffink.'

'Goodbye my spring.'

Nearby was a drawing of a grave – a high hillock; a skull, quite cheerful and resembling a face, crossed bones underneath, and below the bones – a name and surname. The young bandit felt like parting with his life in a romantic fashion, so that his memory would live on, just as it had been described in three brochures on sale by the Ilyinsky Gate: 'A famous bandit and outlaw, the notorious hold-up man Ivan Kazarinov, nicknamed Vanya the Roving Light.'

Next to it, nearby, cheek-by-jowl in the Ship of Death's general cell, the small fry: CRs,[97] Socialist Revolutionaries, and a Menshevik[98] with a scraggly beard, bespectacled, rot-

....

[97]   Counter-revolutionaries.

[98]   The split within the original Social Democratic Party of Russia into the Bolsheviks (the majority-vote holders) and Mensheviks (the minority) had taken place in 1903 along the lines of adhering to humanitarian values and the use of mass terror.

ten-toothed, a coward with no fire or daring within him, a human aphid.

Resembling a fisherman tightly girdled with a leather belt, the commissar of death Ivanov came out onto the balcony, accompanied by his executive – a strong, stocky person with restless fidgety eyes, a perennially lightly-inebriated ill-tempered ogre, Zavalishin – the very same executive who would send the young bandit's soul on to the next world.

Another presence on the bunk was a former tsar's minister, powdered with mothballs, with a thin book in his hands and a neat grey beard, a person accustomed to it all, who had been transported from St Petersburg. Next to him – a polemicist from among the Mensheviks, his pastime gainfully occupied with composing petitions, a venomous individual bent on trying to trip every investigator with a treacherously thorny question. Next along, a profiteer who had been caught selling a consignment of leather for making boots. And yet another personality, seated on the upper bunk and dangling his legs off it – poor Styopa, yet another thug who hadn't yet been otherwise identified. But Commissar Ivanov had been an honoured permanent member of the same merry gang, so he could spot his own kind straight away.

'Hello, Styopa, where're you off to?'

'Mogilyov Province, I guess.'

Styopa looked pallid, oppressed by his eighteen years of existence and an abundance of cocaine.

Soon enough, Styopa would be taken away to a separate chamber. Fare thee well, Styopa, you poor duckling, wayward progeny of good old Mama and Papa.

Zavalishin was observing the pit through drink-sodden eyes, a dependable operator, a martinet on piecemeal pay and a luxury ration, his eyes blood-shot and seeing blood. Prior to nightfall, Zavalishin would drink himself senseless, ready to stand drinks all round, though hardly everyone around him would be willing to share his company. He instilled dread. Say what one might, he remained an unapologetic executioner, willing to do away with his own mother on the strength of an order from above and for the price of a bottle of pre-war cognac. His beard was matted in clumps and the gaze of his swollen eyes, bleared by cheap spirit, lacked focus.

And across the road, if one went through Furkasovsky Lane, was the location of the real hub of the great struggle: the Extraordinary Department of the All-Russian Cheka. There, order and discipline ruled supreme; all personnel were on their best behaviour, and there was no sign of either poetry or unjustified anxiety. Hovering over it all, reigning with unspoken commands, was a clever and brutal genius of struggle and vengeance, a tall gloomy comrade from the first recruitment to the cause, someone who had tasted more than his share of the tsar's penitentiary system, an idealist, a selfless warrior inaccessible to just about anybody, a popular vindicator who had taken charge of the bloodbath – may descendants forget his name.[99]

Straight from the square, a new victim, an enemy of the people and the revolution, would be set down from an automobile and taken in through the door. A form to fill in the small office, then a short time in a small cell lined with bunks, then a re-assignment to a bigger one, a bedbug-infested bunk in the notorious Avanesov's office,[100] and after all of this, by the power of special warrant, across the courtyard, into an old house fitted out as a prison and based on the horrific

....

[99] Felix Dzerzhinsky (1877–1926) was a Bolshevik revolutionary and official. Born into Polish nobility, from 1917 until his death in 1926 Dzerzhinsky led the first two Soviet state-security organisation, the Cheka and the OGPU, establishing secret police for the post-revolutionary Soviet regime. He was one of the architects of the Red Terror.

[100] Avanesov's office – after Varlaam Avanesov (1884–1930), a member of the Cheka commission from March 1919, previously a banking officer.

tsarist model, into the spine-chilling silent premises of the Extraordinary Department from where long corridors, cold and empty, zigzagged towards the offices of the investigators.

That was the fifth station of truth, as it applies in Moscow – forged at the Lubyanka.

COMRADE BRIKMAN

A puny, sparsely-haired man, his chest concave, was writing in a tiny hand, churning out spindly scribbles, myopically staring at the sheet with his left eye, keeping his elbows splayed wide apart.

The telephone on his desk clanged briefly.

'Yes. Yes, speaking. Okay. When was he arrested? Alright, comrade. Just make sure you forward his file to me, soon as you can, otherwise I'll have no idea. Alright then. I'll summon him myself, sure thing, alright.'

The puny man's voice was wheedling, like that of a hysterical woman, with a shrieking undertone.

Having finished writing his 'conclusion', he leafed attentively through the file delivered to him, turning the pages over with the thin-wristed, slender-fingered hands of a child, opened the package containing documents confiscated during the search, gruffly said something under his breath and then his face crumpled:

'What's this again, for Christ's sake? The stupid trifles they've picked up! Those people don't have a clue.'

He made a telephone call, signed an order and passed it on to a soldier of the special task unit who had just entered the room:

'Take this to the commandant's office, comrade. I want him brought to me, straightaway.'

He got to his feet, paced around his room for a while, coughed in the corner, peeped out into the corridor and asked if it was possible to have some hot tea brought in. The tea, weak and lukewarm, was brought in by a stocky woman, her ringlets contained under a kerchief, she herself boisterous and confident:

'Comrade Brikman, d'ya know if there's gonna be a hand-out today?'

'I don't.'

'Rumour has it, it could be cranberry, or perhaps some woollens.'

'I don't know.'

'My word, who does then?'

The guard reported that the prisoner had been brought over.

'Bring him in, then. And you wait behind the door; wait till I call for you.'

The investigator became flustered, sat himself behind the desk, placed the completed 'conclusion' in front of him, picked up his pen, and pretended to be writing.

The door handle rattled and the soldier said from behind the door:

'Go to the left, towards the table.'

In came Astafyev. He was tall, dressed in a somewhat rumpled suit, unshaven, superficially calm.

The investigator raised his head, cast a brief glance at the newcomer, and nodded towards the chair in front of his desk:

'Sit down. Are you citizen Astafyev?'

'Yes.'

'Sit down.'

He spent a couple of minutes perusing his 'conclusion', reading silently, taking time to come up with his first question. Then he inserted the piece of paper into a file, pushed it aside, manoeuvred Astafyev's file closer to him, and asked:

'Are you a professor?'

'*Privatdotsent.*'

'Well, same thing, in essence. A philosopher?'

'Yes.'

'Why have you been arrested?'

Astafyev smiled:

'You should know the answer to this.'

'I do. But what's your take on it?'

'I take it that I've been brought in randomly, for no reason.'

'And thus, you believe we arrest people for no reason?'

Astafyev burst into a sincere laugh:

'I think it does happen. Out of twenty arrests, nineteen are sure to be made for no good reason at all.'

'That's where you're wrong. Mistakes are possible, of course, but mistakes get corrected. We are forced to be cautious since our Soviet power is surrounded by enemies. It's better if ten people languish inside for no reason than we let one enemy go undetected. Don't you agree?'

'No, I don't. I believe the opposite: it's better to let a guilty person slip through your fingers than to deprive ten people of their freedom.'

'There you go, we think differently. The proletariat hasn't won power so as to risk losing it for the sake of such high-minded sentimentality. For as long as the Soviet power is under siege from its enemies...'

And thus, in a thin rasping voice, omitting all commas, the investigator continued to drone on, uttering words that Astafyev had read numerous times in *Pravda* and *Izvestiya* editorials, words that would make you sick to your back teeth with their verities, and lies, their practicality and their incredulity. Listening to him absent-mindedly, Astafyev was painfully aware of a surging bout of boredom, waiting for the investigator to finish. At the same time, he was trying to remember: *I have seen him somewhere, I have heard him speak. Where was it?*

Suddenly cutting his popular lecture short, the investigator asked in the same tone of voice:

'Last week you received a visit from the man in the yellow spats. What's his surname?'

Astafyev answered apathetically:

'It may well be that someone wearing yellow spats did drop in, I can't remember.'

'Did he stay long?'

Astafyev screwed his face:

'Since I am telling you that I can't remember, what sort of a question is that?'

'So, who did visit you last week? List all the names.'

'What are you charging me with?'

'It's not a trial, I'm under no obligation to answer your questions. Once we've found out everything we need, you'll be informed. In the meantime, you must answer mine.'

The large man, healthy and handsome, looked down at the diminutive figure of the scrawny investigator.

'Forget it. How can I answer anything if I'm not even aware of what you're accusing me of? I'll give you a name and you'll go and arrest this person. Who do you take me for?'

'We'll be forced to take you for an enemy of Soviet power.'

'Go ahead, if it pleases you so.'

'Are you aware, citizen Astafyev, of the consequences facing you in such a case?'

'I can guess, but for me it's hardly a persuasive argument. But could you tell me, Mr Investigator, where could I possibly have seen you before? Your face looks so familiar.'

The investigator's body gave a nervous jerk and his voice rose an octave:

'This is totally irrelevant. Are you going to answer my questions or not?'

'Could it have been abroad? Say, in Berlin? Aren't you a former émigré? I have a vague recollection of some emigrant rally... Wait a minute, is your surname Brikman? But if memory serves, you were a Menshevik back then? Am I right?'

Comrade Brikman started fidgeting in his chair, then pressed the bell button and yelled:

'Would you be so kind as to answer my questions?'

Astafyev beamed forth and added in a slightly jeering voice:

'And as far as I can recall, back in Berlin, you were speaking against Lenin. I say, old chap!'

Brikman squealed at the guard who entered the room:

'Take the prisoner back!'

'I need the document, if you please.'

As Brikman was signing the document, Astafyev said, all sincere geniality:

'Don't be consumed by worry, Comrade Brikman. It's bad for you, look how thin you are. Take a leaf out of my book. All of it is pure nonsense and isn't worth the nerves.'

'I don't need your advice, citizen Astafyev. Besides, it's now clear that you'll spend a long time inside, and that's if nothing worse happens. You can go back now.'

After the guard had escorted Astafyev out of the room, the investigator spent a long while writing in his spindly hand, filling out the form with the personal information appended to the file, elbows wide apart and his flat chest pushed heavily against the table. He finished his task, got to his feet, walked around his room, coughed into the corner yet again, felt his pulse, looked back at the door, and drew up to a tarnished framed mirror hanging by the window. The mirror foggily reflected his face – haggard, with a scraggly fair beard, large eyes over the lightly swollen sacks underneath, prominently protruding ears.

His chest had been battered with rifle butts in a transit prison back in his student days, to the extent that he had never been able to breathe freely since. His life was totally devoid of joy, and the only way he could possibly make himself go on, dragging out this life of an unwanted consumptive, was by maintaining his belief in the revolution, and the future happiness of all humankind, the golden age of universal bliss that was undoubtedly guaranteed after this stage of consistent and merciless struggle against the enemies of the working people. Frankly speaking, he had never been a worker himself, and couldn't be on account of his damaged chest. But still, he, Brikman, was destined to become one of the heroes and defenders of the new social order that had been born in Russia but would eventually spread all over the world. Physically feeble, he had to be durable, indestructible, steel-willed – that was the whole justification for his existence.

Comrade Brikman approached the mirror again, tilted his head slightly upwards and tried to stand straight. But once more the mirror presented a puny figure adorned with red feverish eyes. The pockets of his tunic were now bulging forward but his chest failed to fill out the fabric.

Comrade Brikman didn't smoke; the fumes would normally send him off on a long exhausting coughing fit. He preferred his air clean but was afraid of opening the window, since the cold, too, was bad for his cough. He kept in his pocket at all times a little tightly sealed jar that he used as a spittoon.

Today he had lost control and allowed himself to be rattled. That was bad; it should never happen again. There wasn't enough incriminating evidence against Astafyev, but judging by his voice, his conversation and behaviour he was, unquestionably, a truly dangerous enemy. His file should be treated with particular zeal. It was imperative to expose his true colours – my God, was it imperative!

Astafyev's figure popped up in Brikman's mind yet again, barrel-chested, wholesome, sneering.

The investigator picked up the telephone receiver and, tapping the cradle impatiently, started speaking, hurriedly, in his small voice:

'Hello, hello…'

BY HIS BED

To use an expression from the ever-propagating officialese inundating Moscow, Alyona 'initiated contact' with the landlady of the ill Vasya Boltanovsky. This contact culminated in the ladies' joint efforts in procuring some semolina and a little bit of sugar, bartered for some of the millet that Vasya had brought home.

'You're caring for him, Yelena Ivanovna, as if he were your fiancé.'

'Why on earth would you say that? He does need something easily digestible, though. Look how much weight he's lost!'

Changing the patient's nightshirt (clean ones would first be warmed by the landlady's oven), Alyona would pityingly observe the hollows below his collarbones and his pathetically protruding ribs. His helplessness tugged right at the strings of Alyona's heart, filling her with special tenderness towards her patient. Without Alyona, Vasya wasn't capable of doing anything, and during his brief periods of lucidity and extreme weakness, he had to conquer his embarrassment over relying upon her nursing support.

By now the crisis had passed. Vasya was conscious at all times, if hugely enfeebled. During each of his visits, Doctor Kuporosov would take Alyona into the corridor and run through his instructions:

'Keep a close eye on his temperature, Alyona. He must gain some weight, too; feed him in small quantities but frequently. Was it thirty-five point two in the morning? You see, this is as dangerous as a high fever. He may freeze on us this way. Give him his porridge hot, add a lot of butter. Milk is good, too. When he's a little stronger you can give him some meat, say a mince cutlet; you won't find any veal or chicken nowadays. Don't allow him to tire himself, or stay seated in his bed, or talk – let him just lie there. And you yourself, Alyona, don't chatter, don't engross him in conversation. My, my! Such a nice lad, how one pities him.'

Vasya's head had been shaved again, along with his sprouting beard. Resting in his bed, Vasya now looked pleasant and clean, all in white, thin, brown-eyed, a dimple clearly visible in his chin. He only spoke a little, in a soft voice, and mostly offering words of gratitude.

'Thank you so much, Yelena Ivanovna, but why do you have to do it all yourself? Maria Savvishna could help you, at least with the unseemly matters. I really am so embarrassed!'

'What utter nonsense! But now I've got to give your room a proper going-over. You're expecting visitors.'

'Visitors' meant Tanyusha and Pyotr Pavlovich.

Once the crisis of his illness was behind him and Vasya fully regained consciousness, he would lie still, mentally rejoicing at the return of life and trying hard to recall – as much as his head, still rather bewildered, would let him – the visions that had flashed before his mind's eye during the time of his illness, what had happened in his delirious dreams, and what grain of real experiences they might contain. The only thing that had been completely real was this nurse, Yelena Ivanovna, who was always by his bedside and who the doctor had tenderly referred to as Alyona.

Alyona was always present, a part of both his ravings and his lucid moments. Alyona was always there, when his lips were parched and it felt as though the fever were suffocating him, or when his head was burning and his eyes were trying to see through some nebulous lilac circles. But all it took was for Alyona to come closer, and things would immediately become better and easier. Alyona's voice was consolation.

At times, though, Alyona would recede behind a screen of other shadows and visions, and her voice would be replaced by other voices. Those, of course, were the voices of Tanyusha and Protasov. Always together, forever the two of them. Their two voices would be talking in a whisper, sometimes addressing Vasya, sometimes each other.

Tanyusha's voice, always so desirable and longed for, was now heard in unison with another, and so it wasn't soothing; it troubled Vasya. Occasionally he felt like capturing it and making it talk only for himself, pronouncing the most needed words, the awfully important ones, or at least words of comfort and compassion. But that was rendered impossible by this other voice, male, even-pitched, composed, confident, almost jolly. Alyona's voice was only ever intended for Vasya; the other voices were, it seemed, intended for each other, although quite possibly they were discussing and addressing him, too. It was hard to explain, but that was the feeling they inspired. And on hearing those voices Vasya would start thrashing around, his mind wandering, and cry out intermittently.

Another recollection drifted in, if it wasn't a dream. Coming to, Vasya would answer questions addressed to him (whether he felt thirsty, or if the pillows had to be rearranged) and could clearly see the person talking to him. However, having seen this person, he would immediately forget the whole thing. It would somehow sink beyond the sphere of his attention and the confines of the world within which he had been battling death. Still, by now there were longer periods when his head was clear. And so, once, he spent a long time contemplating the face of Alyona, asleep in her armchair, and admiring the healthy glow of her cheeks and the innocent shape of her lips. Another time he inspected, thoroughly, the face of the doctor who was leaning over him, and broke out in a smile on hearing the doctor say: 'Well, my dear fellow, your eyes are much clearer now; time for you to get better.' He could clearly discern Tanyusha, who was staring at him in alarm and with such profound pity that Vasya felt like crying; but Tanyusha's beloved face was now displaying something unfamiliar. And finally, he once noticed – if it hadn't been a dream – both his friends, Tanyusha and the engineer, who were seated right there, beside his bed and close to one another, not speaking but exchanging glances that carried an expression Vasya couldn't decipher.

That was how it happened. Vasya must have been sleeping, soundly and calmly. Then he woke up feeling a wonderful clarity in his head, a feeling of freedom from a painful attack, when one didn't feel like stirring lest the tranquillity and calmness be disturbed. He opened his eyes and saw the distinct outlines of his room and the two faces, illuminated by the lamp, silently watching each other as if transfixed in mutual contemplation. It also seemed to Vasya that Tanyusha's and the engineer's hands were linked. He might not have registered this fact except that when he tried to turn his head abruptly towards the people seated by his bed, Tanyusha made a fitful gesture as if snatching her hands away. So Vasya closed his eyes again and felt his calmness and lucidity receding, giving way to a torturous semi-consciousness, the back of his head growing heavy and his temples feeling as if they were being squeezed in a vice. All of it was coming back to him now, but dizzily; perhaps it never happened at all.

Yesterday was the first full day when Vasya stayed lucid throughout. Still, exhausted by his disease, he slept a lot and didn't get to see Tanyusha.

'Sister, did Tatyana Mikhailovna visit yesterday?'

'She did. She is usually here by three o'clock, when I go home. During this whole time, she has only missed two or three days, and then Maria Savvishna stayed by your bed.'

'How much trouble I've caused everyone! Was I really that ill?'

'It's water under the bridge now. But you were in a really bad place.'

'Has it been many days?'

'Can't you remember? Tomorrow will be the start of the fourth week.'

'So long? And you've always been here?'

'I have.'

'Nights too? So when did you sleep?'

Alyona laughed her bell-like laugh:

'At night of course, or I would steal a nap during the day.'

'In this armchair?'

'When you were very poorly, in the armchair, and when you didn't toss around too much, I would pull the chairs closer and sleep as if in a bed. Maria Savvishna supplied me plentifully with blankets and pillows, so I've been able to make myself a real bed. But I was afraid of sleeping too deeply.'

'How can you do it? You must be very tired. And yet you're a picture of health. It makes me jealous just to see you.'

'It's just that I am very healthy – nothing ever gets to me. I'm used to it all. But you're chatting away and you mustn't – doctor's orders.'

'Talking to you is good for me.'

But in truth Vasya felt exhausted.

When, some five minutes later, there was a light knock on the door and Tanyusha's voice asked in a whisper, 'Well, how is he today?', Vasya didn't open his eyes, although he heard it, and also heard Alyona's answer:

'Today's really good.'

'Is he asleep?'

'Looks like it.'

Vasya didn't open his eyes when a new gentle rapping on the door was followed by a springy male footfall, and Alyona left the room, having simultaneously said 'hello' and 'goodbye'. It felt nicer to lie like that – had he looked at them he would have had to start talking; and before you talk you should think, but that felt horribly hard and demanding.

Through his tired calm he heard whispers, and then the engineer asked:

'I've got to go now; will you be alright on your own?'

'But of course, especially if you have to go. But you'll come along in the evening?'

'As per usual. Well, bye for now, Tanyusha.'

Per usual? And he calls her Tanyusha?

Vasya peeked out and saw Tanyusha gazing after his travel companion with such tenderness as he had never seen before in her eyes; not when she looked at him, Vasya.

And Vasya remembered: *How long did Alyona say it's been? Oh right, tomorrow's the start of the fourth week.*

TRAITORS

To those who were waiting in queues, keeping a place overnight, waiting till the boarded-up door opened in the morning underneath a visibly faded white-and-red shop sign, those who were hoping that, perhaps, they could get some mouldy millet against a children's ration card – to those people the war, still dragging on somewhere, was the least of their concerns, as was the fact that Russia wasn't party to it anymore. Those people had had to grapple with multiple concerns and woes of their own; they had long since forgotten about the war. By now, all that remained in its wake were the graves and the widows, the ruination of whole families and the accursed memory, overwhelmed by the suffering of today.

Mertvago, the lawyer who, once upon a time, had been fixed up by Uncle Boris with a position at the Headquarters of the District Councils, and who had once looked so dashing in the uniform that came with it, wasn't experiencing any particular discomfort – thanks to some family jewels deftly stashed away by his wife. However, he did demonstrate a serious error of judgement by not leaving promptly for Kiev,[101] or some other place even further away, as had some of his more prescient acquaintances. Nowadays, such a departure would be a considerably more difficult enterprise, and Mertvago, while busy with the arrangements, was convinced that we,

....

[101]   Kyiv at the time was under German occupation.

the Russians, had betrayed the common cause of the allies, and that the disgraceful Treaty of Brest-Litovsk[102] (which he referred to as 'sleazy' when at home) spelled infamy for the entire Russian nation.

The traitors were waiting in queues in the wet snow, chewing bread with a generous admixture of rubbish and manure, dousing rancid horsemeat in vinegar in an attempt to overpower the horrible smell, and then proceeding to make it into meatballs which they fried in castor or engine oil.

Be it in the cities or the grain-poor villages, they waddled around clothed in shabby mended rags, forgetting how to smile or to live a life, holding on out of habit and instinct. Confirmed in their degrading crime, they were absent physically as well as mentally from those distant lands where soldiers were still being sent to their deaths, but at least they had been clothed and fed adequately.

Uncle Boris, who had previously worked for Defence, and then briefly got himself involved in sabotaging the war effort, was now employed – as an experienced expert – in the Department of Science and Technology. He would talk about himself in these terms:

'Here I am, working for the Supreme Council for National Economy, but of course I'm not one of them; I work for a science department, nothing to do with politics. It's imperative that we are able to fight the extinction of life and science. Our department is quite autonomous.'

His superior was a young and somewhat befuddled Communist, full of respect for the scientists and afraid of making a fool of himself in their presence, and so Uncle Boris would

....

[102]   The Treaty of Brest-Litovsk was a separate peace treaty signed on March 3, 1918, between the new Bolshevik government of Russia and the Central Powers, that ended Russia's participation in World War I. The treaty was signed at German-controlled Brest-Litovsk, after two months of negotiations.

let himself into his office with his jacket buttoned up to his chin, even if one of the buttons was dangling on a thread and could easily fall off. On entering, the young man would bow, tilt his head to one side and fumble with his hands, not sure what to do with them. This self-conscious boss would invite Uncle Boris to sit down, and Uncle Boris would perch himself on the edge of his chair.

From the point of view of the lawyer Mertvago, whose profession was temporarily of no use to anyone, Uncle Boris was also a traitor, on account of having accepted employment in a Soviet institution. That said, he wasn't excessively critical of him – 'He that is able to receive *it*, let him receive *it*.'[103] Not everyone was capable of maintaining the purity of their principles.

On a normal day, Uncle Boris would arrive at Myasnitskaya Street carrying a case in which he kept drawings of designs for standardising tractors and adapting those tractors to crop farming; he would also be equipped with a strong Swiss-made sack, in case the rations contained groceries. However, since no tractors were being manufactured as yet, and the issue of standardisation didn't involve any particular urgency, Uncle Boris would pop into his department and submit his papers for copying, after which he would direct his steps to Maly Zlatoustinsky Lane where hand-outs were occasionally distributed under the auspices of a different department. The self-serving traitor, Uncle Boris would come home late, hauling his sack that might contain a jar of black molasses, a thimbleful of yeast, maybe five herrings (slightly off), and sometimes a square of thick rubber – enough for having two soles mended. In the eyes of those around him, those who were not experts, Uncle Boris was lucky. In the evening, ready to go to sleep beneath blankets and fur coats,

....

[103]   Book of Matthew, 19:12.

with a fur hat on his head (the miniscule stove would go completely cold during the night), Uncle Boris would tell his wife:

'There's some hope I'll qualify for the academic ration.'

'There is?' Uncle Boris's plain and withered wife would stick out her nose from under the pile of old blankets, excited.

'Nothing's for certain, but there's hope. The motion has been tabled to get the equivalent of a Kremlin ration, but that would only be for the select few.'

'Are you one of those? It would be wonderful.'

'Don't know. It's hard. But maybe.'

The Kremlin ration sometimes contained flour, and real meat as standard.

Even Uncle Boris lived this way. What, then, was to be said about a soldier who had deserted the frontline, taking his state-owned bayonet and some items he had managed to lay his hands on while demolishing a local warehouse? That he had helped himself to state property was perfectly clear to that soldier, and he wasn't at all sure that he had acted nobly. In his village, picking at a rotten horse collar with his rusty bayonet, he was mindful of this theft but was totally oblivious of his treachery and his nefarious betrayal of the allies. Had someone mentioned such words to him, the words that spelled eternal ignominy, he would have rolled his blue, Slavic eyes at them, demonstrating his utter bewilderment.

Homespun coats, peasants' tunics, smocks, frocks with holes at the elbows – the great and polylingual nation, rigid with cold, sick with hunger, robbed in war and in peacetime, exhausted and rendered insane by the years of revolution and the blockade, the entire Russian nation, a beast and an ascetic champion, the tormentor and the victim, had now become a traitor. It had betrayed the Europe that it had never known, to which it had sworn no allegiance, from which it had never received anything, and to whom it had gifted for no purpose or reason, in a Sisyphean feat of futile adoration, millions of lives.

For all the reasons listed above, absolutely nothing of note took place in Moscow and Russia on the eleventh of November, 1918.[104]

Everybody was up early, since there was an irreducible number of things and worries to attend to. The previous night, all had gone to bed early – electricity supplies were erratic and kerosene was expensive and unavailable. The Central Electric Station, running short on fuel, was burning notary acts, deeds of property, share certificates, old credit notes and the archives of the tsarist public offices.

Neither November the eleventh nor subsequent dates proved to be conspicuous in the procession of freezing snow-bound days. Newspapers, which no one bothered to read, carried brief articles on the armistice that had been achieved on the European fronts; but the news was totally devoid of interest and significance in the eyes of those who spent their days queueing and dreaming of fat and sugar. The very same newspapers published, in fits of incredible sincerity, lists of those who had been executed by firing squad the previous week: now this was of interest for family and friends. Others repeated, second-hand, figures they did not believe and several names that rang a bell, however distantly. Just like hunger, or cold, or typhus, the executions had by now become part and parcel of everyday life, inspiring anxiety only at night, when the cloud of fear became particularly dense over the heads of the fitfully sleeping citizens of the freest country in the world.

In the streets of European cities, people were snatching up special editions of their newspapers; they were singing, hugging each other and dancing. Luckily, the sound of this festive rapture failed to reach Russian cities and villages, and

....

[104]   The date of the Armistice signed at Le Francport near Compiègne that ended fighting on land, sea and air in World War I between the Allies and their opponent, Germany.

the ears of those whom Europe was stigmatising with the brand of traitor.

Virtue was triumphant, vice had been penalised.

Should a pantheon of supreme celestial judges have happened to have convened meanwhile, somewhere in heaven, beyond the snow-laden clouds, their verdict would most likely have been similar to the human judgement. The Russian people, the nation of traitors and martyrs, had no one acting in their defence – neither over there nor down here; and immersed in their personal worries, they failed to attend the trials in both divine and human jurisdictions: sentence was handed down *in absentia*.

HE WHO COMETH

Where does love spring from?

Ah, Tanyusha, no one has the answer. People wait for it, but it comes unannounced. They try to describe it, and their time-tested descriptions are full of colour and vibrancy; but what really happens is this: it sneaks in by stealth, wrapped up in a cheap, greyish, nondescript trench coat. Which doesn't make it any the worse, or less yearned for.

It likes catching you by surprise and overwhelming you with its lack of logic. Astafyev once put his finger on it: logic is the death of beauty and mystique. And what Tanyusha said in reply was true, too: 'If you are thinking too much, you are not in love, but when it takes you unawares...'

Tanyusha isn't thinking now, she simply knows. A man has come along and knocked on the door, not a special man, a most common and regular man, only yesterday a complete stranger, while today... will the evening ever come, so that he will be here again?

His hands are rough – all this hard work and frequent use of grey soap. And yet, other hands – smooth, nice and warm, friendly and gentle – are unwanted, unpleasant, not interesting. But to him, the one who has become instantly special, you give your hand willingly, now and forever. And it is impossible to explain any of this, as no explanation has ever existed.

It is eight o'clock. Tanyusha's eyes glide over the lines in her book. The book is silent and feels neglected, not used to being ignored. Granddad is snug in his armchair and of course cannot be expected to sit listening as intently and eagerly. He will never recognise the right footsteps, the sound of his footfall, the one that will linger without fail by the entrance, pause for an instant (why is that?) and then, pause or no pause, announce his arrival with a knock. When this happens, Tanyusha puts her book to one side and, trying not to rush forward, goes to answer the door.

'Who's there, Tanyusha?'

'It is Piotr Pavlovich, Granddad.'

'Oh, that's good. Come in, come in, do you bring us any news?'

'No news. How are you feeling, Professor?'

'Creaking along. It's good of you to drop by; Tanyusha here is tired of waiting.'

'The things you say, Grandpa!'

'Now now, what's wrong with that? Without you, Piotr Pavlovich, it is so monotonous.'

The engineer sits down on the sofa next to Tanyusha and says:

'I was the one who couldn't wait to see you. Because of this useless piece of paper, I had to go round and round, all over the better part of Moscow. Do you know, Professor, that the Donbas[105] is practically at a standstill? And for us, no coal spells total disaster.'

Protasov describes what he plans to do about it, something that Tanyusha knows nothing about and cares even less. But she listens, with pride and attention: that's the type of person he is! If he sets his heart on something, he will get it done, no mistake.

'Plans are all very well,' says the professor, 'but will they allow you to put them to the test? Lest all this energy go up the spout.'

....

[105]   The Donets coal basin.

'It's hard. Very hard. There is complete chaos everywhere and resources are meagre. There is money for other things but when it is a genuine and important cause, I have to plead for every kopeck. But what's the alternative, Professor: let Russia go to rot? One has to adapt to so much – all for the sake of steering life into some sort of a normal groove.'

They drink tea. As they drink it, Protasov tells them how during the war he went on a special mission to Spitsbergen, and how they were ice-bound. He talks about it as if it were a regular pleasure trip, his story amusing and full of graphic detail. The professor is curious whether he had a chance to spot a rare species of bird, one that, admittedly, had been described thoroughly but had not yet popped up anywhere in stuffed form. The engineer did not see those particular birds but, as regards ornithology, he does know a thing or two. And he and the old professor strike up a conversation that is interesting to both of them. The old man has come to life and showers him with facts and terms. Protasov doesn't know certain things, so he asks again. But he knows a lot too, and Tanyusha casts him an occasional proud look and then glances at her Grandpa. She senses that Grandpa is quite taken with the new visitor to their little house at Sivtsev Vrazhek. It fills Tanyusha with pleasure.

When Grandpa retires, always as punctual as a cuckoo clock, Tanyusha and Protasov stay behind, alone.

'I am very grateful to you for my Granddad. His life is so dull.'

'What a great intellect!' says Protasov. 'And what a treasure trove of knowledge. Actually, if you stop and think about it, we do still have people like that in Russia. It's just that hard workers are few and far between. Science is sublime; there are no trifles there, whereas politics is something superficial and accidental: this way today, that way tomorrow; none of it really matters.'

They talk of Grandpa, of Spitsbergen and the engineer's previous life – something that he hasn't yet shared with Tanyusha. What they do not talk about is love, not even in passing. Still, Tanyusha is so interested in everything he has to say, this stranger who has suddenly become so near and dear, and Protasov's tales are so inspired, that the minutes and hours flash by much faster than either of them would like.

Once it so happened that they ran out of things to say. They sat there, for a long while, in silence. Both were thinking about what would happen if they brought their hands closer and, maybe, initiated a tender contact. In everyone's life there are moments that one has to find a way through. This was just such a moment. And that was when Protasov suddenly turned towards Tanyusha, confidently took hold of both her hands, brought them to his lips and kissed them.

And Tanyusha didn't pull her hands back. Instead, she tilted her head towards him, all timid trust and gentleness. And they stayed this way, snuggled together, for quite some time. Minutes ticked away; the cuckoo called, but they remained silent.

The following day both waited to see if a similar moment would happen again. It did, and it all felt even easier – but somehow not enough anymore, though just as good.

Oh, Tanyusha, no one knows the ways of love, even if, since the beginning of time, it comes as it always does.

Protasov walks home beaming, a spring in his step. Tanyusha is now alone and getting ready for bed, her movements fluid and unhurried lest she should spill any from the cup of this new feeling. Afterwards she cannot sleep, reliving these moments and not fully aware of what is going on; her heart has never loved before. Be what it may, life now has a meaning, a purpose, and is brimming with expectations.

He who cometh had put in an unaffected, unexpected, and most timely appearance.

MOSCOW, 1919

The houses of Moscow were stuck together by their frozen walls. A savvy engraver, Ivan Pavlov,[106] was making hectic sketches and carving moulds in wood, keen to immortalise the receding beauty of those wooden houses. He might draw something one day, only for shadowy silhouettes to come creeping along, felt boots and all, in the early hours of the following morning to size the place up, have a good look and listen, and set about prying the planks off, working their way from the fence inwards. The wood would be whisked away on a sled – anything to avoid a clash with the militia.

One silhouette after another, hats with ear flaps pulled down low or wrapped around with a scarf, gloves with holes torn from where the fingers should be, they would be going at it with all their desperate might, while the more audacious among them would even remember to bring along an axe. They would burrow their way deeper inside the house, chopping the staircase into little fragments, ripping the door off its hinges. Like ants, they would whisk away all they could carry, splinter after splinter, plank after plank, leaving sharp grooves in the trampled-down snow and grazing themselves on the protruding wrought iron nails.

The door would then slide down the street, clinging to the fences, for safety.

....

[106]   Ivan Nikolayevich Pavlov (1872–1951), author of block wood paintings and linocuts depicting a 'disappearing' Moscow.

A wooden beam would silently float along, perched on two shoulders.

Doubled in half, they would drag away everything: an old grandmother would grab some splintered offcuts, and someone stronger – a floorboard.

When morning came, nothing would be left in the place where once had stood a little wooden house, except a protruding brick pipe and the little stone inglenook around it, all deep in the snow and mixed up with the remainder of the peeled whitewash. The wooden house was no more. On the other hand, a beneficent smoke now rose in a tidy column over the stone dwellings next door – over there, the people were making themselves warm and cooking whatever they could lay their hands on.

A new day would arise, and stubborn people would crawl out of their houses, sacks and baskets at the ready, looking for the white calico shop sign with its faded red lettering, and take their place in the queue, not quite sure what it was they were queuing for this time. The sign would be flapping in the wind. The doors would open late, and the freezing people would seep through, shivering, and arrange themselves into well-organised lines, with numbers scribbled in chalk on a sleeve or with an indelible pencil on a palm. They would get not what they needed but whatever proved available: a cake of grey soap, a jar of cheap jam, a tiny vial of tea essence. The shopper who had already received whatever it was would leave under the jealous gazes of those who hadn't received anything yet. But the door would already be banging shut – all gone, nothing left, come back tomorrow or the Devil alone knows when.

In Granatovy Lane, a little villa sat a-slumber behind its cast-iron grill, its pretty columns dusted with snow. It no longer had a roof: that had been removed quite some time ago. The walls, too, had been half-dismantled, and the only things still standing were the columns. The villa was nearly extinct: cosy, gentrified, obsolete. A forgotten sign hung over the gate: 'Ring for the caretaker'. The snow in the garden was deep, white, pure.

St Basil's varicoloured cupolas[107] were covered with snow too. Inside, underneath the decorated vaults, a tiny priest in a pointed cap hurried along. In the annex a service was in progress, and old women in black were chewing their lips, all shrouded in shawls. Meanwhile, underneath his brocaded robe, the deacon was wearing a fur-lined body warmer, and felt boots on his old, freezing legs. The incense burner was giving off cheap fumes. 'Let us pray for a clement climate that will ensure abundance of the fruits of the earth, and for times of peace.'

Passing by the printing pioneer Fyodorov,[108] on whose shoulder perched a tiny hungry sparrow, a carter barrelled down from the Lubyanka towards Theatre Square across the snow drifts blocking the desolate throughfare, his horse still alive. He looked fit, and carters were a rarity these days; he could afford to pick and choose whether he wanted a fare. These fellows had no fear: they could transport their own firewood as well as the straw for their horses. Getting oats, though, was excruciatingly hard. These days a carter could earn far better than most, so everyone was respectful towards them.

From the Vladimirsky Gate all the way to the Ilyinsky, along the entire length of the Kitai-Gorod[109] wall, all one

....

[107]　The Cathedral of Vasily the Blessed, commonly known as Saint Basil's Cathedral, is a church in Red Square in Moscow, Russia, and is regarded as a cultural symbol of the country.

[108]　Ivan Fyodorov was one of the fathers of Eastern Slavonic printing, the first known Russian printer in Moscow and the Polish-Lithuanian Commonwealth. A monument to Fyodorov still stands in a small plaza between Lubyanka Square and the Bolshoi Theatre.

[109]　Kitai-Gorod is a cultural and historic area within the central part

could find were cigarette lighters and flints. The lighters were manufactured by the workers at their factories: the workforce was not paid at all – there was nothing to pay them with, and nothing to pay them for. The origin of the flints was obscure. Word had it that there was a merchant who had somehow managed to keep an entire boxful of flints, so now he was the richest person in Moscow. However, if you exchanged winks with the right person, you could also lay your hands on a piece of bootlegged smoked fat; having said this, the transaction would have to take place not here, but in some remote gateway, away from prying eyes. On the positive side, the papers for smokes were available to one's heart content, openly, neatly arranged in the best traditions of offering star merchandise: the sheets having been most carefully ripped out of trade ledgers. Comrades would buy the paper by the sheet and smoke the letters: 'Most esteemed Sir... by way of reciprocating yo... Yours faithful...' It was rumoured that if one were to sell just one volume of such paper by individual sheets, it was possible to live an entire week off the proceeds, and not worry about hunger or any such privations.

The people walking down Tverskaya Street were wrapped up to their eyes, sack-like backpacks on their shoulders. There were service rations, congealed ink, typewriters with no ribbons – but rumour had it some honey had been brought in from Ukraine, and would be available against stamps. Their lips were clamouring for something sweet; jaws had been sent into spasm by the accursed saccharine.

....
of Moscow, defined by the remnants of now almost entirely razed fortifications, narrow streets and very densely built cityscape. It is separated from the Kremlin by Red Square.

Something baffling was written on the side wall of the Iviron Chapel,[110] something about the opiate;[111] there were many other scribbled messages on the walls and stone fences. Futurists[112] had painted murals on the walls of the Passions of the Christ Nunnery, while the façade of the Alexander II Military School displayed lists of luminaries from all over the world. Among the great names were the names of non-entities – although by this time some of the great names, too, had been suppressed and forgotten. Passers-by would read and marvel, but have no time to stop and think.

What's set in stone today becomes warped and faded tomorrow.

The Kremlin stood as ever, encircled by its crenelated walls, and beyond the walls were the people, unaccustomed to the Kremlin. Bayonets at the gates, and passes pierced by bayonets. Still, not all gates provided access, even if you did have a proper piece of paper, stamped and all; the only possible point of entry was through the Nikolsky and St Trinity gates. Above all of it floated Ivan the Great[113] – dead, much like everything else nowadays – the cannon, the bell, and the palaces.[114] It had always felt cold inside the Moscow Krem-

....

[110] The Iviron Chapel, by the Resurrection gate leading onto Red Square, was demolished in 1929 and rebuilt in 1994–1995. It holds a copy of the Iviron icon of Saint Mary.

[111] The author must be referring to a slogan of those days – 'Religion is the opium of the masses'.

[112] Russian Futurism is the broad term for a movement of Russian poets and artists who adopted the principles of Filippo Marinetti and espoused a rejection of the past, and a celebration of speed, machinery, violence, youth, industry, and urbanism, the destruction of academies and museums.

[113] The Belfry inside the Kremlin ensemble, still there today.

[114] Historic monuments inside the Kremlin.

lin, only warming up for Easter, for the sunrise service. But Easter or sunrise services were no more.

The Arbat, however, was still alive, seeing as it was a shortcut to and from the Smolensky Market. A formerly grand lady dragged along a pendulum clock (the spring clanking audibly) and some white shoes. In other words, she was trying to offer scraps from the bottom of her trove – but who on earth would be lured by a pair of white shoes in winter? And plodding back from the market, the formerly grand lady would pull a sack fashioned from a rug, and the contents of the sack would be forever unknown – perhaps frozen potatoes. Such potatoes should first be soaked in cold water, to help them thaw in peace, and then, having excised the black spots, one should boil them in water as per the normal recipe. After all, it wasn't every day that one got lucky and chanced on some dead horse's meat. That said, if you cooked potatoes without skill, you ran the risk of ending up with an ink-coloured mush. And as for herrings, a good way to cook those was to wrap them in a newspaper and smoke them in a samovar pipe. One had to learn the skills; one had to adjust to absolutely everything.

The people were doggedly eager to survive. They chewed oats, half-heartedly bloating themselves with rancid millet, hiding from each other the pastilles of saccharine. In good demand was 'gambled' sugar (it was aspirational, too) – that was the sugar used as a stake placed by soldiers when playing cards; it was cheaper to buy, and with skill and patience it was possible to steam off the slime and the grime, and then, once dry, slice it into cubes. This method worked well really, and after all, sugar was sugar, whatever one said.

By nightfall, people were exhausted, spent, and ready for bed. They would sleep with their clothes on – a hat on the head, felt boots on the feet. Most would curl up somewhere in the kitchen, luxuriating in the warmth feebly lingering after the evening meal. Prior to that, it was imperative to plug the cracks and crevices in the doors leading to other rooms where the glacial winter had taken hold. Should there be a little stove, people would arrange themselves in a star – legs towards the stove. Should electricity be available, it would be used with no thought of economising – everything was free nowadays. There was one fellow who had come up with the bright idea of installing an electric bulb in both of his felt boots, and that was how he slept, at the end of the day – warmer, in a heated garment of sorts. People had grown wise. For all that, electricity wasn't available everywhere, and certainly not at all times: many lines had been cut and shut off. In the absence of electricity, one had to fashion a smoking night lamp out of a bottle, thus enabling work after dark; oil was unaffordable, and such a lamp could run on stinking kerosene. Old shoelaces made the best wicks of all. How important it was to know all of this!

Once the people were asleep, rats would crawl out of the underground through a maze of new tunnels – arrogant, audacious, betailed, beady-eyed. They would scatter round the rooms and kitchens, rattle jars and bottles, send frying pans flying to the floor; they would squeal, fight, and scrabble up to the ceiling, where housewives had left rank butter and the remainder of a chunk of meat suspended from a rope. These days the rats were operating in packs and gangs, and if they failed to happen on some loot, they were adept at biting on flesh that people had left exposed.

In the year 1919, the city of Moscow was dominated by rats. A virulent grey cat would be rented out to neighbours, sometimes for as much as a pound of flour per night. Some, planning for the future, were trying to raise a kitten, sacrificing their own meagre rations, feeding it on the last reserves of food. A cat acquired a status of paramount importance in any household. The coveted aim was to let it mature; it would then feed itself, and possibly even its masters.

The worst enemy was people, the second worst were rats, and the third the diabolically pale lice. Flop houses, train stations, market places – that was where they flourished, unshakeable. At the same time, it was probably not cheaper to die, certainly not compared to living, and it would also involve endless hassle for loved ones.

Still, not everything spelt grief; there were occasions for joy, too. Joy came with each unexpectedly available slice of bread, each undreamed-of hand-out dealt by Fate. Joy was generated by the neighbour who had barely anything himself but still came over, offered compassion and helped to saw a damp beam into manageable firewood. Joy arrived in the morning, on account of the previous night having receded safely, taking away fear and leaving no lasting damage in its wake. Joy was ignited by the afternoon sun: perhaps it will get warmer soon? Joy streamed in with the water that suddenly spouted out of the tap on the second floor. Joy prevailed in the absence of a more bitter grief, or when this bitterer grief happened not to you but to somebody next door.

That year life was unbearable, and man had no kind feelings for man. Women stopped giving birth. Five-year-old children were considered adults, as they had become so in all reality.

That year, beauty departed, and what arrived instead was wisdom. Since then, no one is wiser than a Russian.

UNDER LOCK AND KEY

Astafyev lay on his bunk, watching the shadow that shimmered across the ceiling. The shadow was blurred and quivering, as the light of the lamp post shivered in the courtyard outside the window, the panes of which had been smeared over with white paint.

The Special Department's cell had been designed for one prisoner but was currently used to hold six, so the bunks had been wedged together cheek by jowl. Next to Astafyev, sleeping peacefully, was an ex-general, Ivan Ivanovich Klark, arrested because of a coincidence of surnames, or possibly as a hostage, even if he was an old man, quiet and unremarkable. On Astafyev's other side, his eyes as wide open as Astafyev's, lay an older worker from Presnya,[115] picked up either because of a false accusation or, perhaps, through the agency of his own imprudent tongue. He had just been brought back to the cell from the night-time interrogation in the course of which his case officer, a bully of Latvian stock,[116] kept threatening

....

[115] The name of Presnya District is inherited from the Presnya River, now flowing largely in an underground pipe. In December 1905 the whole district, a centre of the textile industry, was taken over by revolutionary militias. Government troops had to bring in artillery to subdue the revolt. Much of the Presnya District was destroyed, and more than one thousand were killed, mostly civilians caught in the fighting. In November 1917, Presnya workers took over the neighbourhood again.

[116] The Latvian Riflemen were originally a military formation of the

him with execution by firing squad – but on what charges Timoshin never understood.

And so now Timoshin couldn't sleep and was full of anguish – a feeling that was slowly gnawing at his heart. Such emotions, together with insomnia, had been totally alien to him in his previous life; he felt utterly hopeless when trying to conquer these feelings on his own. Tentatively, he whispered his question:

'Well, Alexei Dmitriyevich, you aren't asleep yet, are you?'

'I'm not. I don't feel like sleeping.'

'I'm wide awake too.'

'Did they exhaust you at the interrogation?'

'That's just it. Thing is, I can't get my head round it. They say, "we'll shoot you." But whatever for? What do you reckon, Alexei Dmitriyevich, do they really mean it?'

Astafyev sat up on his bunk, his back to the wall, his arms round his knees.

'Anything's possible. Are you afraid?'

'How can I not be? They'll take my life for no reason, and what about my family? So, you do reckon they're capable of it?'

'How should I know? They may shoot you tomorrow, but equally, they may let you walk.'

'Besides, I'm a proletarian. Though, truth be told, I do own a little house in the country.'

'Are you guilty of anything? What are they charging you with?'

....

Imperial Russian Army, assembled in 1915 in Latvia in order to defend the Baltic territories against the Germans in World War I. In May 1917 large parts of the Latvian regiments transferred their loyalty to the Bolsheviks. They became known as Red Latvian Riflemen, and actively participated in the Russian Civil War. The Riflemen took an active part in the suppression of anti-Bolshevik uprisings in Moscow and Yaroslavl in 1918.

MIKHAIL OSORGIN

'I'm guilty of absolutely nothing, Alexei Dmitriyevich, as God is my witness. But he went on and on: "Why", he says, "You're in cahoots with the factory owner," he says, "You've been hiding him." But our master, he's been on the run for ages; where to – how would I know? And it looks like I've been helping him all along. But this is a total lie, I don't know anything. So why shoot me, Alexei Dmitriyevich?'

'What's your name, Timoshin?'

'My name? I'm Alexei, too.'

'And your father's name?'

'Platon. My father was called Platon, and me, I'm Alexei Platonovich.'

'So, Alexei Platonovich, fear not. This investigator of yours is just throwing his weight around. He's got his own agenda. They won't shoot you.'

'They won't, Alexei Dmitriyevich? But what if they fix it up? This lot, they can get away with murder. You said it yourself: anything's possible.'

Astafyev closed his eyes. Would he be able to sleep at all tonight?

'And even if I was hiding the master, is that reason enough to destroy me?'

'How old are you, Timoshin?'

'How old? Fifty-two, going on fifty-three.'

'Would you like to live long?'

'As long as I'm destined. It's not for us to decide.'

'However long you live, Alexei Platonovich, you won't see anything new. There's nothing to feel sorry about.'

'I've got family in the country. As for myself, I'm not old yet, Alexei Dmitriyevich, I can still work perfectly well.'

'And how much joy does this work give you?'

'No joy, true enough. Still, it's an income. Nowadays, of course, there's no profit, just an eternal fast. We strive to make ends meet.'

'There you go, then. What's there to fear? They want to kill you – so to hell with them. There's nothing to feel sorry for.'

'How can you say that, Alexei Dmitriyevich? Just like that, no rhyme nor reason – and they do you in? Where's the fairness in that?'

Astafyev stifled a yawn. It would be great if it had signalled drowsiness, rather than boredom. Here is a man, living for no good reason, totally devoid of joy, and still clamouring for fairness if you please.

'You know what, Timoshin? Calm down and go to sleep. They are putting the frighteners on you just because they can. You will soon be released. Go and live for as long as you see fit.'

Astafyev had marked his fifth month inside. He'd been summoned three times to be interrogated by the consumptive Brikman. Obviously, the focal point was the man in the yellow spats. What an odd character! Whatever made him put on those yellow spats? However, quite a daredevil, too: they had been hunting for him in Moscow for three months, and had failed. Meanwhile he was even delivering lectures in all those Unions of Liberation.[117] The attempted assassination[118] was all his doing, of course.

If they manage to prove that he'd spent a night in my place, then I'm finished, that much is certain. Who tracked me down?

....

[117]   The Union of Liberation was a liberal political group founded in Saint Petersburg, Russia, in January 1904. Its goal was originally the replacement of the absolutism of the Tsar with a constitutional monarchy. Here the name is used ironically as a reference to verbose liberal-minded groups and associations with no real political clout or relevance to the events of the day.

[118]   At this point in the narrative, it is the autumn of 1918. The attempted assassination must refer to the attempt on Lenin's life on 30 August 1918.

Who denounced me? My neighbour, Zavalishin? Zavalishin is a
Chekist, no doubt on that score. Still, it's not him. He just couldn't
do it. Besides, that night he was out. No, it's not Zavalishin. Most
likely, Denisov, the House Management Committee boss. Ah, to hell
with the lot of them...

Astafyev got up from his bunk and stealthily made his
way towards the window. Against the whitened glass of the
inside pane there appeared a tiny shadow. It slid along the
edge, getting closer to the top window, which opened into
the cell. Astafyev came right up and raised his hand, poised in
anticipation. At the precise moment that the mouse stuck out
its tiny muzzle, ready to sneak into the cell, Astafyev flicked
it lightly between the trembling whiskers, so that the mouse
squeaked faintly and plopped down to the window sill.

Success!

Smiling contentedly, Astafyev settled himself back onto
his bunk. The little bastard would have eaten the bread otherwise. The previous night, failing to find it, the mouse had
sneaked into the box and gobbled up several chess pieces
sculpted out of moist breadcrumbs by the general, a real connoisseur of the craft. After that the queen, the castle and two
pawns had had to be re-moulded all over again.

The mouse had gnawed a channel between the window
panes, and now resided inside the windowsill. It had taken
to making nightly forays into the cell, feeling quite at home
on the table and inside the little parcels of food brought in
by visitors. In the absence of something to eat, it was even
happy to steal its way onto the bunks. Once it had bitten Ivan
Ivanovich, the general, on his big toe – his blanket was too
short and kept sliding down.

Suddenly, Astafyev felt overcome with a passionate yearning to be free. *How stupid! Right here, behind this window, this*
wall, is the street, people, cartmen. Nothing more than two sheets
of glass and several bricks. And the savage will of a few individ-
uals, something that should be possible to cast aside with a word,

a gesture, a persuasive argument. It is simply too ludicrous! To be unafraid of death and yet not thrash around or smash doors or engage in a fistfight or expose one's chest to a bullet.

Gritting his teeth, he clenched his fists and thought: *To scatter the lot of them to the four winds of heaven!*

He felt the sweet delight of muscles flexing in his arms and back, his body only slightly enfeebled by prison. He would throw punches, trample, bite, return blows, disperse the pack of apes with a shard of glass, rush down the stairs dodging the shots, into the courtyard, by the entrance, knock the guard off his feet, break out into the street, disappear round the corner, cheat his pursuers, and then change direction and walk home unhurriedly, observing from a distance the commotion among the Chekists, the melee of automobiles, the impotent frenzy of the outsmarted executioners.

No, home was out of bounds – they'd find him there straight away. He'd make a detour through the maze of tiny crooked streets and head off towards Sivtsev Vrazhek, rap on the glass pane from outside, wait till the top window opened, and shout in a muffled voice:

'Tanya, don't be afraid, it's me, Astafyev, the actor Smekhachev. They're after me, hide me, Tanya!'

And she would answer:

'Oh my God, it's you? But of course, hurry up!'

Once inside, he would waste no words, offer no explanations but take her in his arms, for the first time, resolutely and forever.

A soft whisper came from the adjacent bunk:

'Can't sleep, Alexei Dmitriyevich? Having a tough time of it, too?'

And then, after a pause:

'I saw you flicking the mouse on the nose, very deft. What a peculiar animal – lives by hunting in a prison!'

EFFORTS ON HIS BEHALF

Uncle Boris refused point blank:

'No, Tanyusha, I can't possibly be of any help. I do meet with him occasionally – we have board meetings from time to time, but those are of a purely technical nature, matters of defence. As for personal relations with him – I have none. Nothing beyond "Hello, goodbye". You do understand that our department is completely autonomous and concentrates exclusively on science, no politics at all. For me, Tanyusha, it's just not possible.'

'I do understand that it's awkward for you to do it yourself. But all I need is a reference, just to be allowed to see him.'

'It's all the same, Tanyusha – since it's a political issue, and such a serious one at that.'

'But Uncle, Astafyev was arrested by accident and by error, he couldn't possibly be connected with any of this.'

'I know nothing, and there is no way that you know any better.'

'But Uncle, I'm sure of it! If one interceded on his behalf, he might be released, perhaps even immediately. All that's needed is access.'

'In times like ours, Tanyusha, it's better to wait, not intercede. All you'll achieve will be a smear on your own record – hardly of any help to him. Besides, our surname rings bells. If he isn't guilty, like you say, he's sure to be released.'

'But he's our friend, Uncle Boris, and he hasn't got anyone else to put in a word on his behalf.'

'I do understand, Tanyusha, and I… what I'm trying to say is for his own benefit. It's possible that all this flurry of interest will attract attention, and it'll only get worse for him; whereas now… If it were coming from his family…'

'He's got none.'

'So, there you are, you see!'

'What exactly do I see, Uncle?'

'As I say, the thing is… I've got nothing whatsoever to do with any of it. And the main thing, what I fear most – is that my recommendation… I'm really not in their good books. Well, there's nothing in particular, but they treat us, experts, with suspicion.'

'In other words, you're unwilling to help, Uncle Boris?'

'I am, I am willing, but I can't. I am unable to do a thing. It hurts, really. I'd like to help but I'm powerless. These are the accursed times we live in. Oh, Tanyusha, will we live to see better times? I really can't tell. It's an absolute nightmare.'

Tanyusha fell silent, thought it over, and then raised her head abruptly and gave Uncle Boris an attentive stare. In the beam of her scrutiny, he slumped a little, and muttered again: 'Yes, a nightmare; what else would you call it?'

Tanyusha got to her feet, picked up her purse and said: 'Uncle Boris…'

'What is it, Tanyusha, my love?'

'Nothing. Goodbye, Uncle Boris.'

He saw her right to the exit, dropping slightly behind as they walked. In the concierge's office, where several employees had congregated, he shook her hand and whispered uneasily, obviously eager to appear affectionate:

'I understand, Tanyusha, I understand you. You're so decent and kind. But my advice to you is still the same: wait a while.'

Tanyusha stayed silent. He swept around with his eyes, and, dropping his voice an octave, offered another pronouncement, in a whisper:

'Whatever happens, you know... I would resolutely insist that you... even if you find a way in, that you shouldn't mention me. To me, personally, it's all the same, I'm not afraid, but this way you might send the whole project haywire. After all, I'm an expert, a dangerous presence,[119] a suspicious element in their eyes. You might jeopardise the whole enterprise...'

Without turning her head, Tanyusha said loudly, without a smile:

'Don't worry, Uncle. I won't jeopardise anything for you.'

And she left.

In the evening, when the new friend of the little villa at Sivtsev Vrazhek, Vasya's associate Protasov, came by, they had a long conversation, discussing the business at hand. They pored over a list of names, trying to decide who, and through whose offices, was most likely to prove approachable. Protasov's circle of useful contacts was small. For all that, he did plan several business visits for the following day.

'It may or may not work; still, I should try. I place my hopes on this old acquaintance of mine; I think he's got their ear. Mind you, he's not a scoundrel; on the contrary, he's rather a decent chap. I think we could at least pump him for some information. As concerns a referral for you – this is where I'm really not sure.'

The following morning Protasov was at a friend's, whom he hadn't seen for ages. Their meeting was cordial.

'And what are you up to these days?'

'Me? I'm a sack man.'

'How peculiar. Is it really profitable?'

'I manage to get by.'

....

[119] Uncle Boris's ramblings are not complete cowardice or madness. Engineers and managers from the tzarist regime became one of the very first targets of the show trials, the Shakhty Trial being the first, held in 1928.

'So why aren't you working in your own field? Good people are in demand now.'

Protasov explained his request: to find out, through relevant channels, why Astafyev had been arrested and on what charges. His acquaintance, though far from ecstatic, agreed to help.

'Alright, I'll telephone this character; mind you, one's got to be careful around him, so don't get your hopes up.'

And he picked up the phone:

'Hello, that you? Yes, yes. Recognised my voice? Look, old chap, how did it finish yesterday? Did you stay long? Ah. Oh, I see. You reckon it'll work? Well then, that's excellent. Okay. So that means, not earlier than the day after tomorrow? Whatever you say, I'll telephone. Great, so long... Wait a minute, there was one more thing I meant to ask you... Yes, that's it – would you kindly provide me with a little piece of information, I'm being harassed by the arrested fellow's family, what's his name? It's somewhere here on my desk. What? I don't think so, it feels trivial, he must've been taken in for nothing. It's just that his relatives are bothering me incessantly... His name is...'

It took them about half an hour to get an answer. The response was rather disappointing.

'Nothing definite but very strong suspicions. The case is with Comrade Brikman, and that one likes to sit on his cases.'

'And if someone interceded on his behalf?' asked Protasov.

'It helps, sometimes. Do you know him personally?'

'I don't, but we have friends in common. There's this young lady, she is making inquiries on his behalf.'

'And what young lady would that be?'

Protasov thought it over and then gave Tanyusha's name. He did trust his acquaintance.

'Is she related to the professor?'

'His granddaughter.'

'Good, this is good. The professor is a well-known man, well-respected. Couldn't he get involved himself?'

'He's too old for all of this.'

'So, what are you after, Protasov, a reference for her?'

'That would be great.'

'Alright. Do you vouch for her?'

'Yes, of course.'

'Come on, I'm just saying. Things happen. Are you in love with her? Is she pretty? So, to whom should I refer you? I can only direct you to this person, the one I've just called. I'm okay in his eyes, not so handsome with the others.'

'And who's he?'

The acquaintance stated the surname of this 'character', which was sufficiently prominent for even Protasov to have heard of him. He wasn't the person Tanyusha was eager to get access to, but Protasov's acquaintance, on hearing who she was ultimately trying to approach, burst out laughing.

'No chance, old chap, that's never going to happen. No point in even trying, impossible to arrange. Besides, he shuns all visitors. He'll never even hear you out. My crony is more *au fait* as regards low-grade cases. Also, there's this... he's not a first-rate individual; in a nutshell – a thoroughly nasty piece of work. Still, he's got what it takes these days. A word of caution – one's got to mind one's mouth around him, no idle chatter. Do warn her, this sweetheart of yours.'

'Are you friends with him?'

'This one? We go way back, to the days in exile.[120] We aren't friends, but we do see each other around. Me, I'm not a Communist, politics isn't my thing, but I do sit on various

....

[120] A very common sentence in the days before the revolution of 1917, handed down on charges of hostile political activity. It often boiled down to so many years in exile; specific punishments ranged from a prohibition against living in central cultural and industrial centres to time spent in Siberia.

boards. And you, Protasov, should really enter Soviet employ. Good people are desperately needed now, otherwise there'll be no one decent left. And you, you're a safe pair of hands.'

'That was why they threw me out of the factory, in all probability.'

'Did they? Come on, that was an aberration, a special initiative – they were randomly forcing out all engineers, left, right and centre. Shall I find you a vacancy? You don't work anywhere else at the moment, do you?'

Protasov named an office that had nothing to do with either engineering or mining. He was on their books but hardly spent any time there.

'What nonsense is that? There's nothing for you to be doing there.'

'That's precisely what I'm doing there – nothing. I only drop in from time to time, to collect my tiny package of yeast or a miniscule jar of molasses.'

'What utter rubbish. I'll have you employed as an engineer.'

Protasov mulled it over.

'To tell the truth, I'd like to work. The problem is, I don't quite trust what passes for work now. And I'd really rather not waste my time.'

'The conditions for work now aren't optimal, it's true. But it'll all sort itself out, eventually.'

'And who'll do this sorting out?'

'Who? You will, for one. You, me, the others; in a word – the good people. For the time being, we are being governed by fools and juveniles, that's why it's all going haywire. But have patience, the time will come, the dust will settle and everything will fall into its groove. It takes time, Protasov.'

'I know. However, by that happy time, there won't be a single engine left intact.'

'We'll get new engines.'

'You'll have no resources for that.'

'We'll find a way. What a pessimist you are, Protasov. Are you saying that Russia will be no more, is that it?

'It's possible.'

'No, my dear chap, that's not what's going to happen. It only feels like that now because we are all tired. Me, I'm a level-headed sort who has first-hand knowledge of the powers that be. But I'll tell you this, Protasov: absolutely not, Russia will not perish, it's just not that kind of a country. Then again you, Protasov, don't really believe it yourself, you're just saying it for the sake of saying it.'

They parted amicably, Protasov carrying away a reference for Tanyusha.

Deep down, he's a good sort, thought Protasov. *Of course, Russia won't perish, and of course one should put in an effort to make sure it doesn't. Still, not everyone would be able to clown around over the telephone and be on a first-name basis with all sorts of lowlife. Then again, one mustn't judge him all that harshly; had he behaved differently, he wouldn't have been able to offer help in such a tricky situation, and what's more, without much ado or affectation. It's a real must, though, to work. If only it were a trifle easier to breathe, and there were fewer halfwits to be tolerated...*

THE WOLVES ARE CIRCLING

Amazing, how unafraid the wolves had become!

That winter was heavy with snow, and on his way from the forest to the village, the wolf sank his hind legs deep into snow many times. The moonlight shone on the black track of prints in his wake – not a straight line towards the village, but more like an arch bearing towards the woodland, as if the wolf were involuntarily gravitating towards the shadows.

The track across the bridge was well-trodden, although now, in the winter, the bridge itself wasn't visible; the snow was drifting over the frozen river, bringing the river course up to the level of the fields. Only the withies of the willow stood black, indicating where the mouth of the river was.

By the edge of the track the wolf cowered, and briefly howled in a muted bass. The dogs retaliated – reluctantly, from afar. And the wolf raced forward lopsidedly, his tail rigid.

The second *izba* from the end was the Kolchagins'; it belonged to Andrei and Dunyasha's father. The *izba* was large. Its left side, the one with the front garden, was occupied by Dunyasha's sister and her husband. They had a child.

The wolves had grown bolder because, by now, fewer men were left in the village – some had been killed in the war, the others had stayed on in the cities. Moreover, there was hardly any powder available to shoot the wolves; if any shooting took place, it was mostly at people. Besides, it had become much more difficult to feed the dogs.

Dunyasha's mother was still relatively young, forty-five years of age. Her name was Anna, while Dunyasha's sister shared her name but went by Anyuta. They just about made ends meet. So, when Dunyasha returned from the city, though she brought with her all kinds of goods and a little money, it meant another burden for the family. Of Andrei, they had seen neither hide nor hair.

The Kolchagins' dog was named Spurt; someone had come up with this rather strange name for her. Spurt was getting on somewhat, grubby and on the small side. She could barely sniff out the wolves, but then again, what was she supposed to guard? The sheep were locked in and the cow stayed in its shed, right behind the wall in the old folks' room. There was nothing to guard; all she could do was show solidarity with the other dogs. Spurt had pressed herself against the warm wall and was trying to sleep, although the main sleeping was of course done inside, in the daytime.

That everything was locked in was perfectly clear to the wolf, too. However, what was to be done? He was drawn towards this village that smelled of cowsheds and sheep pens. He was gaunt and hungry, very hungry. Frozen intestines or bones might be dug up from the kitchen middens. Or perhaps he would just take in the rich smell of food. He approached the row of *izbas* from behind, crawling from the side of the vegetable gardens, not the road. Not a single dog yelped – all were asleep.

The wolf flared his nostrils and drew in the air, his muzzle hoary with frost. He shuffled off towards the midden, with its multitude of dog paw prints – the dogs went hungry too, now.

The dogs had merely rooted around on the surface, but the wolf burrowed deeper, sinking in his teeth, helping himself with his claws. He had barely got going when Spurt burst out barking, and the whole canine population of the village broke out in solidarity.

Spurt, as the leader of the chorus, was shrieking and whining, scuttling around the courtyard and leaping on and off the porch at full speed. She was rushing around, flinching away, scared, quivering and bristling, alarmed by the wolf's presence. But as for confronting him directly… surely, that was way too much for her! She preferred to bash against the door and howl herself hoarse.

Nothing stirred in the village; its residents woke, briefly, aware of the proximity of the wolves. But this was something that happened nightly. What was there to look at? All doors were bolted.

The wolf raced from midden to midden, clawing, gnawing. There was a spot where his nose led him to – a sheep shed, directly beside where the dogs were barking. The shed wafted the smell of warm sheep; the wolf salivated, and his saliva froze into icicles.

His ears were bursting from all the barking and yelping, but the village was asleep.

Soundly and deeply.

The wolf's hunger circled around it, from heap to heap, from *izba* to *izba*. The wolf made two full circles around the settlement, drooling poisonous hungry saliva over the prints of his paws.

Reaching the outskirts, he plopped down, licked his chops, and started howling at the village, *cursing it for his starvation.*

Spurt, by Kochagin's *izba*, was cowering and skulking under his curses. The people didn't understand it. But Spurt did.

Woe was upon us!

In the middle of the village stood a pole. On this pole was a bell, scantily protected by a birdhouse roof. That bell should have been rung, to let everyone know:

The wolf has placed a curse on the village.

This curse would bring hunger, so that the people themselves would root around their middens and eat their dogs.

So that they, too, would be seduced by the warm, rich smell of the sheep's manure.

So that they would howl at the moon and wish misfortune on one another.

And would be afraid of their own shadows, and keep their tails between their legs, and become shadows of themselves.

So that they would have nothing to keep under lock and key, hiding it from the wolf's hunger.

May the human hunger be more terrible than that of the wolves!

Let this bell toll, making the people aware of the forthcoming anguish, so that they would thrash around in fear, and gnash their teeth, and drool hungry saliva.

The moon smiled while it listened to the wolf sending his curses upon the village. It did not believe in them. Or perhaps it did, but felt no compassion for either the wolf or the people.

Spotting a young hare hurriedly hopping from the side of the kitchen gardens in which it was still possible to find a cabbage core, the wolf felt reinvigorated and gave chase. The hare was light on its feet, ever so quickly hopping along the frozen crust, while the wolf was heavyset and kept sinking in, biting on his wet tongue. It dawned on him that if he ran in a circular arc towards the forest, he could head the hare off.

He was already devouring the hare with his eyes, emitting small yelps of anticipation, frightening his prey with the blazing glow of his eyes.

Running in circles, they reached the edge of the forest. And there was a brief second when the wolf was about to snap the hare's skimpy tail with his yellow teeth. But the hare ducked into a bush: still visible, but already beyond reach. The wolf craned his neck, jerking his head higher to see better above the snow-laden branches, and started advancing towards the hare's shelter; but the white hare sprang backwards and, pushing his rump forward, scuttled deeper into the forest. No way to catch up with him now, of course.

The wolf plodded, bereft of any hope, all the way to his own lair, to quench his hunger with hungry dreams about the warmth of the sheep and the greed of the humans.

It was morning. The village came to life. Spurt wagged her tail and squeezed inside, eager to take a nap in the warmth of the *izba*.

Her shift was over – the dog's guard duty.

The night passed. The day dawned.

CHILDHOOD FRIENDS

Vasya's heart was in his throat when, on turning into Sivtsev Vrazhek, he came up to the little villa's familiar door and knocked.

He was wearing a short fur coat, felt boots with a red motif, probably made in Kazan,[121] a woollen scarf, and a warm hat with pull-down flaps. After the typhus, he had spent another month in bed – the doctor feared complications. As the severity of his disease subsided, Tanyusha's visits became much less frequent. Her own life was far from easy, since she now had to run the household, cook, do the laundry, and sometimes even trade various trifles at Smolensky Market, while in the evenings, or even daytime – if it was a festive occasion – she played in concerts. Given the general impoverishment, the workers' clubs now paid their performers less, whereas private tutoring jobs were impossible to find, especially in winter, when hardly any classes took place anyway: school premises stood unheated, and the primary concern of children and adolescents alike, like that of the adults, was hunting for food.

There was another thing, though: somehow, Vasya could find nothing to discuss with Tanyusha. When she visited him, she tried to share rumours about various goings-on, but both the rumours and the goings-on were so depressing

....

[121]   The village of Kukmor near the industrial centre of Kazan was a centre for traditional crafts involving felt.

and inconsistent that they really were a very poor source of entertainment for a sick person. Sometimes she would come alone, and at other times together with Protasov, or rather, the two of them would bump into each other at Vasya's by chance. Alyona visited him daily, just as before, although, strictly speaking, by now Vasya didn't really need a nurse. But all Alyona was capable of talking about was the exorbitant prices. There was some awkwardness between Vasya and Tanyusha, something unfinished, and both were perfectly aware of what it was that hadn't been discussed properly. And thus, Tanyusha's visits grew rare.

By the time Vasya finally started going out, the streets of Moscow had long since been drowned in snow, and nobody was available to shovel it off. The snowdrifts, pitted by hooves and flattened by runners, shrouded the pavements underneath. In some places raked-up snow was piled in ramparts, in order to clear a tiny pathway by a gate or an entrance. No one was clearing the snow by the little villa in Sivtsev Vrazhek – the caretaker Nikolai had left for the country back at the end of autumn.

'What's there for me to do here, eh? Just another burden. Life might get easier by the springtime, or, could be, I'll be back by next year. It ain't gonna be like this forever.'

His lodge had been dismantled for firewood. Some time ago, in the days of his tenure, the bathhouse had had to be dismantled, too. Still, it meant that they were well supplied with wood for the winter.

It was Vasya's first visit to Sivtsev Vrazhek, although he had started getting out a week previously. He had kept putting it off. His original plan had been to drop in at such a time when only the old ornithologist would be at home. Then he reasoned that this was all well and good, but he did have to finally meet Tanya again, in her own home, on her territory. After all, nothing had really happened. Everything had worked out the way it should.

He found Tanyusha alone. The professor had gone out for his constitutional, and taken his briefcase with the books.

Tanyusha was happy to see Vasya, if slightly embarrassed. She sensed Vasya's unease, and saw that he was behaving as if he were in a stranger's house, as if he hadn't visited them since the days of his early youth. Tanyusha also knew that she was the reason. But was she to blame, really? Had she ever promised him anything?

He was thinking that talking to her, getting things off his chest, would be difficult, and he was afraid. Yet, he felt it was important. It was imperative to say that he, Vasya, understood everything and that he, Vasya, wished her all the happiness possible. Afterwards it would become easier to meet, and to feel at ease with one another, like in the days of old; okay, not exactly like in those days, but still, to be on friendly terms. So that this discomfort would fade away. It all turned out to be much simpler than that, and the conversation started accidentally.

'So, who lives upstairs nowadays, in your room?'

'For now, no one. Dunyasha left, and her brother, the commissar, vanished even earlier. Those rooms somehow got forgotten and were never entered into any registers. And that's what they are – vacant. But perhaps someone will move in shortly.'

'Someone you know, or just anybody?'

'An acquaintance. It may well be – although nothing's certain – that Pyotr Pavlovich will move in. Although he does have an apartment, with a bath, no less, but these days the water is frozen everywhere anyway, so the bath is no use... Grandpa offered it to him...'

Tanyusha went into great detail, explaining why Protasov would find swapping lodgings beneficial: he would be much closer to his place of work, their rooms would be saved from requisition, seeing as he was entitled to have an extra room for his studies; but then she realised that it wasn't a good idea to go into any of this. Besides, Vasya wasn't listening anyway.

They sat for a while in silence.

Then Vasya asked suddenly:

'Will you marry him?'

She didn't look startled by the question; it was as if she had expected it. Without turning her head, she said:

'I don't know. I like Pyotr Pavlovich. We've become good friends...'

And added in the same voice:

'You disapprove, Vasya?'

She turned her gaze towards him. He sat motionless, looking at the light in the window, and his eyes were brimming with tears.

'Vasya, can it be... are you crying, Vasya?'

Vasya, his gaze fixed on the window, fumbled around for his handkerchief which, as ill luck would have it, he'd left at home.

'There, there, Vasya, is it really that bad?'

He turned away and answered in a trembling, almost childlike voice:

'It's nothing, Tanyusha, you know, it's all the disease's fault, I've become so terribly weaklingey... that's to say, feeble...'

And, having unwittingly created a funny word, Vasya collapsed in sobs.

Tanyusha comforted him the way a mother would comfort a child. She wiped his tears away with her own handkerchief, and caressed his round, closely-cropped head, supporting his forehead as he pressed it against her hand; he was doing that for the first time ever! He might have dreamed about it before, and more than once, but now it had finally happened!

Now Vasya simply didn't know how to raise his head. He felt ashamed of his weakness; besides, he felt the urge to wipe his nose and had nothing to wipe it with. The main thing, though, was that he really had been rendered weak by his disease; that was why it had all happened the way it did.

'You must get better, Vasya, you must grow strong again. You've lost an enormous amount of weight.'

'Forgive me, Tanyusha, all this foolishness.'

'It's nothing, Vasya.'

'I did know it all before, I'd guessed, of course... It's only... But I do wish you every happiness. That's why I've come along, to say it in person.'

'Thank you, Vasya, I know. That is because you're my dear friend, for as long as I can remember, since childhood. Only now let's talk about something else.'

'Let's – what does it matter? I'll keep this handkerchief of yours, may I? I'll wash it later and give it back to you,' he added hurriedly. 'Is the professor going to be back soon? Such a pity I've missed him.'

'Will you stay for a while?'

'Not for long, I must get back home.'

'Are you expecting someone?'

She asked about 'someone' but knew that the only visitor Vasya could expect would be Alyona, who visited regularly. She scrutinised Vasya's face – would it display some new type of embarrassment? But his answer was unaffected:

'Yelena Ivanovna will drop in; she does every day.'

'She's so sweet and warm. It was she, Vasya, who nursed you back to health. But for her, you'd be in a very dark place.'

'Yes, of course. She's wonderful. Above all, she does it all so selflessly, while her own life is far from easy. How much time she has spent on me!'

Tanyusha smiled inwardly:

'You must've become very attached to her during the time of your illness.'

Vasya answered: 'Yes, absolutely!' and thought: *She shouldn't be saying this*! He suddenly realised that it would suit her, Tanyusha, very well indeed if he, Vasya, got attached to Alyona and would need her in the future. Should this be the case, she, Tanyusha, would feel somewhat less constrained, though he had no intention of being a burden to her, which he wouldn't be anyway. Let her love Protasov and marry him. That he, Vasya, had broken down in tears was, of course, silly and ridiculous. But whichever way you looked at it, she shouldn't have mentioned Alyona now, as if trying to give him a consolation prize.

What Vasya also felt was offended on Alyona's behalf. She had without doubt nursed him back to health, and was still taking care of him. She was, of course, compared with Tanyusha, much more down-to-earth – nowhere nearly as well-educated, and when amused, her laughter would taper to a funny nasal sob. But on the other hand, she was very affectionate and kind, very easy to be with. Why, then, drop hints like that, that he, Vasya, could be thus consoled, seeing as Tanyusha didn't love him and was going to marry Protasov?

And so Vasya said:

'Yelena Ivanovna is a no-nonsense person, and is really kind to me. I respect her deeply. Also, she's had quite a few grievous experiences in her own life. I won't ever be able to repay my debt to her.'

Tanyusha realised that Vasya had had to say it. At the same time a very female thought flashed through her mind: *Alright then, Vasya will find a way to repay Alyona!*

And she felt her mood lifting.

The professor came home tired but satisfied. Firstly, the day, although chilly, had been sunny and pleasant. Secondly, as he was delivering a new set of books to the Writers' Shop, he had been shown an issue of an English ornithological journal from the previous year that had accidentally reached their shop. It transpired that the article contained an extensive quote from his book on the migration of birds, and several lines – deferential and polite, in a very foreign way – where the author of the book was referred to as 'a celebrated Russian scientist, an indefatigable researcher of the feathered race.'

In days of old, the professor would read such accolades quite often, not without pleasure, but calmly. But now, in these times of trial and tribulation, completely neglected and isolated from the academic circles of Europe, he felt genuinely overwhelmed. And as he walked home along the Tverskoy Boulevard, hugging to his chest his briefcase with the precious issue, presented to him as a memento, he felt his eyes becoming warm, and a tiny shard of ice chilling his lashes. Inwardly, he felt slightly embarrassed but profoundly satisfied.

Come what may, out there, they still remember the old man!

He also thought: *If only I were younger! We'd wait till it became easier, and then I'd take Tanyusha for a spin around Paris and London. I might even present my report to the ornithological society in English!*

Then an anxious thought came to him: *But I've got no morning coat! I had to barter it for potatoes. I still have a tailcoat, though, on account of the tails – there is no way one could alter it into something simple and useful. But in England it would do the job nicely, especially if the meeting were to take place in the evening.*

Then he thought: *If only I could publish my book! The draft is completely ready, it's just a question of making a fair copy. I've spent over ten years writing it. No point, though, in even thinking about having it published now. Nowadays, no one gets anything published apart from those young chaps, they seem to manage somehow. The titles they come up with are also remarkable:* A Horse Like Any Other.[122] *Christ knows what it means, probably just some tomfoolery.*

Even so, that day the professor's soul was singing.

....

[122]   The title of an anthology by the Imaginist Vadim Shershnevich (1893–1942), published by the Pleiad Publishing House in Moscow in 1920.

He was delighted to see Vasya:

'My my, look at your head, bald as a billiard ball now. Well done for conquering the disease. You should visit us more often now.'

He shuffled around for a while, all smiles, then couldn't contain it anymore, and so pulled the English journal out of his briefcase and shyly showed it to Vasya:

'Look what a rarity fell into my hands – a new issue, though it is from last year, but still. After all, even the university doesn't receive anything from abroad anymore. They also mentioned me, the old antique. It does feel nice, I must admit.'

Vasya leafed through the journal, examined the pictures and said:

'It does indeed. And what a brilliant publication!'

'I couldn't agree more; that's something they do know about. Besides, they've got lots of money.'

Tanyusha made breakfast, but Vasya was suddenly on the move:

'I have to get going.'

'Won't you have breakfast with us, Vasya?'

'No, I can't. I promised to be home by two.'

'Do drop by again, Vasya.'

'Sure, yes, yes. Take care, Professor.'

'Why are you in such a hurry?'

'Things to do.'

'Well, it's up to you. As for me, I'm really, really happy to see you.'

After Vasya left, Grandpa called Tanyusha over and patted her head.

'What do you think of Vasya? He's somewhat subdued these days.'

'I did visit him throughout, Grandpa.'

'Indeed. So how is he? Still pining?'

'Why should he, Grandpa?'

'Well, matters of the heart, stuff like that. Do have pity on him, Tanyusha. He's so loyal, he must be finding it all very hard.'

Tanyusha snuggled up to her grandpa:

'I do believe Vasya will be properly consoled soon. And it will be better this way for everyone.'

THE TWAIN

The little villa at Sivtsev Vrazhek was, of course, the centre of the universe, but life was going on beyond its confines, too, and radiating outwards. People were clasping on to life, each believing themselves to be – and being – its centre.

Andrei Kolchagin, too, was the focal point of his own universe – he, the deserter of the Great War – as it had been referred to previously, or the Imperialist War, as the same people were calling it nowadays; the ex-commandant of the Sovdep in Khamovniki was now the commanding officer of a mixed unit operating in the civil war. Once again, his life was semi-starvation, cold and lice. But there was a difference, too; last time he had been a dumb slave, cannon fodder, whereas now he was a champion of happiness for all of humankind.

True, Andrei Kolchagin wasn't quite sure how this universal happiness was supposed to manifest itself, but these days the hunger, the cold and the lice could be adequately explained: the enemy within had to be destroyed at all cost, otherwise all Kolchagins would face severe reprisals and retaliation. This enemy was very real. This time it wasn't a German Hans, with whom Kolchagin had had no axe to grind, but the very officer who would take swings at him, hitting him on the left cheekbone with his fist. However, what was propelling him forward was not so much anger – that had long since subsided – but fear for the future. However, he couldn't admit it, not even to himself. Fear made for a poor slogan. And thus, very much like the mottos that had been devised for Kolchagins before – 'For our faith, our tsar and our Fatherland!' – nowadays they were inscribing, white on red, 'For socialism and Soviet power!' And just as before, the words, incomprehensible and unnecessary, were filled with personal meaning. Kolchagins were interpreting it thus: save yourself and save what's yours. And Kolchagins were fighting with heart and soul.

Since the days of his desertion, Andrei Kolchagin had had a plethora of experiences: he had partaken of the freedom from commitments that had been forced onto him, experiencing power and an easy life, almost that of an aristocrat. He had also learned how to think – something previously not required of a private. He had fallen in love with the beauty of sonorous words and mastered the skill of uttering them. He had entered into the spirit of a professional warrior, grasped the essence of a heroic deed, and realised the low value of someone else's life and the high cost of his own. And therefore, Andrei Kolchagin was now at the fore, all vistas open to him; no longer a nonentity, an unremarkable soldier in grey, one of thousands and millions of similar soldiers, but a person of note, spoken to like a human being and addressed as a comrade. Just the notion of being able to be promoted to a higher position not because of your epaulettes – something that could be obtained in a cadet school or on account of your aristocratic pedigree – but thanks to your personal valour, your wits and courage: that was what made up Andrei's mind, and the minds of many other Andreis, as to which side they were on, and what identified for them their loves and hopes. Perhaps in reality it wasn't as straightforward as all that, but over there, in the realm of the golden epaulettes, no one had even bothered to check. The experience, earned by Kolchagins back there, had been harsh, unequivocal and true, whereas here and now, everything was new and everything was possible.

Two fraternal armies stood facing each other, collective face to collective face, each with its own truth and its own dignity: the truth of those who believed that their motherland and the revolution alike had been defaced by the new despotism and the new violence, much as it was merely disguised by a new colouring; and the truth of those whose idea of motherland and the appreciation of the revolution were different, those who saw humiliation not in the obscene treaty with the Germans but in the betrayal of popular hopes.

Shame on the nation that couldn't produce any defenders of the idea of a cultured motherland, of a nation true to its word, the idea of a lasting deed and civilised humanity.

Talentless would be the nation that, at the moment of resolving the age-long dispute, didn't make an attempt to crush underfoot the old and reviled idols, undertake a comprehensive rearrangement of everyday practices, ideologies, economic relations and the entire fabric of social life.

There were heroes on both sides; the pure of heart and the victims, heroic deeds and bitterness, lofty humanity surpassing anything proclaimed in books, and feral bestiality, and fear, and disappointment, and strength, and weakness, and blunt despair.

For people and history alike, a single truth, fighting against a single universal falsehood, would have been excessively simple: what existed and what was in conflict were two truths and two codes of honour; and the battlefield, in the aftermath, was scattered with the bodies of the best and the most honourable.

During those days, one of the fallen was a young cadet whom everyone had called Alyosha, a grey-eyed boy, fresh from a gymnasium. He had been involved in killings and got killed himself. He was lying on his back and his blind stare was directed upwards, towards the sky. Why had he been taken so early? If only he could have lived just a few more days, however short! His chest had already been decorated with the ribbon of St George, in recognition of his role in the fratricidal war. But Alyosha was no more.

On one of those days, Andrei Kolchagin, the soldier-commander, a hero of the red banner, was killed, too. Wounded severely in the head, he stumbled against Alyosha's corpse and went down right beside it.

Not asking their names, not passing judgement on their sanctity or depravity, the eternal night solicitously shrouded both of them with the same canopy.

ZAVALISHIN AND HIS REALM

On the days when there were no ops, Zavalishin would wander around his place of work, through corridors and offices, sleepy, seedy, eyes swollen. Everyone knew him but he had no real friends.

Some colleagues gave him a wide berth and never shook his hand in greeting, while others tried to ignore him completely, scared away by Zavalishin's particular trade.

Sometimes he would drop into the commandant's office or the orderlies' room, sink silently onto the bench, and ask about the food rations: when were they to be distributed? Also, when the assignment sheets were expected to be processed. His sheets always looked neat, made out in clumsy but easily legible handwriting, each case duly dated, the numbers of those processed clearly indicated, assignment reference number and other documents neatly attached. In this respect, he was a stickler for labour discipline, and even when drunk never did his job without first obtaining a validating document, properly signed and rubberstamped.

Zavalishin had a bit of stuff going, name of Anna Klimovna, someone he had previously frequented on Saturdays. He had installed her in his flat, but they mostly saw each other during the daytime, around lunch. She was still relatively young, housewifely, imposing. Although perfectly aware of Zavalishin's profession, she showed no particular interest in it. She learnt the facts, was briefly astounded, and got instantly used to it, and moreover, her lover's hefty pay package gladdened her heart. Much as he was reluctant to talk about his work, she invariably had some questions for him: were they expecting long waiting lists, and perhaps his tariffs per head could be reviewed upwards, seeing as everything was so pricey and money was losing its value again. She examined her lover keenly at times when, say, he would come back from work wearing a new suit or new boots. She was informed that by rights, clothes that became vacant were his. She made alterations: if the sleeves were too short, she would let them out; she washed the soiled underwear as well, if he happened to bring it along. And come what may, she was calm, unhurried, and thrifty. When Zavalishin returned home drunk, she would put him to bed, going easy on the scolding: that's the way it went – such was his job, not an easy one and even harder if performed sober. The head of the House Management Committee, Denisov, became her good friend, and was inclined to pay her an occasional visit, should Zavalishin be particularly busy and unlikely to put in an appearance at home.

His heaviest workload normally fell in August and September, when it was time to liquidate criminals. On such days Zavalishin refused to work sober. They always had some vodka, stashed away especially for him; he didn't even have to bother with making arrangements. Sometimes he had to work in daylight. For example, he once went to the clothing depot in Sretenka Street to select a peaked cap against his clothes coupon. He hadn't even managed to find one that would fit when he was sent for. Though the job on which he had been summoned was urgent, he left reluctantly. He completed what he had to do and filled out and submitted his time sheet, but by the time he got back to the depot, all the better leather caps had been picked over. That fouled his mood for quite some time, and he found it impossible to calm down.

The right person for the job and in not inconsiderable demand, he had clearance to go anywhere he pleased, and was particularly fond of the outbuilding in the back yard of house number fourteen, the one that housed a communal cell in the basement nicknamed the Ship of Death. He gravitated towards it for a simple reason: it was where they kept the criminals, the folk that were foolhardy but easy to understand and, moreover, gave no ground for any doubts. Zavalishin didn't know much about politics, and so wasn't entirely clear why some folk were stuck inside while others walked free or were put to death. But in this basement, it all made sense. They looked like the guys next door: either you were a big shot or you were an underdog. They used obscenities correctly, knew each other well, and when preparing to die put on the right sort of bravado, and always, without fail, asked for a final cigarette. Then again, it was very convenient to watch it all from above, from the balcony that ran around their pit. He recognised some by sight: those who had spent a considerable time inside.

Zavalishin's face was also well known. As he drew near, idle, bored, dull and nonchalant, a complete hush would fall over the hold in the Ship of Death, a silence even deadlier than the one occasioned by the arrival of Commissar Ivanov. The latter would call names from the list – an ex-gangster himself, a fact that endeared him to many of those incarcerated.

Zavalishin only ventured there when free, not too drunk, and bored of idleness. As for his own working space, it was a dark cellar with low ceilings, tucked away in the innards of the same house but accessible through a different door in the courtyard, on the side of Malaya Lubyanka, the first door on the left if one were heading from the front gate.

Even so, he sometimes had to discharge his duties in the garage in Varsonofyevsky Lane, next to the Church of the Resurrection. The space there was brighter and roomier but somehow not to his liking, and so it felt less familiar, even alien. In the early days, when operations were taking place outside the city, Zavalishin was forced to share a ride to Petrovsky Park with the condemned, rattling about in the same lorry. That was a complete hassle, uncomfortable, too. Still, being new to the job, he had to prove himself and get used to things; besides, in those days he was not working alone. Later a new procedure was introduced whereby it wasn't people transported out of the city but stiffs; and also, not from the place of the op, but via a mortuary in Lefortovo.

In his own cellar, his principal working space, Zavalishin toiled alone, without any assistants. Then again, what assistance was even possible? It would only create fuss and unnecessary chit-chat. According to the rules, people were taken to his little corridor and pushed forward, towards his open door, while those escorting them stepped back, shutting the door behind them, waiting till he was done. The rest was his personal responsibility, and all worked well; nothing really untoward ever took place. They all walked in on their own two feet, heading towards the light, out of the dark corridor. Previously, Zavalishin had been allocated his assignment forms in person, so that was how he received his clients; he never checked the surnames but kept strict count, neither more nor less than stated on the form.

In his spare time, Zavalishin hardly ever visited his cellar, it wasn't his sort of thing. But sometimes he did wander inside, blind drunk. He would lock himself in, slump on the bench that faced the wall heavily pockmarked with bullets, and howl dismal songs. Sometimes he started shooting, from lack of anything better to do, so as to freshen up the sour stench of his basement with the smell of gunpowder. However, he never fell asleep there – he was afraid of ghosts. He always carried the key to his basement on his person, and only allowed it to be used by the women who did the cleaning, since men would turn up their noses at duties of that nature.

Zavalishin hadn't really met any of his bosses, but then again, he didn't care one way or the other. He never attended rallies, elections or assemblies, and wasn't interested in anything apart from his direct service duties, assignment sheets and various coupons; even his job title was registered as a regular prison warden. Still, his humble status notwithstanding, he knew perfectly well that he was a special case, the one most in demand and most independent, and that was why they fed him, cajoled him, feared him. They could get on without practically anyone else. Anyone could be replaced. But they could never do without Zavalishin and no one could replace him, at least not straightaway. That was why, in the grip of boredom or at times of enforced inaction, Zavalishin could afford tantrums and threaten to resign. When that happened, his rates would be raised, although at times he could simply be placated with a bottle of quality alcohol.

Exceptionally busy days occurred in October, following the explosion in Leontyevsky Lane. That proved to be the peak of the harvesting season.

AT THE MANDARIN'S

It was bitterly cold but luckily Tanyusha had kept a pair of old ankle boots. When she was performing in the workers' districts, she would pull the felt boots over her brogues, and remove them only just prior to emerging on stage. Once she had played her piece, and the encore, she would blissfully sink her feet back into the warmth of her felt boots and thus wait for a lorry to give the performers a lift to their homes.

But she didn't dare put on the felt boots when she was getting ready for her visit to the Kremlin – it was the Kremlin, after all. So, the old ankle boots came in very handy.

A sentry by the Trinity Gate collected her pass, took it into a small gatehouse, and brought it back, stamped. After that, Tanyusha made her apprehensive way along a pathway trodden by the Palace wall, following the bank of clean snow swept away from the path. By the gate in front of the former courthouse she was asked for her pass again. And once more, at the entrance door, but that was the last time. Once inside, she was given directions: climb the stairs and follow the corridor on the right.

She didn't have to wait long. The secretary briefly glanced at the pass, took the letter of reference, and said:

'Just a minute. Do sit down. I believe you will be seen shortly.'

People were passing through reception, back and forth, dressed warmly but behaving as if they belonged there. The rooms were cold, and because of it, appeared especially large and oddly empty. Tanyusha felt herself tiny and lost inside this enormous Kremlin edifice. The passers-by were casting perplexed and curious glances in her direction.

The secretary came out and said:

'Do come in, comrade. This way.'

His demeanour was civil; he even let Tanyusha through the door first. Never before had she visited an office of somebody so highly placed and powerful. In the Soviet agencies where she occasionally had to deal with a variety of petty everyday issues, the offices were all dirty, overcrowded and chaotic, their employees embittered and uncivil. Over here, it was a totally different story. Tanyusha had previously thought that she would step inside something akin to a fortress, where she would be met with bayonets and suspicion.

She entered a large room with a high ceiling and barely any furniture: there was only a couch and three armchairs arranged around a stylish table not covered with any tablecloth. On the table sat a telephone directory and two newspapers. A telephone on the windowsill. The wallpaper showed the imprints of the furniture that had been removed. A book case in the furthest corner, its glass shattered. The room was warm and clean. Tanyusha felt that wearing ankle boots was inappropriate.

A stocky man with high cheekbones and a receding hairline, not very Russian in his appearance, dressed in a service jacket, his trousers pulled over high boots, entered briskly and approached Tanyusha directly:

'How do you do. Was it you that brought the letter? Here, take this chair. What exactly is the problem?'

'I wanted to petition you on behalf of a prisoner.'

'Well, I know, it says so here. What's your connection to Astafyev? Are you related?'

'He's our friend.'

'Who are "we", exactly?'

'He is a good friend of mine and my Grandfather's.'

'That would be the professor? I believe your Grandfather studies birds?'

'Yes, he's an ornithologist.'

'So, what about this Astafyev?'

'He's been wrongfully arrested.'

'How do you mean, wrongfully? We don't go around arresting people for no reason. He has been apprehended in connection with a very serious affair.'

'Astafyev wasn't interested in politics. He's a philosopher, but was recently employed as a performer in workers' districts. We performed together, in the same concerts.'

'What's that, you sing?'

'No, I play the piano.'

'A conservatoire graduate?'

'Yes.'

'Why don't you take part in our concerts? We pay well, and we supply our performers with groceries. Do come and play here sometime.'

'Where do you mean?'

The man in the service jacket raised his milky gaze in amazement:

'Here, in the Extraordinary Commission.[123] We organise concerts. Are you a member of the Socialist Revolutionaries?'[124]

'Me? No, I don't belong to any party.'

'So why are you friends with SRs, like this Astafyev of yours, for example?'

'He's nothing of the sort. He is genuinely not involved in politics; I know him well.'

'Well, we know better. So, what is it you want?'

....

[123]   The All-Russian Extraordinary Commission, abbreviated VChK, and commonly known as Cheka, was the first of a succession of Soviet secret police organizations.

[124]   The Socialist Revolutionary Party, or Party of Socialist Revolutionaries, was a major political party in late Imperial Russia and early Soviet Russia. The SRs were socialists and supporters of democracy.

'I was hoping that, maybe, it would be possible to free him; he has committed no crimes.'

'If he's innocent, he will be released without your petition.'

'But he has been in prison for over a month!'

'So what? Even if it were a year; he's got no business meddling in conspiracies. And you shouldn't concern yourself with him. It's best to give such friends a wide berth. We consider this Astafyev of yours a very dangerous enemy of Soviet power. Better to keep away from him. He isn't your fiancé, is he?'

'No.'

'So why do you care so much?'

Rubbing his forehead, the man in the service jacket added:

'Alright. I'll make enquiries. Whereabouts do you live?'

Tanyusha gave her address.

'So that's that. We don't put people in prison for nothing. If he's found to be not guilty, he'll walk. Otherwise, he'll get what he deserves, rest assured on that score. Do you know Savinkov?'

'Savinkov? No, I don't.'

He got up:

'They'll issue your exit pass.'

The man in the service jacket pulled his hand out of his pocket. Tanyusha quickly retreated and said:

'Thank you.'

He stuffed his hand back in his pocket:

'Good day. Do think it over – come and perform for us, we pay well.'

The secretary in the large reception room took Tanyusha's address once more and handed her a pass:

'Exit through the Trinity Gate.'

White snow covered the Kremlin. Ivan the Great loomed large, a frozen monumental presence. The golden cupolas over the Assumption Cathedral shone brightly. Picking her way among the snowdrifts, Tanyusha felt miniscule again, a complete alien in this world of strangers. The soldier by the Trinity Gate took her pass and speared it with his bayonet.

After Tanyusha had left, the man in the service jacket went to the telephone and gave the number.

'Listen here, Comrade Brikman, where are you with this Astafyev case? Why's that? You should put the frighteners on him. Well, it's up to you. I still believe it would be better to treat the cases separately. Yes. Don't jumble it all in one heap, then we'll see. Yes, what is it? Well, but of course, I'm just saying. As for keeping him inside – why not, let's. Alright. No, I've just had a visit from his fiancée, or whatever she is. Came to plead for him; a pretty girl, by the way. See you, then. But of course, I'm coming in the evening.'

THE PIGGY

Anna Klimovna, Zavalishin's paramour, wasn't a greedy person; no one would call her that. What she was, was thrifty. She also liked to run her household in an orderly manner. Hers was a life of plenty, even if one were to apply standards not from nowadays but from before the war. Zavalishin would come home laden with all sorts of supplies, carrying them in sacks, paper cones and packages, and these contained not the usual rubbish like redberry leaves or clay soap, but the real stuff, allocated to the rations of the most sought-after people: white flour, lime-tree honey, sugar in cubes, to say nothing of various types of spirits. He also provided fabrics, and rubber overshoes, and footwear, even in the right sizes. Besides this he would give Anna Klimovna money, substantial sums at times, though money didn't count for much because it would lose its value by the very next day.

And of course, no one in the house at Dolgorukovskaya Street could hold a candle to him in terms of affluence, not even the House Committee Chairman Denisov, who was accepting bribes right, left and centre, to enable an extra person to register for residence (or, in other words, an extra food ration card), to allow petty trade in various stashed goods from one's flat, and also for no good reason whatsoever except that he, Denisov, was chair of the House Committee and therefore a useful contact for anyone.

In such fortuitous circumstances, Anna Klimovna could have managed a substantial household, and most likely would have, if only Zavalishin, for example, had possessed a little house somewhere on the outskirts of Moscow, or at least a real apartment, even it were as small as only two rooms and a kitchen with a pantry. As it was, they were cooped up in one room; the other two, previously Astafyev's, remained sealed. There was no way to carve a room of any kind out of their paltry hallway, and as for the kitchen, Anna Klimovna had invaded it and cluttered it with her sacks and jars.

Anna Klimovna had half a mind to acquire some chickens and keep them in the kitchen – there were people who did it – but then she had a change of heart, fearing that they would make it difficult to sleep; besides, chickens meant filth, and the smell would be unpleasant too. Why should she bother? She could get eggs with her own money. Still, once she had learned that an old acquaintance of hers, an allotment gardener, had fattened a huge pig and thus made a veritable fortune, she decided to follow suit. It wasn't the fortune she was after so much as a properly established household, so that succulent ham and gammon could be stocked up and smoked in time for a suitable festive season. Anna Klimovna, a native of a southern province, could do it all perfectly well. A piglet like this could easily be fed with the cast-off beetroot tops that the neighbours would be happy to get rid of, along with the swill from the kind refuse that even hungry people wouldn't use as their own food. As for the real nutrients needed for developing fat, she didn't envisage any problem on that score either. And when a young little piglet grew into a big fat pig, it would cover the costs of its maintenance itself. The additional premises could easily be procured, too. To start with, the kitchen would do, since the little piglet would have to be bathed and kept warm; afterwards, none other than Denisov himself, having approved of Anna Klimovna's economic project, promised to make available one of the small well-lit storerooms in the courtyard, seeing as they had stayed vacant anyway.

Anna Klimovna made a foray into a nearby village and bartered some salt, sugar, but most importantly alcohol, for a hefty piglet.

In the beginning, she found herself faced with a multitude of fears: that the pig might grow emaciated, or fall ill, or be bitten to death by rats. As the piglet grew, Anna Klimovna's main concern shifted to keeping it secure from burglars and letting it move as little as possible – just lying around instead, eating without limit, and growing fatter and fatter. On all those counts, Anna Klimovna's efforts met with complete success. Those of the neighbours to whom she showed the pig couldn't but exclaim endless 'ahs' and congratulate Anna Klimovna; and if Chairman Denisov hadn't been personally committed to the pig's wellbeing and safety (he'd been promised a cut) and interested in remaining in Anna Klimovna's good graces, somebody from among the envious residents would have found a way to test the reliability of Zavalishin's door locks.

Zavalishin himself, forever grim and semi-inebriated when at home, showed little interest in the pig. A month before Easter, Anna Klimovna took him to the little shed to take a peep at the large animal, a real tub of lard, clean, nicely washed, pink, barely able to stand upright. And when Easter was two weeks away, Anna Klimovna told him:

'It's time to slaughter our piggy. It takes time to salt the fat and smoke the hocks.'

'It's your idea, so go ahead and slaughter it.'

'How can I do it myself; besides, it's easier for you.'

'What's it got to do with me, anyway?'

'Whaddya mean, "what"? You'll eat it, won't you?'

'Eat it yourself. I'm off fatty things, doctor's orders.'

'You unwell again or what? Why did ya have to see the doctor?'

'Must be cause I'm unwell, eh?'

'And what did he say, the doctor?'

Zavalishin grumbled darkly:

'What did he say, what did he say... He says, if it's like this, and doesn't get better, I'll need an operation, my gut will have to be opened. I wish he'd have his own sliced up.'

'Why the heck do ya listen to him? The things they come up with, them doctors. It may well pass by itself.'

Zavalishin fell silent. He dreaded the word 'operation' for yet another reason – the same word was used in reference to his work at his place of employment. Although the more common currency consisted of phrases like 'to be classified redundant' or 'out, bags and all'. No matter how much he suffered from the pain in his stomach, he simply couldn't bring himself to agree to an operation. Last time he had visited him, the doctor had said:

'Your kidneys are in a very bad way. It's no joking matter. It's better to take your chances now; it may be too late afterwards.'

Anna Klimovna waited till her partner had a free day and approached him once more:

'We must slaughter the piggy today, without fail. Help me, will you? You're more used to it, not to mention you're stronger.'

Zavalishin got up and put on his Colt and holster.

'What's that for? It won't do, shooting it. Much neater with a knife. I've got them sharpened, so that afterwards we can cut its fat in layers. I've got an axe prepared, too.'

Entering the little shed, Zavalishin saw that Anna Klimovna had prepared a table, fashioned out of half a door perched on two boxes, set up a clean bucket, supplied the knives and the clean cloths – everything that would be required for such an 'operation'. She, herself, had changed into a cheap shabby dress, so as not to stain a good one needlessly, and fetched two aprons from the kitchen.

'Put it on, or you'll be soiled with the splatter.'

The little shed had a window, but the door was shut to stave off idle gawkers; the business in hand was a delicate matter, after all.

The fat, scarcely mobile pig was grunting as Anna Klimovna tenderly washed its flanks and tied its legs together.

'Help me lift it to the table.'

They barely managed, and Anna Klimovna, yet again, ran a wet cloth over the fat pink haunches.

Having finished with the ablutions, she wiped her hands dry and said gently, in a small imploring voice:

'You'd be better off without me, it's not a woman's job. The knives are over here...'

But as Zavalishin's beard began quivering and his eyes turned white, she backed off.

'Are you alright? What are you afraid of?'

Zavalishin's whole body was shaking. He retreated towards the door, his right hand reaching for the revolver inside the holster.

'Leave it, I said. How can you do this to an animal? You'll ruin its head.'

Zavalishin pulled his hand out, visibly deflated, and slumped onto the box.

'Do it yourself. I can't slaughter the pig. Listen to how it's squealing!'

'Full of compassion, aren't we? Afraid of an animal. Some man you are, ain't ya!'

'Bloody watch it, Anna, I'm telling you, I can't.'

'Why should I watch it? I'll manage on me own!'

Anna Klimovna picked up the big knife, sharp as a razor, grasped the piggie's pink snout with a cloth, turned it to one side in order to expose its neck, and slashed the knife downwards, weakly and ineptly. The blood gushed forward, the pig jerked with its whole body and shrieked. Anna Klimovna got flustered, raised the knife again but a strong arm grabbed her shoulder and forcibly pushed her away from her victim.

MIKHAIL OSORGIN

Zavalishin, his eyes bloodshot, his face contorted, was waving his Colt around and yelling in a hoarse voice:

'Get off it, out of my way, I'll fucking kill you!'

She emitted a piercing scream, like the pig before her, wriggled free, pushed the door outwards, and tumbled out of the shed. She heard the door banging shut after her on its creaky hinges, and not pausing to look back, raced towards the entrance leading to the House Committee Chairman's lodgings.

Some three minutes later, Denisov and Anna Klimovna gingerly made their way back towards the little shed. It was quiet inside; all that could be heard were the dying squeaks of the pig. They both came to a halt by the door.

Denisov called out:

'Hey, Zavalishin, come out a minute.'

There was no answer.

'Perhaps you should stick your nose in, Anna Klimovna, and see what he's up to.'

'Why don't you stick your nose in instead? I don't want to get shot. He's off his trolley. He's okay dealing with people but not an animal.'

Denisov tiptoed around the shed and peeped through the bars on the window. Directly underneath lay a pink carcass, and further away, half-hidden behind the box, on the floor, sat Zavalishin, his gaze locked on the window. His large Colt was sitting in front of him, on the box.

Denisov sprang back and returned to Anna Klimovna.

'I'm not sure what to do next. He may well be out of his mind, this cohabitant of yours. It might be a good idea to lock him up and get the militia?'

'The padlock's inside.'

'We'll find another.'

At this moment a shot rang out. The pair of them gasped, backed away from the door, and broke into a trot.

The first shot was followed by a second, and a third, and another, and another – Zavalishin was emptying his entire chamber. Denisov and Anna Klimovna hid themselves inside the porch, and several other residents fearfully banged their own doors shut.

Afterwards, Zavalishin's heavy footsteps clunked on the asphalt as he walked across the courtyard – his back hunched, his head hanging down, his hand on top of the holster – heading straight towards his own front door. He let himself in and pulled the door shut behind him.

That was when Anna Klimovna dared to go into the shed. She got in and groaned: the table that she had lovingly erected was bathed in blood, while the pig's head, the beautiful head promised to the Chairman in return for his troubles and protection, was completely riddled with heavy-calibre bullets from Zavalishin's Colt.

'Look what he's gone and done! How can you fire bullets into an animal! He's got no pity, made such a mess out of its entire head!'

And she even briefly broke out into sobs, being genuinely overcome with misery.

VASYA'S BETRAYAL

The clock in the landlady's quarters, behind the wall, struck seven. Vasya Boltanovsky's watch showed ten past the hour already, but his watch was always gaining time, which was actually convenient as it meant he was never late. Still, usually Alyona would come along at half past six. She could have been delayed, of course, somewhere on her way from the hospital.

Vasya marked the page in his book with an embroidered bookmark reading 'Remember me!', took the cigarette butts into the kitchen, picked up stray pieces of paper from the floor, straightened the cover on the armchair. All this took another five minutes. He could, of course, start the kerosene stove himself and brew some tea. He had done everything himself before his illness, but nowadays he was somewhat spoilt by Alyona, who would pop in most days after work, as she lived nearby but her own home was rather bleak. So, a tradition was formed, where they would take their evening tea together, and Alyona wouldn't leave until after ten. After tea they would chat, or Vasya would read aloud while Alyona knitted or sewed. She made a bit of money on the side with her sewing; she also fashioned sensible hats and did a little embroidery. It was she who had embroidered Vasya's bookmark. She also mended Vasya's clothes, and that, too, became a custom, although in the beginning Vasya had tried to protest:

'I can do it all myself!'

But Alyona showed him a sock mended by his own efforts.

'This is not the way to do it! You've just pulled all the stitches together, and the result isn't a darn but something like a cocoon.'

'How is it done, then?'

Alyona undid Vasya's handiwork, pulled a ball of wool out of her bag, and a quarter of an hour later the clump was replaced by a new patch – a wonder to behold.

'The wool isn't an exact match in colour but it's not that important. I don't have anything else on me.'

Vasya looked and gasped:

'Well, this is truly amazing!'

Her conquest of Vasya was complete when she snipped off a shabby shirt cuff, hemmed it, pulled it inside out, and sewed it back onto the sleeve. A stunned Vasya was rendered speechless while Alyona burst into her silvery peal of laughter, then grunted and fell silent in embarrassment.

But still, should he light the stove or wait for a bit?

He didn't have to wait too long because the doorbell rang three times, which meant that Vasya had visitors. Each tenant had a designated number of doorbell rings so as not to have to let in somebody else's guests; there even was a little piece of paper pinned to the front door, listing the instructions on who should be called by how many rings. Vasya would be summoned by three.

That night, Alyona appeared tired and in rather low spirits. She had been delayed by a new intake into their hospital, a large number of typhus cases.

'We're short of beds as it is but they are still bringing them in anyway.'

What's more, Alyona had some unpleasantness at home. Her room was large, exceeding the regulatory size of living space per resident, and now the House Management Committee were eager to install someone else as well, and in this way she would have to share. Another option was for her to move into a boxroom, nearly a pantry. And she didn't know what to do. Maybe the pantry was a better option – at least she wouldn't have to share with anyone.

'Me, for example, I'm left in peace', said Vasya. 'A room like mine is also considered big enough for two, but I can easily obtain a piece of paper from the university.'

'Some people have all the luck!'

But Alyona wasn't one to nurse her grudges, and after the tea her mood visibly improved.

'Do you know that you've got an ink stain on your nose? A lilac one. Will I ever teach you to be neat?'

'Where?' cried Vasya in alarm.

'Where? I told you, on your nose. Look for yourself.'

Vasya glanced into a small wall mirror.

'It's nothing, just a smudge. I was doing some writing today.'

He moistened his finger in his mouth and smeared the stain around.

'Oh, really!' said Alyona. 'Shame on you, some research assistant you are! Come here.'

Out of her little basket – what couldn't she produce out of its depths? – came a piece of fabric. She dabbed it in warm water and then wiped the stain right off.

'There, not a trace. Now go and dry yourself with a towel.'

But Vasya retorted resolutely:

'It's okay, it'll dry itself.'

To Vasya, Alyona's eyes suddenly looked particularly beautiful and gentle. He had overlooked them in the past, or perhaps they hadn't always been like that. And he was very reluctant to leave Alyona's side. As she rubbed his nose with her cloth, he lightly held her hand, fearful that the fabric would be too hot. But when she finished her task, he didn't want to let go of her hand.

Alyona took the cloth in one hand but left the other in his. Her hand was warm, soft and small. And for Vasya, today, this too felt extremely agreeable.

They stood like this until Alyona said:

'What's the matter? Why are you looking at me like you've never seen me before? Why are you staring at my hand? It's just a hand, look – I've got one more, just like this one.'

Vasya took her other hand, too.

So Alyona asked:

'What if I tug you on the ear? Like this? Or even pull both of them?'

She came really close. The collar of her blouse was open, and the neck inside looked neat and white.

At this moment Vasya decided to defend himself; it wasn't the done thing, after all, to pull the ears of a research assistant at the university!

They were not going to read aloud that night. They shielded the light of the table lamp with a large, heavily-bound book, and sat close together.

It transpired that both had accumulated many interesting memories that they hadn't shared before. Alyona believed it was really remarkable that when Vasya had first fallen ill it was she who'd been appointed to take care of him. The doctor could easily have found a different nurse, say, some old lady.

To this Vasya answered:

'Whatever for! It would've been utterly boring!'

'Are you saying you are happy that it was me?'

Vasya grew bolder and gesticulated his satisfaction.

For his part, Vasya remembered that once, when the acuity of his disease had subsided, in the early days of complete clarity, he had once woken up in the dead of the night and lain there watching Alyona, who was napping in her armchair, and trying to guess the colour of her eyes. For some reason he had decided that they were definitely green.

'My eyes? Green? You must have had a funny dream.'

'No, I wasn't asleep then.'

'It doesn't matter. My eyes are blue, really blue.'

'I do see that now.'

'You see nothing of the sort – you're ever so unobservant; it's simply unbelievable. You really don't have a clue. Besides, what right did you have to inspect me when I was asleep?'

'You were sleeping semi-recumbent, in the armchair.'

'But of course I was. Still, you are talking utter nonsense.'

Vasya felt somewhat self-conscious. However, this exchange of memories was so engaging that Alyona stayed longer than usual. On hearing the clock behind the wall strike midnight, she leapt up in alarm:

'Goodness gracious! I've got to get up just after six!'

When they came to part, they didn't merely exchange a handshake, as was their custom. Vasya felt it strange but ever so pleasant.

Getting ready for bed, Vasya pulled off his shirt and it ripped around the collar. He thought: *What a nuisance! Alyona will tell me off tomorrow!*

He wanted, as was his wont before falling asleep, to think about something sad and melancholic, for example, how miserable he was while everybody else was so happy. But this time those thoughts just wouldn't come. Quite the contrary: his face kept breaking into a smile and his thoughts were ever so slightly sinful.

His sin lay in the fact that tonight Vasya had been unfaithful, and adultery had proved sweet and agreeable, but most importantly, it had hurt no one's feelings and not one person had had to suffer any torment.

THE EXPLOSION[125]

On the twenty-fifth of September, after a long interval, the ornithologist once more dropped into the Writers' Shop in Leontyevsky. His briefcase, plump from the books stuffed inside, had tired the old professor out.

'Let me catch my breath first. It's okay, I'll just sit for a minute on this box, please don't worry.'

'We haven't seen you in a while, Professor.'

'True enough, I've had rather a lot on my plate.'

The 'lot' on the old man's plate essentially consisted of the fact that his bookshelves and bookcases were close to empty. All that was left were some reference books, invaluable for

....

[125] The Explosion in Leontyevsky Lane (already referred to previously as a major contributor to Zavalishin's workload) was an act of terrorism committed on 25 September 1919 in the building of the RCP(b) (Russian Communist Party of the Bolsheviks) during a well-attended conference, with the aim of eliminating the leaders of the Moscow Committee. Fifty-five attendees were wounded and twelve killed. The Cheka laid responsibility for this act of terrorism on the underground alliance of left-wing Socialist Revolutionaries and Anarchists. By way of 'reprisal', several hundred hostages were executed – representatives of parties opposed to Bolshevism, officers, members of the intelligentsia and other 'bourgeois elements'. Although the bomb had been thrown by the terrorist Sobolev and not the 'man in the yellow spats' (allegedly Savinkov), this episode is yet another illustration of how numerous and varied the opposition to the new regime was at the time – before being wiped out by the new rulers of the country.

his research, and one copy of each of his publications. As hard as their lives were, Tanyusha made him promise that he wouldn't sell those.

'Should we really hang on to them? Perhaps Alexei Dmitriyevich was right – science is of no use anymore.'

'Pay no heed, Grandpa; he doesn't believe it himself; he just says it for the sake of saying it.'

'But there's nothing else that I, an old man, can be expected to contribute!'

'Stop it, Grandpa, you mustn't talk like that. Don't upset me.'

The old man was profoundly reassured that his granddaughter believed in science, and in him, even if he was old; because it meant that he was still a genuine scientist, and all those green youngsters who had adorned themselves with all types of credentials couldn't compare, much as they were building their careers in troubled times, and as it meant he was king in the land of one-eyed academic men.

'Well, we'll make do somehow.'

However, on the twenty-fifth of September, on this fateful, horrible day, the ornithologist came along to the shop yet again, dragging a tightly-packed briefcase.

'Have you delved into numismatics, too, Professor?'

'Don't know the first thing about it.'

'You've got a lot of rather curious stuff here. Nothing in your line of research, though?'

'To be absolutely frank, these are not my books. I've taken them in on a sort of commission. I'm used to coming here, to trade my books, so I've tried to assemble a batch from what my friends had to offer. As for the valuation, you do it yourself, as per usual. I trust you implicitly.'

'Are you getting a percentage, Professor?'

'I am, can't deny it.'

And again, no one in the shop was surprised that here he was, an old scientist with a European reputation, selling somebody else's books for a percentage. And because no one was scandalised, he felt more at ease and more confident. It meant that he wasn't doing something shameful, and that he could do it again. It could well be that others were doing the same.

Leaving the shop, the empty briefcase tucked under his armpit, the professor looked around, pleased – at the very least, something would be left over for Tanyusha's house-keeping. It wouldn't be much, of course – the books belonged to other people, but on the other hand, he didn't feel so heart-broken over somebody else's books. He had earned a pittance, but still he had earned it, through his own labour, his old man's effort.

The gate of the house next door, set back behind a lattice fence, was guarded by a Red Army soldier with a rifle. Anyone passing through the gate produced a piece of paper – their pass.

The professor, trying to hold himself upright and stride with confidence, set off toward Bolshaya Nikitskaya.

The house guarded by the soldier had another frontage that gave onto a front garden in Chernyshevsky Lane. Inside the garden, cordoned off from the lane by its fence, stood some tall trees, sparsely covered with surviving yellowed foliage. A stone staircase led from the garden towards the first-floor balcony. There was no gate on this side, and so no one entered the house via this entrance.

After it got completely dark, the lane emptied and the windows lit up in the back of the house. An important meeting was scheduled to take place here at eight, and a small crowd of visitors accumulated by the front entrance in Leontyevsky. People were arriving by car and on foot.

Sometime after nine, a solitary person approached the back of the house giving onto Chernyshevsky Lane, looked around him and, guarding his pocket, nimbly climbed over the fence, ducked down and froze.

No one in the lane could possibly see the dark figure as it climbed the stairs towards the balcony and then cast a cautious glance inside the window. The figure's broad back briefly projected itself onto the lowered curtain as a vague outline, while he himself he was able to see, in the crack between the curtains, the edge of a table tightly surrounded by seated people.

Moving away from the wall, the dark figure cast a dark object through the window with a casual arc of its arm.

The blast of the explosion could be heard even on the outskirts of Moscow. Window panes in adjacent streets shattered; further away they merely cracked.

The city's residents, who had long since grown accustomed to night-time gunfire grasped it all in an instant; what had just rung out wasn't a rifle, or a machine gun, and most likely, not even a cannon.

The house with the two facades now had no roof, and one of its walls was gone.

That day, from early morning, Zavalishin had been sober and in grim spirits. He had left the Lubyanka for home before nightfall, as it wasn't one of his working days. At home, he took off his new jacket, acquired after a recent 'operation', and sat down on his bed. In the kitchen, Anna Klimovna was warming up the samovar and preparing a light meal for him before he went to bed.

It wasn't exactly that Anna Klimovna was consumed by greed; she just couldn't reconcile herself to the fact that the doors to Astafyev's rooms were still tightly sealed.

'He's been gone for a while now and may never come back, while his rooms are good for no one. Maybe if you put a word in, they'd unseal the doors? Or then again, you could take those seals off yerself, you'd easily get away with it?'

'Whaddya want with his rooms?'

'You mean, we're gonna go on like this, squeezed into one room and a kitchen? We've got all this good stuff, and nowhere to put it.'

'I can't.'

'Why not?'

'Because I've said so. He might come back, and find his room gone. He's got his things there.'

'Phooey, he's sorry for a toff, this one! Nice of you to care so much about him.'

'Get lost, Anna, don't mess with my head. You've never even clapped eyes on him, unlike me.'

'So you're his friend now, are ya?'

'Maybe I am! He might have ruined my life, but I respect him like a good friend.'

He stayed silent for a while and then added:

'We did drink together, and what of it? He's ever so clever, he had it all worked out. And it proves nothing that he got sent down. And it's not yer place, you dumb piece of skirt, to go on about him. He's a learned sort, way above us; we're peasants.'

'Learned, my right foot… What did he teach ya, this learned mate of yours?'

'That's for me to know. I'm telling you, he may be my bitterest enemy but I respect him, and won't allow a finger to be laid on him. So there. There are more fine books in his rooms than you have rags. And he's read it all, and knows everything. And he would, by the way, drink hard spirit with me, a barely literate common sort, like we were equals. That's not something to sniff at, you know, Anna. But it's not something the likes of you would grasp.'

The samovar had barely started to boil when House Committee Chairman Denisov knocked on the door and shouted from outside, preferring not to let himself in:

'Hey, Comrade Zavalishin, they've sent for you.'

'Who's that, then?'

'A car, they are asking for you, and said you should go out at once.'

Worried, Zavalishin put on his jacket and took down the holster with his Colt from the nail on the wall.

'What do they want with you on your day off?'

'Fuck knows. With us, any day can be a working day.'

'Have some tea, at least.'

'They're expecting me. Splash me half a glass of spirit, from over there, on the shelf.'

And, suddenly enraged because of his anxiety, he yelled at his lover from the doorstep:

'As for this door and the seal, keep your hands off it! Do ya hear me? Don't stick your nose in somebody else's business. A room's too small for her now, this grand lady!'

On his way out, he shut the door with a loud bang.

A VOID

After yet another session of questioning, the fourth by now, Astafyev was transferred to a solitary cell.

The interrogation had been brief. Comrade Brikman, who always felt intensely feverish before the onset of spring, sat there, swaddled in a reddish sweater underneath his usual service jacket, the collar of it excessively loose around his neck.

Making his way in, Astafyev thought: *My, he's really in a bad way, the poor thing. For all that, still trying to keep going, still hopeful.*

'Citizen Astafyev, it looks like your relatives are trying to intercede on your behalf. I've decided to summon you again, perhaps this time we'll be able to see eye to eye.'

'Eye to eye about what?'

'You refuse to accept that you provided shelter to one of the most determined enemies of Soviet power. Do tell me, though, what is your personal attitude towards this power? Do you recognise its legitimacy?'

'Does it need my acceptance? I'm not a foreign power, after all.'

'Your frivolity is misplaced. I'd advise you to answer my question unequivocally.'

'Comrade Brikman, you are unlikely to suspect me of particular tenderness towards the power that, as personified by yourself, has been holding me in prison for over half a year.'

'That is to say, your attitude is hostile?'

Astafyev crossed one leg over the other knee, and leaned back in his chair:

'I wouldn't call it hostile; I don't have a quick enough temper. I'd rather say I'm disdainful.'

'Disdainful towards the power of workers and peasants?'

'Come, Brikman, save me the rhetoric. Which workers and peasants are you talking about, exactly? You should be ashamed of such platitudes.'

The interrogator's whole body twitched.

'Citizen Astafyev, I'll be straight with you: there's not enough evidence against you. Just an unsigned letter to the effect that a man answering the relevant description spent a night at your place. But you, Astafyev, you're a person of intellect, insolent and dangerous to our cause. You're more dangerous than any of those petty, openly hostile individuals. There's a petition on your behalf but I'm still not going to let you go.'

Astafyev felt his temper rising against this puny man who held his entire destiny in his hands. How he wished to seize him by his scrawny neck and keep squeezing till the little man gave up the ghost.

He said, enunciating clearly, out of habit:

'You're grinding your personal axe, Brikman. In other words, you loathe somebody who's healthy and independent. You are an errand boy of this power whereas I am a free agent; you have one foot in the grave whereas I'm healthy, thank God. It's therefore clear that you must annihilate me, although you don't have a thing to charge me with.'

The interrogator jerked again on his chair, went red in the face and hissed, in a shrill whisper, his voice breaking:

'Yes, I've got one foot in the grave, as you have elegantly put it. My chest was pummelled by rifle butts in a prison. I'm a consumptive. What you've just said, citizen Astafyev, is vile, and from where I stand it's below the belt. But I hate you, and the likes of you, not because of this but because of... on account of...'

Comrade Brikman broke into a coughing fit, pulled a small vial from his pocket, spat into it, stuffed it back into his pocket, wiped his mouth on a handkerchief and gave Astafyev a sullen look from his feverish eyes:

'My point exactly,' said Astafyev. 'Some warrior you are. You should get yourself to some warm place in the south.'

Breathing heavily, the interrogator rasped:

'I've no use for your medical opinion.'

As comrade Brikman wiped the sweat off his face, Astafyev looked around miserably, taking in the room. The window glass had not been cleaned in a while. A dusty pile of newspapers and assorted documents had been kicked into the corner, and a lacklustre mirror hung on the wall.

'Some interior you've got here! Why don't you have your windows cleaned, you might even end up letting some light in!'

When he had regained his breath, the interrogator said:

'You may think whatever you like about me. Let me tell you this, though, citizen Astafyev, it's not clear which one of us is closer to...'

He stumbled.

'You'd like to say, closer to the afterlife?'

Instead of answering, the interrogator snapped, in an exaggeratedly official voice:

'Come to think of it, I could release you, citizen Astafyev, if you agreed to work with us.'

Astafyev smiled:

'Are you trying to insult me? You're truly indefatigable, aren't you? But I refuse to be insulted by you, Brikman. You're punching above your weight.'

'Splendid. You may return to your cell.'

He rang the bell. Astafyev got to his feet, patted down his rumpled suit, smoothed his newly-grown long hair and, looking downward, said with an avuncular smile:

'I mean it, Brikman, go somewhere warm, leave it all behind, all this ugliness. I'm not being spiteful. You look terrible.'

In came the security guard.

Alone in his solitary cell, Astafyev took his usual position on his bed: his back against the wall, his hands hugging his bent knees.

There were no books around – the inmates were banned from reading. Nor was there any paper, nor a pencil, nor even a home-made chess set. When still in the holding cell, Astafyev would go through a daily routine of exercises, and taught many prisoners to follow suit. But here he couldn't be bothered. He felt no hunger, although the food was atrocious: soup cooked from dried common roach, overcooked millet with no butter, and a quarter of a loaf. However, out there in the free world many would be envious of such a diet. There was also tea made of carrots and called coffee. He had even been issued with some shag tobacco, which was good, and could excuse many of the transgressions performed by the All-Russian Cheka.

During the early months of his imprisonment, Astafyev thought frequently about being 'classed as undesirable and surplus to requirements.' Eventually, this thought lost its poignancy, and dulled. The worst affliction now was the general weariness of his body and spirit. In the beginning, images of a life outside the prison walls were vibrant and vivid: the rooms with his favourite books, the streets of Moscow, the evenings spent at Sivtsev Vrazhek, the peculiar declaration he'd made to Tanyusha, his concert performances, and his past university career, and even further back in time, his trips abroad. But these images, too, had become vague, and receded. He didn't feel the same yearning for freedom, nor even his erstwhile abhorrence of the prison walls.

Recollecting his conversation with the interrogator, Astafyev thought: *I've worn him out. It would have been better just to hit him. It was wrong of me.*

He remembered that disgusting pocket vial and cringed with the involuntary repulsion typical of a healthy person.

'Why is he even alive, the way he is? What for?'

And what was his own, Astafyev's, life for? What was the point of him staying alive? Didn't it, essentially, boil down to one thing: whether Comrade Brikman would shortly do him in or release him to continue living?

'It is enough that you should suffer, and grumble, and act like an ape. What is your purpose? To be watching all this for three years, or a hundred years, will make no difference whatsoever.'

Marcus Aurelius also said:

'Were you to live three thousand years, or even many tens of thousands more, remember that the sole life which a man can lose is that which he is living at the moment; and further-more, that he can have no other life except the one he loses. And so he cannot lose either his past or his future, for how can you lose something that you do not have?'

Whereas King Solomon had said:

'What has been will be again, what has been done will be done again; there is nothing new under the sun.'

How strange, thought Astafyev. *There are so many merry and cheerful books, so many brilliant and witty philosophical pronounce-ments, but in the end, nothing consoles better than Ecclesiastes.*

A knock resounded in the corridor, followed by footsteps and the sentry's voice:

'Hey you – knock! Go on, knock again!'

The Latvian couldn't immediately work out the cell door from which the sound was coming.

'I told you to knock!'

Astafyev knew what this shouting meant: an inmate push-ing for some special privilege – to be taken to the toilet outside his allocated slot. It sounded as though he hadn't got what he wanted. This poor prisoner must have been suffering grossly.

If the suffering gets intolerable, it kills. If it continues, it means it's tolerable. Summon up all your mental strength and remain calm.

That was how a philosopher was supposed to reassure himself. Yes, a rank-and-file man had a very good reason to hate a philosopher.

In essence, thought Astafyev, *I am utterly devoid of any counter-revolutionary reveries. I would despise my people if they hadn't done what they have done, if they had stopped half-way and allowed the learned chatterboxes to give Russia a haircut using an English comb: a parliament, civil policemen, nicely disguised falsehoods. After all, Brikman is right – I am an enemy, his and theirs. In the long run, it doesn't really matter who is to clamp down on freedom of thought: an ignorant or an enlightened hand; but clamp down it will, and of course, 'in the name of freedom' and on behalf of the people. It must be admitted, though, it's all so very tedious.*

If they had chosen this moment to enter his cell and tell him 'to get ready to meet his maker', Astafyev's pulse wouldn't have quickened.

He thought further: *All these events of ours – the revolution, the executions, the struggle and the hope, and our daily lives, and our spiritual lives – it's nothing more than... a swallow fluttering its wings through the air, its trace visible for a brief instant. But not for longer, no, not for longer. So, is there anything that's real? Only the emptiness. A condensed thought that's turned onto itself. A round zero and a void.*

'A vo-o-o-id.'

Astafyev stretched his legs, closed his eyes, and dozed off.

THE ENCOUNTER

Before nightfall, many a person was brought in from Butyrka Prison,[126] from the camps and other penal institutions. Those arrested on petty charges and those picked up as witnesses were being hurriedly removed from the Ship of Death. The vacancies were to be occupied by those who, in their capacity as hostages and dangerous elements, would be subject to speedy vengeance for the explosion in Leontyevsky Lane. A slipshod job was made of cobbling the lists together, based on notes scribbled by the investigators and at the tribunal's discretion. A reprisal was called for, quick and immediate, a bloody deterrent. There was no time for contemplating mistakes and contingencies. A person's name and identity were of little importance; what was important was to reach a target number of names filled, to tick off the list.

To expedite matters, several lorries were dispatched to Petrovsky Park;[127] a large number, straight from Butyrka, were sent off to the garage at Varsonofyevsky. Still, quite a few had to wait their turn in the basement that was Zavalishin's centre of operations.

Those brought in knew why they were being transported: rumours about the explosion had reached the prison and in

....

[126] A prison in the Tverskoy District of central Moscow. It was the central transit prison in Tsarist Imperial Russia. During Soviet times, it held many political prisoners.

[127] Formerly a pleasure spot and a leisure centre, in 1918 it was used as a place for mass executions by the Moscow Cheka.

the context of today's general commotion and haste, the sentries didn't exactly try to keep it close to their chests. Pallid and highly strung themselves, they were urging the prisoners on, constantly reaching for their holsters with nervous fingers.

All was quiet in the Ship's pit, packed to overflowing. One solitary fellow, sickly and miserable-looking, was moving from bunk to bunk, whispering feverishly, protesting that that he had ended up there by accident and that he, of course, would not be sent anywhere. The others listened to him in silence, making no attempt to reassure him, while their own minds were occupied only with their own fate, and with trying to interpret the footsteps above.

Close to three in the morning, the commissar and three sentries came running up to the banister of the balcony. The commissar, too, looked harassed but cried out in a business-like voice:

'Hey there, how many are you?'

The sentry answered:

'Sixty-seven, all told.'

'What do you mean, sixty-seven? The order was for ninety, to dig the pit?'

He stared in suspicion, then slapped himself on the forehead:

'That's right! Another twenty-three will be sent over from the Special Department. That'll make ninety, right on target.'

Thus reassured, he walked away in a measured gait.

An old general sat on the bunk nearest to the balcony, grizzled and run-down; he was polishing his nails diligently on the turn-back cuffs of his overcoat. One of the prisoners had nowhere to sit; leaning against the wall, he kept pulling out his comb and straightening the parting in his hair. A stocky man spread a piece of paper on the polished table, under the bulb, took out some slices of smoked fat and ate in silence, as if fearful that he would run out of time before consuming every last morsel of what his wife had sent him. Another was seated with his hands propping up his head and covering his face, rocking back and forth rhythmically. A dark man was casting rapid glances around, shrunk into himself, occasionally squinting and baring his teeth, as if trying to smile. Several people lay on their bunks, hands behind their heads. No one bothered taking off their clothes.

Shortly after three in the morning, 'the commissar of death' came running again, the echo of his heels reverberating around the passage – this time without any lists – and yelled at the sentries:

'Get me two of them!'

There was hectic movement on the bunks. The dark fellow flashed his teeth. Someone started frantically waving his hands in front of his face. The old general lowered his head, but slowly continued to polish his nails on the turn-back cuffs. The sentries picked out him and the sickly one, who approached them in a trot in order to explain that he'd been taken by mistake. Both were promptly led away and pushed up the spiral staircase.

Zavalishin was drunk and ghoulish. During the brief intervals in his work, he would slump down onto the bench to the left of the entrance, snatch his bottle and take a swig. Hearing a call from outside – 'One more for you!' – he would raise himself wearily, inspect his Colt and approach the door, leaning on the jamb just inside. Footsteps would be heard from the little corridor in the basement: the guards operated in pairs, one of them walking behind and keeping the barrel of his gun poised against the back of the prisoner's head. Some five steps short of the door, they would come to a halt, and the one behind would yell:

'Hey you, walk straight and get a move on!'

After which Zavalishin would raise his hand...

As morning approached, they started bringing them from the Special Department. On two occasions Commissar Ivanov briefly visited the basement where Zavalishin was hard at work. He didn't come inside though, just called out from behind the door, casting sidelong glances at the asphalt gutter immediately by the wall.

'You there, Zavalishin?'

''Course I am. That's the lot, is it?'

'Have a little patience. Not many left now. Shall I bring a bottle?'

'No, don't. Make it quick, will ya? It's time to wrap it up.'

Soon enough he heard another hail:

'Hey, another delivery for you!'

A drunken voice called back from inside the basement: 'Go on then!' After every third one, a detail would arrive to take them out.

'Hey, a new delivery!'

Zavalishin, trying to balance his body on his feet, came up to the door and raised his Colt.

The thumping of heavy feet ceased, replaced by the soft sound of an even-paced footfall heading towards the door into the basement. When a shirt appeared in the doorframe, Zavalishin barked a command, huskily:

'Turn right!'

The newcomer turned his head towards the source of the bark and Zavalishin's hand sank.

The footsteps in the corridor died away, and the entrance door banged shut. The condemned and the executioner stood face-to-face. Zavalishin's body started shaking so violently that he nearly dropped his Colt.

The doomed man took a closer look and smiled a hair-raising smile:

'Ah, an old friend. So, how *is* life, Zavalishin?'

From white, disobedient lips Zavalishin muttered:

'Alexei Dmitriyevich...'

'The very same, your neighbour.'

Both froze for a second, not saying a word.

Astafyev looked around, taking in the basement, glanced with distaste at the ground by his feet – the slippery floor – and said, harshly:

'Well, all the same – go ahead and do it, why don't you!'

He closed his eyes and waited, gritting his teeth. But all he could hear were muffled grunts.

Astafyev clenched his fists, turned sharply to face his drunk executioner and yelled:

'Do you hear me, you bastard? Do it, quickly! Otherwise I'll snatch your revolver and shoot you like a dog! Do it, you bloody coward!'

Zavalishin raised his hand and lowered it yet again. His drunk eyes were brimming with horror.

In his usual voice, full of mockery and derision, Astafyev offered, loud and clear:

'There you are, Zavalishin. I did tell you that you're good for nothing. What's with all that boasting, insisting you could shoot a person? Now what, shall I go back to bed?'

He passed by the slaughterer, sat down on the bench and dropped his head. As Zavalishin raised his Colt yet again, Astafyev briskly looked him straight in the face and burst out laughing:

'That's the spirit. At last. Well, one, two... go on, you scum... go on... fire!'

OPUS 37

Two portable kerosene stoves were making a frenzied noise in the kitchen, as if trying to outdo one another. The two housewives had just had a row over a needle for cleaning such a stove, since one of them had recently discovered that hers was broken; now they were ignoring each other's presence and didn't even turn round to look at Eduard Lvovich as he let himself into the kitchen.

Eduard Lvovich's cleaning cloth, filthy and full of holes, hung between the door and his stove. He squeamishly picked up the cloth, went to shake it, but halted in embarrassment and instead promptly carried it into his room.

Eduard Lvovich was trying to keep his room clean and orderly. However, he did not possess a floor brush – it had either ended up in somebody's stove or been pilfered. Eduard Lvovich didn't have the energy to run a full-blown investigation among the residents of his flat, now packed to the rafters on account of the new regulations for allocating living space. He reconciled himself to his loss and managed with only a cloth, which he didn't know how to use properly.

With this implement, he first dusted the grand piano's lid, then the stack of shelves and the table. He then bent down with difficulty and waved the cloth over the floor in the direction of the stove. A small pile of dust and some odd threads had accumulated by the stove's door. Eduard Lvovich collected it all onto a hard sheet of music paper and emptied it into the stove.

The cleaning was now complete.

Eduard Lvovich never touched the grand piano's keys with the dusty cloth, only with his handkerchief, which he would subsequently shake and put back into his pocket. The keys were sacrosanct.

He lifted the lid, arranged a sheet of music with his manuscript on the rack, and placed a little pencil nearby. The title read: 'Opus 37'.

Opus 37 was Eduard Lvovich's most recent composition, and as it was finished, the pencil was unlikely to be of any use. Opus 37 was a bizarre piece, devoid of any melody, written in only three days; a piece completely new in form and unexpected even to Eduard Lvovich himself.

In the past he would have indignantly rejected such a morbid, nerve-racking musical creation, but now he found himself its author.

The introduction was clear and conventional – many compositions opened in a similar way. The introduction followed the rules of logic and had inherent coherence. But all of a sudden, a theme, barely outlined and as yet undeveloped, began splintering off... how best to explain it... from some sort of a musical fissure that eventually split the piece right open, from top to bottom. The theme stubbornly tried to follow its natural consistent progression, but the fissure had grown, snapping the stretched-out threads of the musical yarn, fraying its ends, muddling everything into a ball of tragic confusion. It was a moment of desperate struggle the outcome of which was not yet clear.

Now for the main, and the most frightening thing, as far its implications were concerned. The threads straightened out, the ends came unpicked from the ball, a strong-willed voice of authority was already issuing orders (basses!), and suddenly there was a complete paralysis of logic – it turned out that treason was emanating from the strong-willed bass instruments! It had been nothing but a con trick, a diversionary tactic!

When he played this dreadful page, Eduard Lvovich was aware that his old, tired heart skipped a beat, almost stopping, and that his remaining hair stood up on the back of his head, while the ridges of his eyebrows twitched involuntarily. The page was offensive, impermissible – but it was truth personified, life itself! Not a semiquaver could be altered. The composer was a criminal but the composer was also a creator. A listener to and a servant of the truth. The world may go to pieces, all things may be dying, but he had no right to give in. All the threads snapped at once, in one fell swoop; the edges of the musical yarn became a distant dying echo, the theme became petrified and died away, but what was born instead was something new that horrified the author more than anything else: the chaos was acquiring meaning. The meaning of chaos! How could such a thing even exist?

It was in Eduard Lvovich's power to rip these final pages out of his notebook, to crumple them, tread them underfoot, tear them to shreds – this product of an absurd betrayal of all his past, of the traditions faithfully adhered to by the old classical musician, a successor and disciple of the greats. But he didn't have the strength: a criminal loves his crime. Had the outraged ghosts of Bach, Haydn, Beethoven and Mozart surrounded Eduard Lvovich's grand piano and tried to prise his manuscript out of his hands, showering him with curses, twisting the knife with contempt, he would have fought back – with his hands, his little pencil, his dusty cloth; he would have protected this manuscript with his entire body, because for as long as he was alive he wouldn't part with it, not for the sake of the living, nor the ghosts of the dead, not even for the shadow of his own mother. If she had cried and pleaded, he would have exhausted himself crying; he would have died, but he would not have succumbed, not even to her entreaties. There it was – the tragedy of the creative process.

Eduard Lvovich finished playing it through and sprang to his feet, rubbed his hands together, looked around himself distractedly, and started pacing his room, corner to corner, in excitement. Turning round, he snagged his jacket on the corner of his book stand and started. He picked up the copybook that had fallen to the floor, unsure what to do next. There was no doubt that Opus 37 was a sublime piece of music.

Sublime, certainly. But who had dictated it? The Devil? Death? Or perhaps it was the bullet that had once flown into his room at night, shattering the window and lodging itself in the whitewash behind the wallpaper? Was it this bullet that had whispered to him that chaos may and did possess a meaning? That there was meaning in death! There was meaning in insanity, in an absurdity! Nonsense was saddling up the counter-point, flogging it with a whip, and making it serve itself – but how was that even possible?

A white thread had been left by the side of the little stove, overlooked during the clean-up. Eduard Lvovich bent over, scraped it off with the nail of his slender musical finger, and hurled it inside the open stove door. He unbent himself, not without difficulty – his back was giving him trouble. And then, taking a brief glance at the sheet music, he suddenly realised:

It's a conception of genius!

It was so unexpected that Eduard Lvovich gaped, blinked, and said out loud, enunciating every syllable:

'I am a genius. Opus 37 was created by a genius.'

Eduard Lvovich sat on a chair by the wall, resting his hands on his knees. From the kitchen came the hissing sounds of the kerosene stoves and the vituperative murmurs of the housewives. But Eduard Lvovich was oblivious to it all. He simply sat there, momentarily immobilised by the odd, undreamed-of realisation that Opus 37 was a musical insight of genius. This moment was concurrent with the onset of his old age – was it possible? There was also the disquieting certainty: they would not understand, no one would be able to grasp this final revelation of his.

MIKHAIL OSORGIN

No thought of lunch crossed Eduard Lvovich's mind. It was already evening when he pulled his coat – lined with some sort of checked fabric – over his bony shoulders, perched a wide-brimmed hat askew on his head, scanned the room with unseeing eyes, opened the door, and went out. His movements were smooth and noiseless, as if he was afraid to spill a drop from the cup of completeness and revelation.

Eduard Lvovich needed some fresh air. Opus 37 was left open on his grand piano's music rack.

THE CUCKOO CLOCK

The sun would rise, dispassionately, reach its zenith, and descend towards the west. Summer would be replaced by autumn – delightful in the countryside, grim in the cities. Winter would ice over the waterways, blow snow over the roads, bury the fallen leaves. It would become warm, and spring would be back again, enticing people with hope, richly adorning nature with its green tinsel. The cuckoo clock counted the minutes, the two hands progressing unhurriedly and leaving no trace on a circle marked out with twelve signs.

Those for whom the time had come would retire to their eternal rest; new lives would be conceived; new wounds would burst open, ache, scar over; sighs would die down and be replaced with new joy; new fears would arise during the crepuscular hours; people would continue floundering around in the torrent of life, washed overboard from their hastily knocked-together rafts. The river of time would continue flowing with its habitual burble.

The old professor's cuckoo clock measured out seconds, dispassionately and methodically, with the unwinding of the spring, propelled by the heaviness of its suspended weights. On the hours and half-hours, a tiny bird would pop out of its little wooden house, nod its head and emit the appropriate number of 'cuckoos'. The professor would then say:

'What do you think, Tanyusha, isn't it time your grandpa turned in for the night? I'll read a bit in bed first.'

'Of course, Grandpa, do go.'

'Will Pyotr Pavlovich be home late?'

'He's got a board meeting today. It's unlikely to finish before midnight.'

'Aren't you bored without him?'

'Not really. I'll stay around for a while, and then retire, too.'

'Well then.'

The old ornithologist was feeling his age now, but what of it? He was quite advanced in years, after all.

He didn't go out quite as much either, although he had done so today, and chanced upon a little thrill.

At the corner of the Arbat, the professor had spotted a woman, her peddler's tray covered with a clean cloth. And from under the cloth peeped a golden bun – a real one, baked with white flour, just like in the old days. The woman was casting anxious glances around her, lest a militia man materialised from somewhere. One could never know what type of person this militia man would turn out to be, and equally, whether it was permitted to sell buns on a street corner.

The professor fumbled in his pocket for a bundle of banknotes, all of very high denominations – hundreds of thousands and millions – and came up and timidly enquired about the price. The woman answered, cautiously. And so, the professor bought a bun, paying whatever the woman had asked.

After this he hadn't even bothered with the rest of his walk, but instead had headed back home, shuffling his old feet. The first white bun was, of course, for Tanyusha, his sweet doting granddaughter. As if it were a snowdrop! It wasn't for the sake of its taste but for the sake of pure joy: come what may, but here it was, a first genuine white bun, just like in the past life!

'Do me a favour, eat it before my very eyes.'

'We'll share it, Grandpa.'

'Out of the question, it's all yours. Eat it, and drink some milk.'

'Grandpa, this is too much, I won't eat it all by myself. You know what? I'll warm up some coffee, and we'll eat together. Please, Grandpa, don't argue.'

'Well, if only a tiny morsel. It's such a pity Pyotr Pavlovich is out, we could've invited him, too…'

They ate their bun like a communion wafer, gathered the crumbs into their palms, and ate them too.

'There we are, Tanyusha. Even buns have reappeared.'

'Everything is a bit easier now, Grandpa. One can find anything; all that's needed is money.'

'Last year, I think, we did have some white flour, among the supplies Vasya got hold of.'

'We did indeed. I even baked some pies once.'

'I remember that so well, the pies. How is he doing, Vasya? He hasn't been round for some time now.'

'I believe he's doing well. Yelena Ivanovna is talking good care of him. She's very practical.'

'Well, he's worth it, is Vasya. He's such a good person. Yelena Ivanovna is the same – unpretentious and kind. It must be easier for them, together.'

At last Vasya wasn't alone either. Tanyusha, too, had someone to take care of her. It was as if Aglaya Dmitriyevna were calling from beyond the grave:

'What do you say, my dear husband, isn't it time you found some peace, too?'

The little door on the clock slapped open and the cuckoo explained how many more minutes had sunk into eternity.

Grandpa was asleep, his grey beard comfortably spread on top of the sheet. Tanyusha stayed up, waiting for Pyotr Pavlovich to return from his meeting.

It would be curious to remember: what had she been preparing herself for, what kind of a life? It couldn't have been just for the sake of this chance encounter with someone who would always arrive unexpectedly, much as he had been longed for. Surely, it would all come back: the science, the music? It must be temporary, the need for her to try and work out how and with what to feed Grandpa the next day; and how to make happy a dear, sweet man when he returned home, tired after his day at the factory or after an evening session of the board. Are her concerts in the workers' clubs not the fruit of her long studies? Are they not what is real, what matters? True, Eduard Lvovich grumbled, peeved:

'You will kill your t-talent! You mustn't treat m-music in this way!'

He was a huge authority in musical circles, this old teacher of Tanyusha's. But what did he understand of life? Had he ever experienced a harmony of undreamed-of, illogical, accidentally emerging consonance? Had he ever loved – not in the broadest sense, not a musical creation of his, but a real, live person, someone right beside him?

The cuckoo flew out of its door and counted the hours lived through today. Only today, though. It knew nothing of the days and years lived by Eduard Lvovich who, by now, was almost completely bald and increasingly stooping. Perhaps, there had never been a secret in his life; but it was equally possible that the old musician had experienced it, a long time ago.

There had been so many secrets in Tanyusha's childhood, too, but how clear her life was now! Utterly understandable, utterly ordinary. And she, Tanyusha, was completely ordinary, too, like everybody else, just a woman. It didn't hurt her feelings; it felt good. And her love – it had been given to an ordinary man, a rank-and-file person, probably one of very many just like him. He was good, and honest, and business-like, and intelligent – but quite a few men like him must have passed Tanyusha by. Why, of all those men, was it he who had become so close and so dear? Was it just a chance? No, it meant that it had to be so. Did it mean it was to be like that for her entire life?

The cuckoo had nothing to offer in reply. All it could do was measure the past. It had already announced midnight and the birth of a new day. The hand on the clock's face was approaching the first half hour.

However, before the cuckoo flung its door open yet again, the English lock in the hallway clicked with a soft muted sound. He was back. And thus, all was well again...

A SURGERY CASE

A new patient was admitted to the surgical clinic at Ostozhenka. He had been brought in by wagon, accompanied by a woman, dignified and attentive, most likely his wife.

In the administrative office, checking him in, she had said:

'Pray do something for 'im, would ya? As for us, we can pay, I'll promise you that. If necessary, we can even do it in groceries, say, some nice flour, or whatever you need. Much as we are of humble origin, he occupies a good position, with a lot of responsibilities.'

The bearded patient, corpulent and slightly bloated but otherwise possessing a strong physique, was given a bath and installed in a private room, Number Nine. He was groaning from severe pain – it was a case of renal colic, and surgery was urgently required. Barely able to answer the doctor's questions, he stared at him from under his eyebrows, mistrusting and fearful.

After the examination, he enquired through his moans:

'I'm a goner, aren't I?'

'There's no need to talk like that. We'll operate on you and you'll recover. Your kidney is full of stones and pus; you've clearly not taken care of yourself.'

'You'll cut me up, then?'

'Don't you worry. You won't feel a thing under the anaesthetic.'

The operation turned out to be arduous and complicated. After his heavy body had been lifted onto the table, the patient surveyed the doctors and the nurses, looked askance at the mask provided, and asked in a hollow voice:

'Maybe it'll go away on its own? Can't say I fancy dying.'

For a while after the mask was put in place, he bellowed and shook his head, but he soon calmed down. As he was going under, he slurred something unintelligible.

An hour and a half later, he was put on a stretcher and brought back into his room.

When he came round, he just lay there, motionless, with only his eyes roving, unfocused, as if he were drunk. His wife, who came along to visit him in the evening, was told that the operation had been a success but the patient was weak and should be given plenty of rest: let's see what tomorrow brings.

'But is he out of danger? Could he still die? Do take good care of him – don't worry, we can pay really well.'

'There's always some kind of risk. He has undergone some complicated surgery, lost a lot of blood. Did he drink much?'

''Course he did. Where he works, it comes with the territory.'

'Where's that, then?'

'A place of real importance. He mostly worked nights.'

'Still, this drinking to excess – it's bad.'

'I know. I've told him that meself. Might've been what started it.'

The woman left her address: a house in Dolgorukovskaya Street – ask for Anna Klimovna, everybody knows her, the House Committee Chairman knows her, too, they're good friends.

The patient in the clean room, lying still and staring at the ceiling, was Zavalishin. He wasn't in pain, not really, but his head felt dull, and this dullness permeated his entire body. He couldn't be bothered to use his torpid brain; besides, he had nothing useful to think. Seeing a nurse enter, or especially a doctor in a white coat, who would come in and pull back his blanket, Zavalishin eyed them with the same suspicion, his bearded cheekbones twitching.

Around lunchtime on the second day, the semi-conscious patient suddenly started moaning loudly; he turned pale, almost white, so that each small hair on his face became visible. The nurse called the duty doctor. Examination revealed that the bandages were soaked in blood. The doctor ordered the patient to be carried carefully into the dressing station. It turned out that the ligatures that had been applied to the large renal vessels had come adrift, causing a grievous parenchymatous haemorrhage.

With great difficulty they managed to reapply the ligatures to some of the bigger vessels, temporarily clamping the rest, along with the cellular tissue.

The doctor instructed the nurse:

'Stay by his side, keep a close eye on him. He's in a dangerous condition – there's been severe blood loss. In twenty-four hours, when blood clots have been sufficiently developed, we may try and carefully remove the clamps, and then have the wound packed with swabs.'

Zavalishin heard voices, incomprehensible words, and he felt as if he were enveloped in a fog. The ache was dull, his ears were ringing, and a hammer kept banging at his temples. He also felt sick at heart, and the feeling was pernicious; it was gnawing at him, driving away his sleep and his peace.

Anna Klimovna came round again, to ask for news, but they couldn't offer her anything definite or reassuring.

The doctors' hopes were dashed. When, twenty-four hours later, they tried to remove the clamps, it transpired that no clots had formed, not even in the dressed vessels, while the vessels secured by clamps pointed to the degeneration of tissue: necrosis was setting in. The bandages, yet again, were soaked in Zavalishin's wretched blood.

'This is incredible,' said the doctor. 'He's an alcoholic, of course; but still, his blood is particularly resistant; it simply refuses to clot. We can only use swabs now.'

They did not keep it from Anna Klimovna that the patient's prospects were grim. They even allowed her into his room, but asked her not to talk to him and to sit for only a minute by his bed. Anna Klimovna sat on the edge of the chair, peeped sheepishly into her partner's face, saw the white of his eyes underneath the semi-closed eyelids, sighed, and obeying a signal from the nurse, went out.

'Oh dear – he'll die then?'

The doctor answered:

'His situation is extremely serious. His blood is in a poor state, we can do nothing to stop the bleeding.'

'He'll bleed to death, then?'

'It's possible, but let's remain hopeful.'

Anna Klimovna gave a heavy sigh:

'Looks like his fate is sealed. He was such a strong man, though!'

Back home, she told Chairman Denisov:

'They cut him up but it looks like they did it all wrong. I was telling him, let it be. Might've passed by itself.'

'Doctors know best.'

'He might still live for a bit. We should've waited at least till the end of this month – they are paid on the first, and the rations are issued then too.'

'How could you wait? He was in agony. It had to be done, say what you will.'

'True enough. Looks like it was meant to be.'

It was night time. Zavalishin was barely conscious, lying close to the shielded lamp. He felt no pain, and generally could not feel his body, only an occasional cold tingle in his back and legs. His tongue was bothering him, too: a huge, dry, salty lump. When he opened his eyes, he would see shadows scatter across the ceiling and vanish into the corners.

Once, his eyes closed, he thought that he was at home and somebody was banging at the door – steadily, insistently, as if with a soft fist. He felt like calling Anna Klimovna, and started to keen. Then the nurse came to his bed and asked something softly, and Zavalishin remembered that he was in a hospital. Which meant that Anna was at home, alone. She must feel unencumbered now, alone in their three rooms. They now had a large apartment, as no additional tenants had been moved in; they had taken all the books to a shed.

And then he thought he heard a stranger's voice calling out:

'Hey, you've got a delivery!'

Then another voice, a recognisable one, asking mockingly:

'Ah, my old friend. Well, Zavalishin, how's life?'

Zavalishin's body jerked. He wanted to shout, and felt an acute, intolerable pain in his stomach.

When the doctor came running, summoned by the nurse, Zavalishin's stout body was again bathed in blood. The blood drenched all the bandages and was gushing onto the sheet. There was so much of it, so horribly much – of the executioner's blood that was refusing to clot.

Medical science knows nothing about the vengeance of the blood. The patient's woeful case notes had a simple entry – *Dissolutio sanguinis.*[128]

Anna Klimovna came along in the morning to learn that her cohabitor had died in the night.

She didn't cry, didn't even pull out a handkerchief. She only asked what to do next: was she to arrange the burial herself or would the hospital take care of it? But when she went back downstairs, she addressed the woman who played the role of a doorkeeper in a small plaintive voice, shaking her head:

'The main thing is, he occupied a high post, of special importance, even if he was a common man, from the working

....

[128]   Thinning of the blood.

class. A good salary he had, and a ration, and on top of that, they paid him for each job separately, by item, so to say. Every so often a sizeable lump sum. He would receive all kinds of clothes, too. As for his ration, it always had white flour, also honey, and often fabrics, and overshoes and what not. True enough, his job wasn't everybody's cup of tea, but when's all said and done, they did pay diligently, as he was held in high esteem. Our apartment is three rooms with a kitchen, we've got heaps of good stuff, and I've raised a piggy for the Easter holiday.'

And only now, remembering the piggy, Anna Klimovna sniffled for the first time, pulled out a clean handkerchief, and wiped her dry eyes.

AN EVENING AT SIVTSEV VRAZHEK

The steps of the wooden staircase creaked their welcome, the door opened with genuine cordiality, the coat stand received coats and hats with a civil calmness, and the walls of the old house picked out the echo of familiar voices.

On the evening of the professor's birthday, the old villa at Sivtsev Vrazhek assembled those who had never forgotten its erstwhile lavish hospitality. Even Lenochka, once a young girl with amazed eyebrows, by now a mother of two children – even she, a rare visitor, came round to pay a call on the old man and her friend from their gymnasium days.

The first to arrive was the physicist Poplavsky, sporting his shabby black morning coat, contrasting with a pair of new overshoes, recently obtained for the price of a long wait in a queue. According to Poplavsky, beguiled by his overshoes, life had become much easier, and the only hardship was the fact that it was practically impossible to lay your hands on a new book from abroad, even if you were well-connected.

'If it continues like this, we'll fall behind so badly that we won't catch up with Europe for ten years, while – just consider it! – by now, a whole library has been written on Einstein alone.'

Protasov was conciliatory:

'Not to worry. For the time being, what we do know is enough to keep us occupied. Mind you, it would be good to translate at least this knowledge into reality.'

Uncle Boris was supportive of his colleague:

'Hardly the time for new books now. Nevertheless, it would be great to get, at least, some carbon paper and new copying ribbon! We, at the Science and Technology Department...'

Vasya and Alyona came by too. Somehow, Vasya had become a responsible adult overnight, even if he had shaved his beard off – on account of Alyona being in favour of exposing the dimple in his chin. All Vasya's buttons were in their proper place, his shirt collar was clean, his handkerchief properly hemmed and embroidered with his initials. Also gone was his former discomfiture; his conversation with Tanyusha was respectfully affable, and together with Protasov they reminisced about their foraging mission into the countryside. Alyona behaved naturally, but was wary lest she should break into giggles. Still, the ornithologist did get her laughing by the end of the evening, and so Alyona pealed the silver bells of her infectious laughter that tapered to a grunt, and felt flummoxed when Lenochka's eyebrows – the two ladies hadn't met before – swept up in amazement.

Alyona was seated next to the professor, who engaged her in conversation while casting affectionate glances towards Vasya Boltanovsky.

Absent were those who would never come back, whose names were mentioned softly and seriously. Absent was he who had frequently argued, in this very room, with Poplavsky, since the latter had no taste for or understanding of easy-going paradoxes; his tragic departure from the land of the living was still too fresh and recent, an ever-present source of internal grief. Much as life in Moscow had been a never-ending string of losses and tribulations – one should have been accustomed to it by now! – the inhabitants of the peaceful little villa tried to refrain from mentioning the name of Astafyev. The time would come when his name would be added to the necrology, along with the names of young Ehrberg, the ill-starred Stolnikov and many other friends, near and far.

At nine o'clock sharp, the coat-stand in the hallway accepted and arranged on its outmost hook a coat with checkered lining.

Eduard Lvovich, squinting from the bright light and rubbing his hands together, let himself in, greeted everybody, and took his usual place at the tea table, to the right of the seat once occupied by Aglaya Dmitriyevna and now by Tanyusha.

By way of celebrating, they drank genuine tea, while in the middle of the table sat a festive sweet brioche, baked with real white flour, curled on its large dish. There was sugar in one small bowl, and landrine sweets in the other. On offer, too, was butter and a plateful of thinly sliced salami. The menu was exceptional, in honour of Grandpa's celebration.

There was another dish, too, served by Tanyusha especially for Eduard Lvovich, a cause of general astonishment: sweet white rusks, his favourite treat. In the old days both Aglaya Dmitriyevna and Tanyusha had always remembered to bake them for the composer. Over the previous two years he had forgotten what they tasted like, for all that was ever on offer was dry black bread. But today Tanyusha had procured a whole saucer of sweet delights, for the sake of her grandpa and Eduard Lvovich.

'This is for Eduard Lvovich alone! You must eat them all, every last one.'

Eduard Lvovich was flustered, but even Tanyusha's exceptional solicitude did little to dispel the composer's melancholy. It had been quite some time since Eduard Lvovich had felt energised, even when talking about music, even at the keyboard of his trusty grand piano.

The ornithologist, seated in his armchair next to Alyona, teased her gently, insisting that, without her assistance, Vasya would now be unable to stir his tea with a teaspoon.

'He used to be so self-reliant, so much so that he even got himself involved in barter trade with some savage tribes of Russia, together with Pyotr Pavlovich here. He managed to exchange my waders for some gold dust and ebony. That's the fellow he used to be!'

Uncle Boris tried to introduce the subject of the grandiose plans and projects put forward by his Science and Technology Department, especially where it concerned electrification. Protasov chuckled:

'Plans are all very well. Just try to prevent yourself putting a spanner in the works of the basic operations at the factory floor. As for your plans, that's good, there's no harm in those. Your academic designs may even come in handy, eventually.'

Tanyusha presided over the evening, glancing around the intimate circle of the little villa's friends and thinking: *Grandpa's happy. Pleased that he's not been forgotten. It is imperative that Eduard Lvovich agrees to play tonight.*

So, when the plate of salami was empty, and only a few crumbs were left of the sweet brioche, Tanyusha lit the candles by the grand piano.

'Will you play for us, Eduard Lvovich?'

To her amazement, he agreed straight away:

'Yes, I'd like that. I'd like to p-perform a special p-piece... One I've not yet...'

'Something new?'

'Over a year old now. But I haven't p-played it yet, not anywhere. It's c-called... that is to say, there's no name yet, but it's my most recent op-pus. It's Opus Thirty-Seven.'

He blew out the candles and waited till everyone took their places.

Grandpa's armchair was pushed closer to the sofa which accommodated Alyona, Lenochka and Vasya. Poplavsky stayed in the dark corner, on a chair. Uncle Boris and Pyotr Pavlovich remained at the table, and Tanyusha on the rug, by her grandpa's feet, her head in his lap.

Tanyusha was the only one who could see and comprehend the sacrifice made by Eduard Lvovich when he agreed to perform his most recent creation. She listened soundlessly, and suffered together with her teacher, or perhaps suffered on his behalf.

She realised that the old composer had reached a turning point in his work, that a catastrophe had occurred; that he, powerless to reject the musical idea that he'd been serving all his life, had suddenly rocked the columns and sent the temple, created through his own efforts, tumbling down, and that he was now buried under its rubble, writhing in agony. Something new had been born in his life, something that he was striving to understand, overpower and, by all the evidence, exonerate – but to this purpose, he had no words or musical harmonies. All that he had at his disposal was a cry of torment, drowned by the voices of strangers, hostile and alien.

Tanyusha saw how Eduard Lvovich's long fingers clung to the keys, how he was eager to convince himself, how his long pale face contorted, how Eduard Lvovich was gripped with impossible suffering. *Why on earth have I asked him to play?*

He finished with an abrupt chord, immediately leapt up from his stool, pulled the lid back with his trembling fingers, dropped it, shuddered painfully, and froze, confused, with his back to the room.

Tanyusha knew that she had to help, somehow. She came close and gently stroked the sleeve of his jacket, not saying a word.

Eduard Lvovich looked round and muttered:

'Yes, yes, this is the last op-pus, n-number thirty-seven...'

He then rubbed his hands and, without saying goodbye, rapidly strode into the hallway.

Tanyusha followed him there. However, she had no words to offer him, no words that should be said. Did such words even exist?

Snatching his coat off the stand, Eduard Lvovich quickly pulled on one sleeve, but fumbled for a long time, trying to find the other. Tanyusha helped him. He turned around to face her, pulled some sheets of music from his pocket, rolled up in a tube and wound several times with a thin thread, and forced them into Tanyusha's hand:

'Here, it's for you. I've dedicated Op-pus Thirty-Seven, my last one, to you. It's only for you. Yes, that's how it should be. G-goodbye.'

'Thank you, Eduard Lvovich. But why do you have to leave?'

'There's no other way. I m-must.'

He went to the door, took hold of the latch on the lock, turned back, and looking Tanyusha straight in the face, added in a feverish staccato:

'Opus Thirty-Seven is a work of genius. G-goodbye.'

Tanyusha heard Eduard Lvovich lose his footing on the staircase, before his footsteps started receding rapidly.

WHEN THE SWALLOWS RETURN

The guests left early.

'Grandpa, you must be exhausted. Perhaps, an early bedtime tonight?'

'I am a little tired, it's true, but not sleepy just yet. Let me stay with you awhile, I'll rest up and then retire.'

Tanyusha cleared the table, put the furniture back in its place, and put the slip covers back onto the grand piano. Pyotr Pavlovich helped. The professor stayed in his deep armchair, his eyes half-closed. Tanyusha lowered herself again onto the rug at his feet.

The ornithologist patted her head and said:

'When it's so quiet here, and we're all sitting around like this, it feels as though the walls are whispering among themselves. After all, it's an old house, it's got things to remember. This house, Pyotr Pavlovich, was built back in my mother's days, under her personal supervision, that is to say, in the days of Tanyusha's great-grandmother. In those days it was considered luxurious, a big house for a large family. It was beautiful. The courtyard housed all sorts of things: stables, a poultry yard, a bathhouse too, of course. We only recently dismantled the bathhouse for firewood. This is where I've lived all my life, till the very end. Nowadays the house belongs to no one, and the people living between our walls are strangers.'

'They make little noise, Grandpa, and give us no trouble.'

'Well, you're right, everyone must live somewhere. I'm not complaining, only reminiscing. The times have changed.'

He picked up the thread of his thought:

'Now tell me, Pyotr Pavlovich, what will life be like for you, the young? Will it be better than ours, or will it stay the same, or become harder?'

'I believe, Professor, that we will find it more complicated. It goes without saying that no one will live his entire life in the same house; that isn't possible anymore.'

'But on the whole, will the people have it better? We all are in a bad place now, of course. Still, ours are exceptional times, a period of transition. It's necessary to grit one's teeth and bear it, all the way through. And a long way this will be.'

'Our generation will have its work cut out for it.'

'My view precisely. It will take many long years to put life back on track. Poplavsky here is complaining that we've been cut off from Europe, that we'll never catch up now. A scientist can't help but feel it. For a knowledgeable person, that hurts.'

'I don't know about other things, but in this sphere, we'll catch up sooner than Poplavsky believes. What's really dire is the state of affairs in the national economy. It's been reduced to ruins, and the poverty is staggering. There's also a shortage of able people.'

'New people will come; Russia's rich in people.'

'The people must appear,' said Protasov. 'Completely new people who will probably be stronger than before.'

The old man was silent for a while, then patted Tanyusha's head.

'See, Tanyusha, it's good that Pyotr Pavlovich is hopeful. Do try to form some optimistic beliefs too.'

'But I do believe, Grandpa!'

'New people will come and try to do everything in a new way, in their own way. They'll look around, bang their heads against the wall, and then surmise that the new world will never survive without the old foundations, that it will simply disintegrate, that the old culture is not dispensable, it cannot simply be cast aside. So they will pick up the old books, study what has been studied before, make new use of the old experiences. This is absolutely certain. And then, Tanyusha, they will remember us, the old guard, and your grandpa may be remembered, too, and his books will be returned to the bookshelves. And his science will be of use to somebody.'

'But of course, Grandpa!'

'The birds will be of use. My little birds must be useful! There will be place for them in this life. Am I talking sense, Tanyusha?'

'It will soon be spring, Grandpa, and our swallows will return.'

'There's no doubt that the swallows will return. A swallow pays no heed to human disputes; it's all the same to them: who is fighting whom and who emerges triumphant. Today he wins over me, tomorrow I win over him, and then all over again... As for the swallows, they have their own laws, eternal ones. And those laws are much more important than ours. We don't know them well at all yet, there's a lot to learn.'

They sat in silence for a long time. True enough, the walls of the old house were whispering something. Leaning over Tanyusha so that his grey beard tickled her forehead, the ornithologist said, softly and gently:

'Mark it, Tanyusha, make a note.'

'A note of what, Grandpa?'

'The day when the swallows return this coming spring. I may not be around by then, but you – you will record it all without fail, won't you?'

'Grandpa...'

'Yes, yes, do make a note, either on the calendar or in my little book, the one in which I always keep records. That will add another mark. This is ever so important, Tanyusha, maybe the most important thing of all. Will you do it, my dear girl? It'll give me pleasure.'

Grandpa's hand was stroking Tanyusha's head gently.

'Grandpa, my darling Grandpa... but of course... I will record everything, Grandpa...'

ABOUT THE AUTHOR

Mikhail Andreyevich Osorgin (real surname Ilyin) was born in 1878 in the city of Perm in the Urals to a family of intelligentsia. His father a was lawyer while his mother, who spoke several languages and had received a good education from a school in Warsaw, dedicated her life to the family and the children. The family's life was intense, and their cultural interests numerous and varied. They shared a typical set of values adhered to by the educated classes in provincial Russia at the time: the precedence of social interests over private, and an acute sense of justice.

Osorgin's first publication was a tiny piece in the local newspaper, written in 1897 when he still a schoolboy, on the occasion of the death of his form teacher.

Having received his degree from Moscow State University, he briefly worked as a barrister. It was then that he became involved with the party of Socialist Revolutionaries, a popular organisation at the time, rather militant in its methodology and a real rival to the Bolsheviks. However, he never made a career in the party, and shunned internal squabbles and rigid party discipline.

He did not take part in the revolution of 1905, but was nonetheless arrested and spent six months in jail. He was on the brink of starting to serve a five-year prison sentence when, due to a lack of coordination between various penal departments, he was released by mistake, and used the opportunity to flee to Italy.

It was there that he started writing in earnest, becoming a foreign correspondent of *The Russian News* and *European Herald*. In 1916, after 10 years in Italy, he returned to Russia, overcoming significant obstacles, and eager to sign up for the front. However, he was unable to join the army because of his criminal record (the five-year sentence had never been repealed).

In 1917, the Provisional Government invited him to become Ambassador to Italy, but he declined this flattering offer in order to become a full-time journalist and author. He stayed in Moscow during the horrific years immediately after the revolution and the 'Red Terror', like many other members of his class, was arrested by the secret police (Cheka), and spent time in the notorious Lubyanka Prison. He was released under the guarantee of Lev Kamenev, the then head of the Moscow Soviet, but was forced to emigrate shortly afterwards, leaving on the ignominious 'Philosophers' Steamer'.

After a short stint in Berlin (the initial capital of post-revolution Russian cultural emigration) he went to Paris, where he contributed articles, fiction, and book reviews to émigré papers. He was still holding onto his Soviet passport when in 1937, during a routine registration visit to the embassy, this passport was removed from him by force. He never sought or received French citizenship, and lived the remaining years of his life as a stateless person.

Unlike most of his colleagues and contemporaries, Osorgin never held extreme anti-Soviet views. Being highly critical of the system and the government, he believed that Russian literature, whether produced inside the Soviet Union or in the diaspora, was one whole; it was simply that the writers were working under different circumstances and saw the world in their individual way.

Osorgin's best known works were his novels *A Quiet Street* (1930) – *Syvtsev Vrazhek* in an earlier translation, and

My Sister's Story (1931), both translations into English never reprinted.

During the 1930s he spent much of his time in the village of Sainte-Geneviève-des-Bois, in the province of Essonne, where he owned a cottage. Here he rejected urban civilisation, promoting a lifestyle that was closer to nature. He stayed in France during the German occupation and died in 1942 in the village of Chabris, where he and his wife had escaped as refugees. Living on the border of the Free Zone, he had been actively publishing anti-Nazi pamphlets until the very end.

ABOUT THE TRANSLATOR

Sveta Payne (aka Svetlana Dubovitskaya) was born in Ternopol (as it was called at the time when all toponymics were only spelled in Russian, nowadays it is Ternopil), on the western rim of the Soviet Union, in 1961. The territorial volatility of the region, Galicia, gave her a relatively cosmopolitan view of the world. She studied at the University of Lvov/Lviv, graduating with honours in philology, teaching foreign languages, and translation. The love of both spoken and written word led her to gain a command of seven languages.

Her earliest professional linguistic experience was taking parties of western visitors around the geographical and cultural diversity of the Soviet Union, under the auspices of the Peace Committee of the USSR. With *Glasnost*, *Perestroika* and the fall of the Wall, she found herself in an advantageous position, and through an ability for simultaneous interpreting, technical and literary translation between Russian, English and other European languages, she was able to work for western companies that sought to invest in the newly emerging state. During this period, she worked for many major global concerns such as the World Bank, UNDP, Morgan Stanley, OECD, and the European Union's investment and development programmes. However, whilst engaged in bringing her use of languages into the working world, she was always acting on her determination to bring Russian literature to a wider audience by translating Russian poets, writers and film dialogues into English.

During the 1990s she spent progressively more time in the UK, and moved there permanently in 1997 when she married a UK scientist. For some time, she was the UK correspondent for the Russian weekly magazine, *Ogonyok*, writing features on British life and culture. Whilst she went on to work for a number of UK institutions such as the BBC Russian Service and Factiva (news service for Reuters), she also turned to publishing her translations of Russian poets. Her illustrated compilation of poetry by Daniel Kharms, *The Charms of Harms*, appeared in 2011 and is still selling today. As a reverse in the cultural tide, in 1997 Sveta produced a Russian translation of T. S. Elliot's *The Old Possum's Book of Practical Cats*, which has now been through a sufficient number of reprintings to achieve a 'Gold' version. The year 2012 saw the publication of her translation of *The World's Wife*, by Carol Ann Duffy – translated with a view to bringing this work to the attention of the assiduous reading public of Russia. In the same mode she was commissioned by one of the leading theatres of Moscow to translate the libretto of *Jesus Christ Super Star*, to enable a performance of this very popular musical in Russian.

More recently, Sveta has engaged with contemporary Russian writing, having translated a biography of Boris Yeltsin (*Boris Yeltsin: The Decade that Shook the World*, Glagoslav), a novel by Arseny Revazov (*Loneliness-12*, A&NN) and co-worked on two novels by the prize-winning Russian author Victor Pelevin (*S.N.U.F.F.* and *Empire V*, Gollancz).

Whilst still engaged with languages in the business sector, Sveta continues to promote her vision of international cultural understanding, particularly between the English- and Russian-speaking worlds. Her most recent work is a translation of *The Riven Heart of Moscow* by Mikhail Osorgin – of the chaotic changes to Russian society caused by them.

Sveta is now mainly based in London, and divides her residence between the UK and the south of France.

ABSOLUTE ZERO

by Artem Chekh

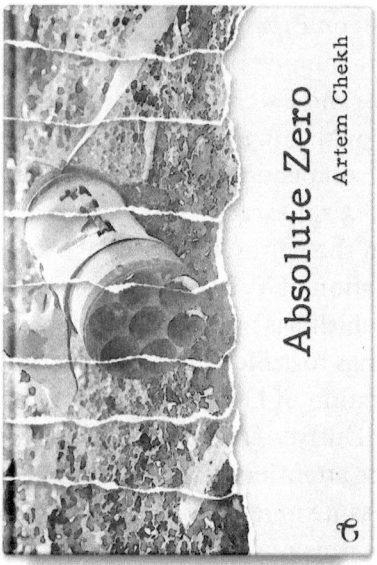

The book is a first person account of a soldier's journey, and is based on Artem Chekh's diary that he wrote while and after his service in the war in Donbas. One of the most important messages the book conveys is that war means pain. Chekh is not showing the reader any heroic combat, focusing instead on the quiet, mundane, and harsh soldier's life. Chekh masterfully selects the most poignant details of this kind of life.

Artem Chekh (1985) is a contemporary Ukrainian writer, author of more than ten books of fiction and essays. *Absolute Zero* (2017), an account of Chekh's service in the army in the war in Donbas, is one of his latest books, for which he became a recipient of several prestigious awards in Ukraine, such as the Joseph Conrad Prize (2019), the Gogol Prize (2018), the Voyin Svitla (2018), and the Litaktsent Prize (2017). This is his first book-length translation into English.

Buy it > www.glagoslav.com

OLANDA

by Rafał Wojasiński

I've been happy since the morning. Delighted, even. Everything seems so splendidly transient to me. That dust, from which thou art and unto which thou shalt return — it tempts me. And that's why I wander about these roads, these woods, among the nearby houses, from which waft the aromas of fried pork chops, chicken soup, fish, diapers, steamed potatoes for the pigs; I lose my eye-sight, and regain it again. I don't know what life is, Ola, but I'm holding on to it. Thus speaks the narrator of Rafał Wojasiński's novel *Olanda*. Awarded the prestigious Marek Nowakowski Prize for 2019, *Olanda* introduces us to a world we glimpse only through the window of our train, as we hurry from one important city to another: a provincial world of dilapidated farmhouses and sagging apartment blocks, overgrown cemeteries and village drunks; a world seemingly abandoned by God — and yet full of the basic human joy of life itself.

Leo Tolstoy – Flight from Paradise

by Pavel Basinsky

Over a hundred years ago, something truly outrageous occurred at Yasnaya Polyana. Count Leo Tolstoy, a famous author aged eighty-two at the time, took off, destination unknown. Since then, the circumstances surrounding the writer's whereabouts during his final days and his eventual death have given rise to many myths and legends. In this book, popular Russian writer and reporter Pavel Basinsky delves into the archives and presents his interpretation of the situation prior to Leo Tolstoy's mysterious disappearance. Basinsky follows Leo Tolstoy throughout his life, right up to his final moments. Reconstructing the story from historical documents, he creates a visionary account of the events that led to the Tolstoys' family drama.

Flight from Paradise will be of particular interest to international researchers studying Leo Tolstoy's life and works, and is highly recommended to a broader audience worldwide.

Buy it > www.glagoslav.com

THE FANTASTIC WORLDS OF YURI VYNNYCHUK

by Yuri Vynnychuk

Yuri Vynnychuk is a master storyteller and satirist, who emerged from the Western Ukrainian underground in Soviet times to become one of Ukraine's most prolific and most prominent writers of today. He is a chameleon who can adapt his narrative voice in a variety of ways and whose style at times is reminiscent of Borges. A master of the short story, he exhibits a great range from exquisite lyrical-philosophical works such as his masterpiece "An Embroidered World," written in the mode of magical realism; to intense psychological studies; to contemplative science fiction and horror tales; and to wicked black humor and satire such as his "Max and Me." Excerpts are also presented in this volume of his longer prose works, including his highly acclaimed novel of wartime Lviv *Tango of Death*, which received the 2012 BBC Ukrainian Book of the Year Award. The translations offered here allow the English-language reader to become acquainted with the many fantastic worlds and lyrical imagination of an extraordinarily versatile writer.

Buy it > www.glagoslav.com

Someone Else's Life

by Elena Dolgopyat

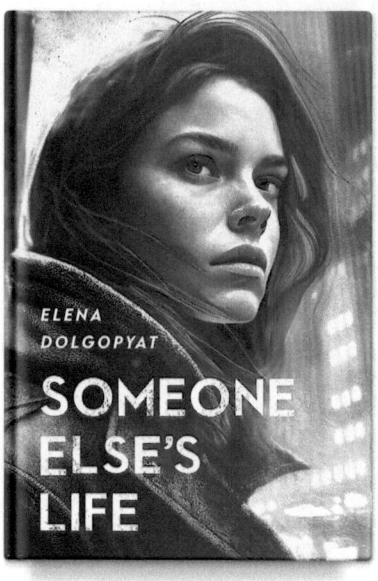

Elena Dolgopyat was born and raised in the USSR, trained as a computer programmer in a Soviet military facility, and retrained as a cinematographer post-perestroika. Fusing her diverse experiences with her own sensitivities and preoccupations, and weaving throughout a colourful thread of magic realism, she has produced an unsettling group of fifteen stories all concerned in some way with the theme of estrangement. Elena herself, in an interview given at the time of the book's launch, said, "Into each of these stories is woven the motif that one's life is 'alien'. It is as if you are separate from your own life and someone else is living it. You feel either that your own life is 'other', or you experience a yearning for a life you have not led, an envy for some other life." In his introduction to the collection, Leonid Yuzefovich writes, "Each of Elena Dolgopyat's stories … painfully stirs the soul with a sense of the fragility, the evanescence, even, of human existence … in her quiet voice, she is telling us of "the multicoloured underside of life". She is telling us of things that matter to us all."

Buy it > www.glagoslav.com

Ravens before Noah

by Susanna Harutyunyan

This novel is set in the Armenian mountains sometime in 1915-1960. An old man and a new born baby boy escape from the Hamidian massacres in Turkey in 1894 and hide themselves in the ruins of a demolished and abandoned village. The village soon becomes a shelter for many others, who flee from problems with the law, their families, or their past lives. The villagers survive in this secret shelter, cut off from the rest of the world, by selling or bartering their agricultural products in the villages beneath the mountain.

Years pass by, and the child saved by the old man grows into a young man, Harout. He falls for a beautiful girl who arrived in the village after being tortured by Turkish soldiers. She is pregnant and the old women of the village want to kill the twin baby girls as soon as they are born, to wash away the shame...

Buy it > www.glagoslav.com

Glagoslav Publications Catalogue

- *The Time of Women* by Elena Chizhova
- *Andrei Tarkovsky: A Life on the Cross* by Lyudmila Boyadzhieva
- *Sin* by Zakhar Prilepin
- *Hardly Ever Otherwise* by Maria Matios
- *Khatyn* by Ales Adamovich
- *The Lost Button* by Irene Rozdobudko
- *Christened with Crosses* by Eduard Kochergin
- *The Vital Needs of the Dead* by Igor Sakhnovsky
- *The Sarabande of Sara's Band* by Larysa Denysenko
- *A Poet and Bin Laden* by Hamid Ismailov
- *Zo Gaat Dat in Rusland* (Dutch Edition) by Maria Konjoekova
- *Kobzar* by Taras Shevchenko
- *The Stone Bridge* by Alexander Terekhov
- *Moryak* by Lee Mandel
- *King Stakh's Wild Hunt* by Uladzimir Karatkevich
- *The Hawks of Peace* by Dmitry Rogozin
- *Harlequin's Costume* by Leonid Yuzefovich
- *Depeche Mode* by Serhii Zhadan
- *Groot Slem en Andere Verhalen* (Dutch Edition) by Leonid Andrejev
- *METRO 2033* (Dutch Edition) by Dmitry Glukhovsky
- *METRO 2034* (Dutch Edition) by Dmitry Glukhovsky
- *A Russian Story* by Eugenia Kononenko
- *Herstories, An Anthology of New Ukrainian Women Prose Writers*
- *The Battle of the Sexes Russian Style* by Nadezhda Ptushkina
- *A Book Without Photographs* by Sergey Shargunov
- *Down Among The Fishes* by Natalka Babina
- *disUNITY* by Anatoly Kudryavitsky
- *Sankya* by Zakhar Prilepin
- *Wolf Messing* by Tatiana Lungin
- *Good Stalin* by Victor Erofeyev
- *Solar Plexus* by Rustam Ibragimbekov
- *Don't Call me a Victim!* by Dina Yafasova
- *Poetin* (Dutch Edition) by Chris Hutchins and Alexander Korobko

- *A History of Belarus* by Lubov Bazan
- *Children's Fashion of the Russian Empire* by Alexander Vasiliev
- *Empire of Corruption: The Russian National Pastime* by Vladimir Soloviev
- *Heroes of the 90s: People and Money. The Modern History of Russian Capitalism* by Alexander Solovev, Vladislav Dorofeev and Valeria Bashkirova
- *Fifty Highlights from the Russian Literature* (Dutch Edition) by Maarten Tengbergen
- *Bajesvolk* (Dutch Edition) by Michail Chodorkovsky
- *Dagboek van Keizerin Alexandra* (Dutch Edition)
- *Myths about Russia* by Vladimir Medinskiy
- *Boris Yeltsin: The Decade that Shook the World* by Boris Minaev
- *A Man Of Change: A study of the political life of Boris Yeltsin*
- *Sberbank: The Rebirth of Russia's Financial Giant* by Evgeny Karasyuk
- *To Get Ukraine* by Oleksandr Shyshko
- *Asystole* by Oleg Pavlov
- *Gnedich* by Maria Rybakova
- *Marina Tsvetaeva: The Essential Poetry*
- *Multiple Personalities* by Tatyana Shcherbina
- *The Investigator* by Margarita Khemlin
- *The Exile* by Zinaida Tulub
- *Leo Tolstoy: Flight from Paradise* by Pavel Basinsky
- *Moscow in the 1930* by Natalia Gromova
- *Laurus* (Dutch edition) by Evgenij Vodolazkin
- *Prisoner* by Anna Nemzer
- *The Crime of Chernobyl: The Nuclear Goulag* by Wladimir Tchertkoff
- *Alpine Ballad* by Vasil Bykau
- *The Complete Correspondence of Hryhory Skovoroda*
- *The Tale of Aypi* by Ak Welsapar
- *Selected Poems* by Lydia Grigorieva
- *The Fantastic Worlds of Yuri Vynnychuk*
- *The Garden of Divine Songs and Collected Poetry of Hryhory Skovoroda*
- *Adventures in the Slavic Kitchen: A Book of Essays with Recipes* by Igor Klekh
- *Seven Signs of the Lion* by Michael M. Naydan

- *Ravens before Noah* by Susanna Harutyunyan
- *An English Queen and Stalingrad* by Natalia Kulishenko
- *Point Zero* by Narek Malian
- *Absolute Zero* by Artem Chekh
- *Olanda* by Rafał Wojasiński
- *Robinsons* by Aram Pachyan
- *The Monastery* by Zakhar Prilepin
- *The Selected Poetry of Bohdan Rubchak: Songs of Love, Songs of Death, Songs of the Moon*
- *Mebet* by Alexander Grigorenko
- *The Orchestra* by Vladimir Gonik
- *Everyday Stories* by Mima Mihajlović
- *Slavdom* by Ľudovít Štúr
- *The Code of Civilization* by Vyacheslav Nikonov
- *Where Was the Angel Going?* by Jan Balaban
- *De Zwarte Kip* (Dutch Edition) by Antoni Pogorelski
- *Głosy / Voices* by Jan Polkowski
- *Sergei Tretyakov: A Revolutionary Writer in Stalin's Russia* by Robert Leach
- *Opstand* (Dutch Edition) by Władysław Reymont
- *Dramatic Works* by Cyprian Kamil Norwid
- *Children's First Book of Chess* by Natalie Shevando and Matthew McMillion
- *Precursor* by Vasyl Shevchuk
- *The Vow: A Requiem for the Fifties* by Jiří Kratochvil
- *De Bibliothecaris* (Dutch edition) by Mikhail Jelizarov
- *Subterranean Fire* by Natalka Bilotserkivets
- *Vladimir Vysotsky: Selected Works*
- *Behind the Silk Curtain* by Gulistan Khamzayeva
- *The Village Teacher and Other Stories* by Theodore Odrach
- *Duel* by Borys Antonenko-Davydovych
- *War Poems* by Alexander Korotko
- *Ballads and Romances* by Adam Mickiewicz
- *The Revolt of the Animals* by Wladyslaw Reymont
- *Poems about my Psychiatrist* by Andrzej Kotański

- *Someone Else's Life* by Elena Dolgopyat
- *Selected Works: Poetry, Drama, Prose* by Jan Kochanowski
- *The Riven Heart of Moscow (Sivtsev Vrazhek)* by Mikhail Osorgin
- *Liza's Waterfall: The hidden story of a Russian feminist* by Pavel Basinsky
- *Biography of Sergei Prokofiev* by Igor Vishnevetsky
- *Ilget* by Alexander Grigorenko
- *A City drawn from Memory* by Elena Chizhova
- *Guide to M. Bulgakovs The Master and Margarita* by Ksenia Atarova and Georgy Lesskis

More coming . . .

GLAGOSLAV PUBLICATIONS
www.glagoslav.com